THE PIERCING

THE PIERCING

Helen McCabe

The Piper Trilogy
Book 2

First published in the UK in 2014 by Telos Moonrise: Dark Endeavours (An imprint of Telos Publishing Ltd)
5A Church Road, Shortlands, Bromley, Kent BR2 0HP

www.telos.co.uk

Telos Publishing Ltd values feedback. Please e-mail us with any comments you may have about this book to:
feedback@telos.co.uk

ISBN: 978-1-84583-899-7

The Piercing © 2014 Helen McCabe

Cover Art: Iain Robertson
Cover Design: David J Howe

The moral right of the author has been asserted.

British Library Cataloguing in Publication Data.
A catalogue record for this book is available from the British Library.

Every eye shall see him, and among them
those who pierced him.

Palais de l'Europe
Strasbourg, 2007

'I should kill him,' Heine Muller muttered. Outside, the setting sun still hurled fiery darts at the building, only to be beaten off by the harsh white light pouring from a thousand offices.

He hurried on through the dusky corridor, when a sunbeam struck him, transforming his formal black suit into a dusty red. He raised the sheaf of papers in his hand to stave off its sudden brightness, then lowering the papers like a flag of truce, he breathed in deeply and loosened his collar. His perspiration owed more to the urgency of his errand than to the heat.

Whatever his boss, Eisenmann, demanded, needed to be delivered in double-quick time. Heine exhaled in an effort to calm himself, brushed his thinning hair back neatly and knocked on the heavy door. A second later, he disappeared inside.

The atmosphere in the stifling office was heavy with shadows. His employer preferred narrow uplighters with red shades, which spattered great bloody circles on the ceiling, but that particular evening, Eisenmann was working with even those switched off. Neither did the air conditioning appear to be working.

Heine dared not speak. He approached the ornate desk, where his master sat hunched, staring at the bright screen of his laptop.

'Here's the list, sir,' he said.

He was even more in awe of Eisenmann than he had

been on their first acquaintance, because, now, Heine knew first-hand what power the man wielded.

That day in 1990, Heine had been a lowly waiter in a smart Cologne hotel, ordered to the conference suite to serve Herr Eisenmann, who was one of the most important businessmen in Germany. How could he ever forget the emergency that had occurred? Eisenmann had been in a meeting when a young Romanian psychiatrist called Marcu had suffered a major heart attack and died in the ambulance on his way to hospital.

Later on, Heine had received a phone call from Eisenmann's secretary, Sigi, who had told him how much his help had been appreciated and asked him if he would consider a job with Herr Eisenmann. He had jumped at the chance. *And look where he was now!* Assistant to one of the most influential men in PACE – the Council of Europe Parliamentary Assembly. Being *chosen* like that had been a jaw-dropping thing!

Eisenmann looked up suddenly and Heine jumped to attention. His master stretched out his hand.

'Give,' he ordered, pushing back the lock of bright hair that had fallen across his forehead. Heine was shocked every time he saw his master's nails, long and perfect. Like a woman's, but not at all feminine. In fact they were hard as armoured steel.

He had not aged like Heine. His hair was not even streaked with grey. Privately, his assistant wondered if he had it bleached, but as soon as the thought came to him he drove it away, in case his employer read his mind. Eisenmann had a way of making you think he knew every tiny thing about you and your past. When he held you with his gaze, you wanted to confess any filthy trick you'd ever played, or sin you had committed. And there had been quite a few since Heine had worked for him at PACE.

Heine deliberately tried to blank such unnerving thoughts, which wasn't difficult, as he had taught himself to think only about serving his master and watching football on the television. He stood silently beside the desk, knowing from experience that he would be dismissed immediately when no longer needed. He watched as Eisenmann picked up the phone.

'Come in, Sigi,' he said. 'I need copies made.'

Every time Heine saw her come in – and it had been a good few years – he lusted after the secretary. But he was beneath her notice. He knew the only person she loved was his master. She was wearing the habitual brown suit, which hugged her figure in a sleek line over her curves. She had great tits and a tight little arse and she scampered about and pandered to Eisenmann's every whim. Her hair was soft brown and silky. He had never seen it badly groomed or ratty.

Heine had no idea how old she was. Sigi always looked the same, but she kept her personal life a secret. Where she slept, he didn't know, but he guessed it was in Eisenmann's bed. He had heard his master call her '*Mausl*' – little mouse, a lovey-dovey name. Another dangerous thought that Heine swallowed immediately.

'The Faculty list,' Eisenmann said, handing it to Sigi. His lips curved into a smile, transforming them from string-thin to full and rich. 'The boy has arrived.' Heine recognised the tone. Thick with satisfaction.

'Good,' she said. Sigi's voice was not attractive, especially when she was excited. It was high and almost a squeak. She and Eisenmann smiled in collusion. Despite that secret understanding, Heine couldn't help thinking what a beautiful couple they made. Then they caught him looking.

'Get out!' ordered Eisenmann. 'And bring round the car. Sharp!'

'Sir!' As he left them, Heine's anger at being on the outside of their secret confidence boiled inside. But he knew it must never spill over into treachery. They must never know how jealous he felt.

Later, as he drove the Mercedes to pick them up, he shivered as a chill struck right through his body. In one terrifying moment, he realised they probably knew already.

1

Faculty of History and Philosophy
The University of North Transylvania, 2007

'Come in,' called Professor Simu Dalca in response to the knock. He stood up as his young visitor entered and shook hands with him briefly. 'Please sit down.' He gestured towards an easy chair. 'I'm afraid it's somewhat dark.' Dalca banned the sunlight from his study on a regular basis.

'Sun ruins the covers,' he explained, gesturing towards his walls, 'especially the leather-bound ones.' Dalca revered his books. To him, the sun was a secret disease, mottling the binding with cancerous spots.

'I agree,' replied the American. But the sun was still strong enough to force its way through the very edge of the slatted shutters, revealing motes of dust spinning in its thick beams. 'It's good of you to see me.'

'My pleasure,' Dalca replied, wondering how long the coming meeting would take. He wanted to get home to Arva as soon as possible.

'Would you mind if I took off my jacket?' asked Philip Durrant. He hadn't been sure if he should have worn a collar and tie for his first meeting with Professor Dalca, but he shouldn't have worried. The man himself was wearing a long, black cotton jacket, half buttoned to expose a wealth of greying chest hair; and loose matching trousers, which looked like befitting wear for someone with the reputation of being the foremost expert in Ancient Romanian Studies. Add to that a beard of Rasputin dimensions and Pip sensed he was facing a less than conventional individual. Not tall; shorter than him, in fact. Morose too, by the look of it. He probably wanted to get home!

'In a couple of months, you won't be doing that. It gets pretty cold over here.' Dalca smiled as he watched Durrant put down his briefcase and place the jacket on the back of the chair. His visitor took time over the task, which indicated to Dalca the boy was meticulous; an essential quality in a professional researcher, but often irritating to the observer. Once the jacket was positioned to the other's satisfaction, Dalca leaned back. 'It's good to meet a new post-doc. Usually, they keep themselves to themselves in the Institute. So what brings you here to the Faculty of History and Philosophy?' He would have preferred to conduct their conversation in Romanian, but the lad probably wasn't up to it yet. Wet behind the ears.

Dalca had looked Durrant up after he had requested the meeting. The American was 15 years his junior, born 1975, Sunny Mead, New Hampshire, USA. He had a PhD in Psychology and, as expected, had studied for his doctorate at a prestigious New York institute that had close links with their university.

He was now about to embark on post-doctoral studies at their own Institution, where it was their policy to welcome foreign graduates. Such liaisons were motivated not only by higher aspirations in research. Foreign money was essential for the coffers.

Romania needed all the help it could get from the academic world, wherever that might be situated. PACE was keen enough to be publishing papers on the subject of cultural co-operation at international level. Indeed, the University had one or two very influential people on their side in the *Palais de l'Europe*: Eisenmann for instance.

Pip had been considering his reply carefully while he withstood the Professor's silent appraisal. That was the way with academics. They deliberated before they spoke. He was the same, but he couldn't help how he felt at that moment. Lit up.

He was sitting opposite someone who, hopefully, would further his research. He had been working on the Marcu Papers ever since the previous year, when he was looking for a subject for his post-doctoral studies. And when he had finally got the chance to come to Transylvania, he had investigated the University's Faculty staff very carefully indeed.

He had never expected to be so lucky. Simu Dalca was not only an eminent historian, but originated from the village of Arva. The very thought of what he might know turned Pip's stomach over. But he mustn't blurt it all out. It wouldn't be professional. Marcu would never have been so clumsy.

'I'm not here to see you as a psychological researcher, Professor, but rather from a desire to know more about your subject,' he said.

Dalca's black eyes pierced him. Their gaze could be terrifying for his students, but could also bring out the best in them. 'That's refreshing,' he said. 'So how can *I* help you?'

'I want to learn as much as I can about the ancient culture of this region and its historical background.'

'Why?' The monosyllable was tight, and Pip wondered if he had been too enthusiastic, appearing like any other young American, overwhelmed by the age of a culture so different from his own.

'I confess to having an obsession with Transylvania,' he said. 'Don't get me wrong. I love my subject, and I hope that what I might learn from you could further my knowledge of it.'

'Obscurity is not my line,' Dalca replied. 'I deal with historical facts and try to make sense of them.' He frowned.

Pip could see he had made a bad start, so he decided to come clean.

'In my last year in the States, after my PhD, I was directed by my professor to some psychological papers he was holding. They had been sent in 1993 to his predecessor, who had never got round to doing anything about them. Professor Wright thought they might arouse my curiosity, given my interest in

Romania.'

Dalca leaned forward. Original papers! It excited him to see the young man's eagerness.

'I know you're wondering why,' Pip continued. He hesitated, '… Something …' Dalca nodded at him to carry on. '… Something inside sparked off the interest. I actually read up all about the country when I was a kid. And the idea stuck.'

'You must have been a very unusual kid then?' Dalca's dark eyebrows were raised.

'I was.' That was part of the old Pip he didn't care to remember.

Dalca caught the expression. The light had gone from the lad's face. The bespectacled young academic had a haunted look, a wan sensitivity that spoke of what? Past suffering? Dalca knew all about that.

'Do you have Romanian roots?'

'No,' Pip shook his head. 'My early enthusiasm was entirely non-academic. I can't explain.' He didn't add, *nor do I want to*. 'And the papers consolidated it.'

'Tell me about these extraordinary papers, Philip,' said Dalca, leaning back in his chair and crossing one leg. 'If they are historical as well as psychological, I might have heard of them. If so, I might be able to throw some light on them?'

'That's why I'm here, Professor. By the way, they call me Pip back home.'

'Okay, *Pip*.' As Dalca settled back in his chair, a timid wind crept across the well-cut lawn and started to rattle the shutters, snivelling to be let in. It was as if it knew a storm was stirring itself in the Apuseni Mountains, bringing its own dark music to mingle with the sounds of gypsy festivals that rose from the villages on the Transylvanian Heath.

The room grew cool and the sharp mind of the historical researcher was working now. Original papers unearthed in an American university. Dalca knew that Durrant had first strike, but what the lad had access to might be of great value to him personally. He couldn't wait to hear. 'So what got you started? Who was their author?' he asked.

'You may have heard of him. Dr Sacha Marcu?'

Dalca felt goosepimples rise all over his legs. The Marcu Papers! So they *had* been conveyed to the States – and now this boy had his hands on them! They had been lying in some dusty vault for 15 years, and had now been handed over to some youngster who had no knowledge of their real historical value. Dalca couldn't believe they were back in Cluj.

The professor did not answer, so Pip took his silence as a negative. 'Okay, I'll explain, if you have time to listen,' he replied. He needed to be careful, his instincts telling him it would be unwise to reveal all he had discovered. The Professor had taken out a handkerchief and was mopping his brow with it.

'Carry on. I have plenty of time. I'd be delighted to hear what you have to say,' Dalca waved. He would have sat there until doomsday to hear what else Marcu had discovered. Marcu's unfinished scholarly book had been the talk of the town in the late '80s, and it was rumoured that his early demise had occurred due to him knowing too much. But then the bulk of his work had disappeared – perhaps stolen by someone close to him. The university saw it as a scandal that Burbor Hospital had not instigated an inquiry into the whereabouts of the missing research, but at that time they had been at odds with the University, which should have been the only proper place for a work of such social and historical importance.

Pip was relieved. The last thing he wanted was for a man from Arva to prove an obstacle in his search for the elusive Grandsire, whose presence he had discovered that red-letter day in 2006; the day Professor Wright had left out the Marcu Papers for him to take home. How could he ever forget the shock he had experienced, when he opened his own Pandora's box?

2

New York, 2006

Pip had been down to Sunny Mead the week before he had opened the box containing the academic papers. His mom had been determined they all celebrate the award of his PhD. Which six of them had; but it had been a bit of a damp squib. Mel, his elder sister, was pregnant with her first kid and got sick all the time. That's what came of starting a family late.

Teddy had said he couldn't make it, while Rose, his twin, had been far too absorbed in herself and her new boyfriend. Mom had been upset by his siblings' lack of enthusiasm at Pip's success. Even his dad had been called out in the middle of the party. He was Chief now, down at the police station, where they were struggling to boost the ranks. They sure were short of officers. 'After all,' said Dave, when he was feeling gloomy, 'who wants to be paid to get shot?' Hence the pressure on his dad.

Pip suspected Diane had organised the unwelcome party because she missed them all a lot and wanted to get her family back together. His mother was different now. Diane had been a very strong woman when he had first left home, but recently, she had begun to worry about him and ring him up a lot. Almost as if he were a kid again and needed looking after. She had even sent him parcels in case he didn't get enough to eat in New York! One of them had contained a tiny silver cross and chain, which Pip had put in his wallet immediately and forgotten about. He didn't need smothering. He was quite well now. He would have liked to have told her, but he didn't want to hurt her feelings.

Frankly, Pip had been more than happy to return to his own domain: a second floor apartment in Brooklyn, with dark period furniture and a big kitchen with a great ice box. From his living room he could look out on the street through the flyscreen and see the neighbourhood going about their business. Just as he had always done from his attic at home, when he was in his wheelchair.

He loved the area he lived in, with its convenient subway link to the Institute and its buzzing atmosphere. What he liked in particular was stopping off for breakfast at the great little diner, which was always packed with interesting people. He often sat there, just watching. Taking it all in.

Nothing escaped Pip even now. He was a born observer, a true researcher, who had never quite got out of wanting to be on his own. He told himself he was a loner, because the accident had done that to him. Anyway, he still had a beloved pet to keep him company.

Cass, the white rat, had been the first in a long line of tame rodents. The latest Cass, who lived in a comfortable cage in his bedroom, was looked after while he was away by a friend of his, who told him that the rat had been pining for him ever since he went to New Hampshire. Pip knew it was true. Cass was the recipient of his private thoughts. He was hoping his friend would take on the rat when he went to Cluj. He didn't keep toads anymore, because Bufo's fate was something he would never forget. At 13, stepping on your dead pet in the dark was not a good memory …

He remembered the first evening back when he had sat with the new Cass on his knee, looking out of the window and stroking her sensitive nose to calm himself. He had been on edge that night with the true excitement of the researcher, and his nervousness had brought back memories, which he didn't want to harbour.

So he had forced himself to remember that waiting for him the next day in the professor's study was a completely new project. No-one else had handled it. It was unknown territory, except to two dead men and Professor Wright, who had handed it to him on a plate.

'Too good to be true, eh, Cass,' murmured Pip.

He remembered what Wright had said: 'I'll look the box out for you. You can take it home if you want. I would have deposited the papers in the Library, but I didn't want them putting in the General Catalogue. Nor the Psychology Library. I shouldn't have done it really, but I always intended to do something about them myself.

'Then I never got round to it. Actually, I've only glanced at them. They look interesting, but I'm too busy now preparing my new book for publication. You, Pip, have a bright future – and an interest in Romania.' He had lifted his eyebrows at that point. 'I think it would be good for you to glance at them. I sense there is some mileage in this. And, of course, it would be great for the Institute if you publish when you come back from Europe. I'll certainly recommend it.'

'Thank you,' Pip had replied with alacrity. 'I'll acknowledge you as my US supervisor, of course.' Wright had grinned, then grimaced.

'Maybe you shouldn't bother! Marcu died very young and Professor Davis, my predecessor, didn't last long afterwards. That was a nasty business. Watch out for vampires!' Unfortunately, Davis had fallen off a ladder at home and impaled himself on his own garden railings. Pip hadn't answered at that juncture, because the remark had been entirely out of character for Wright. He had assumed it was some kind of bad joke. After all, opening the box wasn't going to be like discovering a Pharaoh's grave or embarking on some Indiana Jones venture.

'I'll bring the garlic when I come,' he had quipped …

Wright had left the black box containing the Marcu Papers on the table in front of the window. It measured about 45 by 25 centimetres and was deep. When Pip first saw it, he realised he could hardly carry that home and decided that he needed to extricate the documents.

As he opened the box, he was struck by the particular mustiness that he recognised as ancient. He wrinkled his nose, like Cass did when she was inquisitive. Bizarre. The contents weren't that old.

On the top of them lay a letter with a Romanian postmark. He opened the envelope carefully and found himself staring at hospital notepaper – Burbor – Cluj – and handwritten. Strangely, the words were not in Romanian, but in faulty English written in a small, closed, neat hand, which a graphologist might label as belonging to someone who is objective in outlook and concentrates on details.

The content however belied their technique; an almost hysterical note explaining why the man was writing. Pip squinted at the signature. He couldn't make out the surname, only the first.

Robert, Marcu's charge nurse at Burbor Psychiatric Hospital, declared he had been asked by Marcu to pack up all his research papers and send them secretly to Professor Davis in the event of his early demise.

Pip shook his head. He didn't believe in premonitions, but it had been lucky for him that Marcu had been so organised. Then he reprimanded himself for being happy taking advantage of another's ill-luck. Heart attack and only in his thirties. Pip shrugged, putting the letter back and lifting the lot out of the box onto the table.

All at once, he felt himself stagger under the weight. 'What the hell!' he said as he laid the documents down. They seemed to be burning his hands. Of course, the sun. They had been sweltering in that box, lying in the heat all day. He passed a hot hand over his brow. His head was aching and he hoped it wasn't a migraine coming on.

All of a sudden he was thinking of how he had felt after the storm … He blinked.

He hardly ever thought about what had happened to him that day in Sunny Mead, when he had come to in the ruined lakeside house and found he was like other people again. Funny how everything came back, even when he thought he had made a conscious effort to relegate it to his subconscious. He had even been thinking about poor old Bufo the night before.

You, of all people, should know how the mind works, he reminded himself. *Lighten up. You've been under a lot of pressure lately. What with presenting your thesis and then having to go down to Sunny Mead to the party.* He felt angry about the whole fiasco.

'Calm down,' he said, out loud. 'And don't start reading anything just now. Get it all home first.'

It nearly killed him not to look at the material, and it took quite a while to carefully transfer all the documents into his backpack.

On his way home, Pip felt distinctly nauseous. He thought he might be sickening for something, because he felt almost too weak to lug the backpack up to his apartment.

It was already dark when Pip finally settled down under the anglepoise lamp, his laptop to his left so that he could make notes, and the Marcu Papers to the right. Unfortunately, when he began examining them, he still felt faintly sick and uneasy for no particular reason.

He started by looking at the sheets in chronological order. The bound half-manuscript was particularly interesting. Ironically, the village called Arva was quite near to the Institute where he was hoping to begin his post-doc studies in 2007. That was, if he had anything worthwhile to research.

'*The Feminine Folk Culture of North Transylvania: A Psychological Study,*' he said. 'This is strange. Marcu is so clinical, then he writes something like this: *Chapter One, "Culled from her Head, Written in her Heart's Blood," as told to Dr Sacha Marcu.* Pip shook his head. 'Bit airy-fairy!'

He had a habit of talking out loud. It didn't matter, as there was no-one to hear except Cass, who sat quite still in the corner of her cage, regarding him with her bright pink eyes.

Marcu had been as thorough as he could, given the

tenuous nature of the material. Yet he appeared to have been particularly careful with his analysis of the case notes. He had found an in-patient to tell him what happened in an annual ritual that took place in the village of Arva; a schizophrenic woman who had been sent to him by the local doctor.

Baescu, wrote Pip, and thought, *He's probably retired by now!* The Arvan ritual happened every year in July. It appeared to have a religious basis. According to Marcu's patient, the late Irina Petrescu, the middle of July either ended or began another cycle of misery for the Arvan woman.

When did the whole thing start? Pip found himself wanting to know. He scrabbled briefly through police statements and hospital reports. *Where is the maths for all this?* Back to the interviews. Back to the statements. Marcu had been playing about with the figures, but hadn't had a lot to go on. Only police records. As far as the inspector on the case had known, this kind of atrocity had happened twice – in 1952 and in 1988 – but Irina Petrescu had intimated that the old village women had passed on the knowledge of other past horrific crimes to their unfortunate descendants.

And Arvan men purported to know nothing about what happened to their daughters. They stayed in bed on 22 July! The whole thing was monstrous. *The secret of the marriage bed,* they called it.

As for the policeman who had worked on the 1988 case, the evidence of his own eyes had been horrifying and seemed unbelievable. *Interview Valentin (if he's still around),* wrote Pip.

Appended to the chapters were a series of scribbled notes, as if the writer had felt he must get everything down, *just in case…* Pip thought he knew how Sacha Marcu must have felt. Trying to grasp what was beyond one's reach was both tortuous and irritating for the researcher. And he had never had the chance to finish. That would be death to Pip!

Sacha had evidently come to a full stop before he died, which had occurred on the day he met this man Eisenmann in Cologne. Pip grimaced. How frustrating was that? Anyway, why had Marcu thought the German would help him? Pip studied the letters that had passed between them. Herr Eisenmann had seemed willing to share his knowledge. So he made another note: *Get in touch with Eisenmann.*

As he read on, the brutality of what Marcu had been investigating spooked him. *Grandsire only likes children ... Grandsire has to be satisfied by the rape and murder of virgins!*

One thing Pip hated was child molesters. With good reason. His stomach turned as his inward eye flashed him a picture of six year old Teddy and Rose, hand-in-hand, wandering innocently along the lakeside. He hated it when past moments surfaced from the dark pool of his consciousness. A moment later, he had gained control and read on.

No wonder the mother had gone mad after what had happened to her only daughter, Anka. One of the questions Marcu had asked, which Pip felt was fair enough, was: did the father know? And if he did, why hadn't he stepped in and prevented the girl from 'going-up', as it was called? Another question that presented itself was, why didn't the Church do anything about a pagan ritual carried out on consecrated ground? It was even rumoured that the priest rang the bell to celebrate what was about to take place in his own churchyard.

The priest mentioned by Sacha – Pip felt he could call him by his first name now – was Father Joseph, but he had also cited a Father Pathan. Which of the two was the current priest? Pip made another note: *Village priests, Frs Joseph and Pathan.*

But it was the maths that was the real problem. According to the scribbled notes, and to Irina's evidence, all Arvan girls were forced to get married at 19. Why? Pip frowned then, as he had so many times since he had begun his work on the Papers. He could see that he needed to do something that Sacha had not done: go back to the parish registers and check the births, marriages and deaths. It was strange that hadn't been done already.

He withdrew another envelope that he had not bothered to look at on his first trawl. It bore an American stamp. He presumed it was some communication from Professor Davis to Marcu. He couldn't have been more wrong.

It was another set of dialogues. And clipped to the back of it was a photograph. Nothing could have prepared Pip for what he was about to see. The light-blue eyes stared back at him mockingly, challenging him to remember. How could he forget those haggard features, or the straggling yellow hair that fell upon the bony shoulders. A face that the rest of his family had adored once but had made Pip sick.

The feeling that had plagued him all day forced up the bile and acid in his stomach and, clapping his hand over his mouth, Pip threw the photograph down on the table and staggered towards the lavatory. Seconds later he threw up what felt like all the food he had consumed that day.

He leaned sweating over the toilet bowl, his heart thudding in his ears, his head buzzing. Diep Koppelberg, the music teacher, come back to haunt him. The man who tormented his dreams. Whose black rat was the nightmare that had stuck in his brain for years. How could it be him? How would Marcu have known about *him*? It couldn't be true.

He was a long time in the bathroom, and when he emerged, he felt so weak he had to hold on to the door for support. The ordinariness of his own living room calmed him outside, but inside he was almost as afraid as when he had been a boy. He remembered the fear – the fear of the thing. The terror that it might get him.

He had to look at those papers again. Slowly, he crossed the room and edged towards the table where he had been working. The lid of his laptop was open, just as he had left it. 'How can a photograph hurt you?' he encouraged himself, speaking out loud again. 'You must have been mistaken about Koppelberg. It's somebody else. You were thinking about what happened all last night and you got it wrong, you stupid shit.'

Somewhere in the back of his head, he could hear his rat scrabbling at the bars of her cage. She had been spooked too, just like the original Cass. Shivers of fear ran up and down his back like worm strings as he approached the table, where the documents lay.

He sat down gingerly and, putting out his hand, pulled

his laptop towards him. He stared at the letters on the screen. *NICHOLAS.* Italicised in 16 font. He hadn't written that. He couldn't have! He touched the mouse with a shaking hand and the screen froze.

He had to switch off. When he switched back on and recovered his notes, the name had disappeared. Who was Nicholas? He knew he hadn't typed in that name.

Looking sideways at the photograph and avoiding the staring eyes, he flipped it over quickly. Someone had scrawled on its reverse: *July 1952.*

36 years before Koppelberg. He felt calmer then.

'What was all that about, Pip?' he asked himself. For God's sake, he had a PhD in psychology and he wasn't given to hysterics. Not now, anyway! Some people resembled others. Of course they did! It was a known fact that everyone had a double. A *doppelgänger*, the Germans called it.

So he forced himself to read the accompanying notes that had come via Dr Baescu to Sacha Marcu.

The Rat and the Piper: A case-study of poly-personality traits derived from a series of interviews with WA, in-patient, Weser Psychiatric Institute for Sexual Offenders, N J. USA. 1952.

INTRODUCTION

Walter Arvarescu, a male Caucasian of Eastern European origin, probably Romanian, a sufferer from schizophrenia since his early teenage years, has always maintained that his series of attacks on young children (mainly pre-pubescent girls) were prompted by his principal alter ego, the mythical Pied Piper of Hamelin, and his accompanying bête-noire, a rat named SNIPE. The name is an anagram of the male sex organ and, doubtless, the scapegoat for Arvarescu's savage and insatiable sex drive. In these interviews, the offender blames 'the rat' for his 'failures', a metaphor for his guilt complex after committing the crimes. Walter Arvarescu's intelligence quotient tested on the 99 percentile and his musical and literary abilities are believed to have contributed to his schizophrenic fantasies.

The following dialog entitled 'The Rat and the Piper', is taken from a case study made while he was an in-patient in one of the leading American psychiatric institutions. Dialog 17 is particularly interesting as it was the last recorded before Arvarescu absconded and was never recaptured in spite of an extensive nationwide search. (Dialog 17 was recorded in the presence of Dr W Dietmann, consultant psychologist...)

It was not nice reading. He replaced the notes quietly.

Paranoid schizophrenics often imagined themselves to be reincarnations of the great and good, as well as the mythical. God was a favourite! This man thought he was the Pied Piper, which gave him an excuse for his bestial crimes.

Pip didn't understand the connection between the photograph, the dialogues, Sacha Marcu and what he had been through himself. How could there be any association? It was ridiculously inexplicable, and he needed a clear head to even think about tackling it. So he consigned the terrors he'd experienced earlier to his personal 'Don't go there' file. But he still shivered every time he looked at the madman's face, so he relegated that to the basement of his mind and the very bottom of the envelope.

Later on, Pip realised he would have to find out more about this criminal, who evidently had something to do with Marcu's research. Why else would Sacha have been sent a copy of the letter by the policeman in charge in 1988? Pip still couldn't bear to go back to his notes on the laptop, so he wrote *Valentin* in his notebook.

Yet his brain wouldn't let that name go. It annoyed him like a flying insect that buzzes around incessantly and needs to be swatted. *Nicholas … Nicholas.*

Hold on! Wasn't *Nicholas* mentioned in the dialogues he had just read? He didn't want to look at the papers again, but he forced himself to. All the rubbish about the Pied Piper didn't make sense, but why would it? He promised himself he would look up the Hamelin date though. His knowledge of history was scanty, but he had Wikipedia to rely on for a start. But, again, for some reason, he didn't want to use the laptop until the next morning. He left it, sitting black and squat on the table.

That night the dreams rushed in, kindled by his memory. When he woke up in the morning, he felt and looked as if he had died, and hardly recognised his own face in the bathroom mirror.

He had to face it. He was still hurting. He knew now that he should have done what everyone had wanted him to at the time. See a shrink. But he had resisted every effort his parents had made to help. He had always been stubborn. As a teenager, he had thought he was invincible; and yet, 19 years later, merely looking at a picture of someone who resembled Koppelberg filled him with terror.

It was at that point he decided that taking on the Marcu Papers, whatever they contained, might lay a personal ghost or two. It was not an academic decision, only an instinctive belief. He was not religious. Why he had been led to them, he didn't know – yet. But he had a feeling it was all going to work. Once he reached Romania.

3

Faculty of History and Philosophy
The University of North Transylvania, 2007

'And that's why I'm here, Professor,' added Pip. 'I have been working on the Marcu Papers since last year.'

'Dr Marcu was unfortunate. It was a great pity that he died so young and was unable to finish his research. As an historian, I consider his death to be a very great loss.'

Dalca's face gave no indication of how he felt. He had listened to the boy's explanation, ensuring that he had given no clue as to his innermost thoughts and fears.

He did not add, *It was also a great loss that Marcu's ongoing research should have been handed over to an American university, rather than stay in its proper place, a Romanian institution. He had been the most brilliant student when he was at Cluj.*

Dalca continued, his voice calm, ' Yet, as an Arvan man myself, I fancy there are several for whom his death was a relief.' He saw Pip frown. ' None of us like to have our innermost fears and weaknesses exposed to the world. Marcu used his patients as an entomologist spears beetles.'

'That is harsh,' retorted Pip. He could see the point, but it had been in the cause of science – and history. 'I want to publish *The Feminine Folk Culture of North Transylvania* in its entirety. My professor back home has indicated it is a possibility. To finish what Marcu started. Have you read the first part? It's amazing.'

'So it may be,' Dalca replied. 'Yes, I have read it, and I

have no wish to vilify what he accomplished. However, many people were affected by it – and I think that Marcu knew that would happen when he embarked on the project. I speak from personal knowledge and from a quarter that is entirely non-academic. My mother-in-law – if she had ever met him – would have torn out his heart.' Dalca moistened his lips with his tongue.

'I'm sorry to hear that,' said Pip, his own heart racing in his chest. He knew that the Professor would not have mentioned something so personal if he had no intention of co-operating with him. 'Why?'

'Does the name Murgu figure in your papers?'

Pip reached down and began to open his briefcase. Then he remembered as he flipped through the index in his mind.

'Yes,' said Pip. 'A Simona Murgu gave a testimony about herself and Claudiu Basa. *Statement 25/7/1952.*'

'Then, my young American friend, you and I have something to discuss,' said Dalca. 'But it will not be pleasant …'

'If you could get me an introduction to Simona Murgu, that would be of great help.' Pip was feeling quite excited. 'She might be able to tell me more about the origins of Grandsire.'

Dalca looked at the boy. How long would his optimism last? 'I doubt it,' he said.

'Yes, you're right, I suppose.' All Marcu had had to go on had been the testimony of an already mentally ill patient. Pip sighed. 'I'm always optimistic, but I don't think Marcu was. Hopefully, though, things have changed somewhat?'

He saw Dalca raise his eyebrows. In fact, Marcu had said that no-one sane was willing to speak of the secret; but it would have been insensitive and unprofessional to have revealed such a cynical remark to the professor.

'If *you* approached her, I might be luckier than Marcu,' tried Pip.

'To learn the secret of the marriage bed …' Dalca's voice was so low, Pip could hardly hear, so he only nodded. Then

Dalca raised his tone and shook his head. 'I'm not sure if Simona would talk to you about anything. She's been through a great deal over the last few years.'

'You sound as if you know her well.'

Dalca nodded.

Pip persevered. 'Is Arva a big place?'

'The village is small, but spread out. Even the farmers know their neighbours. The villagers and the farmers are a tight-knit community and do not welcome strangers.' He looked at Pip from under his brows. 'Like all people, they have secrets. But "the marriage bed" is something different.'

'How,' asked Pip, trying to keep any hint of excitement out of his voice or demeanour.

'The secret is a personal mythology. Part of ancient folklore. For instance, the Dracula myth is universal, yet we in Romania purport to own it. But who has heard of Arva?'

Pip was about to reply 'the State Police', but thought better of it. At that point, the Professor's tone irritated him. Arva's secret had given rise to the worst crimes. Why should it be hidden from the world? Marcu had been right to begin the investigation.

'I have been brought up with it,' repeated Dalca, 'but I do not condone it.' His voice was harsh. He must have sensed what Pip was thinking. 'Once, I thought it was a silly superstition bandied about by old women and encouraged by an obsolete Church to keep us on the straight and narrow, but now ...' He hesitated.

'*Now?*' Pip could feel raw excitement tingling through him. Shiver-making. The kind that precipitates a daredevil kid into full-blown fury that takes no heed of the consequence, or a reasonable adult to take ill-advised steps.

'... Now I know better what it leads to.' Tiny droplets of sweat clung precariously above Dalca's upper lip, turning his moustache into the last defence against the tip of a tongue that was trying to moisten his dry upper lip. The boy mustn't know in what way Dalca's own family was involved – yet. 'The skeleton in Arva's cupboard is an ominous shadow that brings darkness to our minds and creates fear and division in our families. We are constrained by it. It was never questioned, until by Marcu – for which he paid a heavy price.'

Pip was about to say, *You think his death wasn't natural?* But he kept quiet. He needed Dalca to keep on track.

Dalca continued, 'God knows if others have tried to uncover it in the past. If they did, they left no proof. And you! Do you think *you* can expose it, unearth it, root it out, where the rest have failed?'

Dalca jumped to his feet and stared down at Pip, his dark eyes gleaming. The calm academic front had been replaced by an intense animation that was well known to his students. 'Anyway, what business is it of yours? I should tell you to leave, Philip Durrant. To go back to your cosy life in the United States. Leave the secret to those who are affected by it. Romania has had many do-gooders who soon disappeared when the going got tough.'

'I'm not leaving,' said Pip. 'If Marcu thought it was worth doing, I do as well; and if he could ferret it out, then so can I.' He had thought Dalca might be dismissive of the project, but not hostile.

Dalca regarded him closely, as if trying to deduce if he was stubborn or mad. Then he said, 'I'm sorry.' He breathed in to calm himself. 'Spoken like a true researcher. I am only trying to dissuade you from a project that is unlikely to succeed. Unfortunately, delving into something like this could be extremely dangerous. Village people are superstitious. And they don't welcome foreigners meddling with legends they have revered for centuries. At least Marcu was Romanian. And popular. I heard he had quite a following in the hospital. They saw him as some kind of saviour.' Dalca sniffed.

'Why?'

'The hierarchy believed he was going to put *them* on the map. And look where it got him.'

'Earlier on you said you'd only *heard* of Marcu. I get the impression you actually know a lot about him,' replied Pip.

'What I know is not all good. Granted he was a clever

man and persistent. Arvan women ...' Dalca sighed.

'Yes?'

'... Feared Marcu. It seemed that all he was doing was watching them for the slightest signs of illness and then having them admitted to a god-awful place full of broken people where he could winkle out anything they knew.'

'You mean Burbor?'

Dalca nodded.

'It hasn't a good reputation. Why Marcu ever wanted to work there, God knows.'

'Perhaps he was trying to improve the place?'

'Maybe. In the beginning. But then, after he began researching, it was the ideal place to transport anyone who fitted into his brief.'

'You make him sound like a monster.'

Dalca shrugged.

Pip's quick mind computed the word. Hadn't Irina called Marcu a monster? That was disconcerting.

'Have you been to the hospital yet?' Dalca asked.

Pip shook his head. He wasn't looking forward to the visit.

'Well, you've a treat waiting.'

'I shall be interviewing Robert, if he's still there.'

Dalca looked blank.

'The charge nurse who worked with Marcu throughout his time at Burbor.'

'Ah.'

The Professor watched Pip put back his notes and close his briefcase. The young man appeared to relax, which must have meant he had learned all he wanted to at present. Dalca was surprised. 'Is that all?'

'No, there's something else. *I* would like to go to Arva. To stay for a while. Perhaps you could fix me up with a room or something?'

'Perhaps. Then my gut instinct to warn you that you should give up the idea of researching the Marcu Papers, has not worked.'

'No chance,' retorted Pip. 'I'm well known for being stubborn.'

Pip's final reaction produced a half-smile. So Dr Durrant had taken the bait. He would not have been who he was, if he hadn't. Dalca's test of his staying power had worked. Pip would not be put off. Well, he had tried. This was no boy, after all, but another young doctor with a purpose. The Professor liked that. He had been looking for such an ally for a very long time. Maybe it was fate.

'There is not enough time to discuss anything else now,' he replied, consulting his watch. 'Where are you staying at present?'

Pip stood up and put on his jacket.

'In the University hostel.'

'Have you a car?'

'No,' said Pip, 'but I could hire one. Why?'

'That would not work well as a permanent arrangement. If you are to spend a lot of time in Arva and travel into Cluj, you'll need transport. The village is remote. You'll need a car.'

'Perhaps I should get one,' replied Pip. He had never been comfortable driving – not since his accident. But – hell – that had been years ago.

'We have a spare room.'

'Really?' It was more than Pip had hoped for. Professor Dalca offering him a room at his home.

'We're not very grand. Does that matter?'

'No,' grinned Pip.

'And I travel into the Department three times a week. The other times I am at home and we can talk.'

'What about a motorbike?' asked Pip. 'I had one back home.'

Dalca allowed himself a brief smile. He waved his hand in mock horror.

'That won't be necessary. I am sure we can find you a small car that would be suitable.'

'This is very kind of you,' said Pip.

'I have an ulterior motive. My daughter will be able to

practise her English. She's an English student. This offer is on one condition.'

Here we go, thought Pip.

'What you are working on must remain a secret to my family.' No sign of a smile now.

'I agree, but …' Pip hesitated.

'… But I promise you, we shall find time to get together. I would rather my wife and daughter thought that you were one of my history students. You understand?'

'Sure.'

Of course, Pip realised, Dalca wouldn't want the women of his family knowing what he was doing. According to Marcu, the men knew nothing about the secret, or ignored it. Pip's quick brain weighed up the possibilities. Maybe they did know, and yet did nothing? It was intolerable. According to Dalca, it was hardly Pip's business – but it was Pip's belief that an individual knowing about a crime and doing nothing to prevent it made him as guilty as the perpetrator.

They stood facing each other in the dimness of the room, then shook hands as if concluding a bargain.

'Then I shall set it in motion,' said Dalca. 'I'll discuss it with Emilia this evening. I am convinced that everything will be okay, as the Americans say.' His sombre face lightened, dispelling Pip's impression that he fell into Galen's category of melancholic man.

'I am grateful, Professor – and excited,' confessed Pip.

'I hope your enthusiasm lasts,' replied Dalca drily. His feelings were distinctly mixed. On the one hand, what he had prayed for – whether rightly or wrongly – had come to pass. Someone wanting to share the burden he had been carrying for years. But on the other hand, could he bear the responsibility of what might be the waste of another young life? Would Grandsire break this young foreigner, or worse?

'Just one other thing,' said Pip. 'You used the word *obsolete* to describe the Church. The Marcu Papers speak of the Arva ritual having a strong link with the Catholic Church and its practices. There was the involvement of Father Pathan, forinstance, and also the processional nature of the ritual.'

'Arva is rare among Romanian villages,' replied the Professor. 'It has been able to keep its faith in spite of persecution. Many villagers are Catholics. I am not, but my wife is. Communism forced Romanian Catholics to abandon the Church and join the Eastern Orthodox, or face a terrible penalty. Catholic churches were destroyed, but Arva's remained. An underground movement kept it going under the persecutions, and the ritual continued.'

'How did that happen?' asked Pip.

'God knows,' replied Dalca. *'Or Grandsire!'*

Pip glanced at him.

'Our church on the hill is now locked up. Hence my use of *obsolete.'*

'Even though things are easier politically?' Pip was surprised.

Dalca shrugged.

'There are reasons.'

Pip could see he wasn't going to elucidate.

'Catholic mass is held in the village hall,' continued the Professor. 'That is where you will find the current parish priest. His name is Joseph. He lives in the midst of his parishioners now, rather than separate from them.'

'Shall I ring you tomorrow?' asked Pip.

'Feel free.'

As Pip left, he fought the urge to run about screaming. He wanted to proclaim his breakthrough to the world. He shook his head in disbelief. He was going to be staying with the Dalcas in Arva! Then the cautious side of his nature prompted him to think that maybe he should keep his room in the hostel, just in case staying with the family didn't work out. He wasn't keen on it, with its rows of box-like flats making up the sides of a huge square, in the middle of which was a small lawn. It was uninspiring, but it served his purpose. He decided to keep it on. Besides, he needed to because of Cass. He couldn't imagine what the Professor and his wife would think if he brought a rat with him! Instead he would go in and feed it.

Then he tapped Dalca's wife, Emilia, into his brain's calculator. She must have 'gone-up' to Grandsire. When? 1968? *And*, Pip frowned, Dalca's daughter must have gone through the ritual too. What had her father said? She was studying English? He was counting. She would have 'gone-up' in – 2004. This was fantastic. *And he was unable to speak about it to either of them.*

He shrugged. Would Dalca have married her off at 19? He wondered then if any distinction was made between professional and peasant. Probably, but Marcu had never touched on it. All his patients had come from the peasantry as far as Pip knew. Farmers and suchlike. Dalca's family wouldn't have come into that category, would they?

'Let's see how it goes,' said Pip out loud as he made his way back to his accommodation. All he could think of now was what the Professor had said about keeping their secret from his family.

That's what Pip had done. He had kept the monstrous secret of Diep Koppelberg's identity locked deep inside him, so that it couldn't harm the people he loved most. But keeping quiet about the music teacher had nearly brought disaster to them all. Finally, Pip had stood up to the monster, with irreparable damage to himself.

Things had to be in the open; brought to light whatever the cost. But he couldn't break his word to Dalca. He had too much to lose. He tried to shrug off the memories and concentrated on his new surroundings. The Gothic spire of St Michael's Cathedral was thrusting its head into the darkening sky above the small, thin pines in the city park. Yet even those scrawny trees reminded him of the deep forests covering the peaks back home. How would he feel being so near to the Carpathians, the mountains he had longed to see for years?

He passed a bench where a young woman was sitting alone, reading. Pip's head was teeming with so many ideas about what might happen when he got to Arva, that he didn't consciously notice she was small, slim and attractive, with sleek brown hair, and wearing a neat, brown suit.

Once he had passed, she took out her mobile and pressed it to her ear.

'He's on his way back to his room now,' she said.

That evening, Pip phoned Robert Riparu and made an appointment to meet him. His immediate impression when talking to the nurse, who was now in charge of the department, was that the other did not share his own enthusiasm. *Probably because he doesn't want to re-visit what happened*, thought Pip. Visiting a psychiatric unit was something he was used to, but after Dalca's bleak reference to Burbor and Riparu's unwelcoming attitude, he had to admit he found the idea discouraging. Yet the visit was essential, given that it was the place where Marcu had carried out most of his research and where Riparu had assisted the psychiatrist in his treatment of Irina Petrescu.

Pip spent some time working on his laptop before he went to bed. He knew it was better to relax before sleep, and had been told that many times by the various doctors he had seen over the years. Post-traumatic stress had subtle ways of returning – in Pip's case, in the form of flashbacks and nightmares.

His head was full of the day's events when he went to sleep; and, later on, he had a visitor. He woke to the sight of the tall figure standing beside his bed, outlined with an eerie brightness. Pip's nerves crackled, while his mind, numbed from sleep, tried to remind him it could only be a dream. But the familiar old smell of fresh earth abused his nostrils.

His hand, one terrified part of his inert body, did not respond when he willed it to switch on the bedside light. This horror could not be dispelled by electricity. It had a fire of its own. The light blue fire of hypnotic eyes. Everything else was dark.

'I don't believe in you,' cried Pip from lips that didn't utter a word. 'Go away!' But the image didn't move. Behind it, he could hear the rat scampering madly about its cage. The logical part of his waking brain told Pip this had to be a nightmare, but he didn't trust it to tell him the truth.

The figure stooped, bending its thin frame over his bed. Now he could see its face glowing. The bright hair that cloaked the skull; the bony nose, a flaming red spot on its side; another bleeding bite on its cheek. The earth smell of the thing overwhelmed him. And the mouth – that dreadful mouth was curved into a mocking smile, showing the red-bud tip of a tongue that flicked in and out through a bar of pointed teeth. Koppelberg had come for him!

Pip's body skin puckered in disgust. *I won't go with him!* he told himself. *I won't!* In panic, his fingers scrabbled for something to hold on to and found nothing. Nothing to cling on to, to pull himself away from that terrifying face, that terrible spectre. He tried to catch hold of his pillow, to hide his face, to protect himself. But he couldn't move.

He lay there waiting, his eyes wide open. When his heart had stopped thudding in his ears and his frightened skin had calmed itself, he willed his arm to reach out, to touch the apparition, but it had gone. Where? His shaking hand obeyed him this time, switching on the light. He could feel fresh air blowing onto his face. The window was open! *That's how it got in.*

Then waking sense took over. He was all right. He was on the second floor. It had been another night fear. The psychiatrist had told him the science behind it all those years ago, when he had needed a hell of a lot of counselling after what had happened in Koppelberg's chalet. They hadn't found a body, and the music teacher had disappeared. He had never been traced. And Pip had been sure he wasn't simply a flute player – although nobody else except his psychiatrist had known that. Since then, Koppelberg's *doppelgänger* had appeared to Pip many times; and, when it happened, each visitation seemed worse than any previous one. Only when he had gone to college and engaged himself in his subject had the night fears subsided. This was the first time Koppelberg had returned for five years. Pip had forgotten how real the hallucination could be.

He scrubbed the sweat off his face with a tissue and drank some water, telling himself he understood only too well how powerful the subconscious mind could be.

He lay there, exhausted, going over the visitation in his mind. The explanation the psychiatrist had given him long before had been so comforting that, afterwards, he had felt that he would like to help other people who suffered in the same way. He had become a psychologist in order to do that. Back then, according to his counsellor, he had been in the *hypnagogic state* when he saw the vision. He had loved that big word as a kid. *Hypnagogic* – your brain paralyses your muscles when you're asleep, but sometimes you wake up and you're still able to see the things you were dreaming. He had believed it all then. But he wasn't a kid anymore. Not that he didn't believe in the theory now, but it didn't seem to work for him personally.

Had he been dreaming of Koppelberg? If he had, he didn't remember it. Each time it happened, he thought he should have grown out of it. But *should* was a word not approved of in his profession. Pip *knew* what had caused this visitation. His discovery of Arvarescu's photograph. It must have been the Marcu Papers that had sparked off the apparition again. The picture of Walter Arvarescu staring out at him with nothing behind those evil eyes, except a hollowness that made him shiver. A photograph of a criminal that couldn't be explained in Pip's terms. How could Arvarescu be Koppelberg? And what had it to do with Arva, where he was about to make his temporary home? It was a chilling thought. Arva and Arvarescu – a connection that was starting to make sense, if only it *were* sensible.

He breathed in deeply. He was relieved to feel fresh air in his nostrils, rather than the raw smell of newly-turned earth. He shook himself. He was all right now. What a fool he was to get so scared. He still felt very cold, and the curtains were blowing out into the room.

He couldn't remember leaving the window open. Pip's legs trembled as he got up and went over to it. As he did, the curtain hooked itself neatly over the frame, blown by the mischievous wind that scattered the pewter clouds, revealing the pale face of the moon.

As Pip leaned over to pull the window shut, he looked down. A cold moment of shock arrested him as his eyes focused on a dim tall figure stood in the middle of the lawn. He *knew* it was staring up at him. Who was it? Pip had never broken the habit of watching people and things outside, ever since he had been the little crippled kid in the attic back home, whose whole world had been inside. Now he used a different gear from those kids' glasses.

The eerie figure still didn't move. Grabbing his night vision binoculars, which lay on the sill, he selected the short range wide illumination and focused. The super-fast optics revealed nothing. No-one showed up. He couldn't understand why. The figure couldn't have moved so fast across that space! Pip scanned the lawn and the surrounding area. Nothing. He put down the powerful binoculars, feeling his hands trembling.

Hardly daring to move, he closed his eyes briefly, then his courage returned. There had to be an explanation. Throwing on his jacket, and checking he had his key, he almost jumped down the stairs and ran through the doors and out onto the empty lawn. He saw something white on the grass. As he approached, he realised it was a piece of paper. Why hadn't it blown away in the sharp wind? Fear crawled over his shoulders and into his arms. He knew it was a message.

Trying to calm himself, he stooped and picked it up. The two words were clear in the moonlight dancing in front of his eyes, mocking him. Pip read the warning:

REMEMBER ME

The man must have left it. He hardly dared look up. But he had to.

'Who are you? What do you want?' he shouted.

Nothing was in his head except needing to know. His voice reverberated against the buildings. Only silence. *Where are you?* thought Pip, while his frightened eyes scanned the area. Who would be sending him warning notes? *He'd had one before.* Perhaps ... He hesitated, fighting the ridiculous notion. Could it have been – Koppelberg! But it couldn't, because he was surely dead, burned to death in the chalet fire! Another thought followed. Maybe the man who had tormented him when he was a kid, had escaped and wanted to get even. He stood there, shaking, trying to control himself.

Or was it Nicholas? Then the memory of the earlier apparition came rushing back to him, compounding his fear. *Remember, it was only a dream,* he consoled himself. *It must have been.* In spite of his efforts, a frisson of terror shook him, resulting in a rush of pins and needles, a warning that a panic attack was imminent. He'd had too many of those. He shook his head as he fought against it.

Come on, you're not a kid now. Don't lose it. You're not scared of dreams. Convincing himself that everything would be all right, he finally regained control. But he was drained mentally, while the knowledge that someone was watching his every move spooked him.

At that moment, he found himself wishing that he had someone to confide in. But who would understand? He was in a foreign country.

4

Pip had not been prepared for the sights he was presented with in Burbor Hospital. His training had been in American psychiatric institutions of a good standard. Although he had seen photographs of the run-down hospitals in Romania, he had not expected it to be so bad. He knew that the country was doing its best to clean up its act, but the reality of Burbor was a shock. He remembered Professor Dalca's ironic remark when he had mentioned going there: *You've a treat coming.*

The hospital lay on high ground and consisted of several brick-built blocks that, from the outside, looked fairly promising, with their neat brickwork and modern outlook across an expanse of well-cut grass. The reality was far from that.

Near to, the paint was flaky and some of the windows cracked. Behind them was wire-mesh, broken and sharp pointed like an ominous cell structure. By one such window, a man was squatting near to the path. He grinned at Pip, revealing a mouth that was toothless except for two rotten stumps. On his head he wore a dirty red woolly hat, and his track suit was stained and baggy. As Pip passed by, the stench of urine floated thick into his nostrils, but to Pip, its smell shrieked neglect.

One of the blocks, named simply *West*, was connected to the *East* by a rusting footbridge. As Pip crossed it, he was struck by the simple horror of all around him. He paused to look down over a large expanse of concrete yard where garbage lay in uncollected heaps, and drew back as the smell of refuse assailed his nostrils. Several dismal looking crows were pecking at the rubbish without enthusiasm. He grimaced. *If it's like this for the people who are visiting, what's it like to be a patient?*, he thought.

In their recent telephone conversation, Robert Riparu had told him that only the most severely ill were in-patients, and those he had seen roaming around the grounds certainly looked serious cases. Some were accompanied by their visitors, who were leading them around or pushing them in chairs. Many wore the lost and vacuous look of the abandoned, while those who approached him appeared to be in bad physical shape, some emaciated, others with the same rotting stubs of teeth and dressed bizarrely. Pip shook his head. No wonder Riparu had been reluctant to meet him. The tone of his voice and his whole attitude had told Pip that he was destined to be an unwelcome visitor of a prying nature.

Once over the bridge, he was directed through numerous corridors, where the only sound was of his feet striking against the grim, concrete floors. These warrens were blank and uninviting except for a few sombre pictures and half-empty noticeboards. The general feeling of utter isolation made Pip wonder how someone could work in such an atmosphere for many years. He thought about Marcu and how he had managed to engender enough enthusiasm to continue with his research in such a dismal environment.

Eventually he found Riparu in a small room adjacent to the ward. Silence was not a good morning sign in a hospital. Usually at such a time, a ward would be full of hospital noises. None of the ward's patients could be seen, nor any busy nurses. Pip wondered if the patients were in a day room. Sometimes, wards were locked so that patients could not return to their beds or have the opportunity of pilfering others' belongings. Breathing in deeply, he knocked.

'Come in.' The voice was toneless, a wraith of sound that echoed in the emptiness.

When the man turned round, Pip's first impression was

that Riparu looked like a ghost himself. He was tall and thin and there was little left of what had been dark, curly hair. Although his face was pale, his hollow cheeks were blotched by two stains of red. He stood up, his face twisting into a smile.

'Dr Durrant.' The smile did not affect the tone.

'Pip, please,' he said in a friendly manner. He was expecting they might shake hands, but the man got up and indicated the chair in which he had been seated.

'Robert. Please sit.'

'It's yours, isn't it?' replied Pip in polite Romanian, indicating the chair.

'I'll fetch another,' said the nurse.

'Shall I?'

'No.'

The short answer only added to Pip's feeling of uneasiness. Chatting to Robert was not going to be easy, not only because Pip wasn't sure if his own language skills were up to scratch but because, although the man was equally polite when he introduced himself as the late Marcu's right-hand man, Pip could feel the same resentment that had been so clear on the phone. It was quite possible that Riparu did resent the fact that Pip had the opportunity to continue the work of his former boss – or it could have been the fact that Pip was American, as Professor Dalca had indicated. Pip knew that such a manner would not be useful to his patients, and he wondered if Robert had much rapport with them.

He looked round the office. It had nothing to commend it. A cell of a room, with several old filing cabinets that had been moved a number of times, leaving their steel impression in a dirty line on the flaking paint of the wall. Pip shook his head at the thought of the miserable accounts they probably contained. Trying to formulate the best way of eliciting information from someone who had been indispensable to Marcu, he was quite shocked to hear a girl laugh outside. It was such an incongruous sound in this atmosphere that he wanted to jump up and find out who she was.

A moment later, the door was being wedged open by a

chair. Robert was balancing it and returning the girl's banter. In spite of what Pip had thought, maybe all was not tears in this ward. The chair was small and hard when it was set down opposite him.

'Only one I could find.' Pip half-rose, but Robert shook his head. 'Stay there. The cushion is easier on the backside.' He grinned. 'Good to see you. Now what can I do for you?' He offered his hand now, and Pip gripped it, feeling a surprising warmth. 'So you would like to talk about Dr Marcu?' His face grew sombre again. 'He was not only my boss, but a friend.'

'His death was a great loss,' replied Pip. 'But we have to thank you for saving his work.'

'We?'

'I'm speaking not only for myself but also for my university.' Pip was aware the sentence sounded pompous. He attempted to soften it by adding, 'I was offered the chance to carry on with Dr Marcu's work by Professor Wright.'

'Not Professor Davis? That is where I sent the Papers.'

'Professor Davis died, I'm afraid.'

'He is dead.' The tone was flat again.

'He met with an accident at his home.' Pip felt that it would be better not to disclose to Robert the manner of Davis's untimely death. The colour had already left his face once more, and his pallor was frightening. 'Professor Wright took over from him and then – much later, of course – he handed the Papers on to me.'

'Perhaps he was afraid the same thing might happen to him?'

Pip frowned at the words. He remembered Wright's flippant remark about vampires and curses.

'I am not superstitious,' replied Pip.

Robert looked at him and sucked in his cheeks.

'Sacha – Dr Marcu and I were on first name terms ...' began Robert.

Pip nodded.

'Sacha was very keen for me to send the Papers to Professor Davis. "Just in case," he said. "*Just in case something happens to me."* When I asked him if he was ill, he laughed and joked, "Of course not!" He didn't *seem* ill.' The words had tumbled out so fast that Pip had found it hard to keep up. 'It was almost as if he knew he was going to die. I'm sure it was a premonition.' Robert stopped and was staring in front of him almost as if he had forgotten Pip's presence.

Who am I to say premonitions don't exist?, thought Pip. The scientific view was that precognition could be put down to coincidence, but those with an open mind were willing to consider other explanations. He thought of the silent watcher again. The incident had shaken him. It had brought back memories he'd kept hidden and made him think about the horrible visions he'd experienced as a teenager. Thank God they were not likely to come true – *except one*, he thought. He was still waiting for that to happen. Trained psychologist or not, sometimes he really believed that it would. The man and the child who had sprung out of nowhere. That vision had stayed with him. The last one he had seen, when he had imagined what was inside Diep Koppelberg's chalet. The next-to-last display case, which had been empty. It had been clean and bright as if it had never been used. Pip had run his hands up and down its sides. It had been made of shiny stuff, of a kind he'd never seen before, and had no sides, like a rectangle drawn in his school maths book.

Then he had seen a speck moving in one corner. But there had been no corner, because it had been changing, disappearing in front of his eyes. The speck had grown bigger and bigger. Pip had been terrified. He hadn't been able to take his eyes off it as it had slowly grown until he had realised it was a man carrying a girl. They had had their backs to him, and the little girl had had her arm round the man's neck. Then, all at once, he hadn't been frightened anymore, because, when they had turned around, they had seemed to be people he knew. The man had even looked like his dad – like *him* … but at this point in his recollection, Pip stalled. He didn't want to think about what had happened next. Psychologically he had worked that one out. He was sure they had been simply two nice people. Ever since then, he had always hoped to meet them again. He hadn't so far, although he would have liked to have done … He wanted to … Then he realised that Robert was staring at him.

'I'm sorry,' said Pip. 'I was thinking. I'm sorry to have brought it all back to you, but I would like to finish what Dr Marcu started. If possible.'

'I'd give up on the Papers, if I were you.' All the warmth that had been in Robert's voice when he had spoken of Marcu had dissipated. However unpalatable the words were, Pip could hear the sincerity in them.

'Why?' He knew he was ready to hear a repetition of Dalca's warning.

'Because trying to find out what is happening in Arva is bad news.' Pip noticed his use of the present tense. 'My boss came to a full stop – and I believe you will too.' Pip grimaced, and Robert must have caught the look. 'It's going to be difficult to catch Grandsire.' He said it almost as if Grandsire existed.

'If I believed that, I wouldn't be here, Robert. But I'm not out to catch whoever goes under the name – that's a police job. I'm here to find out more about him.'

'That's what the boss said,' replied Robert. His tone was morose. 'And look what happened to him.'

'A heart attack.'

'I've never believed that. Marcu was fit.' He lowered his voice. 'But he had enemies.' Pip had never seen any expression transform so fast. Robert's eyes had changed from dull as a dead fish to alive and sparkling. His whole face had taken on a pink hue. 'I think Grandsire killed him.' Robert looked around the room as if he was frightened someone was listening.

'You think Grandsire is a real person?'

'Of course he is. If he wasn't, how could he have raped Anka Petrescu? And got rid of Irina?'

'I see,' replied Pip, disappointment tempering his enthusiasm. Something was wrong mentally with Robert, and if he had been one of Pip's own patients he might have suggested he saw a psychiatrist. How could the man care for his patients in such a state?

'You don't understand,' said Robert. 'You weren't here looking after that poor woman for two years. I was – I *know* things …' He stopped.

'What kind of things,' interposed Pip. 'Did Dr Marcu tell you more about his research that he didn't write down?'

Robert's expression had changed again. Total bleakness.

'I don't know why you've come to see me. I know nothing.'

'Then why did he choose you to send his papers to us?' asked Pip. 'Or were there any left here?' It was a possibility.

'Marcu relied on me. He knew I'd do what he asked. And I did.'

'Yes, and I'm grateful for it,' Pip cajoled. 'What I'm hoping to find out is more about the ritual and its history. Did Irina Petrescu say other things that are not set down in Dr Marcu's notes? It's vital that I know.'

'How should I know? I was only a nurse.'

Pip could see this line of questioning was getting nowhere.

'Look, Robert, you say you and Dr Marcu were friends. Don't you think he would want you to help me?' It was not Pip's way to use manipulation, but it was vital he discovered what else Robert knew. During the ensuing silence, Pip realised Robert was thinking things over. The man got up and shut the door.

'*Just in case,*' he said in a low voice, almost as if he was talking to himself. Pip waited. 'All right. You know I said I thought that Grandsire killed the boss?'

Pip nodded. Maybe he had been wrong about Riparu's instability?

'Well, I think I know who he is.' He put his top teeth over his bottom lip as if frightened to carry on.

'Have you told the police?' asked Pip.

Robert shook his head.

'It wouldn't be any use,' he said. 'They'd never believe me. That's why I decided to talk to you.'

'Why wouldn't they believe you, Robert?'

Robert sat down and stared out of the window. Then he turned to Pip again. The two red blotches on his cheeks seemed to have spread all over his face. 'Do you swear not to tell anyone?'

'I swear!' Pip would have perjured himself happily to know what was coming.

'I think it's the man that Marcu went to see that day.'

'Eisenmann?'

'Yes. The German.'

'But why should he be Grandsire? He was helping Marcu, wasn't he?'

'That's what he said.' Robert grinned, but there was no humour in the expression.

'Have you any proof?'

'Let's say I have some evidence.'

'Evidence?' Pip could hardly believe what he was hearing.

'Yes. After Dr Marcu died, I decided to make some inquiries of my own. I never believed his death was natural. I began what I call my "research". The boss always said I was his right-hand man. I found out quite a few things about Herr Eisenmann.' He stopped and swallowed.

'What kind of things?'

'I can't tell you now. But I have it all saved on my laptop. And some in a file. I could let you have a look but ...'

'But what?'

'I might need ...' he hesitated. ' I'm sorry. Money. Dollars. '

'How much?' asked Pip.

The nurse looked even more embarrassed.

'I wouldn't ask but ...'

'I understand entirely, Robert,' Pip said. 'What I think is that you should bring the material to me and I'll have a look at the extent of it. Then we'll negotiate a figure. The university always pays for *bona fide* research. You can trust me.'

'*Thank you*, Pip.' The man's sombre mood had vanished.

'No, I'm the one to be thanking you.'

'You know, sir, he and I …' Pip raised his eyebrows. 'Dr Marcu and I – we used to talk about Grandsire. He was sure that he was only a name – an entity, he called him. He said he was an archetype that drove all those poor women to their grave. But although it was a clever idea – Jung's, he said – I didn't believe it. I always thought Grandsire was real. You'll know why when you see what I have on him.'

'The next question is, when can I see your material, Robert?' Pip's excitement made him breathless – just like when he had been a kid and had a new pet coming.

'In a couple of days? I'll be off night shift then. I could meet you at my flat if you don't mind the mess. We can talk in private then. Negotiate. Here's the address.' He scribbled it on a piece of paper, then tore it out of a diary on the desk.

'Thanks,' said Pip, folding it and putting it away with care. They agreed on a time, although by then Pip was wondering if it would be possible to find someone to take with him. He needed some back up. He could ask Dalca, he supposed …

Then someone knocked. They both jumped.

'Excuse me.'

Robert went to the door and opened it to reveal a smiling girl. The first thing Pip noticed was her face, which was immediately attractive to him; the next thing was her hair, which was long and dark brown, falling over her shoulders in a simple cut. Her trim figure was encased in jeans and a simple T-shirt.

'Excuse me, Robert,' she said. 'I'm going soon and I think Grandma needs her medication.'

As Robert consulted his watch, the girl was holding Pip's eyes in a friendly gaze. Robert caught the look. 'This is Dr Philip Durrant,' he said. 'He's a clinical psychologist. And an American!'

'Ghita,' she offered, extending her hand. 'Are you going to be on this ward?' She had switched to very good English.

'No, I'm only visiting,' he replied.

'A pity. Burbor needs more doctors.'

'It seems so,' replied Pip.

'Why don't you take a walk down the ward with us and meet my grandma. You might change your mind,' she said, smiling.

'Why not?' asked Pip.

It was the last thing he wanted to do, but now it seemed more palatable in such company. Besides, he felt extremely buoyed up after the conversation with Robert, as unbelievable as it sounded.

'She's better today, isn't she?' asked Robert.

'I'm not sure,' replied Ghita.

The old woman's eyes were like black stones, buried in a face deeply lined from hard work and harsh weather. She was sitting in a small room, bare except for an old upright chair, a table and an uncomfortable-looking bed. The only objects that alleviated the impression of a prison cell were two pictures, one of the mountains, the other a nondescript squiggle.

'I've brought you a visitor,' said Ghita, placing an arm around the woman's thin shoulders, which quivered under a black crocheted shawl. The woman looked up and stared at Pip, her face expressionless. 'He's a doctor, Grandma.'

'No, I'm a psychologist,' corrected Pip, bending down to her. 'How long have you been here?' he asked, not expecting an answer, as the old lady looked as though she was on a heavy drug routine. She continued to stare up at him without speaking, while Ghita adjusted a rough blanket around her knees.

'Come on, Simona, answer the doctor for me,' wheedled Robert.

Pip started at the name, then recovered. It was a common enough name. 'Are you going to tell us how you are feeling today?'

'Not if you're asking,' she snapped.

'Grandma!' reproved the girl.

'Why is *he* here?' asked the woman, pointing at Pip. 'I

know him. I've seen him before.'

'No, Grandma, you haven't. He's a new doctor. He's only visiting,' assured Ghita.

'Why has he come?' She stared hard at Pip, as if she was dragging every thought out of his head. 'What does he want from me?' Her head seemed to be on a string as she twisted it towards her granddaughter, then towards Robert, then towards Pip.

Robert looked at Pip and raised his eyebrows in a warning.

'I don't want anything,' Pip replied, stepping back, uneasiness creeping up on him, stirring up the adrenaline, preparing him for flight.

She was trying to get up out of the chair, but kept falling back. Her cheeks became red with the exertion and those black, stony eyes fixed him with what had now become a glare,

'You do!' she cackled. 'You want to know about Arva, don't you?'

The question shocked Pip. His brain was computing the illogical question.

'And why would he want to know about Arva, Simona?' asked Robert, his voice calm.

'I've seen him before,' she persisted.

'This is the first time I have been here,' Pip replied. He turned to Robert, then to Ghita. 'I'm sorry. I seem to be upsetting her. I should go.'

The old lady was becoming agitated.

'You were in Arva, weren't you?' she accused.

'No, I wasn't.'

'You're the one – the one who took Irina away ...' Her shoulders were shaking.

'I really should go,' said Pip.

A small voice in his head was proposing an irrational explanation. That he was not here by accident. He was treading in others' footsteps. He was part of something that had to be accomplished.

'I'm sorry,' said Ghita. 'Grandma has mistaken you for

someone else. She isn't well ...' She looked at Robert. He took Pip by the arm and led him aside.

'Simona *sees* a variety of people. She thinks you are someone else. She was admitted a few days ago at her own request, and the medication is not taking effect yet.'

'Is she schizophrenic?'

Robert nodded. He didn't look Pip in the eyes.

'Does she come from Arva?'

'You know I'm not at liberty to discuss a patient's personal details.'

'Yes, sorry.'

At that moment, Simona retched an horrific sound from her throat. Robert ran back to her and took hold of one arm while her granddaughter held fast to the other.

'It is him. I know it. He's come to get me. Don't let him take me. Please!' Her wail decreased into loud sobs as Robert comforted her. Ghita came over to Pip.

'I'm so sorry,' Pip told her. 'The last thing I wanted was to upset your grandmother. Who does she think I am?' He needed to hear the girl's explanation.

'Don't worry,' said Ghita. 'This is normal. No, that's wrong. I mean that sometimes she's like this. She thinks you're ... I don't know how to say this ... a doctor from the past – a psychiatrist who was very interested in her condition and was working on some research. Evidently my grandmother was afraid that he would admit her to hospital at that time. She held out for years, as long as she could.'

'Did this doctor have a name?' asked Pip. Although he appeared to be making a joke, he felt very cold. 'What was he was working on?'

'It was Dr Marcu. He was well known to our village. He was researching a project there.'

Pip swallowed, but it did nothing to alleviate the dryness. The woman was quiet again now.

'I must go back to Grandma now,' said Ghita.

'Please–' Pip stopped her. He didn't really have to ask, but he was going to. 'Where is your village?'

'Arva. It's a small place. Quite remote. In the mountains.'

'Did you know Dr Marcu?'

'No, I was only a small child when he died. But my father did.'

'Would I be able to speak to your father?'

The girl looked startled.

'I don't know. Why?'

'It's difficult to explain. A real coincidence.'

Robert was staring at them.

Pip groped in his pocket for his small notepad and pencil. Meanwhile the voice in his head was reminding him there was no such thing as coincidence. He wrote down the number of his department.

'This is my number. Perhaps you could call me? I'm very keen to know more about Dr Marcu. Just leave me a message if I'm not there and I'll get back to you.'

'Very well,' she said, staring at the figures. 'The University?'

'How do you know?'

'I'm a student there.'

'That's great,' he said. 'We could meet up there.'

'I don't know if that would be a very good idea,' she said. 'Even if you're from the Centre for International Co-operation.'

'Why not?'

'Oh, I suppose I'm just being silly,' she said. 'Here's my mobile number.' She wrote it down with a brief smile and handed it to him. 'But please don't ring me. I shan't answer, but I might ring you.' She looked as if she was about to add something, but was diverted by another loud cry from her grandmother. 'I have to go.' Robert had the old woman up on her feet.

'Thank you.'

Pip was about to go out through the double doors, when Simona shouted, 'Stay away from here! It's for your own good, doctor.'

Then her wizened face was transformed by a grotesque smile that, like a wide black slash, opened up and crumpled her wrinkled flesh. She was laughing and singing at the same time, as her granddaughter dried to hush her. The song was like the screeching of an out-of-tune instrument that cut into Pip's head and froze his ears.

Pip stood in the corridor. He had to admit he was shaken. That he should be taken for Marcu was enough, but that he had come across the woman who must be Simona Murgu was a miraculous coincidence, if one believed in them! The old lady was schizophrenic – it looked like she had gone the way of the others – but when she was lucid he might be able to find out some more about both Marcu – and Grandsire.

Robert came out into the corridor. 'You look pale,' he said. 'Take no notice of Simona. She hears many voices. Sees many people. You should know. Strange coincidence she should take you for Marcu, though. You don't look like him. He was blond.'

'How long will she be here?'

'Not long enough to be questioned,' he said. 'Besides, the family wouldn't like it. Ghita is a good girl. She pops in to see Simona several times a week. You wouldn't like to upset *her*, would you?'

'She's certainly a nice girl. I gave her my number. Maybe she'll ring me.' Pip played along with the joke.

Robert grimaced.

'Marcu never had a life. Not even a girlfriend. He was too busy with the Arvan stuff. Don't let it take you over.'

'I won't,' replied Pip. He had every intention of letting it take over every minute of his life, if only he could find out more of the secret that had eluded Marcu. And that he should find an Arvan female at Burbor was amazing. Once again he had the sudden feeling he was meant to be there in Romania. *That he had been singled out.* It was the kind of instinct that makes your skin prickle. Then he thought of the name scrawled across his computer screen. *Nicholas.* A warning. He pushed the negative thoughts away.

'I'm looking forward to reading your material, Robert,' he said. 'How long before you and I can meet?'

'As soon as I'm off night shift.'
'Which is when?'
'I'll ring you,' said Robert.
Pip knew he would. He wanted the University's dollars.

On the other side of the city from Burbor, the flat in which Robert Riparu lived was small and ugly, identical to all the others in the dreary concrete block, with their lines of tiny balconies thrusting out in dismal symmetry. The charge nurse had been a tenant there for over 20 years and was well-known to his close neighbours. But it made no difference. Nobody heard anything that night; or if they did, they kept quiet.

The hooded intruder was used to night visits of that sort. He must have known Riparu's movements and that the nurse was not at home. The dark shadow gained entrance with minimal problems – his immediate incentive was to quell the dog's frantic yapping. He slipped into the living room and pinned down the dachshund with his torch beam. The little dog was standing half in its basket and half out, its lips curled back between the high, short barks. The man approached it, holding out a small bar of chocolate.

'Shut that noise!' he growled.

The dog caught the scent and lowered its eyes. A moment later, it was tearing at the wrapper, attacking the chocolate with its small pointed teeth.

The man had his orders, but he still wanted something out of it for himself. Behind the mask, his eyes flicked around the room. *Nothing of value here*, he thought, disappointed.

He looked back at the dog, then unwrapped another small bar and threw the wrapper down on the carpet.

'Come here.'

The dog looked up, growled and started on the chocolate again.

'You won't be growling for long,' he said. Taking off his heavy gloves, he turned to his rucksack, which he opened with care. He unzipped one of the pockets and pulled on a pair of thin rubber gloves. Then he opened another. He glanced across at the dog. He withdrew a small case, which Robert, if he had been there, would have recognised as one for carrying small surgical instruments, together with another small box.

The intruder withdrew a syringe from the case. His hands shook a little as he produced a vial from the other box and filled the syringe from it. He had to be very careful he didn't prick himself! With syringe poised, he straightened and approached the dog. Putting out a strong left hand, he grabbed the little animal by the collar and dragged it over. It struggled and wriggled, but was powerless against the man's grasp. A moment later, he shot the contents deep into its skin. It yapped once. As he dropped the animal, it went for his legs, but he was well protected. He withdrew another piece of chocolate and threw it on the floor. The dog sniffed, but didn't touch it. Replacing the syringe in the case, the man looked round the room. He knew what he was looking for – what to take with him.

He started to search through the lines of files that stood upright on the shelf above a desk in the corner. He threw each one down as he flipped through. He chose one, which he stuffed in the rucksack. Then he unplugged the laptop on the desk and put that in too. A moment later, the man began to ransack the flat, turning out drawers and tipping them onto the floor. He had to make it look good. The dog was watching, but it seemed all barked out.

A few minutes later, the intruder was on his way.

By the time Riparu came home, the dachshund was lying in his basket. Robert didn't even notice the lack of a welcome, because he was stunned at the sight that greeted him. He looked across at the desk. 'Oh God, my laptop!' After that, he discovered which file was missing. *They knew he was meeting with the American.* He was sweating with fear.

He turned to the dachshund. 'So where were you when this happened?' he swore.

The dog cowered. Then Robert noticed the chocolate wrappers near his basket. No wonder Fritz was quiet. If he'd eaten all that, it would probably kill him! Going over to the dog, he went to pick him up, and to his great surprise and shock, the dachshund bit him! Robert licked the blood off his finger. Fritz had never done that since he was a puppy.

'Poor Fritz, they scared you to death, didn't they?' he soothed. Picking him up and cuddling him comforted Robert for a moment. What was he going to do? He dare not call the police.

The next day, Robert felt even more scared. Too afraid to go to work. He'd had no sleep after his night shift and had spent a lot of the time looking out through the window. If the file had not disappeared as well, he might have believed the robbery had been carried out by some druggie who knew where he worked.

He picked up Fritz, who was strangely lethargic. The dachshund lay still in his lap and shivered at his touch. Fritz had always been a comfort to Robert when he was unsure whether or not he was doing the right thing. It had been 15 years since Sacha Marcu had died, and now the young American doctor had approached him. The lad didn't know what he was getting into. Robert looked at his watch. Today, he had to meet him, to provide him with the evidence that Eisenmann was not the man he claimed to be. Now the proof of the bastard's underground activities had disappeared. The nurse didn't have a good head for facts or figures in spite of his profession. He knew about drugs, about madness, but little about politics or history. He was also sure Eisenmann was on to him.

He thought about the appointment Dr Durrant had made with him. Of course, he had always expected such a call. Marcu would have known what to do. If Marcu had been alive, he would have been the Hospital Director by then. If he had stayed at Burbor, that is. Robert was pretty sure he wouldn't have, even though Marcu had always said he wouldn't desert them.

He had been so clever he was destined for higher things. They had all believed that at the time.

Robert grimaced. And now some other doctor was taking over the research Marcu had spent so much energy on – so much, in fact, that it had brought on a 'heart attack'. Not only did Durrant not understand what he was getting into, he also didn't know how dangerous his research would be. Robert bit his lip. He should never have mentioned Eisenmann. A cold sweat was forming on his skin. *They knew what Robert was doing. They would kill him like they had killed Marcu.* But then he thought of the American dollars. Robert needed that cash. What was he going to do? He should never have built up the dossier. He thought about work. How could he go? Maybe they were watching him. Working in a psychiatric hospital was a damned hard job anyway, especially with patients who were never going to recover. He had no illusions about his profession. The patients were discharged – and then they were admitted again. They were like old friends. Except you couldn't get too friendly with them. Of course you wanted the best for them – to cure them, if possible. Some *were* cured, but others – well – they returned time after time.

Arvan women were different. They hardly ever left Burbor once they'd come in. Simona Murgu had been an out-patient for a long time but, in the end, she'd had to be admitted for assessment. She hadn't been sectioned, but had taken her psychiatrist's advice and entered of her own free will. She was a frightened woman, whose family couldn't cope with her anymore and were hoping there would be a solution to her mental instability. He didn't want any more of it. He just wanted to stay in his flat.

Robert stroked Fritz again. The little dog had been acting very strangely since the break-in.

He wouldn't even touch his water. Suddenly Robert felt very angry. What right had they to break into his home and hurt his dog? He was an old dog. At least the criminal hadn't killed him! Fritz had been a good friend to Robert. His master lifted him off his lap and put him in his basket. He just lay there on his side, panting, so Robert went and picked him up again. It shot through Robert's mind that maybe Fritz was on his last legs. On top of all his other worries, he had to meet the American. He would have to put off the appointment. Besides, he didn't feel too well himself – uneasy and out of sorts, which was unusual for him: it was two years since the last time he had been off work ill.

'Must be catching, Fritz,' he said. 'I know what. I'll call in sick. We'll be sick together, eh?'

5

Planning for his meeting Robert the following day as well as for his move to Arva meant that Pip was very busy. He was anxious to take advantage of Professor Dalca's offer, but the meeting with the nurse had to come first. In the beginning he had seen the interview with Robert as a one-off; a simple matter of a series of questions, but it had now become more complicated.

It wasn't just Robert's request for what amounted to a bribe but also, more serious, his accusation against Eisenmann – or, as Robert had put it, his procuring of *evidence* against the German. Pip couldn't have imagined either of those outcomes. Most researchers assumed the uncommon was bound to arise somewhere along the line of questioning, but this was more than uncommon, and could be harmful to his project. Having to cope with the idea that one of the major players in the puzzle might be a murderer was not pleasant.

'What the hell am I getting into here?' Pip asked himself as he sat and stared at his computer screen. As to the bribe, he had no intention of letting the University know about it, whatever he had said to Robert. If his supervisor discovered Pip intended to reward a man for information compiled illegally, he would be in trouble. Pip sighed, knowing he was going to do it anyway. The second meeting with Marcu's closest colleague had become more important than any worry about cash. He had decided on a figure that he intended to stick to. The money wasn't an issue: he could afford to pay Robert out of his own pocket.

But the thought of what he was getting into was more problematic. This was Eastern Europe and he had no desire to take part in any dangerous exploit. On the other hand, Eisenmann was part of the puzzle he was trying to crack. Marcu had approached the German to learn about the ritual, and he must have thought well of the man and trusted him with the material.

On this, Pip was still trying to decide how he should proceed. If he obtained the *evidence*, what was he going to do with it? Was he going to hand it over to the police? Why hadn't Robert? But it was obvious really: the nurse was too scared.

'Doesn't that freak you out?' he asked himself. He'd had several warnings now that he didn't intend to follow. Of that he was sure. But this latest from Robert – that a man of Eisenmann's importance was a criminal who was responsible for the psychiatrist's death and the rape of a child – was an alarming prospect. Getting mixed up with the Romanian underworld was not something that attracted Pip.

'I think you'd better look at who this guy is!' he said to himself.

When a complete stranger like Robert declared that the man was probably trying to kill him, it seemed a perfectly normal thing to do. Pip Googled the name, mentally noting how dry his mouth and throat had become. Wikipedia was the first, brief entry:

> *'Nicholas Eisenmann, b. 1959 is a civil servant working in the area of culture, heritage and education for the Council of Europe in Strasbourg. He is connected to the advisory council of the ACA where he has worked upon the support strategies for East European countries. He attended the World Conference on Higher Education in September 1998 and assisted the Council of Europe Parliamentary Assembly (PACE) on the subject of*

cultural co-operation at international level.

<u>*Personal Interests*</u>

The promotion of identity and the support of creativity. He has a great respect for the diversity of expression and participation in cultural life. He also finds medieval European history particularly interesting and is an authority on Indian and Chinese mythology.

The photo box was blank. 'No image then,' said Pip. He stared at the keyboard without really seeing it as he tried to make sense of his scanty knowledge of the man. The educational entry might have meant that Eisenmann had dealings with the Romanian universities' exchange of foreign students. As an historian it was feasible that he might be known to a medievalist like Professor Dalca. Pip grimaced. Maybe Dalca knew what Robert knew? The anodyne description of the faceless civil servant who, according to Robert, might be Grandsire, a serial killer, seemed preposterous. That he was listed in the online encyclopaedia meant he was fairly well-known. Robert had said he was 'too important' to be targeted. The nurse's accusation that Eisenmann could have raped a child and killed Marcu was incredible.

Pip shook his head and decided to go and make himself a coffee as the screensaver flicked on. It was a view he had chosen to remind him of home. Not an image of Sunny Mead, but a digital photo of Brooklyn in the fall, taken from one of his apartment windows. Very different from the view he glimpsed through the small window of his study bedroom in Cluj.

He came back from the kitchen carrying the hot drink and sat down again in front of his laptop, warming his hands on the mug. One tiny movement of the mouse brought the screen back to life.

'God!' He jumped back, spilling his coffee on his legs and the carpet. The man was staring back at him from a space that had been empty a few minutes before. The photo box was now filled with the face of a man with straggling yellow hair and staring eyes, who was smiling in the holographic way only computer video images can.

'It can't be …' Pip panted. 'It can't be him!' His eyes darted from box to text. It was the same page. There was no mistake. Arvarescu. Koppelberg. *Eisenmann*. This couldn't be true. He was hallucinating. His hands were wet with coffee and cold sweat. His brain cried out to his fingers to delete the image, but at first they wouldn't move. It took a few seconds for his fear-frozen fingers to work. Then one clicked on the 'minimise' button. His rational self was still working, but weakly. He mustn't lose the image. It might be evidence!

He stared at the bar where it said 'Wikipedia: Eisenmann' until he was calm enough to face it again. Yet, inside, he almost knew what was going to happen. When the screen came up full, the image had gone. A blank box was there again with its bland statement and request:

Nicholas Eisenmann.

No image.

Do you own one?

'Yes!' he said out loud. Then, in his mind, *No, I don't. How could I? Why did I say that?* He sat there, facing the screen, his heartbeat loud in his ears. The image didn't reappear. He put his head back and stared at the ceiling, forgetting that his legs were burning from being scalded by the coffee. He had to try to make sense of everything.

He felt sick as he remembered the events of the last few days. *Nicholas* written on the screen. The note: *Remember Me*. And now, the picture of an unknown American paedophile transferring itself onto his computer. A criminal who resembled the man in the worst nightmare Pip had ever had, but who couldn't possibly be Koppelberg.

In that moment of pure panic, as Pip felt his hold on reality slipping away, the last thing he wanted to believe was that someone or something was taunting him, driving him into a loss of self-belief, into a state of pure fear. Who had tried to do that before? *He knew.* And it made him shiver. He couldn't rationalise how Arvarescu could be Koppelberg. Nor what either of them had to do with Eisenmann. He dared not believe it. He felt like a scared kid again!

Then another picture formed in his mind, the same one that had slipped into his thoughts during his conversation with Robert. The vision he had seen as a kid that had taught him *not* to fear Koppelberg. The smiling man and the child. He had seen them only once, but they had given him courage. If one vision could appear, so could another. He closed his eyes as sweat dripped down his forehead. He wished he could see them again. He wanted to see them again. They'd promised he would. But when? They had given him strength when it was most needed: he had saved Melanie and the twins. Now he had to save himself from going down to a place from which there was no way back. He tried to relax, to make sense of his own feelings. That had been 20 years ago!

His adult self fought his disorientation, reminding him that when you have something on your mind constantly like the Marcu Papers, when you bury yourself in your work to such an extent, you can start imagining anything. Could this have been what Marcu had experienced? He had intimated that his research seemed to be taking account of the paranormal. The signs were there that his state of mind had not always been sound. For instance, some of his language had been truly unprofessional and – maybe he'd had a premonition about what was going to happen the day he went to meet Eisenmann. Or perhaps he had been aware of how dangerous the man was. Pip could feel the goosepimples rising. When he was a kid in the wheelchair, he had felt nothing in his legs. All at once, he could feel the heat coming off them and realised he must have scalded them with the coffee.

Still feeling disorientated, he hurried into the kitchen, fetched a cold compress and pressed it to the sore parts. Later, he soaked a cloth and attempted to clean the spilt coffee off the carpet. He breathed in deeply as he tried to soak up the wet. After he had scrubbed at the stain, he sat back on his heels, trying to be calm. It took him some time to produce everything that was expert and qualified within himself to reject what he had just seen and attempt to rationalise it.

He stared across at the box containing the papers. Perhaps he should take notice of the warnings he'd had and go home? Yet, although he was still scared, he knew he couldn't renege on the project. He owed it to Marcu and, somewhere inside, he felt he owed it to himself. After all, he had been part of a mystery that was somehow linked to this one. Although he didn't understand how – yet! No way was he going to give up the project.

Pip always felt better when he made a decision. He was here in Romania and that was it. No good freaking out. Once again he had the sudden feeling that he was meant to be in this country, finishing what Marcu had begun. It was a strong enough instinct to relegate his fears to the inside. The next day he would meet Robert, and afterwards he would go to Arva. Although he had misgivings about meeting Robert alone, he was not going to let anyone else know about these strange experiences, which could only be the products of his imagination. He would not be frightened off by inexplicable phenomena. He was a psychologist, for God's sake!

Robert didn't ring as he had promised, and it was already evening when Pip decided to go to the nurse's flat. He had misgivings, and regretted not acting upon his earlier idea of finding someone to accompany him. It took some time to get there, and it was not a pretty part of town. Pip felt apprehensive as he got off the bus and looked around. Even the setting sun failed to make such an environment rosy. Instead it lit up every imperfection, deepening the jaundiced tone of the blocks of concrete flats, exposing the cracks in the rendering, turning the washing strung from several balconies a tawdry yellow.

The apprehension was giving way to a palpable nervousness as he attempted to find Riparu's flat. Pip had tried ringing him several times, but now he decided to put away his mobile phone as he sensed that a stranger – and a lost one in particular – might attract trouble easily. Besides, he had a couple of his credit cards on him and his passport, and he had no wish to endure a mugging. A small jumble of hooded youths had been watching him intently from one of the walkways between the nearest blocks, and as he hurried past them he was relieved that no-one challenged him.

He took the stairs to the first floor landing, and once he was in the rectangle that embraced the stairwell, he was getting the set-up of the building. For some reason he kept glancing over his shoulder, but no-one emerged out of the shadows or from the monotonous line of brown doors he was passing. *This is a hell of a place to live*, he said to himself as he approached Riparu's flat. He knocked. No reply. He knocked again. Still receiving no response, he waited for a while. Then, shrugging, he walked back past the numerous doors again. In one way, Pip was glad that Robert was out, and relieved that he had not been the recipient of what might have been dangerous news. In another way, though, he felt cheated, because he needed to know what information the man had.

'I shouldn't have come,' he said. 'I'll ring him again tomorrow.'

As he walked back down the stairs, he wondered if Robert had had second thoughts and decided that to talk to him wasn't worth the risk.

Robert heard the voice of the American who had come looking for him. He didn't dare to open the door. Besides, what was the point? The file and the laptop had been stolen. Added to that, he had a horrible headache, which wouldn't go away. If he had been imaginative, he might have described it as head-splitting. It seemed to pierce his brain from back to front. He stared down at the dachshund lying in his lap. The small body was stiff and stone cold; the eyes glazed and dull. He knew he should bury his pet, but when he tried to get up, his legs wouldn't work properly. Their weakness was owing to – what? He had no idea.

Inside, Robert felt a deep sorrow at the dog's demise and

at his own lethargy. He didn't know how long he had been sitting in the chair, nor how long he was going to be. His whole body was racked with intermittent pain, which he didn't like, because he didn't know what to do. He was used to helping other people, but none of that seemed to matter now. He had to stay here with Fritz – safe in his chair. He was afraid to leave his apartment in case *they* got him. He knew the people who had killed his dog would still be around, watching. If he went out – or called the police – or even spoke to the American, it would be the end of him. He would just sit and wait until things were better. The thought of what might happen to him made him sweat. He hadn't been to bed and he didn't know what time it was. His hair was wet from perspiration. His shirt collar was soaked and the rest of his clothes were comfortless owing to the damp. He thought he must have a fever.

His finger was unbearably sore. He looked down at the place where Fritz had bitten him. The wound was inflamed and oozing. Robert tried to remember the last time he'd had a tetanus jab. But he found it extremely hard to concentrate on anything at that moment. Anyway, what could have been the matter with Fritz? He was a house dog, whose life was tied to the apartment. A dullness seemed to have fallen upon Robert that even the thought of the American's dollars could not cheer. He would keep on sitting there in the dusk with Fritz until he felt better. But he didn't …

A day later, one of Robert's neighbours told his friend he had heard several loud screams coming from Riparu's flat. 'Like an animal being slaughtered,' the man said, staring at the adjoining wall.

6

Pip received no call from Robert the following day either. He was puzzled by this, given the nurse's earlier eagerness to cooperate, but he had other things to think about – for instance his move to Arva. He had received a call from Professor Dalca early on.

'Hello, Pip,' the Professor began, followed by the usual pleasantries. 'I've spoken to Emilia and she's agreed to have you stay with us.'

'That's great,' replied Pip. 'When am I expected?' The thought that he was going to see Arva at last exhilarated him.

'As soon as you can pack up at the student hostel.'

'That won't take too long. I've decided to keep my room here, just in case you get tired of me over there in Arva.'

A short silence followed the quip, making Pip wonder if he might have offended the Professor.

'I doubt that will happen,' replied Dalca. 'So, when would you like to come to us?'

'As soon as possible? Today?'

'Yes, I'm sure that will be convenient. I'll speak to Emilia, and if it isn't, I'll let you know. Will you need a van for your things?'

'Not at present. I'm leaving most of them here. I travel light. What's your address?'

Dalca laughed politely.

'I'll expect you for supper then, unless you hear

otherwise? Have you a pen?'

'Great.' Pip wrote the address down with care.

Another silence, then:

'You remember our earlier conversation? About you being one of my history students?'

'Yes. No problem.'

It was a pity, but Pip had to go along with Dalca's request. He didn't want to get on his wrong side.

'You should take a taxi out to us – that's until we get you fixed up with a vehicle.'

'I prefer the bus,' said Pip. Doubtless the Professor thought he was wealthy. 'I assume there is one?'

'Yes, but only twice a day. It leaves the bus station around 15.00 hours – and I said "around". It drops you off at the bottom of the hill by the church.'

Pip's heart thumped as he thought about the prominence of Arva church in his research.

'I'll catch that.'

'If you're not here by midnight, we'll come looking for you,' joked Dalca.

'I should make it by then,' replied Pip, participating in the fun. 'I look forward to meeting your family.'

'They feel the same. Goodbye, Pip.'

'See you later, Professor.' He thought he ought to stick with the Professor title. The Romanians seemed more formal somehow. Back home, he and his supervisor were on more familiar terms. Maybe he would shorten it to "Prof" soon, or even get as far as "Simu".

A cab would have been preferable, Pip reflected, as he endured the experience of being crammed into what could only be called a commuter bus, containing not only people with their numerous belongings, but also one or two chickens and other livestock. He found being the centre of interest unattractive, but maintained a friendly grin for as long as he was able. Once or twice it was reciprocated as passengers got off at various stops and he watched them disappear down a deep forest lane or through a gate into empty grassland without a sign of habitation. One young woman touched him on the shoulder as she went past. She had dark brown hair and was wearing smart clothes – a brown city suit – and carrying a briefcase. It was as if she was acknowledging that all Romanians were not provincial; that, however rural the setting, professional people were carrying on with everyday life. He watched her as she got off the bus, and wondered where her house was. Her sleek brown head bobbed up and down as she walked along the side of the vehicle and the driver stirred its engine into juddering life again. Then Pip looked back and was surprised to see she had disappeared from sight. *She's probably walked right into the forest*, he thought. *Rather her than me.*

He had read an account on the internet of the research the University was carrying out on wild animals in the neighbourhood. Evidently bears were common. He assumed the woman must have walked through some hidden gateway that led down a path to her house.

Satisfied with the explanation, he thought of Ghita, the girl he had met in the hospital, and wondered if he would be lucky enough to see her again. That set him thinking about Robert and his accusation against Eisenmann. *Maybe I should have gone back to his flat?*, he wondered. *Or perhaps phoned the hospital to check if they knew where he was? Maybe he'd changed his shift?* A sudden uncomfortable thought came into his head. *What if something's happened to him and it's my fault?*

'No,' he said, then realised that he had spoken out loud. Immediately he was conscious of several pairs of curious eyes fixed on him as they bumped on over the rough road. *They probably think I'm an idiot*, he said to himself.

He had asked the driver to tell him when they got to Arva – but how could he miss the place? It was dominated by the church on the hill with its squat tower and surrounding forest trees, which protected it with a dark cloak all the way down from the top of the ridge. He recognised it from Marcu's photographs. The building was set against a sky that was a vision of dark orange ornamented with wispy grey clouds. Pip alighted and looked round.

Soon the bus had emptied and the other passengers were hurrying down the roughly tarmacked road towards the sparse lights of home. Only Pip lingered. It was getting late, but he felt a sudden desire to see the church close to. But if he did, maybe the Dalcas would think he wasn't coming? He changed his mind. Taking out the paper with the address on it, and shouldering his backpack, he followed the rest of the stragglers towards the village.

Then, as if by instinct, he felt he had to turn around. His eyes flicked upwards, and he saw a light dancing on the hill.

'Someone's up there,' he said. 'Maybe it's the priest.'

He frowned. Hadn't Dalca said the church was locked these days? So the torch must have belonged to someone walking around in the graveyard. The thought of what had happened in that cemetery, and was still happening, made him hurry in the direction the others had taken. Not a soul was visible now, and the dark was already advertising itself by lowering black clouds, ready for their onslaught on the murky orange of the sky, which seemed to cling to the distant mountains.

Pip had no taste for wandering in a poorly-lit, unfamiliar place without a map, and he wished he had asked Dalca for full directions. He passed several houses, all of which were shuttered and apparently uninhabited. He stopped in front of one that was small and white-plastered, with a sloping roof and a smoking chimney. A man and a woman sat outside on a bench under a porch made of corrugated plastic from which swung terracotta plant pots. The woman, dressed in a pink cardigan and an old skirt, had her head in her hands while the man stared into space, a pipe drooping from his lips. Pip went over to the dilapidated fence.

'I wonder if you could help me?' he asked, holding out the address. The woman looked up, gave a little scream, then rushed into the house. The man stared on as if he hadn't heard. 'Do you know where this is, please?' The man didn't answer. Evidently Arva was not the place to ask for directions.

Pip continued. Soon the tarmac turned into a rough concrete, cracked and full of deep holes. He thought he must come upon a street name soon, but nothing seemed to be marked. He could hear a horse's hooves approaching and stood aside to let the wooden cart through. It was coming at a fair trot, and Pip had the impression that if he had still been standing in its way, it would have run him down. The occupants – a young man driving and a woman in a flowered headscarf seated behind him – didn't even look his way.

'Friendly,' said Pip, trying to decide on his next move.

He wandered on into the village, looking for any building of importance, or even a bar where he could ask. Most of the houses were ill-kept, many with shuttered windows. Each had a neglected air, and in some cases the brickwork was crumbling.

'Now, why would Dalca live in a place like this?' Pip asked under his breath.

He found himself querying his eagerness to move to what seemed a truly godforsaken place akin to the ghost towns of the Old West back home. He felt as if a gunman might spring out at any time and mow him down.

Instead, a car's engine startled him. An incongruous sight, given that the vehicle was a bronze Mercedes, which rounded the corner ahead and slid to a halt before him, blocking off the narrow street like some menacing predator.

Local Mafia? thought Pip, his hand near to his waist, where he hid his money belt. He tried to look as if he was oblivious to the car's threatening presence, and turned sideways to pass it by on the pavement.

Then the window rolled down with a fluid hissing and a woman's voice said,

'Are you lost?' The tone was both squeaky and supercilious.

'I don't think so,' he replied, squinting at her in the gloom. Her looks were as mousey as her voice was high. Her eyes were as brown as her hair, which was streaked with grey highlights. She smiled, revealing small teeth with particularly sharp incisors.

'Are you going far?' she persisted. 'I can help. I come from round here – but it's up to you.' She shrugged, arching her eyebrows and showing the tip of her tongue between her teeth.

Is she trying to pick me up? he thought, more than surprised.

'Ask him who he's trying to find. We don't bite!' The voice from the back was sarcastic. The car had tinted windows and, in the dusk, Pip couldn't see the other occupant properly, but he had the impression that the man was white-skinned and blond.

'The Dalcas,' he said, feeling extremely foolish.

'Ah, the Professor,' said the man. 'Follow this road around the corner and turn left into the square.' Then, to the girl, he instructed: 'Drive on!'

'Thank you,' said Pip, but the window was already gliding up and the Mercedes engine hissing as the girl accelerated away. Pip caught a glimpse of the car's rear hub cap as it passed – and blinked. It bore a bright yellow circle in its centre, with one winking eye. Bizarre, thought Pip. Some kind of logo? As he watched, the car seemed to disappear like a mirage. Its body and roof were bathed in a shimmering orange glow, although the sun had almost gone from the sky.

He frowned, took off his spectacles and cleaned them with the little cloth he kept in his pocket. His eyes were playing tricks. Probably eye strain. Maybe he needed some new glasses? But as he hurried round the corner, he found the impression of the wheel logo disturbing him, pricking his memory like a sharp needle. But he couldn't catch the echo in his mind. It was frustrating. He was sure he had seen it somewhere before. But where – and when? Shrugging, he walked up the empty road into the dusk.

The directions the man had given were good. The road led

into the small village square, and the Dalca home spanned one of the corners. He couldn't miss it. A tin plaque with the name of the street that he wanted had been hammered into the side of the building and, below, the house number was fixed on the side wall next to a wrought-iron gate. The house itself was in bad repair, paint flaking off and the plastered brickwork crumbling at street level. Yet it was far superior to any other Pip had passed so far. It was imposing, with a wide ornamental ridge above the arched windows, stretching up to the roof and carved in a geometric design.

'Wow,' said Pip, standing back to look. 'That's more like it.' Taking off his backpack in order to squeeze through the gate, he walked along the path at the side of the house. The door was substantial and made of a dark heavy wood, but it too had seen better days. He lifted the carved knocker and brought it down on the door.

'You made it then?' Professor Dalca opened the door to his knock. He was dressed less flamboyantly than when he and Pip had met at the University. This time he was wearing old jeans and a checked shirt, and his face looked white and strained, in sharp contrast to his black beard. In fact, he appeared to have aged since their first meeting. *Dalca has a lot on his mind*, thought Pip, *and it doesn't look good.*

'Yes,' he said out loud. 'A guy in a Mercedes directed me.' He noted a sudden flick of surprise in the Professor's eyes. 'He had a woman driver, who was smart. She said she came from round here. They seemed like business people.'

'Come in and meet my wife,' said Dalca, ignoring Pip's indirect angling for information.

As Pip walked in through the door, an aroma of meat cooking wafted into his nostrils, and he remembered lying to his mom when he told her he was remembering to eat properly.

The smell grew stronger as Pip followed the Professor along the broad hall corridor. The floor was tiled, and Pip's interested eyes noted that some of the tiles were cracked in places. So too were the weathered plaster walls, on which were stencilled shapes that proclaimed an Eastern influence.

'It's a large house,' he said as they reached the far door.

'Emilia inherited the place,' replied the Professor. 'It has been in her family for generations. I moved in after we married.'

So it's his wife's, thought Pip. *I can see why they need a lodger. To keep the place up.* The ceramic tiles continued into the living room, but here a large plum-red rug stretched like a carpet from wall to wall. Pip's impression that it had been expensive once, but was now faded in places from wear and tear, was borne out when he glanced down to where his feet, and many others, had almost obliterated a square containing a cockerel. The bird's bright plumage was no more.

The drapes were half-drawn over shuttered windows, and they too suffered from age. The gloomy effect was complemented by two worn tapestries on facing walls. In fact, the only brightness in that large, dim room came from a glowing log burner. The small television screen was covered with a black cloth. *They're not TV addicts, then*, he thought. A woman, who had her back to the door, got up and placed a book down on her chair. She turned slowly. The Professor went forward.

'Emilia, this is our new boarder. Philip Durrant.'

She had bushy greying hair and very dark eyes. Her black dress accentuated her slight frame, which was slim to the point of thin.

'Nice to meet you, Mrs Dalca.' Pip offered his hand, and felt her cold fingers slip in and out of his quickly.

She's not been warming herself by the fire, was his wry thought. His first impression was that Emilia Dalca was unsociable. She exuded anxiety, and the cool handshake reinforced his next assumption, that she was not particularly pleased to see him.

'Don't let my husband work you too hard, Philip,' she said, smiling briefly. 'I hope you like boiled pork.'

Emilia watched the American eat. This young man was different from the usual lads Simu brought home, and she wasn't sure why. Woman's instinct, she supposed. She had never met an American before, but she had a feeling that he would be trouble. You only needed to look at the world news. She wasn't highly educated like her husband, but once Simu had seen a great deal in her. That was another story. He had needed her help, and she had given it for several reasons. Arvan women had to be careful whom they married. He had been a good husband in his way, but too studious for his own good. He was an intellectual who didn't take much notice of anything but his academic work, which Emilia knew was leading him now down a dangerous path. Sometimes, when she was in despair, she even wondered if he had already known too much of the secret when he had courted her. But then she dismissed the idea as monstrous.

Philip Durrant was of the same species: scholarly, serious and slightly stooped, probably from poring over endless books. And, like Simu, he was most surely dedicated to some cause or other. He wouldn't have been chosen by her husband otherwise. He was fairly good-looking, with deep blue eyes behind his spectacles and dark curly hair, but she knew he was deep. Not happy either. She could see it in his eyes. As if he was remembering something that wasn't good. If he was looking for happiness, he wouldn't find it in Arva. It had never been a place to enjoy oneself.

She felt a shiver down her back. All the trouble with her mother, then her daughter's non-compliance, was getting her down. She knew that. And she mustn't let depression take over. Whatever happened. Her nerves felt like tight little strings as she thought about it. Sometimes a voice in her head told her that she would end up like her mother if she didn't do something about it. She watched her husband tear the coarse brown bread apart and dip it into the stew with white tapering fingers come from a lifetime of book work. He had never had to labour on the land, fetching and carrying heavy loads, like her own father. Simu was an Arvan, but very unlike the breed.

She felt it was his duty to protect their daughter, and not only hers.

She must have made a sound as she swallowed back her tears, because both men stopped eating and stared at her.

'Are you all right, Emilia?' asked Simu.

She nodded and concentrated on the food she had cooked, but could hardly get down her anxious throat. Her husband's kind tone was very different from earlier. She had tried to stop him bringing a stranger into their home. She had warned him *it wasn't safe.* She had been as angry as he was when she had shrieked back at him that their daughter had to be protected, especially before her wedding – which hadn't suited Simu at all. Then the old argument had started again. He didn't want his precious daughter marrying *only* because she would soon be 19. He said it was reasonable that a man should know why. He wanted the mastery, like all Arvan men, but his *whys* were different from a simple carter's or a farmer's. It had become his mission to find out the truth about 'the secret of the marriage bed'.

But Emilia was strong, like her sisters before her. They knew what was right. She wasn't going to be the one to split and let slip what the men of Arva had been trying to work out for the last five hundred years. That way led to sure disaster for the Dalca family in particular. Look what had happened to the Petrescus: Irina, the mother, had gone mad and died; the father was broken; and the child dead!

Emilia was determined she would not go mad, like Irina, or her own mother. She had a duty to remain sane for as long as she lived. She carried a burden that was the heaviest any Arvan woman could, and would fight with every bone in her body to uphold it – for her daughter's sake. Emilia nearly choked on a potato as she thought again of the horror that had been the Petrescus' lot.

'Sorry!' she mumbled as her husband and her guest stared at her.

She would *never* tell, and Simu would know only what was appropriate for an Arvan male to know, professor or not.

He had come round to her way of thinking in the end. At least, her choice of suitors, young Anton, was a fellow student of their daughter's and fairly acceptable. Besides, her daughter had known him all her life. The lad understood what they were all going through, because he was Arvan too. He knew what was right – how to treat her. On the other hand, they were just kids, and Emilia was very much afraid that the lad's feelings might get the better of him. As for their daughter, she had to get on with it, like it or not.

A moment later, Simu was standing beside her with his hand on her shoulder. 'Shall I take your plate, dear?' He had a meaningful look in his eyes, warning her to remember they were not alone.

'No, it's fine,' she replied. 'I'm just tired from a busy day.'

'Not on my account, I hope,' said Pip. 'I'm used to looking after myself.'

'It has nothing to do with you,' she replied, forcing a smile. 'Your room is ready when you are. I hope you'll find it pleasant.'

She envied this serious young man, who she knew, whatever past traumas he had been through, would never experience the burden the Dalcas carried. He could know nothing of the sleepless nights they shared, and had not the slightest idea that he was lodging with the most unfortunate family that ever lived.

'Are you finished?' she asked, ' Or would you like some more?'

'Best stew I've had for a long time,' Pip said, wiping his mouth. *The only stew*, he thought. 'It was great.'

Emilia was wary of any flattery from a stranger. It boded no good.

Simu rose from the table. 'Come, Pip,' he said, 'you must try some of my plum brandy. Ghita will be home soon and it will give you the courage to meet her.'

'Ghita?' asked Pip, startled to hear the name of the girl he had met at Burbor Hospital.

'Yes, our daughter,' explained the Professor. 'She is out with her boyfriend at present, but she'll be back soon.'

'Fiancé, Simu,' corrected Emilia.

'Oh, yes, I keep forgetting about Anton,' he said, and the sarcasm was evident.

Hours later, Pip collapsed fully-clothed on the patchwork goose-feather quilt and stared across at the tall wooden wardrobe for inspiration. The red and white diamonds of the sheet cover danced up and down before his eyes, making him feel a little sick. *I reckon I got the best room; I can't be that unpopular then*, he thought, savouring the feel of the deep, soft bed and wriggling on his back against the pillows. He tried to think logically, but it was an effort. His mind was still reeling from the revelation that Ghita was the Dalcas' daughter. Which meant that Simona Murgu was Emilia's mother, and the Dalcas must have direct knowledge of what went on in 1988 and 1952. No wonder Dalca didn't want his womenfolk finding out who Pip was! Why hadn't the Professor admitted his family connection to Simona Murgu in the first place? Obviously he retained some of the Arvans' characteristic reticence with outsiders.

What had the Professor said at their meeting? Pip grimaced. *The villagers are a tight-knit community and do not welcome strangers.* He must have been thinking of his wife! She certainly fitted the pattern. If only Mrs Dalca knew that Pip was there to help them, she mightn't have been quite so... He searched for the word, but couldn't quite focus on the right one. *Hostile*? Not quite? *Suspicious* was more like it. He wasn't really surprised at her attitude, given the mathematical scheme of Arvan culture, which was a little hard to grasp at present, because both his head and his legs were slightly out of tune with everything, after drinking several generous measures of the Dalcas' plum brandy. He frowned as he attempted to calculate.

So Ghita was engaged to someone called Anton, and it was plain to see that the Professor wasn't happy about it. If Pip was right, there were two possible reasons why he hadn't done anything about it: either Ghita was in love with the guy; or the Dalcas had to marry her off to someone at 19 in order to fulfil a sick and antiquated tradition. If it was the second reason, then the girl, a university student, who must have brains, was going to go along with it. Why? He had got the distinct impression she was feisty, which was reinforced by the fact that she hadn't come home yet. Mrs Dalca had kept on looking at the clock and then at Dalca, who still hadn't taken any notice. If Pip had been sober, he would have picked up straight away that the atmosphere was choked with forbidden secrets. But he had been too busy partaking of the plum brandy. Finally, they had all gone to bed.

'Man, you have walked into a shit load of domestic,' muttered Pip.

Sympathy for himself overwhelmed him, followed by a befuddled remorse. No way would he want their problems. All he had to worry about was the occasional visit by a demon, and the problem of how he was going to crack the Marcu Papers. A moment later, he fell fast asleep. He was woken only some time after midnight by the sound of doors banging and several raised voices, two of which definitely belonged to women.

Dalca heard the open shutters creaking like only ancient wood can when remembering the agony of the axe cut. The curtains rose and fell as the wild fingers of the autumn wind caught and pinned one of them against the chattering louvres. He turned over and thrust his head into the duck down pillows. He knew Emilia was awake, full of resentment. Another night, another row; while, on the other side of the wattle and daub, lying in an inebriated sleep, was Pip, a foreigner who might hold in his hand the key that could unlock their troubles.

Dalca was not a believer in a higher power – he had asked himself too many times why the deity should allow such evil if he were all-powerful and benevolent. Given what had happened in their village in the past, he had no difficulty in believing that a lower power was at work – now that he himself was already playing a part in the struggle against the evil that was Grandsire. He asked himself once more if fate had chosen the American too, just as it had ordained his own birth.

How many times had Emilia said bitterly that he was *too intelligent*? That he thought he was better than everyone else? He could hear her words: 'No other man in Arva would keep on questioning his wife until he drove her to madness – or death! You know I can't tell you!' He was determined to discover the true 'secret of the marriage bed' – an abomination that had been spread and promoted through the ages by a succession of mad women.

Dalca was not an uneducated carter, like his late father-in-law, but an academic, a man of persistent questioning. He would not be duped. He had also sworn to himself not to let Emilia's cant affect his daughter. He sensed Ghita didn't really want to marry Anton; that her mother was pressurising her. Emilia's emotional blackmail was taking its toll on the young couple, like her constant reminders that if Ghita didn't toe the line, something dreadful was going to happen to them all. Then her grandmother was held up to her as an example! Until recently, he had not realised quite how much Ghita was influenced by Emilia. She was a modern young woman in everything but the burden of tradition. She had 'gone-up' to Grandsire in her 16th year like the rest of the Arva girls. He had never believed she would, but she had.

He tormented himself that he had permitted it. But if he had withheld his permission, she would have been bullied by her peers and disowned by her own mother. He had known the score when he married Emilia. Every Arvan woman told her husband just enough. *That there was no danger on 22 July, given that the rules were observed.* So Arvan men went along with it. Even a sophisticated history professor like Dalca – because he loved his wife and his child. God, how I hate this place, thought Dalca. He gritted his teeth as he thought about the annual rite. 'Going-up' to Grandsire was as important to the women as a religious procession or their First Communion.

He blamed the parish priest for it, and all those past so-called holy men who, if they had not condoned it openly, had closed their eyes to the outrage and let the ritual continue. Why had not one of them spoken out against it? He himself had written to the bishop and received a non-committal letter in reply, saying that it was not the Church's role to interfere in the people's culture. So Dalca had set himself against the priests and begun a personal crusade to find out the historic origins of the 22 July ritual; and, some years later, he had firmed up his theory.

Then Marcu had appeared on the scene, investigating something entirely different. He had brought into the open the fear that all Arvans were too afraid to acknowledge; that within the women of the village was a tendency towards mental illness, whether inbred or not. Behind that lay the reason Emilia had taken Dalca on. He was a man many women would have not considered, on account of his background, but who had the potential to overcome it. Which he had. But now, after her mother's slow deterioration, she seemed to have lost faith in his ability to save them.

Marcu had been the first to set down, in his Papers and subsequent unfinished book, an examination of what he believed lurked in the female Arvan psyche. Then the psychiatrist's work had come to an abrupt end with his early death. What kept Dalca awake at night most of all was the desire to discover the warped destiny that Emilia prophesied for the Dalca family – and make sure that whatever caused it would not befall his Ghita.

So what was Emilia hiding? He had to know. He needed facts and figures to back up his historical research about the Grandsire and add to what he already knew. The arrival of Philip Durrant had almost been miraculous; but, from the philosophical point of view, miracles do not prove the existence of God. Fate again.

If Irina Petrescu had not died, then perhaps Marcu might have found out the truth. He had published a description of the ritual in the early chapters of his research, but had come to no conclusion. He had intimated he could soon be ready to publish more. So what else had he discovered? Then, after his death, his personal papers had disappeared and could not be located in Romania – because, as Dalca had now found out, they had been languishing in some American university.

Pip was now in possession of them, and he had approached Dalca. But would he be generous enough to share his knowledge after he had gleaned what he could? Both men needed the other's scholarship. How could the psychological mystery and the historical mystery be fitted together?

And why should the two of them succeed where others had failed? Marcu's approach to Eisenmann had proved his downfall and culminated in his death. Dalca's knowledge of Eisenmann was not confined to a meeting they had once had regarding cultural exchanges. The powerful German's involvement in Arva's tragic history had later become known to the Professor through sources he could not disclose. Could Pip handle Eisenmann better than Marcu had, and discover what his predecessor had really wanted to know? For instance, the boy had already contacted Riparu – someone Dalca had never known existed. Maybe Pip might get to the policeman who had investigated the most recent crime? He had the credentials. What other leads had he discovered in those Papers? The possibilities were many. The boy had to be protected. But how was Dalca going to do that? Having him in Arva under close scrutiny was a start.

The Professor lay staring up at the ceiling. He was sure Pip's enemies were already gathering, earthly or unearthly. He had lived in Arva too long not to know that both must be considered, as well as the proof of history.

7

'You like your coffee black?' asked the Professor, ready to pour out what looked like a cousin to the River Styx.

'The blacker the better,' Pip replied, grimacing. His headache was deserved.

'Salami?' asked Emilia, offering him the plate.

'No, thank you,' he said, trying not to look at the round, fatty eyes.

'Eggs then?' Emilia again.

'Just the coffee.' Pip sat warming his hands on the cup and glancing at the empty chair opposite. The daughter was evidently still sleeping. He wished he was too, because his head was thumping.

'You need to get used to Romanian plum brandy,' remarked Dalca. Then, to Emilia: 'Where's that girl?'

'I've taken her a cup of coffee. She is up. I've heard her in the bathroom.' The words were borne out by a sudden groaning of the plumbing.

'She should hurry or she'll be missing lectures again!' said Dalca.

'Why? Has she missed them before?' snapped Emilia.

It was obvious to Pip that the small talk was forced. Reading between the lines, neither of them was best pleased with the other, or with Ghita. He recognised the signs, having been through family strife himself. By then, he couldn't wait to see the girl. Then the door opened and he knew he was staring too hard. Long, dark brown hair, trim figure encased in jeans and a T-shirt. Exactly as he remembered from the hospital. Dalca doubtless wouldn't be happy if he found out that they had met before, and Pip realised his cover could be blown by one careless word from the girl. But she was as good an actress as he was discreet. She just glanced at him and perched on the chair opposite.

'Do you want to know who our visitor is?' asked her father.

'Can't wait.'

Pip couldn't tell whether her eyes showed a hint of mischief or danger.

'One of my post-doc historians.'

'Really, Dad.'

Pip held his breath, wondering if her father lied to her often.

'Hi,' she said, extending a slim, brown hand across the table.

'Hi. I'm Pip Durrant.' He took her hand. It was not cold like her mother's had been. At that moment, Emilia was following their every move.

'And I'm Ghita. You're studying history? What period?'

'Mainly medieval.' He was not given to untruths, except when necessary. He wondered what Ghita's agenda was for going along with the lie. He needed to know why!

'Are you both ready?' Dalca was looking at his watch.

'No, I'll take the bus,' Ghita said.

'You'll be late again,' he accused.

'Dad, it's not school. I'll get in when I like.' Which sounded like a danger sign. Her parents studied her, but Pip could see they weren't going to start another fight in front of him.

'Well, if that's what you want,' said the Professor. 'What about you, Pip?'

'I need to settle in a bit – and I intend to go and see the priest.'

'Father Joseph?' asked Emilia. Pip could see something

approaching alarm in her eyes.

'Yes, I'm researching into some aspects of the medieval church. Isn't that right, Professor?'

Dalca nodded, but looked less than happy.

'Your research sounds very interesting, Dr Durrant,' commented Ghita. 'We must discuss it.'

He felt her parents must have caught the sarcasm in her tone. In fact, the whole family was looking at him now.

'I'd like that,' he countered.

'You've never been particularly interested in history.' This brief comment from Emilia directed at Ghita was a signal for Pip to get up from the table. He pushed his chair back at the same time as Dalca.

'Thanks for the coffee, Mrs Dalca,' he said. 'I have to go now and get my notes together.' He didn't particularly want to talk to his host, but Dalca went through the door before he did and was about to pick up his briefcase in the hall.

'A word,' said Dalca, detaining him. Pip had a feeling he knew what was coming. 'It would have been better if you hadn't mentioned the priest,' he added in a low voice.

'I realise that.'

'You need to be careful. Both my wife and Ghita have ways of finding things out. This is our secret. Remember. Leave me to the explanations about our collaboration.'

'I'll be more careful,' promised Pip. He didn't have to guess what the reaction would be if the Professor found out that Ghita knew who he really was. He was still working on how he would combat that as Dalca walked off down the hall. He had certainly got off to a bad start. Next moment he was hurrying upstairs. He wondered what was being said about him in the kitchen, but he didn't care, as the kind of reckless excitement he had felt as a boy was overtaking him again.

When he reached his bedroom, he pushed back his hair from his forehead, where the sweat was forming. Once inside, he breathed in to calm himself and looked around. He had been so drunk the night before that he had hardly taken in anything of his surroundings. The massive wooden wardrobe looked disapproving as he approached it and peered inside its hollow emptiness. The quilt lay humped in the middle of the bed, squashed into his shape where he had fallen into his dreamless sleep. He straightened it. Then he walked over to the mirror and felt his chin, noting the dark stubble.

'Well, that wasn't a great start was it, Pip?' he said to himself. 'Better take a raincheck on the brandy tonight.' He was rummaging in his rucksack to find his washbag when he heard a rustling. He looked round to see a piece of paper appearing under the door. He guessed who the note was from even before he read the words.

I don't know what you're playing at. I'll meet you by the bus stop in 20 minutes!

He decided he didn't have time to have a shave or wash. Otherwise he might not have another chance to get Ghita on her own. But he had to make his exit look authentic. Pulling on his jeans and throwing on his parka, he placed his laptop in his everyday bag-cum-briefcase in case he got the time to see the priest. Then he stuffed the contents of his rucksack back in. With his head still thumping, he ran down the stairs – only to meet Emilia in the hall. Her presence was demanding.

'Are you going to see Fr Joseph right away?'

'I hope so.'

'Have you made an appointment?' Her eyes flicked towards his briefcase.

'Not yet.' Pip was desperate to go. Had her mother seen Ghita write the note? Did she suspect they were meeting?

'I'm afraid he'll be preparing for Mass now.'

'Well, I'll catch him afterwards.'

'Are you a Catholic, Dr Durrant?'

'No, but I'll hang around until the service is finished.'

'Do you know where to find Father? It's not at the church! That's closed.'

'Yes, the Professor told me Mass is held in the hall at present.' He was sure she was trying to detain him now. 'I'm sorry, but I need to go, Mrs Dalca.'

'Very well.' She let him pass, and he could feel those

miserable dark eyes watching him walk down the hall. 'Just a moment!'

He stopped. *What else?* he thought.

He turned to see that she had gone back into the kitchen. He wanted to dash out, but it would have been inappropriate. A moment later, she re-emerged. 'Here. This is the key for the door. Then you won't have to keep disturbing us.' For someone feeling less guilty than Pip, the sentence would not have borne a double meaning.

'Thank you,' he said.

'Shall I show you how to use it?'

'I'll be fine. Thank you.' He was halfway through the door when she shouted, 'Supper is at seven!'

He didn't look around in case she was watching him. He began to run across the square in the direction of the street he had walked along the day before. How far was it to the bus stop? He couldn't remember. Whatever happened, he had to meet Ghita. What if she caught the bus before he made it? As he passed the spot where the Mercedes had blocked his way, just for one moment he thought of the couple inside. He reached the perimeter of the village, his eyes fixed on the church. At the bottom of the hill was the bus stop. When he reached it, no-one was around. Not a soul. He had missed her. He swore. Puffed out, he sat down on the side of the road in disgust.

When he got his breath back, he got up and walked across the road. He looked up the stony path that led to the church. Maybe nobody had been up there since the village girls 'went up' in July? He imagined them walking up the path at dawn, clutching their red and gold flowers and their poopy dolls – children and dolls alike dressed in the ancient way, ready to do what they were bound to by the ritual. The thought sickened him.

'It's obscene,' he said out loud, thinking of the unfortunate ones who hadn't come back the same as they had 'gone-up'. Pip had those names off by heart. Catina Albu, 1952; Anka Petrescu,1988. Names that formed a litany of sorrow. Victims of Grandsire. How many more innocents had walked that way in the past? He had to find that out. To look back as far as he could, with Dalca's help. Maybe the Professor had already researched it?

As he began to walk up the rough track, he wondered what had really happened to the girls who'd been the prey of the Grandsire. He was determined to see where it all happened – the tomb with its arch cut in the stone and the figures of the dancing children around its lid. Pip shivered in spite of the physical warmth derived from that mad dash to meet Ghita. The idea that he, of all people, might be the one to find the answer, seemed incredible. He needed more names, more evidence and lots of time.

'Dr Durrant!' The voice made him jump. He swung round. She had come up behind him.

'Ghita!' he said, relieved. 'I thought I'd missed you.'

But he knew he was in for a roasting. She stood there, her eyes sparking, which made her even more attractive. The slight wind was stronger now and blowing her hair everywhere as they faced each other on the path to the church.

'You're disgusting,' she said, 'deceiving my parents. Lying to my father. Pretending you're an historian, while, all the time, you're a doctor!'

'Psychologist,' reminded Pip.

'Don't argue with me! It's the same kind of thing.' She was really angry now, and Pip was sorry for her, because he knew he was going to have to tell her that her dad was in on it. She was too intelligent to be treated like a child. 'You're like *him*, aren't you?' He was shocked by the scorn in her voice.

'Who?'

'Marcu. Even my grandma saw through you. And she's ill.'

He wanted to point out that that was why Simona had thought he was Marcu, but stopped himself.

Ghita scraped the toe of her trainer in the dust, her angry eyes strafing his face. 'All that man wanted was to destroy us.'

'That might be what you've been told, Ghita, but it's not true.'

'And he'd stop at nothing to do it!' Evidently she had been indoctrinated by her mother.

'Marcu was trying to help. Like I am.'

'We don't need your help. Why don't you go away? You'll have to, when I tell my dad.' She said it with such conviction that he wondered how she would feel when she realised her father had betrayed her.

'Then why didn't you tell him this morning at breakfast, Ghita? You could have.'

At that moment she looked so young and vulnerable, Pip could hardly bear to let her know that Dalca was lying.

'I wanted to hear your explanation,' she said.

That sounded more hopeful. With Ghita on board, he might stand a chance of finding out what she knew.

'Okay. I'm a psychology post-doc being employed by the University to take over Marcu's research project.'

'How did you get to my father? He would *never* have agreed to talk to you.' She was so vehement that he could see she really believed it.

Pip sighed.

'You're wrong, Ghita. I'm afraid he knows all about it. Besides, do you think I could fool *him* into thinking I'm an historian?'

Her fine brows arched together as if she was trying to make sense of what he was saying. Then she frowned.

'He's Arvan. He wouldn't betray us. You're lying.'

'I'm not. He made me swear I wouldn't tell you or your mother.' Pip had stepped over the line. Now he was facing the prospect of incurring Dalca's anger, of getting slung out of their house – and without the Professor's information, he might be unable to proceed.

But, at that moment, it didn't seem to count for much against a pair of brown, anguished eyes searching his face. Pip had always tried to be measured and logical, ever since he had learned that imagination carried a penalty. He also believed that to tell the truth was the best. Ghita's shoulders had dropped, making her appear more vulnerable than ever.

'Your father is trying to help you and your mother,' Pip added. 'Like me, he's trying to find out about Grandsire, so that nothing bad will happen to your family.'

All at once, they heard the rumble of distant thunder. They both looked up at the sky, which was morning blue without a hint of rain. But the wind was getting up. Ghita looked frightened.

'What are you afraid of?' Pip asked. 'I'm sure I can help.'

'My father can't do anything. He doesn't know the secret. He always thought my grandma was mad. Even before she went into hospital. So how do you think you can help? I don't want to discuss this anymore. Least of all here! I hate this place.'

The vehemence of the last sentence worried Pip. Had she already been hurt in some way? He put out his hand and touched hers. It was cold.

'Don't!' she warned. 'I have to think what's the best thing to do.'

'None of this is your fault,' he said gently. At that moment, Pip felt something like Judas, but it seemed to matter more than anything that he gained Ghita's good opinion. 'We can talk about it anytime you want,' he added.

'We can't,' she said.

'We need to, Ghita. If only you knew how important it is to finish this research!'

She rounded on him again.

'You think I don't know? Every moment of my life has been spent discovering something I didn't want to. It goes on and on. It never stops.' Tears started in her eyes.

'I understand.' He had made her cry, and that was the last thing he had wanted.

'How could you? You just want to get hold of my mother.'

'Ghita, I am who I am,' he said. 'I shall find out.'

'You can't stop anything happening to us,' she retorted. All at once, she broke free and ran away from him down the steep path. He followed, trying to catch up, thinking how pompous he had sounded. Who was he, anyway, to solve anything?

'Where are you going?' he shouted.

'Don't ask,' she yelled. He slowed. As she reached the end of the opening to the path, an old, small car appeared and screeched to a halt.

'Ghita! Wait!'

The car door opened, and Pip saw the driver – a boy with dark hair. A second later, Ghita jumped in, slammed the door and the car accelerated away. Pip exhaled in annoyance. The driver must have been waiting somewhere. It was probably Anton.

'Christ,' he swore. He dropped his briefcase on the path and put his arms behind his head in a gesture of rage. 'Well, you made a mess of that, didn't you?' He was very angry with himself. 'You not only blew your cover, but you frightened her off.' What if she went straight back and accused her dad? He would be out on his ear. He had been an idiot.

When he had calmed down, Pip began to consider Ghita's attitude. She had been angry too, but as scared as hell. Of what? Pip didn't know yet, but he was damn well going to find out.

Still thinking about Ghita, he walked on down the uneven path. Then instinct told him to look left into the forest, which revealed something he had not noticed when he had climbed up – a dilapidated old building, half-hidden in the trees. It looked as if it had been burned down and left to rot. It was an eerie-looking place and he couldn't understand why he hadn't noticed it before. He had probably been too fixed on the idea of looking at the church.

He shivered and pulled the zip of his parka right up to his neck. The temperature had certainly dropped, and he thought of Dalca's amused words when he had taken off his jacket at their first meeting. *You won't be doing that in a couple of months. It gets pretty cold over here.* Deciding to investigate, he began to walk towards the ruin, where it squatted beneath the forest trees like a crouching animal. It was when he reached it that he realised there were the remains of outbuildings behind.

It had definitely been some kind of smallholding. Strange place for a farm – in the forest right next to the church. Where was its grazing land? Maybe the people had kept only pigs or suchlike?

He walked into the ruins, glancing around at the old charred timbers, covered with lichen. He kicked one and found it alive and crawling with woodlice. Something coloured was lying beneath it. He picked up a stick and poked at it, bringing to life a charred piece of cloth, which was big enough to reveal the image of a rooster. It was decaying now, but must once have been a bright hand-made tapestry.

He walked around inside what remained of the roofless building. Occasionally, a piece of blue plaster revealed itself. He was trying to imagine how the farmhouse might have looked, and who its occupants might have been, when he caught sight of two objects; one, lying on top of a mound of earth, was a grotesquely high boot that Pip recognised as having probably belonged to a disabled man; the other was a little holy water stoup, lying on its side with its brass bowl half-buried under the earth. He loosened the earth around the bowl and examined it. Its base had once been a representation of an angel with its outstretched wings holding the bowl.

Then a picture began forming in Pip's mind, becoming more clear as he concentrated. The Marcu Papers. What did they say about Claudiu Basa? The old man who lived by the churchyard, who kept pigs? Convicted for bestiality?

Immediately a house flashed into his mind, his imagination bringing it to life with the clarity that only those who have experienced visions recognise. It was an extraordinarily sharp picture. He saw the clearing and the single-storey farmhouse built into the hill; its sloping roof green and moist with living lichen; its two white windows framing the dark-eyed glass. They had known it well in Arva as the house by the path, where the old cripple lived.

Pip stood in the ruins with the imaginary house rising above him. He felt as if his body was crooked, like it used to be when he couldn't walk; when he was a cripple, living in his attic away from the life downstairs. He looked down at his feet and saw he was wearing the ugly boot. Then the stick in his hand transformed itself into a thick, knobbly cane. As the vision grew clearer, the coldness of the grave washed over his body and his real self faded away as he slipped into the world of Claudiu Basa, the lame farmer who lived next to the path that led to the church. He could hear the shrieking of pigs and then the clatter of a child's feet running down the path, flying down from the church towards the inn at Sancipia. He could see the girl now, her arms outstretched in terror like a windmill's sails; a plump child with her braided hair sticking out from under her headscarf, her face contorted with pain. Her black apron and white skirt were red with mud and blood. He could feel the pain she felt through all of his crooked body.

'*Moarte*, murder,' he muttered. His voice was old, guttural and unfamiliar. Dropping the cane, he fell down on his knees and clapped his hands over his ears to shut out the chattering voices that surrounded him, taunting him, telling him things he didn't want to hear.

Then all went quiet and Pip was standing in the ruins, shaking. What had just happened more than frightened him; it filled him with dread. He knew that he had seen the Little and Chosen – the name the women of Arva gave the victim. Chosen for Grandsire. His head was reeling. He hated what was happening to him again. *I don't want to see these visions! I shouldn't be here!*

Coming to, Pip grabbed his briefcase and ran, weaving through the trees towards the path. The only thought in his head was to get away from the farm and back to the road. The tangled brambles tore at his clothes, their spiky fingers trying to keep him from leaving. His breathing became short and he had to stop for air. At least he had reached the path! He closed his eyes in relief. When he opened them, he felt better. Turning, he looked up at the church. Why, he didn't know. Then, through a haze of perspiration, he saw a tall black shape standing near the church gates. Someone had been watching him!

The sweat was running down his face. His shirt felt cold on his back, and he shivered again in spite of his parka. A moment later, the shape disappeared.

'Maybe it's the priest,' he said out loud.

He hoped that the man hadn't seen his crazy progress through the trees. Then an unwelcome thought crept into his head, a thought so preposterous that to entertain it would be utter foolishness. But it wouldn't go away. It the man wasn't the priest, could he be – *Grandsire*? The thought stuck. Then it began goading him. *If you go up there, you might find out.* He swallowed to moisten his mouth. *Why shouldn't you?*, it urged. *It was only a man you saw. Go on. Don't be scared. You want to see. Really you do. You're grown up now. You can do it. Grandsire will be an old man now. He can't hurt you.* The thought lured him a few steps up the path.

Pip thought of passing the farm again and shuddered. But he shook off the fear. The vision was only in his imagination. He *was* grown-up. He wasn't the frightened kid he had been years before in Sunny Mead. He was strong. If it was the priest, he would be able to chat to him. Maybe find out more about this place.

Pip was hurrying up the path now. Perhaps the man had disappeared into the forest, though? He couldn't have been going into the church. The gates were barred.

But they were not. The chains were off and the padlocks hanging down. *Who has the authority to open them?* thought Pip. *Only the Church.* The man he had seen *must* have been the priest. *Where is he now?* Pip could feel the sharp breeze cooling his face as he stared across into the churchyard. The weak early morning sun, which had been swimming through a wispy haze, had now disappeared behind an angry-looking cloud, making the place even more forbidding. Pip stood at the entrance; then, after a few moments of hesitation, he decided to go in.

As he walked up the path, he saw that on each side the churchyard grass was wild and overgrown. Graves that must once have been tended were now consumed with couch grass and brambles, through which peered the forgotten faces of the dead pictured on the stones. Hundreds of sightless eyes followed his progress as he walked in the direction of the church. The path twisted and divided into thin, stony strings that led to different areas of the churchyard. All at once he glimpsed, out of the corner of one eye, a black shape that moved quickly out of sight. He swung around and saw it again, passing between the gnarled trees. Although he felt scared, he walked towards it, telling himself he wasn't a kid and the shape wasn't a vision.

A moment later, a tall monument with a broken column on top revealed itself. The area had been hidden by two enormous forest trees. He swallowed. This couldn't be anything else but the place he had dreamed about, that had brought him from the States. *Grandsire's Grave*. The Marcu Papers explained that the cross had been struck by lightning during a storm and had never been replaced. He breathed in, ready to go and look. The man was there somewhere, and Pip was going to find out what he was doing and how he had got in.

Pip walked towards the trees, thinking this was the path the children took on their July pilgrimage to lay their flowers and do homage to their village's founder. He knew the tomb lay on the other side of the obelisk, facing east. Each detail had been described so well by both Marcu and Inspector Valentin. The tomb was hewn from shiny mountain rock, with figures of dancing children fretted on the lid. Such carving seemed a sacrilege in itself. Worse that happy children should mark the spot where the crimes against those poor little girls had taken place in 1988 and 1952.

God knows how many others before that were taken by the monster who calls himself Grandsire, thought Pip as he approached. A strange compulsion to view the tomb for himself was urging him on, in spite of the thought that whoever or whatever he had seen must be waiting for him on the other side. When he reached the obelisk, his stomach flipped over in shock. The man jumped up almost as if he had risen from the hidden tomb, which he must have been crouching behind. Pip felt instinctively that this man was not the priest. It wasn't because he wasn't wearing the collar, or because his suit was black and streaked with fine red dust. *He just knew.*

'What are you doing here? This place is private.' The stranger's voice was smooth, but authoritative. Pip noticed that his skin was pale and pure, like the finest porcelain. His hair was deep gold and thick, like a girl's, but there any touch of femininity ended. The man caught his stare with eyes that were as unblinking as a snake's. The darkest Pip had ever seen. Black. His body was strong and well-muscled under the suit, and his whole frame exuded a sense of power.

'I was looking for the priest,' replied Pip, ignoring the question.

'You won't find him here. He lives in that ugly pile of bricks and concrete they call the village hall.' The two men appraised each other. 'And you are …?'

'A tourist,' lied Pip. 'I was on a walk, saw the gate open and thought I'd just come in and take a look. Neglected, isn't it?' He looked around as he said it, and had the uncomfortable feeling that the man knew he was lying. Besides, most tourists didn't carry briefcases!

'This is private property,' returned the other. 'I'd *run* away if I were you.'

Pip couldn't miss the sarcastic inference, or the threat. So the man had seen him panicking.

'And you are?' Pip was determined the man should see him in a different light.

'I have permission to be here.' A nasty edge had come into the stranger's voice. Evidently he had no intention of revealing his identity.

'And where do *I* get permission?' asked Pip coolly.

His brain was working now. The man came slowly round the obelisk towards him. Pip could see his hands were red with what looked like rust. His fingers were long and slim, like a musician's.

'I have a higher permission than any you'd be granted.' The voice had become almost a snarl. Pip could see that the man's hip pocket was bulging. Maybe he had a gun?

'I'd like to take a look before I go,' he replied.

'At what?'

'Where you were,' Pip said.

'Why?'

'It looks interesting.' Pip drew in his breath, put down his briefcase and stared at the broken obelisk. 'How did that column break off?'

'I have no idea.'

'So you're not local?' Pip was moving closer.

The man didn't answer. What had he been doing on the other side of the tomb? Pip had to see the door. Had the man opened it? He knew there was one on the side facing west. *The Arch of Darkness*. It was well documented. The terrifying thought that this stranger might be Grandsire kept slipping in and out of Pip's mind. How could he be? Why should he be? But who was he? Pip knew he was being watched and again had the feeling that the man knew what he was thinking. So he looked down at the sharp little stones under his feet. Under here the poopies had been buried. The girls had to bury the dolls before performing the ritual song. Were there any left now? He shivered inside.

'What are you looking at?' asked the man, his voice level and cold.

'Nothing. Just watching where I'm walking.'

The stranger grinned, revealing particularly sharp white teeth. But the grin had no humour. Was the man going to try and stop him? Pip stood his ground. It was his own fault if something happened to him now.

'You're trespassing,' the man said.

'No, I'm interested, that's all.'

As Pip passed him, he was close enough to feel the man's body heat. A second later he was facing the tomb. It was chest high, and its glassy top was like a table. Strange thoughts flitted around in Pip's head. Allusions to its significance. An altar where innocents were sacrificed. A Communion table. A place of horror. He bent down to look, and could make out the arch carved into the stone. Then he gasped. Not carved into the stone now, but apparently receding. It *was* a door! Forgetting the silent watcher standing behind him, he pushed at it, and it gave way. He noticed the red rust covering his hands. That's what the man had been doing. Opening the door! He straightened quickly and looked across to where the stranger stood. The man had gone. Pip was torn over whether he should follow or continue his inspection of the tomb. He rubbed his hands down his jeans and walked away from the Grandsire's Grave, his feet scrunching on the little stones. He thought he could see a hint of black and followed it, but no-one was there. The stranger must have left in a hurry. What did that mean?

Pip returned to the tomb and bent down again towards the crack in the door. A sudden gust of air made him jump back. Stagnant air! The scent of ancient stone and putrid, musty earth. Then he saw a worm of water, wriggling and trickling out. It glinted red. Rust! He swallowed in relief. For a moment he had fancied it was blood.

'Stop it,' he growled at himself, dismissing the idea angrily, fighting against his imagination, determined to be rational.

The tomb must be flooded. Then he wondered, if it hadn't been, if he would have had the courage to go in. All at once he felt queasy. He pulled himself together.

'Probably the plum brandy,' he said out loud.

Immediately he heard what seemed to be faint laughter. He'd had enough. His mind was playing tricks again. Pip walked away from the tomb, past the great trees and onto the path again. He was doing everything he could to calm himself in case another vision took him unawares. The professional view of visionary experience was that it was contact with the supernatural, heavenly or diabolical.

Why had he believed he had got over his post-traumatic stress when such experiences kept intruding into his personal life? He couldn't discover what kind of message – if any – he was deriving from them at present.

'Things are getting on top of me,' he said out loud to reassure himself. 'It's this place. But I am not going to see a doctor over here. I have to keep myself in check!'

Although his feet were making for the gate, all he could

think of at that moment was what he had just seen – the door to the tomb. Was that where Grandsire lay in wait for his victims? Then he thought of the stranger. Maybe he *was* Grandsire and had come back to revisit the scene of his crimes. But it was a mad thought. The man was too young. But wasn't that just what Simona Murgu had said in her statement to the police when they had questioned her about Claudiu Basa? Claudiu had said he had seen Grandsire twice, in 1952 and in 1988, and he had never looked any older!

It was preposterous and it couldn't be true. Why could he even think it? But however much he fought against it, Pip was beginning to believe, in spite of himself, that things were happening in Arva that no-one could explain. The kind of things Marcu had said he had experienced. Perhaps Pip should tell Dalca about the stranger? Or the police? He kept on thinking about their meeting as he hurried down the path. Maybe the man was just a local, but he didn't look like one. He had a sinister air about him, a strange familiarity that Pip couldn't place. But Pip had never seen him before.

As he reached the gate, he gasped. It was closed – and locked. The chains and the padlocks were in place. The creep had locked him in! It was unbelievable. He was shut in Arva churchyard. A moment of panic overtook him as he rattled the railings. Seconds later, he began to think logically. How could he get out? The railings surrounding the perimeter of the churchyard were at least six feet high – and sharp. He would impale himself if he tried to climb over. He needed someone to open the gates. But who?

He took out his mobile phone from his briefcase. He only hoped he would get a signal. But he was very high up, which should help. His first thought was to phone Dalca. But the Professor was in Cluj. What about Emilia? That wasn't a good idea, but it might have to do if he couldn't think of anyone else. At least she could fetch the priest.

Then he remembered he had Ghita's number. She had told him not to ring her, but this was an emergency. Where she was and whether or not she would bother to answer he didn't know, as their parting earlier on had been less than cordial. And she had also said she hated this place. But he had no option. As he pressed the keys, somewhere in the distance his ears seemed to catch the sound of faint laughter on the wind.

8

This time the black shape was a slightly-built priest in a flowing cassock. And he was accompanied by Ghita. Pip felt extremely foolish as Fr Joseph undid the chains. But he didn't care about the priest's disapproving expression. He only had eyes for Ghita, who looked as if she had been crying.

'Thank you,' he said to both of them. But it was Ghita he cared about. He wanted to know what had happened to her that morning. Had he upset her that much earlier on?

'How did you get in here?' Everything about Fr Joseph seemed unapproachable, and his voice was no exception. As he walked through the gates, Pip felt like a naughty schoolboy.

'The same way I got out,' he replied with sarcasm, knowing that his tone was unworthy of what he felt, which was sheer relief. It had been an unnerving experience. 'Actually, when I arrived, the gates were open.'

'Impossible,' replied the priest, his dark brows lifting above his hollow eye sockets. 'Only I have the keys.' He had a pale complexion and looked as if he needed a good meal. Yet, something in the priest's gestures, and the way his light grey eyes flicked from side to side, distanced him from Ghita and Pip, whose professional sharpness caught the smell of fear exuding like sweat from his emaciated frame.

'I'm sorry, Father, but someone else has. He was here, and I talked to him.' Pip heard Ghita give a little gasp. The priest was staring hard at him now as if he didn't believe what he had heard. Then he bit his lip.

'And I suppose this man locked you in?' The sarcasm was harsh.

'He must have. No-one else was here.'

'Except you,' stated the priest.

'Please, Father,' said Ghita, 'Dr Durrant is staying with me and my parents. He's not likely to have made this up. He's my father's student.'

So she's sticking up for me now, thought Pip. *That's encouraging*. He didn't really care what the priest thought of him anyway. All he needed was to get away from that place and give himself time to think about the nerve-racking encounter with the stranger. He didn't know if he should describe it to Ghita though. She still looked scared.

'I see you have a champion, *doctor*.' The priest shook his head as if he couldn't believe it, and Pip thought how uneasy the man looked. 'How is Anton by the way, Ghita?'

You bastard, thought Pip, assuming the cleric was implying that Ghita's championship of Pip had been a betrayal of her relationship with her fiancé.

'Very well, Father,' she replied.

'I didn't see your mother at Mass this morning.'

'She's not well, Father, and I'd be happy if you didn't mention what happened here to her. She'll be upset.'

'Of course, if you don't want me to.'

Ghita looked at Pip in relief.

As the priest bent to check on the padlocks, Pip struggled against the insane desire to kick him in the butt.

When Fr Joseph had finished, he straightened.

'In any case,' he added, 'I am determined to discover who else thinks he has the authority to open these gates. That prerogative lies only with the Church.'

His voice was faint now, almost tremulous.

'The man was quite clear about it. He said he had a higher permission.'

Pip had meant to shock him, and he seemed to have succeeded, as immediate alarm showed in the parish priest's face.

'There is none higher than the Church!'

Pip would have liked to have replied *What about God?* But he didn't intend to get into theological arguments.

'There's the government, I suppose,' added Ghita suddenly.

Fr Joseph turned on her.

'You think this man was from the government?'

'I think that's unlikely,' said Pip. 'He seemed to know his way round the churchyard.' The two of them were staring at him now.

'What did this person look like?' asked Fr Joseph.

'He was wearing a black suit. He was blond and tall. Very tall, and his eyes were ...' Pip decided he wouldn't add *black like a snake's.* Ghita was already frightened. And he was sure he knew why. They both thought he had seen Grandsire! So his instincts had been right. But the man had not been a ghost. Or a vision. He had been flesh and blood. Of that he was convinced.

'I don't think we need to hear any more,' said the priest, and his voice was shaky.

'Strangely enough, I was hoping to talk with you, Father. I came up to look round while you were at Mass. Mrs Dalca told me where to find you.'

'And now you have,' said Fr Joseph. 'I don't think I can be of any use to you.'

'I think you can,' replied Pip. 'As Ghita said, I am researching, and I am very keen to look up parish records.'

'I am afraid that I can't help you there. Many of our ancient ones are held in places other than this. For example, Hungary, Serbia, Poland and even Germany.'

'The ones I'm after are not quite as ancient,' replied Pip. He was not going to let the priest off the hook so easily. 'I would be grateful for a chat.'

'I cannot help you with this.'

'But you might be able to with other things, Father,' was Pip's cool reply. During their whole conversation, Ghita hadn't said a word. 'May I make an appointment?'

'I'm free after Mass tomorrow. Come along to the hall,' he said.

Pip was taken aback by this, given the priest's hostility. He caught Ghita's surprised glance.

'Great,' he replied.

'I have to go,' said Fr Joseph, consulting his watch. 'I've spent too much time already. I hope that something like this won't happen again?'

'Certainly not,' agreed Pip. 'Next time I'll ask you for the key.' The priest frowned at him, then turned to Ghita.

'Thank you, Father,' she said.

'And give Anton my best wishes. Doubtless I'll see you both at Mass on Sunday?'

'Of course.'

'Goodbye then, Ghita. Goodbye, Dr Durrant.' With that he turned and made his way quickly down the hill without a backward look.

'What the hell have you been doing?' asked Ghita. 'If my mother finds out, there'll be murder.'

'That won't be anything new here, will it?' asked Pip, and was immediately sorry. 'I wasn't doing anything. I couldn't help going in when the gates were open.'

'Is it true they were?' Her voice faltered.

'Well, I didn't fly in,' he joked.

She caught at his arm and looked round as if she was afraid of them being heard.

'That's not funny!'

'Why?'

'You know very well,' she said. 'I don't understand how you got in, but did you make it up about the man?'

'Would you rather I had?' he asked gently.

'Probably.'

'Well, I have to disappoint you,' he said. 'I know you're scared, but you don't have to be. Nothing happened. He was just there, that's all.'

'You spoke to him!' she almost shrieked.

It still surprised Pip when someone with intelligence was afraid of what they believed was supernatural.

'I'm not going to ask you who you think he was, Ghita, but I can tell you he wasn't anyone to be scared of.' He thought how adept he was becoming at telling half-truths.

'Why?'

'For one thing, he was only young.' She didn't look convinced. 'Anyway, enough of him. We'll find out who he was in the end. When you came up you'd been crying. Why? It wasn't to do with me, was it? If so, I'm sorry.'

'You think a lot of yourself, don't you?' she said, the old feistiness appearing. 'I'm upset about something quite different. I went to see my grandmother. Anton took me – and Robert wasn't there.'

Pip's stomach lurched.

'Why? Where was he?

'He's in the hospital. Not Burbor! The city hospital.'

'What happened to him?'

Her eyes seemed huge as she regarded him. They were filling with tears.

'My grandmother was right. You're bringing us bad luck!' She swallowed.

'Ghita! What has happened to Robert?'

'They say … they say … he's dying.'

'Dying! Christ! Why?'

'He has rabies! The nurse who took over from him told me something about his dog biting him. It must have been in the garden with a fox. It happens here sometimes.'

'Does it?' His brain was sorting through the horrific possibilities. *Rabies*! What a way to die!

'Yes, this is Romania. You look shocked. How do you think *I* feel? ' Her anger showed. 'You didn't know him like I did. In fact, you didn't know him at all.'

Pip couldn't bear to think what might happen if he told her that Robert and he were closer than she thought, and that someone, somewhere might have set this up. But who and how?

Eisenmann. He remembered Robert's words so clearly now: *I always thought Grandsire was real. You'll know why when you see what I have on him.* But Pip never would now. The German must have got to Robert first.

'What are you thinking?' asked Ghita.

He brought his attention back to her.

'I'm thinking we should get the hell out of here and find ourselves a cup of coffee or something stronger,' he said.

All at once, she grabbed his arm.

'Come on,' she said, 'I know where we can get a drink. But, remember, this doesn't mean I've forgiven you!'

They ended up at what looked more like a tumbledown garage, at the end of a cart track on the outside of the village. It had a tin roof and a rickety door. She must have seen the look on his face when she explained, 'This is where the kids go. They won't tell if they see us together, because it's a place that we all keep secret.'

More secrets then, thought Pip, feeling ancient as he entered. A bunch of rangy teenagers were staring at him suspiciously. All were smoking and dressed in the usual tattered jeans and T-shirts, one of which said 'NYU' on the front. He wondered if any of them were carrying knives. Zero tolerance probably wasn't a phrase they understood. Ghita went up to them and they huddled together. Pip waited awkwardly. A moment later, things had changed, with grins all round. She came over to him. 'I told them you were an American student and you'd buy us all a drink,' she said.

'Sure will,' he said, relieved, thinking how old he really felt. 'What do they want?'

'I'll get them,' she replied, and he could have sworn her eyes were glinting with mischief. 'You just pay the bill!'

He hadn't been wrong about Ghita. She was a smart operator. He wondered what would have happened if he had refused the request.

'What happened to the coffee?' he said, when she

returned carrying two small glasses.

'You look like you need a vodka. I do,' she retorted.

'Okay,' he shrugged.

She lifted her glass.

'To Robert!'

She swallowed it down in one. He followed suit, and her tongue crept round her lips in a tiny smile as he did so. 'Better than plum brandy?'

He couldn't answer, because it was pure fire water.

'Robert,' he toasted, when he had caught his breath. How would she react if she knew that he might be indirectly responsible for Robert's death? But he didn't intend to tell her.

They sat in silence until she said, 'This doesn't mean we can be friends.'

'So you said. I'm sorry but, honestly, I'd like us to be. Whatever your dad says.'

'He'll say a lot,' she replied.

'That's if you tell him we've been talking.'

'I shan't have to,' she replied, puckering her eyebrows. 'Mother will probably get it out of Fr Joseph. She's like that.'

'How?'

'Someone will have seen me going to the priest's,' said Ghita. 'And they will tell her and she'll confront him. And he won't be able to get out of explaining. You wait and see.'

'He didn't seem timid.'

'Well, he is, I can tell you. He's frightened someone will write to the bishop complaining about him, and then he'll get carted off somewhere, like ...' She stopped.

'Like?'

'Never mind. I wish you'd never gone up to that place. You've caused a hell of a lot of trouble to Fr Joseph, and to me.' She looked as if she really meant it.

'I told you the gates were open and I walked in. You know I wouldn't pull a stunt like that, lock myself in, phone you and bring you all the way up there.'

'Do I? If you're like Marcu – and you are – you'd do anything to find out what you want to know.'

'Well, if that's your opinion of me, I'd better go,' said Pip.

'Yes, you should.'

'Where do you get a cab round here?' She lifted her eyebrows and grinned.

'Nowhere. This isn't New York. It's the bus or nothing. What are you doing?'

Pip got up from the table and knew they were all watching him now.

'I could say it's none of your business, but ...' he shrugged, '... but I may just go and see Robert.'

'They won't let you in!' He could hear the confidence in her tone.

'We'll see.'

'Why would you want to go and see him anyway?'

'Once again, that's my business.'

She was standing up now too, holding out her hand.

'Money?'

'Oh, yes, I remember, it's on the house,' he said in English.

He took out his wallet, wondering what he would do if they jumped him. He offered some notes to Ghita.

'That's too much,' she said. 'You want to watch out, carrying that much cash.'

'I can look after myself.'

She smiled in response.

'Just like you did when you got locked in the churchyard? Here, this is enough.' She took a note. 'Evidently, you can't look after yourself, so you'd better hang around with me for a bit longer. Don't look so surprised. I want to see Robert too. Wait there.'

He watched her walk over to the bar, thinking how well she gave what she got. As she was paying, she was talking to a young man whom he hadn't noticed before. He must have come in through a back door. Pip watched her pay and then bring him over.

'This is Anton.' Her fiancé! Near to, he wasn't bad-looking, but he didn't look happy. 'He'll take us into Cluj.'

Pip could see it was the last thing the guy wanted – and he knew why. But it seemed Ghita was the boss.

'Hi, Anton.'

The boy nodded but he didn't answer. A moment later, the three of them walked out together. Pip had been right. There had been no battered old car outside when they had come in. It was now parked there in a mud hole, and was covered in sludge. Probably a death-trap, thought Pip. He had never been that keen on cars since his accident, but as long as it got him where he wanted to go, he was willing to take the chance! He climbed in the back and, as they screeched off, he decided that Ghita must be thawing a little, or she wouldn't have invited him along for the ride.

And what a ride it turned out to be! Much worse than the bus. The guy had never heard of braking. Pip had a shrewd suspicion that the bad driving was for his benefit. *Still, it's better than a punch in the mouth,* he thought. Neither of them spoke to him, so he spent the journey imagining what the priest had told Emilia and planning what he was going to say to Dalca when he saw him next. Pip was also calculating his best approach to Ghita when she started asking questions about Robert. Whatever the outcome, he was probably deep in the shit. But his self-pity waned as they drove into the gateway that led to the city hospital; a much bigger place than Burbor, and almost as grim from the outside. Pip stared up at the rows of identical windows and wondered behind which one the last act of Robert's tragedy was being played.

They soon found out. Anton was left behind in the car as Ghita managed to get herself and Pip into the foyer of the isolation unit.

'Are you relatives of Mr Riparu?' the nurse asked.

'Yes, I'm his niece, and this is a doctor,' replied Ghita. She sounded so sincere that anyone would have believed her – except the nurse.

'He has no relatives,' the woman replied, her heavy features registering suspicion. 'Before he went into the coma, he told us he was alone in the world. Maybe you'd like to talk to the police.' She was eyeing them up and down as if they were criminals. *She probably thinks we're after his money*, thought Pip.

'What have the police to do with it?' asked Ghita, her voice quarrelsome.

'Death from rabies is notifiable.'

'He's dead?' asked Pip.

'Not far off. Anyway,' she added, looking him up and down with even more suspicion, 'if you're a doctor you'd know all about rabies.'

He did. He had been an animal lover since he was a little guy. Robert's deterioration must have come on fast. Sometimes it could be really quick if the bite was bad, but usually it took two to four weeks for the infection to take hold. After that came the hallucinations and the extreme thirst, followed by an horrific fear of water, then manic behaviour, culminating in paralysis, coma and death.

His brain was computing again. Maybe Robert had had the infection already when they'd talked. He had thought how morose and lethargic the man had been in the beginning, then how he had started to light up with excitement when he had given Pip to believe that he knew who Grandsire was. Maybe his claim to having evidence was all fantasy? Maybe he had nothing on Eisenmann? Perhaps he had made it all up for American dollars? It was a sickening thought, but if true, it meant that Pip had nothing to fear from Eisenmann! He snapped out of his thoughts as he heard the edge in Ghita's voice:

'So we can't see him?'

'Certainly not.'

'At least if he dies, will you let us know, if I give you a phone number?'

The nurse shook her head.

'Sorry, you're not family.'

'Well, how can we find out?' persisted Ghita.

'You can't. But if you come back ...'

'We're wasting our time here,' snapped Ghita. 'Robert and I were very close in Burbor.'

'*Ah*, Burbor,' said the nurse.

She thinks we're psychiatric cases, thought Pip.

'Come on, Ghita,' he said, attempting to take her arm. 'We're not getting anywhere.'

She pulled away.

'Don't tell me what to do,' she retorted. 'This country is ridiculous. Would this happen in America?' she appealed.

'It might,' said Pip, trying to be patient. He wanted time to think about the possibilities.

'Oh, you never *do* anything, do you?' Ghita rounded on him, her eyes glinting like they had the first time he had seen her. He wished he could be like that. Spontaneous. She reminded him a lot of his sister, Mel. All fire, and wanting answers straightaway. 'I'm going,' she said, turning.

'Where to?' He followed her down the corridor.

'To find my father,' she said. Pip grabbed her arm, oblivious of the stares of passers-by. 'Let me go, please.'

He did. There was nothing he could do to stop her blurting it all out to Dalca. She didn't say a word as they strode on. When they reached the main door, she breathed in hard and glared at him.

'Anton will drop us off at Uni. What you do then is your business. I suppose I'll see you later. There's always the bus.'

'Right!' said Pip, following her to the car.

Everything – the way she walked, what she said – he wanted to see and hear more of. Ghita was really something. If things hadn't been so serious, he might have been amused at her treatment of him. At least, he would have taken it lightly. But that would be inappropriate now, seeing that a man was on the point of death and there was a good chance it was all Pip's fault.

After Ghita and Anton had dropped him outside the University, Pip had stood there for a few moments watching the constant stream of students going in and out. He didn't join them. As a post-doc, he had only himself to answer to, and his timetable was flexible, interspersed with the occasional visit to his supervisor to see how the work was going. *At present, it's going nowhere*, he thought. *And will it ever?* He had begun to realise that what had happened to Robert had hit him hard. According to Ghita, he was a Jonah, the harbinger of doom. What had she said? *My grandmother was right. You're bringing us bad luck.* Was he?

He had been told at least three times now to go back to America and jettison the project.

He walked into the square by St Michael's Church and sat on a bench, where doubtless many other students had come to philosophise. As a rationalist, Pip saw belief in luck as a fallacy. When A happens, then B has to happen. In his case, if in Simona's eyes Marcu was a monster, then Pip must be one too, as he was engaged in the same kind of business. If he had been a believer, he might also have gone along with the idea that if he met Eisenmann, he might end up like Marcu – dead! But it was Robert who was dead – almost. Again, if he had believed what Ghita said, then he might have been the one to cause Robert's death – although she didn't know it.

For a psychologist, luck also had connotations of ritual and obsession. And ritual was very much his present business. Luck could also be seen as a form of superstition. That was what Marcu had discussed in his Papers about the women of Arva. The Little and Chosen was a victim of bad luck. But he knew from his examination of the cycles that what happened in Arva was not coincidence. And yet, neither Marcu nor he himself had been able to make sense of it. And that was where superstition kicked in …

Pip shook his weary head. He wondered if he should go to Burbor for what remained of the afternoon and see if he could speak to Simona Murgu again. She might be more sane this time; yet if she saw him, it might distress her, so he was not convinced it would do any good at this point. He had a shrewd suspicion that the old woman had lapsed into the kind of medical state that nothing could be learned from, except by the kind of day-to-day intensive attention that Marcu had been able to give to Irina Petrescu. But an interview with her later was still a possibility. The thought that if he went there he might run into Ghita again really put him off. He had other demons to attend to presently.

So, his head still full of impending possibilities, he got up and walked on to the student hostel, where he spent the first two hours of the chilly autumn afternoon going over his notes and planning his campaign. He was glad that he had kept a bolt-hole to which he could retreat, and indeed might need to when Dalca found out what had been happening.

Later, he caught the bus and braved another rickety drive to Arva. That evening as he alighted he had no desire to deviate with a stroll up to the church. He just made for the village as quickly as he could. Using the key Emilia had given him, he entered a completely silent house. No sound from the television issued from the room at the end of the corridor, and when the ancient wooden stairs creaked with his weight, no one stirred. He concluded that Emilia must be out and that neither Dalca nor Ghita had yet returned home from the University.

Enjoy the calm before the storm, Pip thought as he sat on the small chair in his bedroom at the desk that had been provided for him. The question now was, when he was confronted with his misdemeanours, should he defend himself? He was definitely guilty as charged, but how much his crime was his own fault was questionable. If he hadn't met Ghita at Burbor then things might have been different. He would still have been undercover as Dalca's post-doc in medieval studies, but how then would he have escaped from the churchyard? His analysis of the morning's shambles made him smile – but only a little. After all his philosophising, he was almost sure of one thing: he had been meant to meet the stranger at the tomb. The puzzle of the man's identity had been annoying him all day, like a buzzing gnat. He thought of it just like that, and he didn't know why. Buzz, buzz in his ears. There had been something faintly familiar about him, like when you meet someone and you're sure you've seen them before, but you couldn't possibly have done.

At that precise moment a door banged, making Pip jump. Someone was back. What should he do? He couldn't holler down the stairs, 'I'm home.' Instead, he lay down on the bed and awaited developments.

He was awakened by a sharp knock on the door and a brief 'Dinner's on the table.'

As he rolled over, blinking, he heard the sound of footsteps receding. He shook his head. What had happened? He had fallen asleep, of course; and this time it hadn't been from the effects of plum brandy. Probably mental exhaustion? He jumped up. One look in the mirror confirmed more than designer stubble, rather the early signs of a beard. Again, no time to shave. At that moment, Pip didn't care how he looked. He only wanted to get things over with and hear his sentence from the Professor's lips.

It was pork again, this time seasoned with some herb that Pip couldn't recognise. Ghita was not present and Emilia spent the whole meal in silence, although occasionally she caught Pip's eye, then looked away. The whole uncomfortable hour was spent exactly as Pip had imagined it would be. Added to that, a draught was whipping under the table and freezing his feet. *The beginning of winter, then,* he thought. *This house is going to be pretty uncomfortable; but, by the looks on their faces, I shan't be spending it in Arva!*

When the meal was finished, the Professor said, 'We're going to the study now, Emilia. Pip and I have something to discuss.'

His wife nodded back in a dismissive gesture, as if she couldn't care less where either of them went. *Here it comes,* thought Pip, pushing back his chair and preparing to follow Dalca. He picked up his plate to take it away, but Emilia shook her head at him. He was evidently not welcome in the kitchen either, which at present seemed to be the only warm place in the house. *Winter is sure coming on,* thought Pip.

The Professor's study was exactly how Pip had imagined,

almost a copy of the one they had met in at the University when he had first arrived. However, no sun crept in there that evening. It was cold when Pip followed the Professor inside, and was situated below stairs in what he would have called the basement back home. But it had none of the comforts of the traditional American den. No furniture to relax in, nor anything indeed that Pip might recognise as comfortable. This large, bare room, inhabited primarily by books, seemed a witness to a life given to unrelenting scholarship. Pip couldn't imagine how Dalca found anything, as his eyes swivelled from untidy heaps to haphazard sheaves of papers. Only the books were neat and the files arranged above them, row upon row. *Probably his life's work*, thought Pip. Whatever Dalca was researching was now being worked upon with more than enthusiasm, given the state of the table, chairs and floor.

'Don't step on that!' barked Dalca. Pip withdrew his foot carefully, and the Professor lunged to retrieve several sheets of paper.. 'I know exactly where everything is.'

Pip realised that Dalca was not apologising for the clutter, but rather accusing Pip for thinking it was disordered.

The Professor began to shift a another pile of papers off a chair and place them on the central table.

'Bring it , please,' he said, indicating the chair. 'We shall be better off here.'

Pip carried the chair over.

'Sit down.'

Then Dalca continued to do exactly the same for himself, revealing a chair that had once been a fine specimen of some craftsman's carving, covered in worn red leather. A moment later, they were facing each other over what Pip realised now were piles of documents. Pip waited for the storm to break as the Professor surveyed him with piercing eyes.

'I'm disappointed in you,' he said.

'I'm disappointed in myself at present,' Pip sighed.

Dalca nodded his acknowledgement of the confession, but by the way the Professor was regarding him Pip knew he wouldn't be able to justify himself.

'Emilia tells me that you were up in the churchyard and you had to send for the priest to let you out. What was all that nonsense about getting locked in?'

So Ghita had been right and Fr Joseph had been intimidated by Emilia. Pip was beginning to dislike the priest as much as Dalca did.

'She also tells me that you phoned Ghita?' the Professor added.

'It's true,' replied Pip. 'I had no other option.'

'You could have rung me.' He gave Pip no time for an excuse. 'Exactly how did you get my daughter's number?'

'She gave it to me.'

'When?'

This was where Pip had to decide whether to lie and claim that it was when they were together at the bus stop, or to tell the truth that he had met Ghita at Burbor. She had probably told her father anyway.

'Well?'

'I met her at Burbor, but, at that time, I didn't know who she was.'

The Professor leaned back in his chair and then, all of a sudden, banged his fist down on the table.

Pip ignored the gesture and continued, 'It was only when you mentioned her name at dinner that I realised she must be your daughter. It was a bit late then.'

'Late is the word,' was the menacing reply. 'So what did you talk about with her after I left?' Pip's dilemma was far from solved.

'Just the normal things.'

'Such as?'

'Look, sir,' said Pip, retreating to formality, 'what is the point of this interrogation? I'm sure you're aware of what we talked about. I had no option but to tell Ghita that I was here under false pretences. She's too bright to be deceived.'

'So you think you know my daughter that well after such a short acquaintance?'

'I don't know her at all, except I'm sure – she's scared.'

Pip breathed in quickly. He could see that Dalca was getting angry.

'What do you mean?'

'Ghita was as scared as hell up there outside the churchyard.' The two regarded each other.

'You told the priest someone else was inside – and that he locked you in.' Dalca's voice was low and cold.

'I did, although Fr Joseph didn't appear to believe me.'

'Describe this man to me.' Pip noticed that Dalca was clasping his hands together, revealing white knuckles. His look was directed anywhere but at Pip.

'He was tall and blond. He wore a black suit and his eyes were the most piercing I think I have ever seen. Quite black.' Pip did not add *like a snake's*, but he was watching for Dalca's further reaction. The Professor's hands remained clasped as if he couldn't let go.

'And what was the man doing?'

'I'm not sure, but he seemed to be examining the tomb.'

'Which tomb?'

'Grandsire's.' Surely that might provoke a reaction.

'How did you know which one it was?' It seemed a facile question.

'I saw the broken cross. Marcu and Valentin gave a detailed description of it in the Papers.'

'What were *you* doing there?' Still Dalca showed no sign of emotion.

'When I saw the churchyard gates open, I wanted to see it for myself.'

'That wasn't very sensible,' said Dalca. Pip could see he was attempting to turn the conversation away from the stranger.

'Do you know who the man might have been, Professor?'

'A local?' Dalca shrugged.

'He didn't look like one,' Pip persisted. 'But he told me he had permission. He was patronising. According to him, I had no right to be there. Where would he have obtained such permission?'

'Maybe he was a man of the Church?'

'He was not a priest.'

'I mean someone from the Catholic Church. There has been much conflict about Church property and its maintenance. As I told you, tensions arise fairly often, and relations between the government and the Church are quite fragile. The Romanian faithful have long memories.' Dalca unclasped his hands. Reading his body language, Pip felt he was now confident in this explanation for the man's presence.

'Might he have something to do with the government?' asked Pip.

'I prefer to think the Church.'

'If so, Fr Joseph knew nothing about it.' Pip frowned.

'Maybe he was a grave robber, then?' The sarcasm was evident. Dalca began tapping his fingers on the desk; another sign he was beginning to be annoyed by Pip's persistent questions.

'Whoever he was,' replied Pip, 'Ghita was afraid when I mentioned him.'

'Ghita is young. Who knows what goes on in her head?' replied Dalca. 'Did this man say much?'

'No, but I had the impression he resented me being there, and not only because I was, in his words, trespassing. In fact, he was entirely unpleasant – almost to the point of threatening me.'

'I told you foreigners are unwelcome around here.' Pip could see that whatever Dalca thought, he was not going to enlighten him. 'If you see him again, let me know and I shall make some inquiries. But it is certainly strange that he had a key to unlock the gate. Maybe the priest is holding out on you and had given him permission?'

'Why would he lie?'

'Why wouldn't he?' Dalca half-smiled. 'He's a priest! Perhaps you should follow the course that you intended to this morning and arrange a meeting with him.'

'I already have.'

Dalca lifted his eyebrows at Pip's response.

'So – going back to Ghita – you went against my wishes?'

Pip nodded.

'I'm sorry.'

'Did you discuss this project with her?' His voice had a dangerous edge now.

'Not exactly. I did ask her why she was so afraid. You see, when I was at Burbor, I also met your mother-in-law, which made things worse.'

'Simona!' muttered Dalca.

'The old lady took me for Marcu! She behaved as if she recognised me! It must have been quite frightening for Ghita.'

Dalca put up his hand.

'And so you told her who you really were?'

'No, Ghita thought I was a doctor. At that point she had no idea who I was. She was as much in the dark as me,' Pip appealed. 'Until breakfast today.' He could hardly believe how much had happened in so short a space of time.

'So you're trying to tell me that you didn't reveal yourself on purpose?'

'Of course not,' replied Pip, 'I wouldn't do that. It was an unfortunate coincidence.' When he had said the word, he reminded himself he didn't believe in coincidences.

'So what shall we do now?' asked Dalca. Pip wasn't sure if the question was addressed to him, or if Dalca was referring to what action he was about to take.

'Forgive me, Simu … but …' Pip realised it was the time for sucking up – and also the first time he had called the Professor by his first name. He was a psychologist, and once again his training in handling awkward social situations had proved itself useful. '… but I believe we should enlist Ghita's help and maybe your wife's too.'

Dalca jumped up from the chair, leaving it spinning, and turned his back on Pip, one hand on his hip. Then he turned.

'Emilia?' The word was thick in his throat. He leaned forward. 'You know *nothing* about us here. What we are going through. What I am suffering.'

'I've only been here a couple of days, but I can feel the secrets in this house,' retorted Pip, staring back. 'I know it's not my business, but why don't you let them help – and get things out in the open?'

For a moment he thought Dalca was going to hit him, but instead the Professor sat down again and dropped his head into his hands. Pip felt slightly embarrassed that he had provoked the gesture and stared at the pile of documents in front of him, marked *Genealogy*.

'This is Arva,' said the Professor, looking up. 'Those who have tried to *get it out in the open*, as you put it, are either mad or dead. This is what I wish to spare my family. You are only a boy – a foreigner. You have not lived through it.'

The atmosphere, which had been so heated, now cooled rapidly. A frisson ran through Pip. He might have been in charge of the discussion until this point, but all at once Dalca's words, which seemed to have been wrested from deep within, cut through his manoeuvring, raising it to another level. He felt uncomfortable for thinking only about himself and not about the consequences of his actions on others. Like Marcu, he had a single-minded ambition to discover the secrets of Arva. He realised that any goal that became an obsession, whether satisfied or not, took little account of others' feelings.

Children had died because of a secret that could not be revealed. Girls like Catina Albu and Anka Petrescu, whose mother, Irina, was dead – although that death could not be laid at Marcu's door. Marcu himself had died, without reaching his goal and – as Robert's fate came into Pip's mind – innocent people were still dying. Maybe this was the time to say something that showed Pip appreciated how Dalca felt? Of course the Professor didn't want to expose his family to whatever dangers that might come to light.

'I'm sorry if I have upset you, Simu, but I know from personal experience that secrets are best out in the open. Once, *I* kept things to myself, and I shouldn't have. I nearly gave up.' Back when he had fought against the evil that had been Diep Koppelberg, he had been near to despair. 'Secrets bring terror, and the result of terror lasts for a very long time. It doesn't go away.' It felt puerile for him to be giving advice to a man of

Dalca's stature and experience; a man who, at that moment, was watching him closely.

'And still hasn't?' asked Dalca.

'I can't explain.' Pip shut down. He didn't want his personal confession turning to Dalca's advantage.

'Fair enough,' said the Professor. 'Well, Pip, you have heard me ranting, and you do not know quite how near you were to me turning you out onto the street. But you appear to be speaking from the heart. I like that in a young man. But listen to an old one. It is best we don't involve the women in my house – yet. When the time comes, we may have to. But we have work to do before then.'

Pip swallowed. He had pulled it off. He wasn't going to be kicked out. He had made the right decision when he had told the truth – although he nearly hadn't.

'I think we should make a fresh start,' said Dalca, holding out his hand. Pip shook it.

'I'd like that and – I'm sorry.'

'Apology accepted. Well, what did we come here for?' Dalca regarded his piles of papers. 'First of all, neither of us has any real idea what the other knows.'

'I'll fetch my laptop,' said Pip, 'then we can compare preliminary notes.'

The Professor nodded and Pip got up and walked to the door.

All that bullshit from Dalca about 'speaking from the heart' and 'liking that in a young man' hadn't really convinced Pip. He still intended to find out what Dalca knew before he gave the Professor access to the whole of the papers containing Marcu's notes and observations. He realised that the alliance he and Dalca had agreed upon had, at present, the essence of two dogs sniffing about each other. Fetching his notes had at least given him time to think. It might be some time before he could accept that he had the Professor's cooperation as well as his trust.

He knew that an obstacle for both of them would be taking into account the unknown quantity that Marcu had labelled 'the entity that was Grandsire'. For example, Pip's own experiences over the last few weeks had to be seen in that context. Was he ready to expose himself? To confess that he felt deep inside that he had been chosen to deliver what Marcu had failed to? That somehow his own past was tied into what had been happening in Arva for centuries? Just admitting it to himself seemed ridiculous. In his experience, an academic like Dalca, who dealt only in historical facts, would never excuse such a confession on the part of a fellow scholar. It would mark him as not only unscientific but also unfit for serious research.

Yet Pip felt some hope. He had picked up certain words and emotions expressed by Dalca during their short acquaintance that appeared to point to the fact the Professor himself had experienced intangibles that could not be rationalised. Only trust between them could remedy the situation. Pip had not begun well. He had already betrayed the Professor's confidence. Sometime soon, one of them had to make the first move. But would that be Pip? At present, he didn't know.

When Pip had left the room, Dalca leaned forward in his chair again and, elbows on the table, rubbed his forehead with his thumbs. He had to think what to do and to get it right. He had gained the young academic's confidence once more. He was immensely relieved that he did not have to throw him out. He realised that they were both adept at verbal sparring and that this would probably go on for some time. *That's if we survive*, he thought. He closed his eyes momentarily.

What would Pip have thought if he had known Dalca was entirely sure of the identity of the stranger in the churchyard! Would it have made Pip's blood run as cold as Dalca's own had when he had first discovered the stranger's identity? A unique origin that was destined to remain hidden and had been so within living memory. The fact remained: their enemy was near, and that in itself was enough for Dalca to know that both he and Pip were in peril. It must have suited *him* to leave the boy alone, which was surprising. In fact, Dalca didn't yet understand why. It would have been so easy for him to have removed Pip from the equation, as others had been removed. Dalca conjectured that it probably pleased him to toy with them both for a little longer, so that they could lead him nearer to the knowledge he was seeking. Soon, Dalca was going to have to tell the American the truth about their enemy, which would be even more dangerous. Yet there seemed no other option. He needed Pip, and *vice versa*.

He could hear the lad coming back down the stairs. The time for playing games was over. Now the hunt for Grandsire was beginning in earnest.

He went out into the hall just as Pip reached it. 'Excuse me a moment,' he said, and went into the kitchen. Pip waited.

'Emilia,' he heard the Professor say, 'Dr Durrant and I have a great deal to discuss. We do not want to be disturbed by anyone. If we need coffee, I shall ask for it.'

'Very well,' was the dull reply.

Pip could imagine how his wife must be feeling. Entirely shut out. He knew what that was like. A rush of sympathy filled him. Although she had shown nothing but suspicion of him, he felt he knew something of her suffering.

The Professor emerged and Pip followed him to the study door.

'Now, let's get on with it,' said Dalca, holding the door open.

Pip went through into the sanctum. He was ready to do battle with whatever demons faced him.

9

'To recap,' said Dalca as they settled down, 'we are both in possession of certain facts. Mine come from historical research, yours from the Marcu Papers. Are we agreed?' Pip nodded. 'Good. May I begin with a question?'

'Feel free,' said Pip. He would rather have asked one first, but he was so eager to know Dalca's information that he was willing to wait.

'What do you want most, besides getting the Marcu Papers published?' Dalca leaned over the table, his whole attention focused on Pip.

'That's easy,' he replied. 'I want to find out who Grandsire is and if he committed the crimes that I have set down in here.' He tapped his laptop. 'The rapes and subsequent deaths of Catina Albu in July 1952 and Anka Petrescu in July 1988.' As he repeated the familiar dates, his mind suddenly zoomed in on the latter. All the horrors that had happened to him and his family had occurred in that same month in the summer of '88. Another coincidence? Rather that the fact had been wiped from his mind.

'Something the matter?' asked Dalca. He could see his colleague had thought of something he had never considered before.

'No,' lied Pip.

The memory could hardly have any significance – except that he couldn't erase the staring eyes of Walter

Arvarescu out of his mind, or forget the criminal's extraordinary likeness to Diep Koppelberg. Then suddenly his mind was reeling from another significant realisation; Arvarescu had escaped from the New York prison in the summer of 1952. Two dates that tied in with the Arvan crimes. What could it mean?

'Shall we continue?' said Dalca, who would have given anything at that moment to know what Pip was thinking. 'So discovering Grandsire's identity is of prime importance. Then you and I are of the same mind.' He smiled. 'I think we can also say that the police would be interested in finding that out too. Secondly?'

'I want to know how and why Grandsire is linked to the Arva ritual.'

'Grandsire the man or …' Dalca paused. Pip saw him hesitate – and rejoiced. Was the Professor about to admit that Grandsire was more than human?

'Or?' queried Pip. 'What else could he be?'

'I am referring to his fundamental nature.'

Pip felt he could at least come clean on this one. 'Marcu called Grandsire an *entity*. Do you think that description fits, Professor?'

Dalca's eyes never strayed from Pip's face as he answered.

'I admit I believe there is more to Grandsire than a maniac who rapes and murders children.'

'So do I,' replied Pip. 'But how can that be, when the murders span so many years?'

'Slowly, Pip.' Dalca put up his hand. 'Before we discuss that point, I would like to hear what else you consider of importance.'

'The "secret of the marriage bed" is paramount.'

'Again your ambitions are the same as mine. So we must help each other.' Dalca straightened and lifted his arms behind his head – a gesture Pip did not recognise but was well-known to his students. Dalca had relaxed and was deciding his next move.

'I believe *you* know a lot more than I do about Grandsire's nature and the women's secret,' Pip said. He felt it best to be blunt. 'You said so at our first meeting, when I first mentioned Simona. At that time, I had no idea she was your mother-in-law.'

'Then your belief in my knowledge is misplaced,' retorted the Professor. 'But I may be able to help with the question of identity.' Pip narrowed his eyes. Did Dalca really know who Grandsire was? 'And I have studied the possibilities that present themselves about his nature.' He stared straight at Pip. 'But as for the "secret of the marriage bed" ...' He shook his head. 'It is inaccessible.'

'But your wife knows the secret?' Pip found it hard to believe Emilia had not let anything slip. But as Marcu had said, Irina Petrescu was the only Arvan female that had ever disclosed even a minimum.

'Emilia will never tell me, nor any man,' retorted Dalca.

'What about Ghita?'

'Ghita knows nothing, nor will she until she is married – an event that is fast approaching. And I don't want her to marry, any more than I wanted her to take part in the ritual.' Dalca's lips set in a line.

'Why didn't you prevent her "going-up"?' asked Pip. 'You knew the dangers! And you can still stop the marriage!'

'She would have been ostracised. I could not allow that to happen. As for the marriage – she is 19. I have no control over her in that respect.'

'What if something terrible had happened to her when she "went up"?' Pip was incredulous. How could the Professor have allowed it?

'Emilia told me it would not. She assured me it *could* not.'

Pip realised he must be talking about the conditions of the ritual: that Grandsire was interested only in pre-pubescent girls.

'And you believed her?'

'I did.'

'You were taking one hell of a risk,' said Pip, wondering what he would have done in the circumstances. 'Look how Anka Petrescu deceived her mother.'

'We are not the Petrescus!' Dalca flashed. 'Emilia would not have let anything happen to our daughter, any more than she will now. My wife was secure in her knowledge – a knowledge to which I as a mere male – and an Arvan – have no access.' Pip could hear the bitterness in the tone. He was beginning to realise how much everyone in the village, professional or peasant, was a victim of this perverse tradition. 'But we go on too far. Let us concentrate on one thing at a time. First, the Grandsire and his origins.'

At that moment, the lights flickered. Both Pip and Dalca looked up at the central pendant as the light died and the blackness of night enfolded them. Pip heard Dalca swear.

'Power cuts,' said the Professor. 'The first sign of winter. It will be worse when it snows.' His grim voice thrust through the dark. 'Hold on one moment. I have candles in the desk drawer.'

Pip waited. He didn't feel at all comforted by the thought of a power cut at this juncture of the conversation. He listened to the Professor scrabbling about. How the hell would he find a candle in all this mess?

Then, just as Pip's eyes were adjusting to the dark, he noticed a dim light creeping under the door. He got up from his chair and watched. There was a fumbling outside, resulting a moment later in the door opening. Emilia! She was carrying a branch of flickering candles in her hand. She came over and set it on the desk.

'Emilia, thank you,' said Dalca, looking up from his foraging. 'Now the electricity is off, I suppose coffee is out of the question, dear ...?' Pip noted he had never spoken to her so civilly before in his presence.

'I have made some already.'

Then she turned round and walked out of the door, revealing another branch of candles, which she lifted up from the floor. Pip went over to his chair and sat down again. He felt rather foolish and particularly glad of the candlelight. He would have hated Dalca to know that the dark had spooked him. It was not his particular friend, for many reasons, and still revived the old fears.

While Dalca was settling his papers, Pip considered the look he had seen on Emilia's face. She certainly didn't approve of them being holed up in the study all evening. *She's probably been listening at the door*, he thought.

'Right,' said Dalca. 'When the first snows fall, this will be happening all the time.' He steepled his fingers as the candles threw strange shadows over the ceiling and walls of the cavernous study, transforming their bodies into huge, crouching shapes.

'Returning to your question,' said Pip, 'I know very little about Grandsire's origins, but I have been doing some calculations.'

'To add to Marcu's?' Dalca could hardly contain himself.

'Yes, to a certain extent. But I would rather you told me your ideas first.' They both hesitated, more rivals than allies, and Pip felt it necessary to add, 'I promise that if you allow me access to your information then I shall be free and open with mine. You have my word. If we are to get anywhere, we have to work together.'

Dalca nodded.

'Very well, I have built my theory upon research but, before we start, I warn you, that there may be times when you will consider suspending your belief in me as a professional historian.' Pip frowned. 'And I must enlist another promise from you, that should anything happen to me, then you will continue with this project. It is vital that my family is preserved. Also, I must have your assurance that nothing I say tonight will go further than this room.'

Pip knew that Dalca was speaking about Ghita rather than his wife.

'I promise,' he said, and he meant it, although uneasiness made him shift a little in his chair – and instinct warned him to get up and run from this duplication of the situation when Marcu had handed over the safe-keeping of his papers to Robert Riparu *just in case* something happened to him. 'But what could happen to you?'

Dalca stroked his chin.

'It is always a researcher's fear that his work will die with him.'

Pip understood the expression very well.

Dalca continued, 'You speak of calculations. If any of yours have affinities with mine, I beg you to elucidate as we proceed. Wouldn't that be best?'

'In other words, we must trust each other?'

'Yes.' Dalca nodded.

'Then I agree.'

'Very well,' said the Professor. 'Grandsire as an entity rather than a murderer – or both.' A sharp rush of wind blew one of the candles out. Dalca took no notice. 'As a medieval historian, I have been looking back at the origins of this village. We shall talk of the ritual at a further meeting.'

Pip nodded. His hands were sweating.

'So what are the roots of the Arva settlement?'

The Professor paused. 'The ancient past of this area points to the fact that our ancestors, the Dacians, who made their home here, were descended from the Romans, who ruled over them for some 175 years from AD 101 to AD 275. This justification of our Daco-Roman roots came from the Catholic Church in the 17th Century.

'The Continuity Theory,' said Pip. 'I had not heard that the Church was part of this national awakening.' The debate over whether the Romanians were Daco-Roman or Magyar in origin had been waged since at least the 10th Century, and had been the root of fierce nationalism.

'Thank you,' said Dalca. 'I am surprised you do not know about the Church's involvement, but the explanation for it will come later. I am not a Roman historian. My interest takes account of the medieval settlement of this area and the birth of this village, which I have traced back to the 14th

Century–'

He broke off at a soft knock on the door. He got up and opened it. Emilia was standing there with two mugs.

'How long will all this take?' she asked. 'Ghita is not in yet.'

'I expect she is with Anton.' He took the mugs. 'We shall be at least another hour. You can go to bed, if you like.'

'Not until she's in,' said Emilia, closing the door.

'She worries,' said Dalca, handing a mug to Pip. The coffee was lukewarm, but still welcome, and the candles were burning down. 'Where was I?'

'The 14th Century.'

'Sometime in the 14th Century, and I cannot be precise, Arva was founded.'

'By whom?'

'That is not set down, except I have read that one source reveals that the founder was of Germanic origin. As you may or may not know, at that time, migration was taking place from Germany to Eastern Europe in the quest for land and opportunity.'

'Had this man a name?' asked Pip. He felt as if he couldn't breathe.

'He may have been called Nicholas.'

At that moment, light suddenly flooded the room as the electricity came back on, making them both jump.

Dalca quickly regained his composure. 'Do you wish to add anything at this point?' he asked, his keen eyes probing Pip's face.

'It's a common enough name,' replied Pip. He stared at his laptop. How could he ever forget it?

'Far from common, by the look of it,' said Dalca. 'You asked me to trust you. I think you should reciprocate.'

'I don't think …' began Pip.

'What does the name mean to you?' persisted the Professor.

Pip swallowed. Dalca was right. To him, the name was extraordinary. He could hardly bear to think about that day in

July 1988 when he had entered Koppelberg's chalet by the lake and had a vision of the boy *Nicholas*, the little Crusader with the red blood cross on his tunic. Then there was the emergence of *Nicholas* in *The Rat and the Piper* dialogues between Arvarescu and his psychiatrist. And finally *Nicholas* Eisenmann …

Dalca extinguished the candles, and Pip came back to the present.

'All right,' Pip said. 'I experienced something strange a week or so ago.' He told the Professor what had happened, trying to make the incident sound as matter-of-fact as possible. 'The whole thing was inexplicable,' he concluded. 'How could the name Nicholas appear on my laptop? Occasionally I wonder if it happened at all.' He felt he couldn't add about the photo appearing too. Dalca would never have swallowed that!

'I am sure it did,' was Dalca's amazing reply. 'From what you have told me, Pip, I can see you are as bound to this thing as I am, but in different ways. You are a seeker, as I was once. Now I am only the vessel.'

'What do you mean?'

'I knew from the first that it was not coincidence that brought you to work on the Marcu Papers, which I had thought lost forever.'

'How?' asked a startled Pip.

'I am sure now that you have the feeling you were chosen to take on the task.'

'In a way, but I have no idea why.' It was no time to lie.

'I think you might find the answer if you look inside yourself, Pip,' said Dalca. 'Examine your own history. From our first meeting, I realised you were different. No student I know has ever described himself as having *an obsession with Transylvania*. A love for history perhaps. Or in your case, a love for psychology.' His gaze was unwavering. 'To me you seemed *possessed*.'

'This is ridiculous,' said Pip. 'Why are we having this conversation?'

'Because it is true. You were sent to us.'

'For God's sake, Professor!'

'Not for His sake. I have no love for Him. But I love my family – and Arva.' He coughed. 'Sorry, it's the dust in here.' Pip knew it was really emotion, the kind he was feeling as he tried to face what Dalca had said. He tried to be his logical self, but inside his head was a mixture of fear, confusion and memories – and especially the terrifying vision of the boy Nicholas that Koppelberg had shown him in the summer of 1988.

'Shall we break now?' asked Dalca.

'Not now. I need to know more,' insisted Pip. 'You think this Nicholas is Grandsire? That some kind of ghost has been murdering children?'

Dalca moistened his dry lips. 'What happens in the Arvan ritual is beyond our mortal reason,' he said. 'The girls were attacked, for sure. I have not read the reports of their rape. I have no access to police records. But I have heard about their strange deaths. Do you know about that?'

'Only what I have read in the Marcu Papers about Anka Petrescu. The police chief said she looked like an old woman when she died. But I didn't believe it.'

'This is what I have heard too,' said Dalca. 'But one hears many things in Arva – usually in the ravings of crazed old women.'

'You mean Simona?'

Dalca nodded.

'With your permission,' ventured Pip, 'I would like to talk to her again.'

'She will only talk to you if she wants to,' he replied. 'However, I shall not forbid you to see her. But Ghita must not be present.'

'I wouldn't want her there,' said Pip.

'You and my daughter seem to have hit it off,' said Dalca.

'Sadly that is not true,' replied Pip. 'In fact, quite the opposite. I think Ghita dislikes me almost as much as your wife does.'

Dalca inclined his head.

'I also intend to interview Inspector Valentin, the police inspector who was in charge of the Petrescu case. If he agrees to see me, maybe he will retract on the account he gave to Marcu about seeing the child before she died?'

'Perhaps,' replied Dalca. 'And now – may we return to your calculations?'

'They began when I examined Marcu's maths,' said Pip. He realised the two of them were on a different footing now. Although they desired different things – he the completion of Marcu's work, Dalca the welfare of his family – they were now discussing both academic research and the possible existence of the paranormal. It seemed the only way they might discover what really happened in the churchyard was to share the evidence. He breathed in:

'Marcu began looking at the birth dates he had been given by Irina Petrescu, and at the occurrence of the crimes. According to him, there was also an incident in 1916, but I know nothing about it – yet. I am hoping that the policeman may be able to help there. 1916, 1952 and 1988. So it seems that something happens here in a 36-year cycle. Why 36 years? What does that signify? I know that Marcu in his discussion with Robert Riparu queried if it could have some kind of astrological significance, but he drew a blank.'

'He was a scientist,' said Dalca. 'I know something about the significance of the number 36. I think I can help there.' At that moment, they heard raised voices outside, and Dalca looked at his watch. 'But not tonight, I think,' he said. 'Ghita is proving to be exceptionally troublesome at present.'

'Maybe it's because she doesn't want to marry Anton?' Pip's indiscreet remark, born of disappointment at their meeting breaking off so abruptly, did not bring the angry response he expected.

'You should tell her mother that,' replied Dalca with a wry smile. 'Enough for tonight. 'We will continue this conversation another evening. If we are spared.'

Pip stared at him, hoping he was joking.

Dalca must have noticed the startled look. 'Don't worry. It is a saying that Roman Catholics often use. You see, something of Emilia has rubbed off on me. Patience, Pip. We have many years of secrets to take into account and, so far, we have had less than three weeks.'

Pip thought it was best to take to his room while the arguments went on in the kitchen. In any case, he had plenty to think about besides Ghita's relationship with her parents. He had been extremely disappointed that his discussion with the Professor had ended so abruptly; but, as Dalca had said, this had been going on for many years. How many exactly? He needed to start work on the dates as soon as possible.

Irina Petrescu had been born on 22 July. According to Marcu, that was significant. If Fr Joseph was willing to help – which admittedly seemed unlikely, given his attitude – Pip would be able to examine some of the parish records. If the ones he needed were held elsewhere, he would have to instigate a search for them on the internet or otherwise. He would try to find out about the Albus and the Petrescus. As for 1916, he hadn't much to go on, but he was going to try. He would leave it to Dalca to tell him the significance of the number 36. Fr Joseph was the next person he had to see, followed by Chief Inspector Valentin. Valentin must have retired by now, but Pip was fairly sure the Police Department would be able to point him in the right direction.

When Pip lay down, thoughts were buzzing around in his head so much that at first he couldn't sleep. Besides, he was afraid that he would have another hallucination. But he could no longer hear the raised voices from the kitchen – the house was silent except for the wind buffeting the walls outside – and at around two in the morning he did eventually fall into a sleep, which was not punctuated by any visitation and was terminated only by a knocking on his door.

'Do you know what time it is?' He recognised Ghita's voice. 'Father wants to know if you are coming with us to the University.'

Pip jumped out of bed and, throwing on his dressing

gown, ran over and opened the door.

'Sorry, I overslept,' he said.

'You were lucky you got any sleep,' she replied, 'after the row that went on.' She looked pale, and her expression was almost as wan as her complexion.

'I know it's none of my business,' said Pip, 'but why do you keep on upsetting them?'

'As you said, it isn't your business,' she snapped. 'Are you coming or not?'

'No, thank you, I'm going to see Fr Joseph.'

'Oh, yes, I forgot.' She raised her eyebrows. 'Good luck to you. But be careful. Mother will grill the poor man afterwards.'

'As I found out last night. By the way, thanks for not running to your dad.'

'It wasn't because of you,' she replied.

'Thanks anyway. I wish we could talk, Ghita,' he tried.

'I've nothing to say at present.'

At that moment, a voice called from the bottom of the stairs.

'Ghita! What are you doing?' It was Emilia.

Ghita made a face.

'I have to go. I'll tell Dad you're working from home.' She half-smiled.

'Thank you. See you tonight.'

'I doubt it,' she replied, closing the door.

Pip went over and sat down on the bed. Ghita's behaviour was puzzling. She had seemed so friendly when he had first met her at Burbor. Of course he had upset her, but there were still hints that she wanted to open up to him, whatever her attitude. For instance, her comment about having nothing to say *at present*, followed by a half-smile that seemed to tell him she was only pretending to dislike him. All these signs counted in his suspicions that she was either playing a part or was too scared to talk. But what was frightening her? Her mother, who wouldn't give her a minute's peace? Or what she believed Pip was going to find out?

He shook his head and sighed, realising that getting Ghita to confide in him had become as important an aim as speaking to the other people on his list. He had to admit it was not only because he wanted to learn more about Arva, but also because he sought her good opinion – which was certainly a first for him, as he hadn't needed anyone for a very long time.

'So you are seeing Fr Joseph this morning,' said Emilia.

She even knew that! She was also clock watching. 'You should go soon. You shouldn't keep him waiting. Mass will be nearly finished.'

He could see how Ghita felt – as if she was under the Inquisition.

'Going now,' he said, grabbing his briefcase.

'Dinner's at seven. Don't be late,' she called after him, and he knew it was a reproof for him having slept in. *How the hell am I going to be able to put up with this until next year?*, he asked himself as he closed the door behind him; but, inside, he knew he was going to have to, because in that dark house lurked a secret that he intended to uncover, even if his life depended upon it.

10

Pip hung about outside the village hall. The stranger in the churchyard had been right about the makeshift church. It was an ugly-looking building with a corrugated roof, which looked as if it would not withstand even a summer storm. Waiting for Mass to end gave him time to contact the Police Department regarding Inspector Valentin. Their response was as he had expected: they asked him for his credentials and promised to ring back. Naturally, they would want to check up on him at the University.

Finally, the service was over. The congregation had been sparse, and made up mainly of headscarved old women in black and several ancient-looking men. When Pip entered the hall, a young boy was taking off the altar cloth, underneath which was an ordinary trestle table. Pip went over to him while he was carefully folding the white linen.

'I've come to see Fr Joseph,' he said.

'He's gone home.'

So much for his promise, thought Pip. 'Where can I find him?' he asked.

The boy gave him directions that led him through the back of the hall and down a path towards a decent-looking one-storey brick house, which seemed much newer than any simple dwelling he had seen in Arva. *So they look after their priest well,* he muttered as he knocked on the door. It was a little time before it opened to reveal Fr Joseph, who was not wearing his cassock, but a pair of black trousers and an open-necked shirt. His expression revealed little but weariness, and he had the appearance of a workman rather than a member of the clergy.

'Come in, please,' he said. 'I have been expecting you.'

Pip walked behind him into a room that evidently doubled as living quarters and study. Two walls were fitted up with large wooden bookcases straining to hold a variety of books, none of which appeared to be new. The coffee table, which stood between two chairs, was bare except for a breviary and a small statue of the Virgin Mary. A large crucifix hung on one wall with a bunch of what appeared to be herbs adorning the feet of the crucified Christ. The atmosphere of the room was stuffy with the faint smell of incense mixed with cooking cabbage. Pip's first impression that the man lived in luxury had been inaccurate. He was evidently frugal in his tastes.

'Please sit down, Dr Durrant.' The priest indicated the well-worn chair. That morning Fr Joseph seemed very far removed from the indignant cleric who had reprimanded Pip in the churchyard. In fact, he seemed quite approachable. 'How can I help you?' He sighed, but Pip sensed it was not from boredom, but rather anxiety as to where their future dialogue was about to lead. Yet, however reasonable Fr Joseph promised to be, Pip did not want their conversation reported to Emilia Dalca.

'Thank you for seeing me, Father,' he said, 'but I want to make it clear that our conversation must remain between us alone. Can I rely on your integrity?'

'What you say to me in this room will remain here and only here. Did you suspect that it would be otherwise?'

Could he count on the man? Pip wondered. If their discussion had been in the confessional he could have, but he had only his instincts to lead him to trust this melancholy cleric.

'I don't want this getting back to the Dalcas,' he said, holding the priest's gaze. 'I know we didn't hit it off yesterday, but I felt you were against me. Even that you didn't believe me about the man who locked me in.'

'I had no option at that time,' Fr Joseph replied. 'I was not doubting your word, rather sparing my young companion further anguish.' It was a surprising reply.

'Ghita?'

'I know my parishioners and their troubles well. But I do not know *you*, Dr Durrant. Or, indeed, if you can be trusted.'

Pip was about to defend himself, then changed his mind as the priest continued.

'Yet if Professor Dalca has taken you into his home, then I must conjecture you are trustworthy.'

'In what way?'

'Taking a stranger into one's home can often cause friction, but when it is for the right reasons, then it is a charitable act.'

'Have you any idea of the reasons why I am here?' asked Pip.

'Scholarship? To further one's knowledge is creditable. I set great store by it.' He indicated his books. 'But as a mere parish priest, I do not have the opportunity these days to pursue my own historical studies.'

'Are you an historian?' Pip had not expected the conversation to take such a turn.

'Certainly not of Professor Dalca's calibre, but I studied Church history at the seminary.'

Pip wondered how this scholarly priest had ended up in Arva and what he must know and feel about the obscene ritual that involved his parishioners. He was either a hypocrite, or he had his orders from his superiors.

Then Fr Joseph added, 'When I finished my degree I was sent here. Does your enquiry relate to the Church itself?'

There was much Pip could have said at this juncture, but he chose his words carefully.

'Not really. As I indicated when we met before, I have an interest in the local records of this parish. How far do yours go back?'

'And as I told you, the church records are not held here. In fact, you may find it difficult to obtain any details. I'm afraid that Romania is far behind in getting its genealogical information onto microfilm. Requests to do so are usually ignored.'

That's helpful, thought Pip. He added, 'If you remember, I said that initially I would like to look at more recent records. In fact, I am specifically looking for those of 1916.'

'The First World War,' said the priest, looking startled. 'What is your interest in that particular year?' His face had become extremely pale. The mention of 1916 had certainly provoked a response.

'I want to know about registered births and deaths in the village that year.'

'Who *are* you, Dr Durrant?' The question was not unexpected. 'What is your real reason for being here in Arva?'

'I can tell by your expression that you have some suspicions already,' replied Pip. 'I am in the process of researching a project that another began, but never finished.'

'*Marcu!* God rest his soul!' The priest crossed himself.

'Yes. I have the Marcu Papers in my possession. They were sent to the United States after his death for safe-keeping at my university. My Professor offered them to me as a post-doctoral project that might lead to possible publication in the future. After a year's research, I have discovered within them an historical cycle.' Fr Joseph's eyes flicked away. 'This is an avenue I intend to pursue to its conclusion. Suffice to say, I am investigating what has been happening in Arva over an extended period of time.' Pip paused. 'You understand my stay here would be compromised if this was common knowledge. Need I remind you of your earlier promise?'

The priest shook his head and stared across at the crucifix, as if trying to gain courage from it. A few moments later, he said,

'In what way do you think I can help you?'

'You have been parish priest here for a number of years.

In fact, you were here in 1988, weren't you?'

'I know what you are going to ask me, Dr Durrant, but I can't help you.'

'1916 was an identical year in the cycle, wasn't it? As was 1952. The rebirth of Grandsire? And wasn't your predecessor, Fr Pathan, the parish priest in both those years? I have heard it said that the parish priest rings the bell at dawn on 22 July. Did you do that in 1988, Father? Do you still keep up the old custom?' Pip pressed on like the Grand Inquisitor.

The priest put up his hand.

'I beg you to stop. We should not speak of such things. You should not have come here. You must go. For your own safety.'

'I am not afraid,' declared Pip. 'Are you?' He was thinking that this man must have heard a thousand confessions. What was going on in his head? He pressed on. 'I have so many unanswered questions. Why is the church on the hill locked and barred from the faithful? Why is it open only on 22 July each year? Why does the Church allow the ritual, Father?' Fr Joseph did not answer. 'Shall I go back to my first question? What happened here in 1988? You of all people must know. And what is the Church's involvement?'

'Did Professor Dalca send you?' The priest's tone had changed. He seemed ready to fight back. 'I think you should ask him about his part in all this. *There are those close to him who know the answers.*'

Pip assumed this must be a reference to Emilia, as the one closest to Dalca.

Fr Joseph went on, 'The man has no belief in God. It is only my reliance on my Maker that has protected me so far. You must understand that my reticence is the only way I can continue as parish priest here!'

'You mean your silence, your obstruction of the truth. No, the Professor did not send me. I am here on my own behalf – and Marcu's. I know this much already. That the girl Catina Albu died in mysterious circumstances in 1952; and that 36 years later Anka Petrescu also met a terrible end. I promise you I shall find out about 1916 and who the victim was then.'

'You will not,' said Fr Joseph. His tone had changed. 'There *was* no victim in 1916.'

'How do you know?'

'I cannot reveal my sources.'

'From a confession?'

'What is revealed in confession must forever remain a secret. It is the Church's function to hear and to absolve whatever sins have been committed,' he replied. 'The Church cannot prevent evil. Its role is to teach and guide.'

'But it is not the function of the Church to protect the guilty,' retorted Pip.

'The perpetrator of these terrible crimes does not need the protection of the Church, Dr Durrant.'

'You speak as if the crimes were all committed by the same person,' said Pip.

The corners of Fr Joseph's lips twitched. To Pip's practised eyes, it was not the beginning of a smile, but rather a sign of nerves. Afterwards he pressed his lips together, as if he had finished everything he had to say. Pip was determined that would not be the end of their conversation.

'I *shall* find out about the Grandsire.' Pip's tone was unrelenting.

'Unless he finds you first!' was the retort. 'May I offer you some advice? When you advance, you cannot find your enemy, but when you retreat, he will find you. You look puzzled. Shall I make it clearer? When you look for him, you cannot find him, when you rest, he will be upon you. Be careful!' The remark was spoken with such passion that Pip was startled.

Fr Joseph continued,

'Yes, evil still walks this earth, Dr Durrant. It takes many forms and appears in many places. It has little respect for geographical boundaries.' The priest's voice had taken on a high note, almost like an incantation. 'Evil is very real. It is all around us, and it can be found especially in man's lower nature. Every human being has a dark side. Protect yourself and go home. Grandsire is nearer than you think. He is everywhere, Dr Durrant.'

It crossed Pip's mind then that the man might be deranged.

'Are you talking about Satan?' he asked.

Fr Joseph looked at him in the strangest way, almost as if he pitied him.

'Lucifer has been destined to incarnate in human form at certain key times in history. You should know that, Dr Durrant. He sees himself as a saviour, come to redeem humanity. The innocent, who follow, are his prey. But he is a false light.' The atmosphere in the room had become uncanny.

'You are talking about the Anti-Christ? Are you trying to tell me that Grandsire is Lucifer? That he has chosen Arva as the place to reincarnate every 36 years?'

The incredible thought was not one Pip wished to entertain. He asked himself what Marcu would have done if he had heard the priest speaking like this. Probably had him committed to Burbor! But this was no time for levity, even if it remained unspoken. Pip breathed in to calm himself.

A moment after this outburst, the priest turned to the crucifix, made the Sign of the Cross and began to pray out loud. Pip stood there awkwardly. His impulse was to walk out, but he had not finished the inquisition yet. When Fr Joseph turned back towards him, his face was bloodless, as if any life he possessed had deserted him.

'I have said too much. And I shall pay for it. Now I have gone this far, I might as well help you on your way a little further. Be aware, Dr Durrant. Professor Dalca holds the key to your quest. One of my sources was Claudiu Basa, the lame farmer who lived by the church. I heard his last confession, which I can never divulge, but one thing I may tell you is that he died on the day his mother was born. The answer to that riddle you must discover for yourself. Now, I wish to return to my prayers.' At that, he knelt down.

'Thank you,' was all Pip trusted himself to say. He knew

he had overstepped the mark in his questioning of Fr Joseph. In fact, he felt enormously guilty. A moment later, he stood outside the front door, gulping in the fresh cold air. He looked up and could see snow had fallen on the hills. As Dalca had said, winter was on the way. Meanwhile, his head was sifting the conversation he had just had. One part of his brain told him he ought to be afraid as well, the other that the priest was talking nonsense. The warning Fr Joseph had given him about Dalca especially spooked him. What did the Professor know that he wasn't letting on? He had agreed they should trust each other. As for the riddle – *Basa died the day his mother was born* – he would have to think about that carefully.

He felt particularly uncomfortable when he remembered Fr Joseph stating that he would pay for having said too much. How? What was going to happen to him? Did he think Grandsire aka Lucifer was about to appear and drag him down to Hell? However incredible the thought seemed, it made Pip shiver, because he had seen the look on Fr Joseph's face. At the same time, Robert flashed into his mind. He had been about to say too much as well?

What have you got in store for me *then, Grandsire*, Pip thought. If he had really meant it, he might have been terrified too. But, as a scientist, he could not believe in this talk of the Devil. No, Grandsire must be flesh and blood. He knew his visions weren't real, and that demons don't send messages on computers.

According to Robert, Eisenmann was the culprit. 'Maybe I should go see him soon?' he muttered, setting off to make his way back down the path, through the hall and onto the road. But the hall was now locked. He walked round it, searching for an exit, and was rewarded by the sight of a narrow path leading back to the road on the other side. The small gate was swinging open. He walked past the line of curtained hall windows back onto the road – and caught his breath.

The bronze Mercedes was parked opposite with the girl driver seated inside. He began to walk away, eyes downcast but glancing at the wheel hubs. This time he couldn't see any logo, no yellow circle with a winking eye. He must have imagined it! Then the girl was getting out, beckoning to him. He stopped.

'Dr. Durrant!' she called. She was wearing the same neat brown suit as before. When he had squinted at her in the dusk he had thought she was quite pretty. In the daylight and near to, he could see that her chin was a little too pointed, her eyes small and inquisitively bright. He thought she looked like a little animal with her brown hair sleeked back behind her ears. He liked animals, but he didn't like her! She was holding something in her hand.

'How do you know my name?' he asked, glancing uneasily at the car. Was the man who had spoken to him before inside and listening?

'Everyone in Arva knows who you are,' she replied, smiling. He frowned as she offered what she was carrying. It was a business card, gold on one side, red on the other. Pip stared at it, hardly believing what he read. *Nicholas Eisenmann*!

'My boss would like to meet you, Dr Durrant. He thinks that you and he might have something to discuss that would be of mutual value.' She smiled. Her teeth did not look perfectly white and even. 'I am Sigi, his secretary. If you would like to ring our office number, I will be delighted to make you an appointment.'

'I'm not sure ...' replied Pip, still turning over the card.

'Very well,' she said. 'But a word of warning, doctor. It is rare that Herr Eisenmann asks for a meeting. In most cases, people are very keen to meet *him*.'

'I'll think about it.' Pip saw her brows wrinkle, making her eyes look too close together. 'But thank him for asking.'

'I shall,' she said, and turned. A moment later she was scurrying back to the car. Pip watched as she drove off at some speed.

Well, she didn't like that, he thought. *Who does Eisenmann think he is to summon me to a meeting? How does he know I am here? What does he want?* In the light of the knowledge Pip had gained in the last few days, it was going to be some time before he got round to meeting the man. He wanted to learn as much as he could before he exposed himself to the kind of danger that Marcu had apparently faced. But Pip didn't like the idea that everyone in Arva knew why he was in the village. Who had told them? Certainly not Emilia, because she was supposed not to know. Ghita? Had she told her mother? Or her friends? Or her fiancé? He hated that word. What about Dalca? He didn't want to think that the Professor would betray him. If none of those, then who?

Maybe Sigi, as she called herself, was lying? And how did she and her boss know about him anyway? He frowned as he groped for the memory of what she had said the first time they'd met. *We come from round here.* Didn't Eisenmann live in Cologne, where Marcu had met him? The thought was most unsettling. He looked at the card again. The man must be really important. His office was in the Palais de l'Europe in Strasbourg. That confirmed what he had found out from consulting Wikipedia. Pip didn't like to think about the photo that had appeared in the blank box beside Eisenmann's name – the image of Arvarescu and, worse, the face of Koppelberg. Pip considered what course of action he would take if, when he met him, Eisenmann turned out to be Koppelberg. If the picture he had seen turned out to be real.

What *was* going on?

Robert, the one man who had seemingly had the answer, was probably dead by now – something Pip didn't like to think about. Only one other person might know the truth. Dalca. Perhaps he knew Eisenmann? Sigi and her boss had directed Pip to his house.

'As soon as Dalca gets home tonight,' said Pip under his breath. 'I'm going to ask him. And it won't be the only thing I want to know.'

But as he walked along the road back to the Dalca house, another thought came to him. Maybe what Sigi had said meant something else? Perhaps this was Eisenmann's home ground? If so, he would know what went on in the village. But Marcu mustn't have had any idea of the man's roots when he went to see Eisenmann. The notes he had taken that day had never been recovered – if he had made any, that is. Only Robert might have known that – and he couldn't be asked. Pip breathed in. *Things are getting pretty serious*, he said to himself. *Look out for yourself!* Then, for no apparent reason, the joke Professor Wright had made before Pip left for Romania jumped straight into his mind: *Watch out for vampires!*

'So you saw the priest,' said Dalca. 'What kind of a welcome did you receive?'

'Fr Joseph was very helpful,' replied Pip, not surprised to catch a sudden hint of alarm in the Professor's eyes.

'That's a first for him, then.' Dalca stroked his wild beard into place. He looked extremely unkempt that evening, even more so than Pip, whose own growth had gone well beyond designer stubble. Looking at Dalca convinced Pip he needed to shave soon. Usually he didn't care much about his personal appearance, but seeing the state the Professor was in, which evidently reflected his state of mind, had reminded him. Dalca seemed agitated now. 'So what did he tell you?'

'He thought you'd sent me. I soon put him right on that.' Pip then related what the priest had said about studying Church history, adding the fact that records of births, marriages and deaths were held elsewhere. 'That's about it, although he spoke highly of your scholarship. In fact,' Pip paused, 'he seemed to think you know more about what's been going on in Arva than he does. How do you feel about that?'

'What exactly *did* he say?'

'That those close to you knew the answers. I assumed he meant Emilia, but I'd like to know for sure, considering he took the trouble to warn me what might happen if I discovered too much.'

'And what was that?' Dalca was hunched now, his arms crossed across his chest in a defensive attitude.

'You warned me what might happen to me some weeks

ago and told me to go home. Let's say he was more specific in his advice. If I was a nervous kind of guy, I might have been scared off by now. I don't want to think you're the one who's going to do the scaring! Who *is* close to you, Professor?' Pip didn't mention the riddle. That could come later when he had worked it out for himself. 'It's time to show some of that *trust* you're so keen on. Otherwise you're on your own; and, if I'm right, you wouldn't like that, would you? Because you need me. But if you think I am going to do your dirty work for you, you're wrong. It's time to level with me, Professor, and you can cut the flattery.'

'You're pretty smart, Pip.' Dalca stared back at him. 'But if you weren't, you wouldn't be here. I confess I have not been entirely fair to you. I have held some things back that I would have told you eventually. Last night, when we talked, I mentioned the significance of the cycle and the number 36. Where do you suppose I learned about it? On the internet? No, Pip. I grew up with it. As did my ancestors. Can you guess who they might have been?' Dalca stood up.

'I'm in the business of facts, Professor, not guesswork,' replied Pip, thinking he would be really spooked if Dalca went on to tell him that he shared a family tree with Grandsire! But in this country anything was believable. At that moment, the lights flickered. 'Christ, not another power cut,' he said.

Dalca sat down again.

'You Americans have a way of making light of things,' he said.

'I guess we're just not Romanians,' replied Pip, breaking the drama of the moment. 'Tell me about your ancestors.'

'They are the Roma,' said Dalca.

Pip stared at him, his brain computing the surprising information.

'The gypsies?' From what he had read, gypsies were exempt from the ritual, so why the hell had Dalca allowed Ghita to 'go-up'? Why was he allowing Emilia to bully her into a marriage she didn't want? And above all, why had Emilia married *him?* The Roma were some of the poorest people in

Europe, so how had one of them risen to be a Professor of Medieval History? What had the gypsies to do with Grandsire? Pip's head was buzzing with so many questions and possible answers that he could hardly cope.

'My origin makes me about as unpopular as you in the eyes of my neighbours.' Dalca smiled, but the smile did not reach his eyes, which were remote. Now Pip recognised from where the Professor had inherited his dark looks. 'I may have done well for myself, but I am a gypsy, and I am proud of my heritage and the special knowledge it has added to my own scholarship. I can see you are wondering how I managed to get such a good education.'

'I guess it's none of my business,' replied Pip.

'Nevertheless I shall tell you,' replied Dalca, 'as there are to be no secrets between us.' He delivered the sentence with a wry smile. 'The facts are brutal. I was adopted by a wealthy couple from Brasov, who had no children of their own. My mother, a young gypsy from the Arvan camp, could not feed me, so she sold me to them, but only on the strict understanding that when my adoptive parents died, I must learn of my heritage. My adoptive father was an honourable man and agreed to the condition.

'After my adoptive parents' early deaths, I discovered a letter explaining all, and the terms of the agreement. At first, the discovery was painful, but it brought me back to Arva, where I also met Emilia. I do what I can for my people now. They need a champion. I fight their causes, and for this they have taken me as one of their own. As I am of their blood, they trust me.

'Enough of me, though. Let us get back to business. The number 36, or six squared. You may wish to take notes of this. In simple terms, 36 is an unlucky number. You can do the maths. If you take each number from one to 36 and add them all up, the total is 666.'

Pip frowned as he tried to take it in.

'The Devil's number?'

'Exactly. And you told me that Marcu thought the dates he set down might have some astrological significance?'

'Yes?'

'Do you know anything about the zodiac?'

'Only that there are 12 signs. Remember, I'm a scientist,' said Pip.

'Yes, and each of those 12 signs has three decanates, making 36 decanates in total in the zodiac.'

'But there's nothing in astrology, Prof. You should know that. You're an academic, a professor of history.'

'Yes, of medieval history. In those times, both kings and ordinary people took notice of astrology. Don't cut yourself off from everything, Pip, simply because you do not believe in it. My race has always seen astrology as important.'

'I realise that,' replied Pip, 'and I'm willing to take it on board, if it makes any sense of what has been happening here in Arva.'

'Good. It does. I suggest that when you have time, you look up the Ancient Chaldean Magical Square of the Sun. You may find the maths very interesting. Or the Talmud Yerushalmi. In the Jewish faith, the number 36 has always had great significance. Or the Sixth Septura Tiphareth.'

'I will,' said Pip, trying to get it all down on the laptop. 'But what about the ritual? Surely it's Christian?'

'Now that is where things get difficult,' said Dalca. 'It may be Christian – and Catholic – but by its very nature it is a perversion of all that the Church purports to stand for.'

'So why is it allowed by the bishop?'

'There's an answer to that,' Dalca replied. 'Very soon, I shall take you to two people who might open your eyes to other possibilities. The priest may not have the records, but they have been recorded by those who, though innocent, have played their own part in this age-old evil.'

Pip was startled by the sudden passion in the Professor's words.

'You don't think Grandsire is the Devil too?' Immediately he regretted the slip.

'Did the priest say he was?'

'Kind of.'

'*Kind of!*' Dalca stabbed at Pip with his finger. 'You're still joking. I trust you won't be when you discover the truth for yourself.'

Pip put up both his hands.

'Okay. It's just my way. In fact, Fr Joseph wasn't quite explicit as to Grandsire's nature, but I would say he is scared as hell himself.'

'A very apt description, Pip.'

'Another thing I'd like to ask you, Professor, now we're being truthful. Where does Nicholas Eisenmann fit into all this? You know what?' Pip produced the card from his briefcase. 'I've received an invitation from him.' He handed it over.

'Who gave it to you?' Dalca was staring at the card as if he couldn't quite believe his eyes.

'His secretary, a woman called Sigi. She was waiting for me when I came out of the church hall.' To Pip's utter surprise, Dalca made a hurried Sign of the Cross. 'She suggested that it was some kind of honour that I had been invited to meet her boss.'

'*Don't go,*' said Dalca. 'It is too early. You have much to learn before you take on Eisenmann.'

'Am I meant to take him on then?' asked Pip, who realised he knew the answer as he said it. Then he added, 'You seem to know a lot about him. How come?'

'Promise me that you won't reply to his invitation?'

'Who's running this show?' quipped Pip, although he felt particularly uneasy.

'Very good, Pip, but once again, you may not feel like joking very soon,' warned Dalca.

There was an awkward silence for a few moments, which Pip broke by saying,

'I feel like a coffee. Do you think Emilia might make us one?'

Dalca set his lips in a hard line, as if at a loss to understand Pip's flippant attitude, but went to make the request of his wife. If he had known Pip better, he would have realised that when he was joking, it meant that he was anxious.

After the coffee arrived, the two men settled down to talk some more about the ritual. 'The Arvan ritual is a perversion of the Catholic rites,' Dalca repeated. 'Although I have never been present – all men are forbidden to witness it – I understand from Irina Petrescu's account, which Marcu set down, that the girls and their mothers have to recite the Rosary the night before, in Mysteries of Six of course. Then, in the morning, before they take the walk up to the church, the girls are turned round on the path three times. I will speak of that later. All Arvan girls go through this ordeal, although I believe not one of them wishes to take part and that all are made to do so by their mothers, who in turn were forced to do so by their mothers before them. The historical records give little indication as to what takes place later, up at the church, but it seems that it is often observed by the incumbent priest.'

'Including Fr Joseph?'

'Yes.'

'Good God,' said Pip. 'Do you think he was present when Anka Petrescu was attacked?'

'We don't know – she never spoke a word about it afterwards. Nor could she. Nor could any of the other girls who "went up" that morning!'

'Did anyone hear the bell ringing?'

'The houses are all shuttered on 22 July. If anyone heard, no-one mentioned it. The villagers are very superstitious people.'

'What about you? Did you hear?' asked Pip.

'No.' Dalca paused. Pip waited, but the Professor didn't seem inclined to add anything else.

After a moment, Pip said,

'Then I ought to go and speak to Fr Joseph again and ask him if he was there.'

'That would be unwise. Best leave well alone. My reason for telling you all this is that you understand what is the nature of the ritual.'

'Witchcraft,' said Pip.

'It goes deeper,' replied Dalca. 'More like resurrection.'

Pip frowned. 'Another belief is that children and only children stand between two worlds, the natural and the one above nature – by which I mean the spirit world. The children are the visionaries.' Pip swallowed, thinking about himself. 'Innocent children are the ones who are chosen. That is why they are in demand during such practices. They are special. In the Arvan case, predator and prey become one. The old becomes young again, while the young becomes old.'

'And you think this is the reason why Grandsire wants only children?'

'I'm afraid so.'

'It's sickening.'

'I agree,' said Dalca.

'So let me get this straight,' added Pip. 'The Grandsire reappears in this magic cycle of 36 and regenerates. Does this mean he's going to come back again in ...' Pip calculated. '...In 2024?' He grimaced.

'It is possible,' agreed Dalca.

'Well, he has to be stopped!' retorted Pip.

'The cycle has been continuing for hundreds of years and has not been stopped yet. It would need a very special child to do so.' Dalca was staring hard at him.

'You think a child should bear that burden?' It was Pip's turn to speak passionately now. He knew all about children's burdens. 'Do you even care?' he added.

'I care as much as a father can, but I am secure in the knowledge that my own child "went up" and "came down" unharmed.'

'But what about her children?' burst out Pip.

'According to Emilia, as long as the rules are obeyed, then nothing will harm the girls. In any case, when they are married they learn the secret too, and make sure their offspring remain safe.'

'Well, it hasn't worked, has it? It's gone wrong – too many times. How many exactly?'

'That is what I am engaged on researching at present, but I doubt if I shall ever discover the facts. I have done some retrospective counting and have studied the records. I have gone back as far as I can to document the reoccurrence of the terrible crimes in this village, and I have found evidence that a virgin was taken as far back as the 14th Century.' Dalca sighed and steepled his fingers.

'And you think that the person, or entity, called Grandsire attacked her like all the rest since?'

'Is there any other explanation?' asked Dalca.

'Yes! I feel sure that in each year a crime was committed, a different man was responsible. A man who masqueraded as Grandsire. A child murderer. A pervert – not a ghost of some kind!'

The professor smiled.

'I understand why you suggest that, Pip, but here a suspension of belief is needed. You see things through scientific eyes, but I prefer to think that, each time, Grandsire himself has been the murderer.'

Pip shook his head, feeling both annoyed and impatient at the Professor's attitude. When they had first met, Dalca had said he *dealt in facts*. Now his attitude seemed to be exactly the opposite.

'But supposing that were true, how could he be stopped?'

'I told you. The child would need to be very special! A visionary.' Pip's stomach turned over. 'What's the matter?'

'Nothing,' Pip replied.

'I know that when we began our discussions,' Dalca continued, 'you were trying to discover my feelings in respect of a supernatural involvement. Now it is you who have to consider the possibility that in the future this little village may spawn a Messiah. But a female one. Which in itself is a perversion.' Dalca didn't smile. Pip ran his hands through his hair, trying to take it in. 'Children are very special, Pip. You have none of your own, but you will understand when you do.'

'If I lived here I'd never have any,' replied Pip. He felt both angry and helpless, while, inside, his realistic self was telling him the whole concept they were discussing was nonsense. He gathered his thoughts. He was imagining how

Marcu must have felt, when he added, 'Okay, if I go along with this, how far back does it extend?'

'From what I can deduce, Arva was founded in 1376 – which is, of course, a significant year in the cycle. Before that I can discover little.'

'1376?' said Pip. The date seemed to ring a bell in his head, but it couldn't think why. 'I'll look it up and see what happened.'

'You do that,' replied Dalca. 'I shall be delighted to hear your conclusions.' He consulted his watch. 'Time for bed, and Ghita is still not in. She will be the death of her mother.'

'Where does she go?' asked Pip, thinking of the secret bar they had visited.

'She is with Anton, and according to my wife he is a good boy. She will be home soon. As I say to Emilia, she is 19 and cannot remain a prisoner in her own home. After the wedding, things will be different.'

'When will that be?' asked Pip.

Dalca smiled.

'I leave wedding arrangements to Ghita and Emilia. I have other things to think about.' He sighed. 'I think we might take a trip out to the gypsy camp tomorrow.'

'Yes,' replied Pip, but he still wanted to choke Dalca for failing to do anything to prevent Ghita's wedding. 'I also want to contact the policeman on the case. Inspector Valentin.'

'Let's hope you will have more success with him than you had with the priest.' The sarcasm was evident. 'Goodnight, Pip.'

'Goodnight, Professor.'

It was only when Pip returned to his room that he let fly. 'You're a bastard, Simu,' he said out loud. ' You know what's going on, but you won't do anything about it. Well, if you won't, I shall. I'll nail Grandsire. At least the one in 1988. Or I'll give the police the ammunition to do so. If the murderer really is Eisenmann, I shall find a way.'

Feeling better, he sat down in front of his laptop with the date 1376 still buzzing in his brain, and started to look for leads.

11

A red-streaked dawn threaded itself through the night clouds, then flamed into life, illuminating the Carpathian mountains and turning their snowy heads into blood.

Fr Joseph, weary from a sleepless night punctuated by prayer, shivered with the cold as he closed down the boot of his small car, which was loaded with his few personal possessions. His most precious was locked into a small black case. The chalice that had been given to him by his mother at his ordination. His mind was made up. It was best to leave and throw himself on the mercy of the bishop. If he was sent to Cologne, it would be no more than he deserved. Sinful clerics who had dabbled in alcohol or drugs, or who had broken their vows in so many ways like his late predecessor, Fr Pathan, were sent to their Order's house of correction there.

He felt under his shirt for the chain around his neck, which held the keys to Arva church. He was done with the village now, although it had been an even worse burden to Fr Pathan: Arva had been Hell for Pathan, but only Purgatory for Joseph.

Fr Joseph started up the car engine and drove slowly through the silent village, along the ill-kept road. No need to be careful that morning as there was no traffic, but he kept his lights switched on as the dusky red of dawn was as dangerous to drive in as was twilight. He squinted through his windscreen up above the forest trees to where the church was beckoning him. He had one more task to perform before he left Arva forever.

After parking the car at the side of the road, Fr Joseph's climb up the stony path felt like the journey to Calvary. He was sweating with the exertion, as he had been a day or so ago, when he had arrived to free the American. He had no idea how the enemy of their Church had managed to get inside the sacred precincts. At least he had not revealed the stranger's identity to the young doctor. Fr Joseph was still at a loss to understand how the man had managed to obtain a key to the gate, but he had and, therefore, Fr Joseph needed to check on the church in case it had been desecrated. Another thing Dr Durrant did not know was that the key to the gate also unlocked the church itself.

When the priest reached the iron railings, he was about to bend to the task when he heard dogs barking from the village far below, their frantic noises eerily echoing across an otherwise silent landscape. He became more tense when he thought he heard movement in the deep forest beside the path. His immediate thought was of a wolf pack. The village sheepdogs might have caught their scent. It was a well-known fact that at least six thousand wolves made their home in the forests of the Carpathians. At the onset of the previous winter, two of his parishioners had had a run-in with wolves intent on taking their sheep. The wolf pack had moved on down into the farmland as the first snows fell, at about this time last year. Fr Joseph knew wolves were notoriously shy creatures that hunted only livestock, but in that lightening dawn, sense had deserted his head.

He continued to unlock the gates and tried to ignore the howling behind him that had first been faint, but was becoming louder as it was brought down upon him by the chilling wind. All of a sudden, the wolves became terrifying. He had always hated wild animals as a child, because once as a frightened child he had dreamed that he had been torn to pieces by a pack. The memory fast returned of burning eyes and terrifying jaws that housed lolling tongues, bloody from his flesh. His mother couldn't comfort him that day so long ago and now there was no comfort. He was a man set apart from the rest of humanity. Called by God and betrayed by Him too.

His hands were cold and sweating as he tried to lock the gates behind him, fumbling as if the wolves were on his heels, as if his last day was come. He knew that the high fence would not keep them out, because there were holes in it, holes they would discover. Other terrible imaginations followed, of beasts dragging up the dead, of souls who were not yet with God, miserable souls who wandered the world. He had always admired the holy martyrs who faced such terrible deaths with patience, now those torments they had endured came fresh into his mind. Those men and women were destined to see God's face. Would he? Once his faith had been strong. Now he realised he even questioned the existence of God.

What was left for him? Punishment in a clerical house of correction and then, eternal punishment, the worst of all. He gritted his teeth, which were chattering. When he had left his presbytery, he was afraid, but now he was terrified. Why had he come up to this desolate church at all, which once had been a sacred place, but now had been desecrated by Pathan, one of the many priests who had gone before him, who had broken their priestly vows as he, himself, had done when he rang the church bell perpetrating that eternal cycle of pure evil. How many times had he averted his hypocritical eyes from the forbidden areas, cutting out of his mind the part he had played, and had been too weak not to acquiesce with tradition. His presence in the church on that summer morning in July 1988 had never been revealed to the investigating police by his parishioners. They had colluded in his guilt when he had performed the tradition according to their wishes by ringing the bell in the tower. He had been curate then to his predecessor, who had not had the strength to climb to the bell's platform. He remembered how afraid he had been when he climbed up the rickety tower. He had wished then it would break under the weight of his great sin: that mortal sin he had committed, by allowing little Anka to be killed.

Joseph stopped, oozing with disgust at himself as he remembered how he had allowed the rites of the Church to be desecrated by an innocent child taught by an ignorant mother. He shivered. '*Moarte, moarte*, Murder.' The words he had heard from old lame Basa's lips when Joseph had heard his last confession. How many times had the ancient farmer seen his parish priest, who should have been his comfort and his teacher, pass him on the way up the path that fateful morning, but Basa, like the rest of the villagers, had kept that terrible secret.

Basa had been a man set apart; someone who had claimed to have seen the Grandsire three times. What he had told Joseph was more than any mortal man could bear. Joseph wondered how Basa, an outcast, shunned by all, could have learned the 'secret of the marriage bed'. As the time passed, Joseph had learned much more as, one by one, the women of the village had shunted their age-old filthy secrets on to his shoulders in the confessional. He had absolved them, but who would absolve him from that hell? He could tell no-one what he had heard. Not even the Pope himself!

Joseph leaned on the wall of the building, shaking all over. He was a priest in name only now. There would be no forgiveness for him from the Lord. He might as well be dead because the Evil One had entered into him.

As he leaned against the cold stone of the building that had once been the House of God, he cursed it, then sank down outside the door, scraping his thin, white hands against the blocks, causing them to bleed.

Getting up, he staggered inside. The church lay, totally untouched, festering under a thick film of dust, festooned with cobwebs and smelling of mustiness. No Christian church robbers would enter here. They were too afraid. But there was One who would. Fr Joseph's teeth chattered. He felt half mad himself.

The candlesticks still stood on the altar, draped in spiders' webs. The altar where Pathan had said Mass. The pulpit where he had spoken to his flock. Lied to them. All intact.

Fr Joseph looked round. No human had touched the altar, nor desecrated the sacred vessels. He shook his head and wiped it with a bleeding hand. 'No human.' The words were only a gurgle and stuck in his throat, which was dry because the spit wouldn't come.

At that very moment, the door clanged shut. The priest pressed his hands together, too terrified to turn. Any sense of security he had in his head was gone. Rolling his eyes upwards, he saw through the high windows that the tops of the trees were tossing. It was a sign that a storm was here. His legs wanted to move, but they were paralysed as they sensed *something* approaching. Joseph closed his eyes in one futile gesture of fear and pleading, like a doomed man in his blindfold, waiting for execution. Then, opening them, he looked towards an altar that held no hope for him.

A moment later, he was caught from behind and felt the iron fingernails digging into his neck. His head was twisted upwards as he saw his old enemy's face and his voice broke through the spit.

'You!' he gibbered. Then he was spun on to his back and clawed hands were dragging him along the nave. His feeble struggles ceased as his heels scraped along the stones, then he was spun again and again, like the little girls were turned before their deaths. He heard the cackling laugh, then a dusty blackness enveloped him. The coarse material with its suffocating thickness cut off all light and was drawn tightly, closer and closer into his face, bruising his lips and forcing open his mouth. He could see nothing, only hear the faint panting from his failing chest and feel the interminable dragging. No time for a prayer nor any act of mercy.

'Climb!' the voice ordered as he was pulled up onto his feet and pushed into a vertical position, hood pressed against the wood. His scream was muffled as the hand caught hold of his leg and pulled it almost out of its socket to place his foot on the first rung.

At that moment, his brain switched into self-preservation. He began to struggle again, but that all-enveloping body and merciless weight was placing hand over hand and foot over foot, climbing with him, forcing him up upwards – to the bell platform. Cold with terror and almost fainting, he realised they were welded together in that narrow space. But *he* couldn't fly! Then his enemy disengaged itself.

He felt metal cut into his throat as his key chain was torn from his neck. A moment of silence, then a heavy object replaced it. A rope. In one moment of clarity, Joseph knew it was the end. 'God, have mercy on my soul,' was his last thought.

A flash of daylight assailed him. He blinked as the hood was torn off his head – and the final earthly blow to his legs took him off his feet, launching him into space where there was only air, above him, below him, around him.

Seconds later, Fr Joseph's body came to a juddering halt, neck broken. His adversary leapt down the stairs and stood beneath the twitching corpse.

'You know the secret now, priest,' he said, looking up with burning eyes. Then he turned on his heel, swung his dusty cloak about him and left, his expression a gloating mask of triumph.

Pip slept until late, but nobody came to wake him. He glanced at his watch and realised that he had already missed breakfast. So he lay in the comfortable bed, his head full of Dalca's disclosures about Arva as well as those personal to him, which at this point he wouldn't admit to himself or anyone else. Delving into the year 1376 had taken a lot out of him. He took a long time to get up, trying to forget it – for the present.

Finally, he shaved. Then, when he was almost dressed, he heard the light knock and went to the door. 'Ghita! I'm sorry. I overslept.' To his utter surprise, she ran straight into the room and sat down on his bed. 'What's wrong?'

'It's all right. Mother's gone out. She's really upset.' Ghita shook her head.

'Another row?' She looked so dejected and he was keen

to show sympathy.

'No. She went to Mass and Fr Joseph didn't turn up.' It was the last thing he had expected her to say.

'How do you mean?' His empty stomach turned over quite sharply.

'He didn't turn up for the service, and when she and a couple of her friends went over to his house, he'd left.'

'Left?'

'You sound like a parrot,' she snapped. 'Yes, he was gone. He'd taken everything. Even his priestly vessels. And he had left a letter for everybody. It was addressed to the parishioners.'

'What did it say?'

'I don't quite know, but Mother was in a state. Dad's talking about phoning the police.'

'Why? Does he think something's happened to him?'

'One of the farmers noticed his car parked at the bottom of the hill to the church! I wish you'd stop asking questions,' she said, rubbing her forehead in an almost childish gesture. She looked up. 'This isn't funny, but … have you ever thought that every person you visit, something bad happens to them? Who are you going to see next?'

'No, Ghita, it isn't funny, and I hope you're not going to say that to the police!'

'Of course I'm not. You're almost as unpopular as Dad, but I wouldn't do that.'

'Why don't people like your dad, Ghita?'

'That's for him tell you,' said Ghita, getting up. Pip wasn't sure if she even knew about her father's gypsy background, so he kept quiet. 'Still, in spite of all I've said to you over the last week or so, I like you – a little. At least nothing's happened to me – yet.' Her smile was watery.

'Well, I'm glad you do, because you aren't so bad yourself.' They stood quietly for a moment. Then Pip said, 'I think I should go find your dad.'

'No, don't do that,' she said. 'He wouldn't appreciate it. You'd only be in the way. Come down and I'll make you some breakfast.'

At that, Ghita walked out of the room, leaving him in a state of disbelief. Ghita had said she liked him. And the priest had disappeared.

'*Suicide*,' announced Dalca to Pip, 'It seems quite clear. The priest's note proved it.' Although he appeared adamant, there was something by the way he delivered the words that made Pip believe the Professor was trying to convince himself of the fact. 'Let's be sensible here,' Dalca continued. 'He had written to his parishioners asking for their forgiveness and confessing to them that he had sinned against the Lord. A typical suicide note.'

'I'm not convinced. For example, what do you think Fr. Joseph had done to them then,' pressed Pip. 'He seemed a caring pastor. As for sinning?' he shrugged... 'He heard their confessions, he said Mass, and he seemed dedicated to their welfare.'

'You're annoying me,' replied Dalca. 'What about ringing the church bell on the 22 July? Luring children into the churchyard, doing what all his damned predecessors had done.' His tone was bitter. 'And what's more he encouraged the village women not to tell what was going on up there. You're going to tell me now he probably suffered for it because they told him in confession. It's an abomination.'

'He probably did. That's confession for you. Yet, would that be enough to make him kill himself? I don't think so, because I know how that man was when I visited him. He cared for them and they obviously for him. Imagine, he must have been the only one whom they could confide in. Other individuals might hate him for that. Take you for instance, Professor, like lots of men in Arva. How many of them would have liked to have heard that secret his wife was keeping from him?' Dalca just steeped his fingers and his face looked grim.

'I am only making a case for someone *killing* Father Joseph,' added Pip. Someone or *something*. The man was terrified, but sane, when he warned me to keep my nose out. You and I both know that probably somebody found out that he had said too much. We both know who that might have been.'

They were silent for a while.

'Well, at least the police believe it was a classic suicide case as they found his car at the bottom of the hill and that he had gone up to the church for some specific reason so early in the morning. And he locked himself in! They would see that as classic behaviour,' replied Dalca.

Pip was determined to get Dalca to admit that Joseph had been murdered. Once again, he wanted to believe it was Grandsire or Eisenmann. In fact, it mattered to Pip a lot because he needed that backup from Dalca, that reinforcement to convince him even further they were dealing with something that he had always shied away from; the fact that he, himself, was in mortal danger. He could be next! Pip needed them to be working together and not for Dalca to renege upon their earlier conversation. It gave him courage.

All at once, Dalca added, 'The police will find out there was only one set of keys.'

'Joseph's wasn't the only set,' said Pip. ' I know that.'

'Are you going to tell the police about your stranger?' asked Dalca.

Pip was silent.

'Very wise,' replied Dalca. 'Shall I continue? He locked the gates behind him, climbed up onto the bell platform and hanged himself. But his key wasn't found at the scene. He probably threw it away, just in case anyone came through the gate and found him by accident. A thorough search of the churchyard is now taking place,' said Dalca. 'Anyway, that's my understanding of the situation.'

'I wonder what brought that on?' said Pip. Dalca was looking at him in the same way Ghita had.

'Maybe you touched a nerve,' replied Dalca. 'Emilia is beside herself. There is a chance they won't send another priest to Arva. The breed is in short supply.'

'What will people do?' Pip wondered what it must be like

to have a faith and not be able to practise.

'Probably have to go into Cluj. Or perhaps the village might get served from there? Who knows?' Dalca shrugged, then grinned. 'The lot of them might even turn Orthodox?' Pip knew it wasn't his place to tell the Professor off for such an insensitive remark.

'What about Ghita's wedding?' Pip wasn't sure why the remark had slipped out, or why he wanted to know. But he did.

'Ah, the wedding! Cluj again, I fear. I shan't be going in to the University this morning. I may have to comfort Emilia from time to time, but we could continue with our discussion. I think a visit to the Roma today would be unwise.'

'I'd rather not, if you don't mind.' Pip didn't want to be around the house at that moment. 'I'm going to try to contact Inspector Valentin and set up a meeting.'

'Well, do be careful,' replied Dalca. He had a hint of mischief around his mouth, but it was not reflected in his eyes. 'I wouldn't go visiting too many people if I were you – or the Romanian population might dwindle even further!'

'I don't want to offend you,' said Pip, 'but I do think that remark was in poor taste.'

'It was meant in fun,' said the Professor, 'but in my opinion, this time you have done Arva a favour. Would you like a lift?'

'No thank you, I'll take the bus if I need to,' retorted Pip, picking up his laptop.

'Very well,' replied Dalca. 'And now I must go and look for Emilia.'

As he left, Pip wondered exactly why the Professor hated the Church so much and yet was still so knowledgeable about it.

Gregori Valentin received the telephone call from his old office as he was finishing his lunch of chicken soup and salami, which was as boring as his morning had been. He had been retired from the police force for ten years now, and he had never accepted it. Of course, while he had been working, he had grumbled constantly, saying he'd had his fill of rape and murder and wished it all would end, but without the daily buzz he had not relaxed into old age with grace.

He had always been morose, mainly on account of his work, as well as being a martyr to frequent stomach upsets. Privately, he put his illness down to stress over the grim sights he had seen, but he would never have admitted that to anybody. One sign of weakness on the job and an officer lost face. Except for his stomach he was a fit old man, although his hearing wasn't that good. As he rarely had visitors, it didn't matter. So to receive a telephone call from the office was joy to his day, although he had to listen very carefully as the young civilian clerk conveyed the amazing news that an American psychologist wanted to interview him about a murder that had taken place in 1988.

'Shall I tell him you'll phone him?' asked the young woman – and waited. She had no idea that at that particular moment Gregori was suffering from a sudden attack of heartburn that drove every thought from his head. 'Are you still there, Inspector?'

'Yes, sorry,' he replied. ' What does he want to know?'

'Search me,' replied the clerk. 'To discuss the case, I assume. Shall I give you his name and number? He checks out at the University. He's staying in the student hostel. Would you like the address?' Valentin thought about it for a moment. 'Hello?' The young woman seemed less chatty now and more impatient as she gave him the details. 'Have you written all this down?' She probably thought he was senile!

'Yes, thank you.' He had written it down with care.

'Goodbye, Inspector.'

The phone clicked off. He stared at it, then at the piece of paper. *Dr Philip Durrant.* Now what could he want? A murder in 1988? There had been several that year.

'Hmm,' said Valentin out loud. 'Psychologist, eh?' That wasn't quite the same as a psychiatrist, and he knew about them. They were as nutty as their patients. He'd had enough to do with Dr Marcu. A tiny pain stabbed through his stomach as he thought of the late doctor. He had been a strange one, but he had been very grateful to Valentin for his input on the Petrescu case.

The Inspector's mind lingered on what had been the strangest of all the crimes he had investigated in a career that had spanned 40 years. The thought of it made his stomach turn over. That was when his digestive trouble had started. He had popped indigestion pills throughout the whole of that investigation. Of all the horrible things he had seen, the little girl who had turned into an old woman in a week, was the worst. He remembered the transformation of round cheeks into sunken hollows; the puckering of the firm, youthful skin into wrinkles; and the appearance of age spots on the beetling brows. How could he ever forget that sight in the farmer's house? Or the wailing of her demented mother? *1988*.

Could Dr Durrant be investigating the Petrescu case? He hoped not. Things about that case had puzzled him for years. In fact, they had made him into the man he was now. Of course, he would never know unless he phoned. Valentin sat down at the table, drummed his fingers on the stained wood and stared at the telephone. He sniffed. Life was so bloody boring at present, in spite of his research. After making a strong cup of coffee, which he knew was bad for him, he went over to the telephone, picked up the receiver and dialled the number.

Their conversation was pleasant, but brief. When Durrant mentioned the death of Anka Petrescu, the light went out of Valentin's afternoon. So he had been right.

'Arva? In 1988?'

'Yes. The Petrescu case. I'd be extremely grateful for a few words.'

'I'm not sure I can help you,' replied the Inspector. 'What do you want to know?'

'Well, the Marcu Papers are now in my possession and they contain several notes from you. I would like to clarify a few things. Of course I would like to obtain the police records.' The young man sounded hopeful.

'I can't talk about those,' said Valentin. 'The case is

ongoing.' He didn't add, *but I have my theories.*

'I quite understand, but anything you could tell me from a personal point of view as the chief investigator would be very helpful.' The voice was both determined and persistent.

Valentin moistened his dry lips with his tongue. What harm could it do now to talk something over? Besides, he was eager to know how much Marcu had known but hadn't disclosed.

'Why not,' he said.

'Great!' replied Dr Durrant.

Valentin shook his head. Another youngster, probably, who didn't know what was what. They agreed to meet at a café in Cluj three days later, as the psychologist said he was busy with other appointments. When Valentin put down the receiver, he still felt as uneasy as when he had first learned from Dr Durrant that it was the Arvan crime he wanted to discuss.

'I wonder what you'd think, lad,' he said to himself, 'if you knew what I've discovered? Maybe I'll tell you and maybe I won't.' He groaned as he felt a burning sensation followed by another sharp stab. He had promised himself so many times that he would go into hospital and let them do their worst with his ulcer again, and the pain was getting so bad that he knew the time was coming when he would have to have an operation.

He had no-one in his life in whom he could confide. His isolation had grown into an immense burden after he had retired. He had divorced early on in his marriage. Like most policemen, his personal life had suffered on account of the job.

He breathed in and looked round at the material he had amassed on the Petrescu case. His small flat had become a repository for his still growing research on the Arva murders, past and present. The policeman in New York who was now retired himself had also become a firm friend. Together, they had shared newspaper and magazine cuttings, long emails, and conversations on Skype, to satisfy their ongoing interest in serial killers and ritual murders. Added to that were his files on the history of the region going back to Charlemagne. He had also delved into unknown territories of the paranormal and made a lengthy study of local folk beliefs and witchcraft. Therefore, his piles of files, boxes of papers, articles and written records, as well as his scholarly books, had become Valentin's life's work of which he was secretly very proud. He didn't know whether or not his former colleagues had given up on trying to find the Arva serial killer, but *he* hadn't. One day, all the files he had compiled on Grandsire might be of some use.

Why hadn't he shown them to the police? He shook his head again. He knew the breed. Anything that wasn't factual was pooh-poohed by them. He didn't blame them; he would have reacted the same way in his time. But now things were different. He was allowed to have imagination. After he had received that puzzling information in 1988 from his colleague in New York, consisting of the photograph and the details of Walter Arvarescu, he had read the *The Rat and the Piper* – the record of the conversations between the American paedophile and his psychiatrist.

Valentin had been so interested that he had asked the girl in his office to find a copy of *The Pied Piper of Hamelin,* written by the English poet Robert Browning. At that time he hadn't questioned how quickly she had found it. Now, when he analysed everything that had happened back then, he thought it strange that she had managed to bring him a German translation so quickly. She had been different from any girl that had worked for him before. He remembered her very well. She had had all the men after her. She had always worn a neat brown suit, had brown hair slicked back and a tight little arse. But she had been arrogant. She had come from Bucharest, and wouldn't have anything to do with anybody! She had thought they were all hobbledehoys in Cluj. He wondered what had happened to her.

The killer's name and the poem had entranced him and, since then, he had been trying to put two and two together. When he had retired he had started by researching the name Arvarescu, and then the origins of the poem. But there had been no-one to listen, or to discuss his research with. If Marcu had lived, he would have been the ideal person. Dr Baescu, who had attended the case, would have been another, but he had retired like Valentin and was not living in Cluj anymore. In any case, he and the Inspector had worked together for only a short time after the attack, and when the doctor had defended the villagers' culture, Valentin had been particularly obstructive. He regretted that now, but it was one of the reasons why he hadn't tried to contact Baescu. Now another doctor had taken over Marcu's research. Maybe now was the time for Valentin to let go, and turn the files over to him.

He got up from the table and went over to the black stove, which squatted, its doors wide open, begging for wood. As he fed it, he warmed his hands, then he looked over to the neat line of shelves that took up one side of his small living room. He was punctilious in his tidiness, which came from his training. The only deviation was the weighty pile of magazines and newspapers that he kept by his easy chair for quick reference. Police habits died hard. He liked to keep abreast with the world of crime.

He walked over and ran his finger across the shelves, took the first box file down and carried it back to his seat by the stove. The temperature had dropped considerably that week and Valentin was not looking forward to the winter. It would soon be snowing. He settled down and opened the file.

It had been a difficult task to begin his own research, as he wasn't an academic; but he was in possession of certain facts that the general public was not. For instance, the rape of Anka Petrescu. He had photocopied the pathology report, which had clearly stated that the traces of blood found on her doll had come from a rodent. The rape itself *had* taken place, but no semen traces were found. None of it added up. So he had started looking for other explanations. Unnatural ones that, as he had discovered more, he could explain only as supernatural. He had been a realist until he began to read books on the occult and the nature of rituals.

In fact, Valentin had become an avid amateur historian. It had taken him a very long time to find out about the settlement of Arva. Combining this with his research into the supernatural, the poem's date, its sources and the leads within it – rats included – he had come to the conclusion that in 1376 the sinister Pied Piper, who was known by many names like the demons of old, had abducted a band of German children and brought them to Transylvania. Valentin was now almost sure that the place he had brought them to was the village of Arva. The date fitted with the presence of the Saxon population in the area. The only problem was that no-one would believe a word he said if he told them his theory that Grandsire, as the village women called him, was probably the Pied Piper. But as for the Piper's reincarnation at certain intervals, Valentin couldn't get his head around that. If he had mentioned it to a soul, he would probably have ended up in Burbor himself!

Once, since his retirement, he had returned to Arva and attempted to have a meeting with the woman, Simona Murgu, who at the time of the death of Anka Petrescu had stated to him that Grandsire had committed the crime and that he would never be caught. She could have known the historical truth, probably through an oral tradition passed down through the ages. Maybe she also knew the secret of Grandsire's reincarnation during the ritual. At that time, he had thought she was deranged. She had even had a fit of maniacal laughter while standing over the corpse of her one-time lover, old lame Claudiu Basa. And no meeting with her had ever taken place, as Valentin had learned that what he had suspected was true: Simona had ended up a psychiatric case!

He flipped through another file, thinking about the American tourist, Wally Arvarescu, who had been in Arva that day in 1988 and should have died when the plane that was taking him back to America caught fire and crashed. His remains had never been identified. Valentin was now on the point of believing that he might have been the reincarnation of Grandsire. When the Inspector had shown the photograph of the New York paedophile to the woman from the Inn Sancipia, Ruxandra Dobos, she had given a positive identification, linking the face in the photograph to the tourist Wally Arvarescu. How that could be possible he did not know, because the paedophile

Wally Arvarescu who had disappeared in 1952 could not also have been a 36-year-old tourist called Wally Arvarescu. Unless he was a time traveller! Neither had it escaped Valentin's notice that in 1952 the rape and murder of another innocent child, Catina Albu, had taken place in Arva.

Valentin wasn't sure if he could even broach the subject at his meeting with Dr Durrant. The young man would probably deal only in hard facts, in which case he would certainly not be open to paranormal suggestion. But it all depended on what kind of person the doctor was.

Valentin had learned over his years as a policeman that his instincts could be trusted. He made an immediate decision. He would write down his proposition as to Grandsire's identity and send it to Dr Durrant in a letter. Then it would be up to the academic to decide whether they met or not. It was all going to be too difficult otherwise. Valentin didn't want to look a fool, but if his evidence was to be discounted, then it was better in writing than face to face.

It took him some time to summarise his argument. When he read it over, it still seemed plausible, but he realised his correspondent might feel differently unless he was able to suspend his belief in reality. The Inspector put a note with it, saying that if Dr Durrant felt after reading the summary that it was best they did not meet to discuss the case, he would understand. He addressed the envelope and searched for a stamp. He was lucky to find one left in his desk drawer. He looked across at the stove and grumbled at its capacity to eat wood. Bending over, he opened the doors and fed it again. Immediately, tongues of bright flame licked and curled around the small logs, making them blaze up momentarily.

'That's better,' he said, 'I don't want you going out.' He put the letter inside his jacket and donned his heavy coat. When he opened the door of his flat, it was colder than he had imagined outside, and the weather was murky. He pulled up his collar against a keen wind coming from the mountains, which assaulted his face with icy blasts as he made his slow way towards the post box.

'Ugh, winter!' he muttered. 'How am I going to put up with it?' The Inspector had always had good eyesight, but the autumn twilight was playing tricks with his vision as he crossed the unlit road. If he had bothered to wear his hearing aid, he might have heard the sound of the approaching engine, emitted from a car that had no lights switched on in the gloom.

A minute later, Valentin sustained a tremendous blow to his side, and a bright light exploded behind his eyes. He was already bleeding in the brain and internally as he was hurled, semi-conscious, over the car bonnet. A moment later, his head crunched onto the rough road surface, leaving his dying body a crumpled, broken mass in the gutter.

Back at Valentin's flat, the hungry stove digested the crackling logs, causing them to emit flying sparks, one of which settled on the heap of reading material placed in a neat pile beside the Inspector's chair. The sheet on the top curled into black ash as the fire spread itself like a living thing. It wreathed into a flaming red-gold shape as its burning teeth nibbled at the synthetic material of the adjoining chair and set it alight. The thin curtains were the next shivering victims to be consumed by the hungry fire, and soon the whole of the flat was set alight. The late Inspector's precious files and scholarly books were gobbled by the predator, which divided as it grew. The old varnished furniture was the next to die, and soon there was little left of what had once been a small, comfortable home.

A shocked neighbour called 981 to alert the Fire Brigade. After the fire was drowned, a search was made of the premises for Inspector Valentin, but no body was found.

12

'I have made a discovery that is guaranteed to make both of us happy,' said Dalca on the morning of the day when Pip had arranged to meet Valentin. 'I have to go in to the University, so unfortunately it is you who are going to have to do the work.'

'That's what I'm here for,' replied Pip, wondering how anyone could possibly be happy in Arva. 'What is it?'

'I have located the church registers.'

'How did you get hold of them?' Pip's mood lifted. 'The priest told me that he didn't have them.'

'Then he was lying,' replied Dalca. 'But don't let us speak ill of the dead. Let us look at his demise as a bonus.'

Once again, Pip marvelled at the Professor's insensitivity – but then, wasn't he just as pleased at the chance to get his hands on records that might lead to more evidence on Grandsire?

'Where were they?'

'I had the good fortune to go to the house with Emilia, and while my poor wife was sobbing and clearing some of Fr Joseph's personal things, I came across a box – a very large one – which I opened. Naturally, she said I shouldn't touch the documents, but I told her it would not be safe to leave the church records there in case they fell into the wrong hands, as the place is bound to be unoccupied until another priest comes – if ever. She believed me! I am very glad that Emilia was on such good terms with the late Fr Joseph.' He grinned. 'So I had one of the villagers bring the box back here on his cart. The documents are in the study. How do you feel about going through them?'

'I can't wait,' replied Pip. 'But what about our visit to the gypsy camp?'

'That can wait another day. In any case, I shall have to alert Anya that I am coming. Her grandmother, Eva Kirchma, is one hundred years old and must be prepared to meet visitors.'

'We're going to meet a hundred year old lady?' Pip was incredulous.

'She still has her faculties.'

'And remembers a lot about Arva?' asked Pip. His enthusiasm had deserted him since the priest's suicide, but now it was creeping back.

'Too much,' replied Dalca. His own happiness had dissipated. 'Come through to the study. The documents are waiting for you.'

As Pip lifted out the registers, Dalca explained, 'In Transylvania, church records began in the early 1600s, and transcripts were made as early as 1784. The priest was right when he told you that some of these can be found in archives in Hungary, Poland and Germany, as well as Serbia. Hopefully, what we have here are the Arvan registers for at least the last one hundred years.'

'The same time that Eva Kirchma has been alive?'

'Just so, Pip.' Dalca's dark eyes searched Pip's face.

'I want to look at 1916 in particular and, of course, 1952.'

'And 1988. I understand. I wish you well. I have told Emilia you are not to be disturbed as you are extremely busy.'

'Thank you.' The last thing Pip wanted was to be confronted by Emilia while he was working on the registers.

Once he was settled with laptop at the ready, he discovered that births and baptisms were recorded under the names of the child, its father and usually the mother. Added to this was the date of the christening and the name and sometimes the place of residence of the godparents.

He thought he would work with the birth records –

earliest first. Looking at Marcu's notes, he decided to find out something about 1916. The priest had said there had not been a victim that year. All the names in the records were unfamiliar to Pip. He had nothing to go on at all. He didn't know why, but something was telling him he ought to look even further back. The birth records went back only as far as 1900, but soon he came across he name he recognised: Claudiu Basa. The lame farmer who had lived by the church. Pip shivered a little as he remembered the vision he had experienced in the ruined house. Basu had been born on 27th July 1900. That would have meant he was nearly 16 and on 22nd July 1916.

Pip thought about the priest's riddle. Claudiu *died on the day his mother was born.* All at once, his quick brain had worked it out. The *date* that his mother was born. That was what the riddle meant. The date rather than the day! What had seemed so difficult now seemed so easy. Pip had no way of knowing the date of Claudiu's mother's birth, but if he could find out when Claudiu had died, then he would know.

He turned to the deaths and burials register for 1988, which held the name of the deceased, the date of death and/or burial, sometimes the names of the parents or spouse and occasionally the place of origin. When had Claudiu died? He remembered Marcu had said that Inspector Valentin had been to see the farmer, but found out he was dead on arriving at the house. Simona Murgu had been there and had laid out the body. That must have been near to 22 July 1988. Pip made a note to remind himself to ask Valentin to corroborate it. He looked for the year 1988 and, after scanning July's entries, found that Claudiu had actually died on 22 July.

'Strange!' he said out loud.

But if Fr Joseph had been right, it meant that Claudiu Basa's mother was born on 22 July – year unknown.

Then he started thinking about Irina Petrescu. According to Marcu, she had been obsessed about her birthday, which was 22 July 1952. The psychiatrist had noted that she felt it was her fault that Anka had been chosen as Grandsire's victim. Pip's brain was computing again.

'What about Catina Albu then?' he asked himself. She had been in her fifteenth year, just like Anka, when she had been raped and murdered. If he could find *her* mother's birth date … But unfortunately, Pip didn't know her mother's maiden name, so he couldn't look her up. The death register only mentioned her as Albu. Maybe Dalca would know about that? He made a note to ask him … Then he realised that Irina Petrescu had been born on the same day – the day Catina Albu had been the victim.

He could see it now. The significance of 22 July was paramount. Not only was it the day when Grandsire, or the man who called himself Grandsire, returned, but it was also the day when Irina Petrescu was born. There had been no victim in 1916, which was very strange, given that it might also have been the day when Claudiu Basa's mother was born. He couldn't find out – yet – about Catina Albu, but was there any other connection between the victims? Catina, Anka and the crippled Claudiu Basa. He narrowed his eyes. The link was probably there to be seen, but he couldn't see it … He concentrated. Then all of a sudden it came to him: *Grandsire only likes girls!* Claudiu was male. If he hadn't been, would he have been Grandsire's victim as well? Was that why there was no victim in 1916? Was that what Fr Joseph had been trying to tell him?

Pip leaned back in Dalca's chair and closed his eyes. He could hear his heart thumping in his ears. Of course, all this could have been coincidence, but he had never believed in flukes. To prove his assumption, he needed to find out about Catina Albu's mother. He was captured then by an intense desire to look into other dates from the past. He turned to his laptop and set it to compute the dates back in cycles of 36 years: 1880, 1844, 1808, 1772 … How far back should he go? The computer continued, producing a table of dates going back through the 17th Century, then the 16th, the 15th, the 14th … Suddenly a date flashed up that caught Pip's eye: 1376.

'My God!' he said out loud. 'Arva was founded in 1376!' Fr Joseph must have known about the significance of the dates and concealed the registers. He would never have done so without the permission of his superiors. How long has the Church known about it and done nothing?' Pip was shocked by the enormity of his discovery. Instead of elation at his possible success, he felt sad. He had progressed further than Sacha Marcu in one single afternoon. Yet maybe his predecessor *had* tried to get hold of the parish records and had been told by the priest that they were elsewhere and, afterwards, had failed to find them. It had only been good luck that Fr Joseph had died. Then Pip realised he sounded exactly like Dalca ... He wondered how much Dalca knew. In fact, how much did all Arvan men know?

He glanced at his watch. Lunchtime! He was reluctant to stop now, given his breakthrough. However, the decision was made for him. The knock on the door was sharp.

'Just a moment!' he called, replacing the registers and closing the box quickly. He opened the door to reveal Emilia. Her habitually pale face was flushed and she appeared agitated.

'I'm sorry to disturb you,' she said, 'but you have visitors.'

Pip raised his eyebrows. He wasn't expecting anyone.

'Who is it?' he asked.

'The police,' she said in a low voice. 'Two officers are waiting in the kitchen. I shall stay in here. I have things to do.'

Pip had no idea what she meant, but only one thing was on his mind. Why would the police want to interview him. It must be about Fr Joseph – or perhaps even Robert?

'Will you ring your husband for me, please?' he asked.

'Very well,' she replied.

Pip walked down the hall slowly. He had done nothing wrong. But the police over here were not friendly and he was a foreigner. He needed some back-up.

The police were there for over an hour. When they had gone, Pip stared at the letter. It had been found at the scene of the crime. Hit and run, they had said. He remembered the policeman's look as he had asked, 'Do you have a car, Dr

Durrant?'

'No,' he had replied, thankful that he hadn't bought one after all. Then they had informed him that Valentin's flat had been destroyed by fire. The rest had been routine. They had asked where he had been at the time and what his business was with the late Inspector Valentin. Of course, they must have already known, as they had opened the letter. But what they had thought of it, he dared not think. Doubtless they had wanted to know why the late Inspector was communicating with him. He had told them that the information was meant to be used in his psychological work for the University, and they had seemed satisfied with his answer. Valentin had set down carefully all his research on the crimes committed in Arva. This would have been common knowledge in the Police Department, but what would not, was the fact that the late Inspector had believed a supernatural to be responsible for the crimes.

He expected they would think Valentin had gone mad. Little did they know that the Inspector's line of thinking ran concurrent with Pip's own investigations. Valentin had confessed in the letter that how Grandsire was reincarnated was beyond him, and that he feared Pip would not wish to see him after he had read it.

Ironically, Pip would never have the chance to talk to him now. That Valentin had died was more than a tragedy. He was now the third person to have paid the ultimate penalty for becoming involved with Pip's research. Maybe what Ghita and her father had said was true. Pip had brought them all bad luck. It was not a pleasant thought. He remembered the day of his first meeting with Dalca. The Professor had warned him then – that something might happen to *him* if he persisted in his quest to find Grandsire.

Pip examined his feelings. How afraid was he that he would be next? It was a difficult question. Even more troubling was the information that Valentin had believed the Pied Piper of Hamelin to be the Arvan murderer and to have founded the village of Arva in 1376. He leaned on the kitchen table and put his head in his hands. 1376. What *did* he personally know about the date? A moment later, his memory was sifting through an enormous amount of material. He was afraid that another vision was coming on. His head hurt. 1376. Where had he seen the date before?

Then he clutched at the memory he had kept shut away for so long in order to save his sanity. The tall display case in Koppelberg's chalet, marked 1376. It was all coming back now. The statue man coming alive. The glass case melting to let him slip through into the Piper's medieval hell. The drowning rats, the laughing children merrily following the Piper. Their parents weeping on the battlements. He recalled how he had crept along slowly on his crutches, wanting to be with the happy children, but had been left behind as they made their way to paradise! And the great black rat that had survived the river. Pip was lost in a waking dream, when he felt a hand on his shoulder – and jumped. He looked up in a daze.

'Dalca!' he gasped. 'Thank God you're here.'

The Professor shook his head.

'Emilia asked me to come home because the police were here. What did they want?'

Pip filled him in, and Dalca looked as anxious at the news as Pip felt.

'It goes on,' the Professor said, shaking his head.

Pip didn't understand what he meant and didn't ask. Instead, he handed Dalca the letter. When the Professor had read and returned it, his face was pale and his expression drawn.

'Maybe I should – go home?' Pip said. 'You warned me and I took no notice.'

'Do you want to?'

'No, but I'm beginning to believe that ...' He couldn't finish the sentence.

'That Grandsire reincarnates?'

'Something like that,' replied Pip. 'But when I look at it realistically, I know it can't be true!'

Professor Wright's words flashed through Pip's mind: *Watch out for vampires!* He didn't believe in *them* either, nor their ability to continue living through the ages fuelled by the blood and flesh of mortals. He had to set aside the legends, forget the visions, and be sensible. As he tried to convince himself, a voice in his head was reminding him of the little girl turning into an old woman. In his letter, Valentin, the hard-headed police inspector, had corroborated Marcu's story concerning the 1988 victim. But he could hardly believe that either. Was there some medical explanation? He had heard about progeria, a rare disease that hastens ageing. He didn't know enough about it, but it was a possibility.

But what he had found out from the parish registers was fact. The perpetrator of the latest crime must be still at large. Maybe the belief that a woman who was born on 22 July would give birth to Grandsire's victim had been handed down the female line from family to family, and at each stage of the cycle some madman had taken advantage of them? If Pip discarded the project, and did not expose the secret, then this kind of thing could go on in the future. But did he want to be the saviour of Arva? Even the thought was ridiculous. He looked at Dalca, who stood silent, hands clenched by his sides.

'No, I don't want to give up,' Pip repeated. 'I'm here and I'm staying, especially after this morning. Professor, do you know by any chance the maiden name of the mother of the 1952 victim – Catina Albu?'

'No, I don't. Remember, I was brought up elsewhere. Why?'

'Come through to the study,' said Pip, getting up, 'and I'll explain.' But an unpleasant surprise awaited them. The box containing the registers was not on the desk where Pip had left it. In fact, it was nowhere to be found.

'Emilia!' said Dalca and went off to look for her. When he returned, his expression was grim. 'She phoned the bishop in Cluj yesterday and someone came and picked up the registers while I was out and you were with the police. Damn her.' The tone was vicious.

'She was only trying to do the right thing,' replied Pip. He wasn't sure why he was defending her.

'No, she was making sure I didn't find out anything,' snapped Dalca.

'Anyway, I've made most of the notes I need,' added Pip. They sat down and Pip told Dalca his discovery about the dates. The Professor seemed strangely preoccupied during the conversation. He had also turned very pale, and Pip wondered whether he was ill or only under stress. 'Did you know about these dates already?' he asked.

Dalca shook his head.

'So, you think those who are born on 22 July are destined to have children who are Grandsire's victims?' he asked. His voice was quiet and level.

'That's right. But to give my argument more weight, I need to find out about Catina Albu's mother. I'd also like to check on anyone else born on the same date. How can I do that now the registers are gone?'

'You could ask Simona about the Albus.' The tone was flat.

Pip was shocked. Dalca was suggesting that Pip question his mother-in-law, who the last time he had seen her was in no fit state for visitors.

'I may do that. And you know of no-one else who might help?'

'We can't ask Emilia, can we? Nor the priest.'

It was Pip's turn to shake his head at Dalca's sarcasm. He knew if he kept going he would find out. It was often like that in research. You think you are on to something and then you came to a dead end. Like Marcu.

'Well, I think we should prepare ourselves for the gypsy camp tomorrow, don't you?' finished Dalca.

Ghita came home early that evening. They all had dinner together and the conversation was more amicable than Pip had yet experienced in the Dalca house. Pip put it down to Emilia being glad to see her daughter and Dalca grateful for not having to face another row. It was also his first experience of sampling *mamaliga*, a steaming yellow cornmeal mush, which was one of the staples of the Romanian diet. When they had eaten that, which was filling and had been consumed with crusty hunks of bread, Pip had a hearty helping of Emilia's home-bottled fruit. Finally, Dalca proposed a nightcap.

'I'm sorry. I have work to do.' At that moment, Pip thought he couldn't manage a plum brandy! 'Do you mind?'

'Not at all,' replied Dalca.

Then Ghita added,

'I have work to do as well. Perhaps you could help me with some of my English translation, Pip? The passages are extremely difficult.'

The cordial atmosphere in the room vanished at that point. Emilia was fixing him now with what he had come to recognise as her habitual expression – a hostile stare. Whatever her mother thought, he was going to take up Ghita's invitation.

'I'd be happy to do so. Shall we go into the study?' He looked at Dalca for back-up.

'No, I'd rather we went upstairs,' she replied. 'I have all my books in my bedroom.'

'Okay,' he said, not looking at either of her parents, as he was conscious it was probably her intention to irritate them both.

'It's all right, Mother,' she said. 'I'll leave my bedroom door open.'

The hint of mischief in her eyes excited Pip more than he could remember. In fact, he had almost forgotten the last time he had been with a girl – but he began to hope he was going to *be* with Ghita.

Neither Emilia or Dalca answered and, as Pip was climbing the stairs behind her, his brain was searching for the reason she had invited him. Was it because she liked him? She had said she did before she had made him breakfast. In fact, her response had been the nearest to flirting he had experienced in a long time. Pip had always been so obsessed with his work that research had taken precedence over relationships. Now he began to consider a different future than the one he had so far mapped out for himself. As they reached the top of the staircase, he told himself off for even thinking about getting involved with Ghita. Aside from the fact that she was technically engaged, she was also 13 years younger than he was, and probably considered him old. So why did she want to be alone with him? Did she have some hidden agenda? He decided, as she opened the bedroom door, that whatever she wanted from him he would go along with; but he knew, whatever it was, it probably wouldn't be accepted by her parents.

She left the door open. He stood inside looking around the room with surprised eyes. It was minimalist: cool off-white walls with no posters or girlie paraphernalia like his sisters used to have at home. It was a room that he could have been comfortable in, with a carved white-painted wooden desk and typing chair underneath, an anglepoise lamp, her laptop and shelves of books and more books, the bindings of which gave the only colour to a serious student's room, which, as far as he knew, Ghita was hardly ever in. He kept his eyes *off* the bed, until she beckoned him over.

'Come over here, it's more comfortable than the chair.' They sat beside each other. 'I wanted to talk to you alone,' she said, glancing at the open door.

'I gathered that.'

'I'm not being nosy, but what did the police want?'

He sighed. She was going to grill him.

'They delivered a letter to me from Inspector Valentin.'

'The policeman you were going to see?' Her large dark eyes searched his face.

He took off his glasses, and taking out the small cloth from his pocket to polish them, he cursed himself for being so gauche with someone so beautiful.

'Why did *they* deliver it?' she added.

'Valentin is dead.' He came straight out with it, and as he heard her gasp, he cursed himself for being a blundering male. She put her hand to her mouth and dropped it again, then stared down at the white counterpane with even wider eyes. 'I'm sorry, but it's true.' He made sure his tone was gentle. 'He was the victim of a hit and run. At the same time …' he hesitated, '… his house was destroyed by fire.'

'How terrible. He was killed and his house burned down?' she repeated. Her expression was one of complete incredulity. He knew how she felt. Like he had, when he had been told. Pure disbelief.

'Yes.' He was going to add, *His luck certainly ran out*, but he didn't. Instead he waited for her to call him a Jonah again. This time she didn't.

'I think you should give up what you're doing and go home,' she said, looking straight at him. He hadn't expected that reaction.

'Do you want me to?' He winced inside. The question was extraordinarily superficial.

'It's not what *I* want. It's self-preservation.'

'You think I'll be next.' His mouth had gone dry and he moistened his lips with his tongue. How often had he asked himself that in the last few days?

'I hope not.' Her tone was utterly sincere. 'Please tell me how far you've got with your research?' The words came out in a rush.

'I can't tell you the details, but you know I'm trying to finish what Marcu started.'

'This is Romania,' she said, 'and there are people here who don't want you to.' She looked away and stared at the window, where the pale curtains moved slightly in a breeze that had crept through the wooden frames. Ghita got up from the bed, went over to the door, closed it, then came over and sat down again. Pip wondered how long it would take before Emilia came up.

'How do you know that people don't want me to go on with my research? How can you be sure?'

'I just am. You should go home, Pip. I'm frightened.'

He put a gentle hand on her arm and she let it lie there.

'Don't be scared on my behalf. As I told you before, I can look after myself.'

Her smile had been sarcastic when he had said that the

last time. Now she remained unsmiling. 'But can I?' she asked.

He was shocked. The self-assurance he had so admired had left her now. Her expression resembled the one she had worn when he had told her about the man in the churchyard.

'What do you mean?'

'You should ask my grandma,' she replied, 'but she wouldn't be able to tell you anyway. Do you know what, Pip, I'm scared of her. Once ...' she hesitated, '... Once, she tried to kill me!'

'To kill you?' he repeated, horrified. 'Surely not. What did she do?'

'She said everything was my fault. She put a pillow over my face. I remember struggling for breath. It was horrible. I was only about nine. If it hadn't been for Mother coming in, she would have suffocated me.'

Pip knew she was telling the truth.

'Your grandma's a schizophrenic, Ghita. I'm sure she didn't know what she was doing.'

'That's what Mother said, but *I* know she did, Pip. She was sorry afterwards and tried to hug me, but I wouldn't go near her. It took a long time until I let her touch me again.'

Neither spoke for moment, then Pip said,

'But now you go to visit her all the time. Why?'

'Yes, I go, and the worst thing is, it's in case one day she tells me the reason why she did what she did. How can everything that happens and is going to happen to my family be my fault!' Her voice was passionate. 'I don't know why I'm telling you this. I'm going crazy.' She shook her head.

Sudden fear overwhelmed Pip. How many women in Arva had said that in the past?

'You're not,' he replied. 'What about Anton? Could you tell him?'

'He wouldn't understand.'

'Wouldn't he?'

'He's scared himself, but he doesn't show it. We don't talk about things like that. But you know all about these things.'

'I wish I did,' replied Pip, rubbing his forehead. 'But

there's still so much to learn. You could help me too.' A little voice in his head accused him of being manipulative. He ignored it.

'I can't help you,' she said, her lips set in a grim line. 'Mother won't tell me anything until I get married.' She pulled her arm away, but he caught it again.

'For God's sake, Ghita, that's not why you're getting married, is it? ' He felt shaky with anger. 'Listen to me, you don't have to! You can do what you like.'

'I can't. Don't you see? Once I know I can make things right.' She was breathing in quickly now as if she were in pain. 'Once I know the secret, I'll tell!'

He stared at her.

'You mean it?'

'I do. And I'll tell *you*, if that's what you want! Then you can go back to America and leave us all to it.'

The enormity of what she had said overwhelmed him. This was temptation handed to him on a plate. If Ghita married, she would tell him the secret!

Then he remembered Fr Joseph's words. *Every human being has a dark side.* This was his, pressing him to take part in something he abhorred – to tacitly accept the idea that Ghita should be forced into marriage with someone she clearly didn't love, in order that he might learn 'the secret of the marriage bed'.

'Then it will all stop.' she added. 'The ritual will end. Girls won't have to do those horrible things any more. Why don't you say something?'

'I don't know what to say,' he replied.

'Why?'

'Because …' He had no idea how to explain his feelings – and he didn't have to, because Dalca walked in without knocking. He stared at them both.

'I thought you were going to help Ghita with her translation.'

'I wasn't feeling very well, when I got up here,' she replied. 'Pip suggested I had a rest. I was tired. Probably too much *mamaliga*. He's been cheering me up, Tată.'

Pip assumed it was a pet name she used for her father. He saw Dalca's expression soften.

'Well, I think you should get to bed now if you're tired. What do you say, Pip?'

'I agree,' he replied. 'I hope you have a good sleep, Ghita. I'm sure you'll feel better in the morning. Hopefully, I can help you with your English translation then.'

'I don't think so,' replied Dalca. 'Remember, we have an appointment.'

As Pip walked out of the door, he fielded Ghita's imperceptible shake of the head. There was no need for her to warn him not to say anything about their conversation to her father. He had no intention of doing so. All he wanted to do at that moment was to go back to his own room and think about what she had told him.

13

Great flakes of snow whirled over the landscape, carried by a powerful wind off the mountains that stormed its winter way towards the village. Superstitious housewives in outlying farms closed their shutters hurriedly to prevent demons coming down from the wind and possessing their bodies. But in the basement of the Dalcas' house, the two men heard only the faintest sound of the wind's wild laughter.

After breakfast, Pip had been summoned into the study by Dalca. He was sure he looked as tired as the Professor. He hadn't slept well as he was turning over so many things in his mind. The few weeks he had experienced in the medieval atmosphere of a country so far removed from his own, were already taking a toll on him. But he told himself once more that he had chosen this research path and would not think of giving up. He owed it to himself and to Marcu – as well as to the women of Arva.

'I hope you're ready for today,' said Dalca. He was smart. He looked as if he recognised how Pip felt. *Lucky he can't read my mind as well as he can my face*, thought Pip.

'I sure am,' he replied as enthusiastically as he could.

'Before we set off for the gypsy camp and you meet Eva, I want to fill you in a bit more regarding the ritual.' Dalca steepled his fingers. Pip recognised the body language. It meant he was in charge.

'Great,' replied Pip, switching on his laptop. He sat back

and waited for the surprises.

'The old lady knows more about the Arvan ritual than I do,' said Dalca. 'My knowledge is limited to what I have discovered through my own research and through being the husband of an Arvan woman. However, she has had first-hand experience.'

Pip felt the old excitement run through him. It had been absent of late, giving way to other, more disturbing emotions.

'I can't wait to meet her,' he said, trying to banish from his mind the scared look on Ghita's face when he had gone to her room the night before. 'You mean that she has taken part in the ritual? I thought gypsies were exempt.'

'They are, but it does not stop them observing.' He paused, then continued. 'There is One who has seen ... But I think we should leave that for later!'

'I hope he'll be there!' Pip felt slightly irritated that Dalca could say something, then immediately renege on it, but his excitement was growing. He was actually going to meet someone who had observed the ritual! How much would Marcu have given for that? Perhaps he had had no-one to introduce him to the gypsies? Pip wondered if he had discussed them with Eisenmann. It really needled him that he had no record of Marcu's final meeting with the German in Cologne.

'*She* will be present,' replied Dalca. 'She is Eva's granddaughter, who cares for her.'

Another grandchild, thought Pip.

Dalca continued, 'Now – back to the ritual. We have spoken of this in an earlier conversation, but what I am about to tell you now is somewhat different. You know I believe the ritual is a perversion of Catholic rites. In my studies of the occult, I have come to the recent conclusion that our Arvan ritual fits many of the cultural traditions of Eastern Europe.'

'I didn't think the occult was part of your course,' said Pip, and regretted it immediately when he caught Dalca's disapproving look.

'I told you before that you joke too much,' said Dalca, 'but I shall put it down to your youthfulness and inexperience.'

Ouch, thought Pip, wishing he could explain that it was part of his nature to be flippant when faced with serious issues.

'Sorry. Please carry on.'

'As a perversion, the ritual is sacrilegious. Have you ever heard of a witches' Sabbath?'

'Certainly,' replied Pip. 'It is where witches congregate to make a pact with the Devil, isn't it?' He didn't feel much like laughing at that moment. Valentin had been studying the occult, and look what had happened to him!

'Quite so. And the rites this Sabbath entails are sacrilegious practices that pervert sacred services and often take place on holy ground. During these frolics, children are bewitched and devils make music and dance – amongst other things! Am I making sense?'

'Yes,' said Pip. 'You're making parallels with Arva churchyard, the bewitching of an innocent victim and Grandsire's song that the girls have to learn and perform on the day?'

'Good. And the dancing?' Pip frowned at the question. 'I can see that idea is new to you. Did you know that turning someone around three times was a magical practice?'

'No, I didn't, although Irina said that the turning around before her daughter took the stony path, signified the Trinity.'

'And what could be regarded as more *magic* than that fiction, which was plucked out of the air by Tertullian in the early part of the 3rd Century?'

Pip was not surprised at the viciousness of the remark. Again he wished he knew why Dalca was so violently anti-religious.

'Yes,' the Professor continued, 'such turning around is documented. Other strange occurrences and signs took place involving children – often they were changed by demonic possession. For example, the belief was held that, in some cases, they took the place of their parents.'

Pip stared at him.

'You mean that it was believed a child could change into an old person?' He was thinking of Valentin's account of his visit to Anka Petrescu's house.

'Perhaps. I am telling you this, so that you understand what we are up against. I told you earlier that the villagers are superstitious, and I did not mean only those in the village itself, but also those in the surrounding neighbourhood. There are other elements to the Arvan ritual too. Often witches have been accused of causing storms and bringing hail to destroy the crops. This was, of course, the peasants' explanation for natural catastrophes.' He smiled.

'You're referring to the legend of ice piercing the clouds? When the priest rings the bell?' Pip brought up the passage from Irina Petrescu's testimony on the laptop. '*The bells were pretty, piercing the ice in the clouds.*' He looked up. 'But the footnote says, *A local superstition that tolling bells will disperse hail and prevent it from falling and the crops being spoiled.*'

'That is the perversion. The reality of the priest ringing the bell to disperse the hail is perverted, as witches really welcome it. That's what you believe if you are superstitious. Everything is turned upside down. A violent storm can also be viewed as another sign to prepare us for Grandsire's resurrection. All over Europe, uneducated people still believe in storm demons, who bring bad weather, cause illness and attack people in various ways.'

'A summer storm broke the cross in Arva churchyard and afterwards no-one would replace it,' Pip said, almost mechanically, because at that moment his mind was split between his visit to Grandsire's tomb and the catastrophic storm in Sunny Mead when, as a 13 year old, he had crawled through the long grass by Kiefer Adams' storm drain to the chalet by the lake, frantic he would not be able to save his siblings from Diep Koppelberg.

'I can see you are thinking that over,' said Dalca, trying to guess what was on his mind. 'It is also a fact that when witches were tried, priests – who *purport* to be godly men – were present. For example, when witches were tried by water, it was believed to be similar to the rite of Baptism.'

'So, if the priest was not godly ...' said Pip, dragging

himself out of the past, 'then he could be seen as instigating and even approving of evil.'

Dalca nodded.

Pip breathed in as he formulated the hypothesis. 'To sum up, the Arvan ritual has its roots in a witches' Sabbath in which Grandsire *aka* the Devil is conjured and comes to claim an innocent victim in certain years.' His common sense would have dismissed all this as nonsense, but with an open mind and a psychologist's training, he could see it had possibilities in the beliefs of a supernatural peasantry. As a realist, he was not ready to swallow Dalca's explanation. On the other hand, how could he make sense of what he had experienced in his visions? Or what had appeared on his laptop? Added to that, inexplicable things continued to occur in Arva in a 36-year cycle. Evil things. That *was* a fact. If only he could prove how many times these particular rapes and murders had occurred in the distant past! But he had no records to support him in his search. He remembered Marcu's frustrated jottings about taking account of the paranormal. Now he knew how his predecessor must have felt.

'Am I right, Professor? Is that what you are saying?' he repeated.

'Something like that,' said Dalca. 'But it is only a theory, which needs fleshing out. This may well come later. As to the identity of Grandsire, who may or may not be the Devil, have you ever heard of the *tisztátalanok*?' Pip shook his head. He did not recognise the word.

'Who or what are they?'

'The evil dead, whose greatest happiness is to possess a particular area or even a house.' Pip shivered at the thought. 'They are spirits who are caught between here and the hereafter, who enter the bodies of the unwary, freeing their prey of time and space dimensions. Many of these spirits pose as skilled musicians, whose music enchants all who hear it. Finally, their victims are possessed and journey to another world. Are you all right, Pip?' Dalca stopped.

'I'm fine,' he replied, but he didn't feel it. All he could

think of at that moment was Diep Koppelberg.

'We should take a break now,' said the Professor. 'I shall go and make coffee. Then we shall set out for the gypsy camp.'

Pip nodded, but didn't speak.

As Dalca entered the kitchen, he was considering the effect his words had provoked. He had an uncanny instinct that Pip, though presenting himself as rational and an unbeliever, had experienced the supernatural in some form. But he realised that the boy would never admit to it unless he wormed it out of him. Maybe confronting him with the supernatural in the form of Eva Kirchma's story was the only way to bring Pip's experiences to the surface? Dalca had always found it was better to face such experiences head-on, as he himself had been forced to do.

Once again, the Professor found himself believing that this foreigner had been sent to them on purpose. But who had done so? Unlike Emilia, Dalca had no belief in God, only fate. He feared that now the Marcu Papers had been located, the young American, whom he had brought to Arva, stood a good chance of losing both his project and his life. Yet he still hoped that the only human who had personal knowledge as to Grandsire's identity, and also the power to destroy Pip, might have made a fatal mistake. Instead of succumbing to the enemy, Pip could prove himself to be the village's redemption, resulting in the destruction of their mutual enemy. Why Pip had been chosen for the task was not yet clear to Dalca, but he realised that the choice could not have been accidental. If he could only learn what had happened in the young doctor's past, he might begin to understand.

'Should I bring my laptop along?' asked Pip.

Dalca shrugged.

'They have electricity, but I don't know if they will be happy for you to use it. Maybe a notebook?'

'Okay, I'll go and get one. But I'll bring the laptop anyway.' He had become paranoid about anyone accessing the information contained in the computer. Not that Emilia would know how to – but Ghita was a different matter, although he didn't like to think that *she* would try in any circumstance.

The temperature outside had dropped since breakfast. He looked out of the window and was amazed to see a light film of snow on the village roofs. *I'll need my parka today*, he thought, and brought it out of the wardrobe. Then he found a reporter's pad and made sure his pen was working, but also took two pencils just in case. At the bottom of his backpack was a sealed foolscap envelope containing the letter from New York regarding Arvarescu's photograph and several other items he had detached from the Marcu Papers in readiness for the visit to Valentin. On a whim, he slipped the envelope into his laptop's carrying case.

Then he sat down and brought up the data he had scanned in on the Marcu Papers. As a good researcher, he needed to check that he had read the information properly before progressing to new notes. Dr Baescu had told Marcu that Eva Kirchma had been the village prostitute. It would be embarrassing to make a mistake about such sensitive information! He wasn't sure if he should raise the issue with Dalca. Zipping up his parka, he ran down the stairs and paused for a moment.

He could hear Emilia in the kitchen, but there was still no sign of Ghita. She had probably been so tired after their session the night before that she had slept in. The front door was ajar.

The Professor was already waiting for him in the car, with the engine ticking over and the fog from the exhaust billowing into the cold air like a ghostly cloud.

'I was surprised to see the snow,' said Pip.

'It's not much,' replied Dalca. 'Probably blown down by the wind off the mountains. But more is on its way. You'll need that then.' He indicated Pip's parka. He himself was wearing a heavy sweater and black trousers under a dusty black overcoat, which needed replacing. The overall effect was funereal.

'How far is the camp?' asked Pip.

'Several miles. Gypsies usually live on the outskirts. They're not welcome too near habitation.'

Pip glanced at Dalca, recognising the bitterness in his tone.

They continued on the road through the village, which soon led between open fields covered in snow. On one side the meadows sloped their way towards the mountains, with only small spinneys of woodland to break the undulating monotony. *Now might be the time to mention Eva Kirchma*, thought Pip. He realised he risked a sarcastic response, but he needed to know before they arrived at their destination.

'This is probably an indelicate question.' Pip's Romanian was good, but the finer nuances of the language were lost on him. He was just going to have to come out with, *Was she always a prostitute?*

Dalca didn't take his eyes off the road as he considered the question.

'She is over one hundred years old.'

It had served Pip right. He realised that Dalca's tart reply was also an effort to satirise his inadequate use of tense.

'I mean in the past,' Pip persisted.

'I believe so. But when you meet them you will be sorry for asking me that question.'

They were passing a horse and cart at that moment, and Pip realised it was the same vehicle that had driven straight at him when he was looking for the Dalca house. The young man was driving again and the woman passenger was wearing a flimsy dress and the same flowered headscarf. Both were attired inadequately for such a cold morning. As they passed, Pip noticed a new addition – a small, pretty dark-haired child of about three with a stick in her hand, who was balanced in a precarious position at the back of the cart and trailing the stick along in the dust.

'Gypsies,' said Dalca.

'Are they going into Arva?'

'No, begging in Cluj. I am sorry to say that most of the

Romanian gypsies' revenue is derived from that occupation. They will use the child.'

'If she doesn't fall off the cart first,' was Pip's dry response.

'She will not. She has been left to explore for herself ever since she was born. Gypsy children are encouraged to be independent. Do you know that some five or six year olds can recognise what is valuable scrap metal and what is not? '

'I didn't know that,' said Pip.

'I have not seen that particular family before,' said Dalca. 'They are probably nomadic. Eva and Anya are what we call sedentary gypsies, who remain in one place, unless of course they are kicked out. A few have remained in this area since the Second World War. They were the lucky ones. Others were transported first to Transnistria and then on to places like Auschwitz.'

Pip went cold at the thought.

'But not Eva Kirchma?'

'She had her protectors,' said Dalca. 'I am not in the mood for more questions on that subject. I do not like to think of the Holocaust and the loss of half a million of my people. In any case, she might tell you herself.'

Pip could appreciate his attitude, although he would have liked to hear more. He had had no idea that so many gypsies had been exterminated.

'Over there,' said Dalca, indicating. Pip looked just before they swung left onto a cart track. He could see smoke rising. 'This place is not pleasant,' the Professor added.

As they approached, they could see no parked caravans as Pip had imagined, but a jumble of shacks with tin roofs, protected by a patch of woodland. As they drove nearer, he could see that several roofs were slipping off, and his impression was that the shacks were little more than sheds. However, he noticed there were still television aerials. The encampment reminded him of shanty towns in South Africa or Asia that he had seen on television.

'It doesn't smell too good either,' said Dalca, 'although

there are some efforts being made to clean it up, so the sewage doesn't run into the drinking water. You look shocked. You'll be pleased to know that our destination is a little more comfortable.'

Dalca parked the car, and Pip's nose was hit by the raw smell. As they walked towards the shacks, dogs started barking in unison. Then several headscarved women appeared, one or two carrying babies. When they saw them, they nodded at Dalca, but before they turned and went back into the sheds, Pip was the recipient of several curious glances. 'They thought we might be tourists,' explained Dalca. 'Rich pickings, I'm afraid. In spite of numerous warnings, foreigners arrive looking for the picturesque and are relieved of their wallets. Watch your laptop.'

Pip held on to his carrying case tightly.

They continued until they came to an area where several miserable-looking wooden carts were parked and several horses grazed. 'Over there,' said Dalca. Pip was almost as surprised as when he had seen the priest's house. A large trailer was parked by one or two sheds. Washing strung across from the shed to the motor home was flapping in the wind. The once-white vehicle was not smart but was incongruous amidst the poverty, and was more the type of thing Pip had been expecting to see in a gypsy camp. As they approached, a middle-aged woman appeared in the doorway. To Pip's surprise, she ran down the steps towards them. She was small, but dainty and dark of complexion; so dark that Pip thought she was Asian.

'Simu!' A moment later, she and the Professor were exchanging kisses, cheek to cheek. But what they said to each other gave Pip no hint as to their relationship, given that he couldn't understand a word.

Dalca turned. He was smiling for the first time that morning. 'Anya, this is Dr Durrant.'

The woman held out her hand. She was definitely of Asian descent. Maybe in her early sixties, thought Pip.

'I am pleased to meet you,' she said simply. Pip could imagine her eyes had once been wonderfully dark, but now they had sunk in slightly under hooded brows, yet her skin was almost unlined and stretched over fine cheekbones. Anya had once been a very good-looking woman. He wondered if she had followed the same profession as her grandmother, then dismissed the thought as unworthy.

'Me too,' he offered his hand.

She turned back to Dalca and spoke again in what Pip now realised must be the Romany language.

'Don't worry, I'll translate if necessary,' said the Professor.

Anya ushered them both into the trailer. As Pip entered, he could see what Dalca had meant by *comfortable*. The trailer was well-kept inside and clean. There were no luxuries, but it was welcoming, with a well-worn rug on which were printed tiny red roosters. Something stirred in Pip's memory, but then his eyes were drawn to a large armchair in which slumped what appeared to be the humped body of a very small person, almost completely covered with brightly-crocheted blankets.

'Grandmother is asleep,' said Anya. 'But she'll wake soon. I have prepared her for your coming. Tea?'

They drank the dark beverage from dainty china mugs, which Anya took down from a cupboard beside the small television set. When they were settled, Anya said, 'Simu tells me that you would like to know our history, doctor.'

'Pip, please.'

'Pip,' she smiled.

'Short for Philip.'

She nodded at the explanation.

'Simu did not tell you my nickname.?' She glanced at the Professor. 'It is Black Anya.'

'Thank you.' Pip hoped he did not look embarrassed. He couldn't imagine anyone introducing themselves in that way in the States, or anywhere else in fact.

'You call me just Anya,' she explained. Her eyes told him she had noted his discomfiture.

'Sure,' he nodded.

So he had been right. Many gypsies were dark-skinned.

He knew the story of their origins. It had once been thought that their people derived from Egypt, but now it was believed they could be traced back to medieval India. Pip was convinced this woman's ethnic background pointed to a more recent link with India. For the hundredth time that morning, he felt both excitement and apprehension as to what these women were going to tell him about Grandsire. Then the hump in the armchair stirred.

Pip and Dalca sat facing the old lady, whose black, bird-bright eyes appeared to be the only living thing in her face. Yet Pip wanted to hear more than anything what still lingered in that century-old brain. He had never before met anyone as old, and he marvelled at the depth of the wrinkles that criss-crossed her parchment-thin skin like river tributaries. What struck him most was, although her complexion was spotted with age, it was white. Her long dewlap trembled as she spoke Romany to her granddaughter in a trembling voice. Anya looked from her grandmother to Pip.

'Simu has explained everything to me, and I to my grandmother,' said the girl. 'We both know the importance of this meeting and its possible outcome for all of us, but both she and I need your promise that what passes between the four of us in this room today will remain a secret.'

Dalca cut in:

'Anya means that when your work on the Marcu Papers is complete, you must never divulge your sources. I know this might present a difficulty, but I am sure you will be able to overcome it in time.'

Pip understood by Dalca's expression as he said this that he had in mind the fact that, by the end of the project, Eva Kirchma would probably have passed away.

'I understand.' Another promise, another secret.

'I shall translate Eva's words,' said Dalca, 'and add any explanations needed as we go along. Later Anya will have her say. Your notebook?' Pip withdrew it and his pen. 'Later, you can add the narrative to your data. You wanted to learn about 1916? Now you will. We must get on, or Eva will be tired again.' He smiled at Anya. *He is certainly a different man here from when he is at home*, thought Pip. *I wonder why?* He leaned forward in the chair, pen at the ready, his heartbeat accelerating with the excitement of the true researcher.

14

1916

Eva was grown-up for a ten-year old, although she was not quite sure how old she was or on what day her birthday fell. But she knew where she was going. Both gypsy and *gorgio* understood that if they were in danger and the Austrian enemies came down from the hills, the village people would make for the safety of the church on the hill. Fr Pathan had been clear about that. He was a gentleman as well as a priest and treated them all the same. Her mother said it was because of his race. It was rumoured he was the son of a nobleman from Portugal and a dark woman. But the only things Eva noticed were his proud bearing and his dark curls. She loved him with the heart and soul of any little girl for a man as much above her as he was. He did not treat her like a slave, which her mother had been to men.

It was very early in the morning and summer lightning had been making the landscape crackle for two whole days. Eva had little knowledge of how the fire from the sky could bring down the trees at will. She had crept out of her bed to make her way to Arva church, because she had listened hard when on the night before her mother had said 'The priest will be ringing the bell tomorrow.' She wanted to hear again the pretty noise that she had not heard for many months. Most of all she wanted to see the priest ringing it. That was why she was out at dawn. For what reason the dark father was ringing the bell was no concern of hers. She only wanted to see him. If he would not let her into the church, then she would wait outside until he came out. The only fear she had was of meeting enemy soldiers in the woods. But she had heard her father say that their own forces would be driving them back over the border soon, and then everything would be all right. She knew war was a terrible thing.

It was hard work going uphill, and the stones hurt her bare feet. Gypsies know all about birds, but she could hear none in the red dawn and thought they must all still be asleep. 'Fr Pathan will wake you up,' she said, staring at the massive forest trees that bowed their heads to the wind. Eva was afraid of the gale that brought demons down with it, that would take you back up and throw you around in the clouds. She was more afraid of demons than of soldiers!

The gate was open. She liked the churchyard and sometimes would walk through it looking at the pictures of dead children. Sometimes a big boy came to the churchyard with his pigs. He was as ugly as a wind demon, and Eva was afraid of him. He had a leg that he dragged behind him. She hoped she wouldn't see him that morning; and anyway, the bell would frighten the pigs and he would have to run away after them.

A strange mist was creeping through the churchyard, wreathing the church tower itself. She had not seen any mist in the meadow below. It made her hurry in case the evil ones had come down from the clouds and were waiting for her. When she reached the church door it was locked. 'Father?' She rattled the latch, which was so large that she needed her two hands. 'Father, are you in there?' No reply.

Then the bell crashed above her. She was so scared that she ran crazily back down the path and crouched behind a bush. She would wait there until Fr Pathan came out. Maybe he would carry her home. She smiled, but the smile soon died on her lips, because she saw the boy from the farm outside the church gates. Why was he there at this time in the morning? At that moment she hated him.

She watched his black hat bobbing as he crept behind the tombstones.

Eva shrank back. She was afraid what might happen to her if he saw her. And the wind was getting up, howling. She knew it was the demons as the rain began to fall, spotting her face with huge drops. 'Father, come out and help me,' she prayed, but the bell was still booming, and it didn't sound pretty any more. The storm was cracking around her and Eva shut her eyes. When she opened them, she saw the tall man, wrapped in a cloak, with a hood falling over his face. She guessed it must be a soldier. If he saw her, he would run her through with his sword. He was standing in the shade of the trees where the big tomb lay – the one with the cross on top and with the children dancing round the edge. She loved it. Why were they dancing? She wanted to dance like that in a circle. Why didn't the soldier make for the church porch, as the rain beat off him and the sky flashed fire? She watched, terrified, as his hood slipped down and he threw off his cloak. *He was not a soldier.* She had never seen clothes like his before, striped yellow and red, fitting him like a viper's skin. And he had his head turned to the sky, his yellow hair streaming free. Eva knew he was very angry. She could hear him roaring like a bull, mingling his voice with the thunder, stretching his hands to the sky as if he was bringing the lightning down. She couldn't hear the bell anymore. She put her hands over her ears and closed her eyes, but the stranger's voice was still piercing her and his image would not disappear.

Then she felt the tread of footsteps and squinted up in horror. The man stood looking down at her. At that moment she thought she was going to die. He stooped. His wolf-blue eyes reflected the lightning as they bored into her face, strafing her shivering little body. Now she saw he was much more ugly than the crippled boy. His cruel, sharp teeth showed as he snarled at her. Then Eva knew. *He was a demon.*

All she could remember afterwards was looking up at the sky, which was a still, pure grey, and feeling the hush about her. Eva thought she was dead and closed her eyes tightly again.

Then, cold with horror, she felt herself lifted high into the air. She screamed and opened her eyes to look into the kind, dark face. The demon had gone!

'Father,' she sobbed. 'Father.'

'Eva,' the priest said, placing his soft lips against her cheek. The terrified child snuggled deep into his arms. From that moment, Eva Kirchma was lost.

2007

The old woman's eyes were closed as she finished speaking. A sombre silence followed, and no-one spoke. 'So she has seen Grandsire,' said Pip, shaken by the face-to-face account. 'And the boy must have been Claudiu Basa?'

'Just so,' replied Dalca. Then Pip was calculating again. So Fr Joseph had been right. There had been no victim in 1916. He breathed out in relief. He wasn't sure how he felt. It was a mixture of elation and disbelief. A little voice in his head was telling him it was about time he took the idea on board that Grandsire was, as Eva had said, some kind of demon.

'What did Eva mean by saying she was lost after that?' he asked.

Dalca and Anya exchanged glances.

'The priest became her lover,' replied the Professor, 'and she had his child eight years later. So much for his vow of chastity.'

Pip had not been expecting that. Then he wanted to ask how, then, she had become a prostitute, but he decided this was not the time. In any case, he was too stunned. He had met someone who had seen Grandsire close to. He breathed in. He had to know.

'Would it be possible to ask ...' he hesitated.

'You can ask anything,' said Anya.

'... If your grandmother would look at a photograph?'

Dalca stared at Pip. His eyes clearly asked, *What photograph?*

'I'm sure she would,' said Anya. 'Her eyes are still good. But this is not the right time. Telling the story has taken its toll.'

Looking across at Eva, Pip realised that she was dozing again.

Anya must have seen Pip's disappointment, because she added, 'I'll make sure that she sees it before you leave. Besides, she has other things to tell you. You are honoured. It is a long time since her last confession.' Pip didn't know how to respond. 'I think this is the time for us all to have some *tuica*.'

'Only recently distilled, I may add,' Dalca smiled. 'And made from plums!'

The alcohol burned its fiery way down Pip's throat. 'Are you feeling better now?' asked Anya. 'You had gone pale. Doubtless you have other questions to ask – for instance, about …' She hesitated. '… About my grandmother's personal life?'

'It isn't really my business,' said Pip.

'It may not be, but it is relevant to the situation. My grandmother had been promised as a young child to a boy of a good gypsy family. This is done in our culture, maybe even as young as six or seven. Naturally, after her … affair – I think that is how you would say it?' She raised her eyebrows. 'Neither family, hers or his, would own her. She became even more of an outcast than gypsies usually are to those who mistrust them. Forgive me, that was not meant to be offensive. Pathan would not marry her, and could not keep her, so she took the only path open to her. But she bore no more children after Magda. I think you understand why she may have called her baby by that name? After the fallen one?'

Pip sighed and nodded.

'It was not easy to be my mother,' continued Anya, 'although I never knew her. Her end was particularly difficult, but I shall leave my grandmother to tell you. She is awake again. She likes some *tuica* too.' She went over and held a small glass to Eva's lips. 'This part of her story will be more unpleasant, but she has declared that this abomination in our midst must be destroyed.' Pip heard Anya's voice falter and braced himself for what was to come.

Dalca sighed. 'We are about to hear of a cruel time, Pip. The First World War in Romania – which country did not then exist in name – was very different from in the West. It was waged against the Austro-Hungarian Empire, of which it had been an unwilling part. The Romanians signed a treaty with the Allies on 17 August 1916 and entered the war on 28 August 1916. They had allies of their own, and together they drove the Austro-Hungarians out of the Carpathians, but their success was short-lived. However, I do not wish to bore you with details of my country's defeats.

'But in 1942 …' He hesitated. 'This will be painful for us all, but even more so for the three of us – Eva, Anya and myself. In August 1942, a decree was issued for the confiscation of the goods and properties of both Jews and gypsies. Those such as Eva who could prove they had been sedentary for ten years were offered some hope that they could stay. The rest were deported to Transnistria for settlement in groups of 1,200 to 1,600. By the end of August, 13,000 gypsies had crossed over. By September it was the turn of the sedentary gypsies in rural and urban territories to be shipped out. So what do you imagine happened to Eva and Magda?' He stopped. Pip sat in silence.

'We should ask her now,' said Anya.

Dalca nodded, and a moment later, Anya was whispering in her mother's ear. Although Pip was struck by the horror of it all, at least another visitation from Grandsire could not be added to the mounting terror of the Nazi war machine. If Pip's calculations were to be trusted, Grandsire was not scheduled to appear again until 1952.

'My daughter, Magda, was beautiful,' began Eva in a trembling voice. 'Far more so than I had ever been. And it was good for our trade. She had followed me into it, as she had no option. And there were many soldiers who came to use us – and not only our own. But in the June of 1942, she was visited by a German. Considering they treated us as animals, their custom was not expected. When they had gone inside the van, I heard her screaming. Very loudly. I had been sent outside at pistol point. The soldier was drunk.' The old woman hesitated for a moment, and Anya turned her head away.

'By the time I managed to get in, he had done his business. I remember he still had his pants down. He was fat but powerful, and my girl had stood no chance. Although she was a prostitute, until then she had taken only men that did not make her vomit. Bruised and broken, she was cowering with terror on the floor. I dared not go near her at first, as he was waving a pistol about; but in the end, I did. I threw myself on the floor beside her. I remember praying to God that we would survive. But it was not God who helped us!' For a moment her voice faded, and Pip dared to glance across at Dalca, who had stumbled somewhat over the translation. His face was pale and his eyes glittered.

'Then the door of the van burst open,' Eva resumed. 'I was trying to comfort my Magda, my arms around her, trying to protect her broken frame from yet another assailant. In the dim lamplight I could see only a pair of shining boots. We clung to each other, hardly daring to breathe, but I could feel Magda's sobs vibrating through the whole of my body. I looked up, and the newcomer had his back to me. He was wearing the cloak of a high-ranking officer. He did not speak, but the next moment, the van shuddered with a shot, and the beast who had raped Magda was spreadeagled upon the floor.

'I wanted to struggle up and kiss the boots of our saviour, but I was too afraid. He turned around, and then it was my turn to scream. He stooped and stared at me from wolf-blue eyes, smiled at me with white, sharp teeth. His blond hair fell across his forehead under his peaked cap.

'"No screaming, Eva," he said. "You cheated me before. Now you owe me!"

'I don't know how he knew my name, but it was the same man I had seen in the churchyard all those years before. *And he had not aged.* "I shall come back to reclaim what is mine," he said. He straightened, and his shadow fell over both of us. We felt its darkness in every bone. That shadow tormented us with the evil of war, the cries of the suffering, the knowledge of all things black. It took many days for us to recover.

'The body of Magda's attacker was taken away later by four silent soldiers, and in spite of the deportation of all our neighbours, no-one bothered us. It was not until September that Magda got sick. Not with an illness from the filthy water and lack of food, but from being with child.

'She carried it within her until, after a terrible labour, she brought it forth – a little girl. She died two days later, leaving her child an orphan ...'

Eva tried to move forwards in the chair, but she was too weak and fell back. A weeping Anya rushed to her. Together she and Dalca made the old lady comfortable. Pip did not know what to say. He felt useless at the story of such suffering, and his stomach curdled at the thought of the German officer. *He had not aged.* The words echoed in his head as he remembered Simona Murgu's testimony as to what Claudiu Basa had told her in 1952.

I saw him 36 years ago. And he looked just the same then. Just as young. Claudiu Basa had seen him in the churchyard at the same time as Eva Kirchma. Pip felt sick. Was the stranger *he* had seen in the churchyard only a few days earlier the same man? But he didn't want to think about it. Not yet. Not until Eva had seen the photograph. Then he remembered with relief that the eyes of the stranger he'd seen had been black, like a snake's, not blue.

He jumped as he felt a hand on his shoulder. 'Is it too much for you?' asked Dalca.

'No. Is there more?' Pip was doing his best to stay calm, although he felt as if he had been through the whole horrible experience himself. He also had the instinct there was worse to come.

'I'm afraid so.'

Pip swallowed. He didn't want to hear more, but on the other hand he was eager for some explanation. One thing he did know was that Anya was Magda's daughter. How could she be so normal?

'I brought up my grandchild,' Eva went on, 'and she stands before you now. They called her "Black Anya" because of her complexion. Whereas her mother, Magda, was fair, with a pure skin the colour of porcelain, Anya was dark; a throwback to her cursed grandfather. One would never have known she was the product of our drunken conqueror.' Eva spat the word out as if something bitter had come into her mouth. 'Pathan continued to be priest here. He had long given up any thought of me or his daughter. He was ashamed of his sin, but he was not granted the consolation of a Christian confession. Besides, we were gypsies. Once I had loved him, now I felt nothing, but when I heard the church bell, I spat upon the ground. We were outcasts to our own. Even our clients reviled us.'

'Grandmother, we have had one blessing. Someone to lean on.' Anya's gentle rebuke brought Pip out of the story. He wanted to ask who the person was, whether the small comforts they possessed at present had been bought from prostitution or this unknown benefactor.

Eva took no notice. 'Once I was beautiful,' she said, 'but soon it was left to my granddaughter to care for me and to bring in the bread. And her story is as terrible as mine.'

'What about the man – the Nazi?' asked Pip. He couldn't help himself. '*Did* he come back?'

The old woman was silent. Her bird-bright eyes stared into nothing.

'Not yet, Grandmother. Do not show him yet. Rest now,' said Anya, covering her with the blanket.

'Show me what?' asked Pip, eager but afraid at the same time. He saw Dalca lean forward and grip Anya's arm as if to detain her.

'He will understand later, Simu,' she said in a strong voice. She turned to Pip. 'I have known for many years that what happened to us all was ordained, like many things that happen here in Arva. We are an unfortunate people, gypsies and *gorgios* alike. At least we gypsies do not have the agony of watching our young ones sacrificed. But we must be the witnesses. Like Eva, I was drawn to the churchyard in the summer of my tenth year. 1952.'

Pip shivered inside. A Grandsire year. Had Anya seen

the rape of Catina Albu? She must have seen the question in his eyes. 'Yes, I saw the little victim,' she said. 'The dawn was red, but it was streaked by floating dark clouds. I remember them in particular, because I thought they were bringing back the storm that had raged all night. The lightning had cracked about our van and torn off three tin roofs in our camp. It had brought down some forest trees, and I'd climbed over one's trunk on my way to the churchyard. I must have looked like a small, dark fly caught in a web of branches. Hidden by the bushes, I crept along the side of the path.

'Then I saw a girl "coming down" from the churchyard. She was plump and pretty. I was angry because I'd missed seeing the girls "going up". She was kicking the stones and looked miserable. Then I watched her leave the path in front of me and make her way over to the farmer's house by the church. When I was in sight of the farm, I could see her sitting down by the front door as if she was waiting for someone.'

'Simona Murgu,' breathed Pip, hardly daring to glance at Dalca.

'I was wondering whether or not to go home, but at that moment I noticed a man, wearing a tall black hat, darting out from behind the pigsty at the back of the house. The girl in front did not see him.'

Pip caught his breath. His imagination was walking all the way with Anya.

'He was dragging his leg, but he was running as if he was late. I followed him. He was so fast that he darted in through the churchyard gates before me. I knew who it was. The cripple who watched the girls "go up" every year. Claudiu Basa. He was an outcast like the gypsies. I wanted to see what he did. If it was true that he was the Grandsire.

'But he hid himself on the edge of the churchyard, like a black tea leaf in my grandmother 's fortune-telling cup. I knew it was so that he could get away. I crouched behind a bush and waited, with the bell booming above me.

'Then another girl came into the churchyard. She was small and pale, wearing a pretty white skirt and blouse with embroidered sleeves, a black apron and a headscarf. She was carrying a doll dressed exactly like her. She was so pretty that I envied her. When she was near the tomb, she began to sing, and her voice cut through the dawn like a shepherd piping to call his sheep. Sometimes I hear the song in my head, as clearly as I heard it that day. The bell was still ringing to greet the morning, but it didn't drown the shrill notes of the song. I looked up to the church tower and cursed my grandfather, who did not care about us anymore, who let terrible things happen.'

Pip felt colder than ever. He shivered again.

'Then another man appeared from behind the tomb, creeping round it like an evil shadow. I prayed to God that the cripple would help me and the girl, but I could only see his hat bobbing up and down. He must have been craning his neck to watch. Now the girl was bending and burying her doll in the stones. I felt my hands sweating and my heart pounding. I wanted to scream to her that the demon was coming up on her from behind. And then there was a sizzle of lightning and she stumbled, and he fell upon her like a wolf falls on a sheep.'

'Did you see his face?' Pip burst out.

'No. I saw her feet though, and I heard her screaming, when the stones came alive.'

'Alive?' Pip swallowed. He was living through it all with Anya.

'Like a river. At first I thought it was water … then rats … or a river of blood. Or maybe just the red dawn on the stones. The man straightened and she was in his arms! He lifted her high into the sky and I was dazzled by the brightness around him. Whether it was the sun or something just as bright, I didn't know. Then he threw her, and she flew out of his arms and crawled along the ground towards the gate. A moment later, he turned. His hair was gold. I saw the glint of something under his cloak. I knew he was looking at me, but I was dazzled by the sky. I tried to run, but I couldn't. I thought he was coming for me next. I was nearly fainting with fear. I couldn't see for the brightness, and when I could, he was gone.

'I ran down the path, my feet scraped by the stones. I

didn't know what had happened to that poor little girl. I only knew I couldn't help her. Where she went I didn't know. But now I do. She flew to the Inn Sancipia. I had seen the Little and Chosen. I had seen the Grandsire.

'I ran past the farmer's house, cracking the branches as I ran. They must have heard me inside the farm, because I made such a noise. I didn't know where the first girl – the pretty and miserable one – had gone, but I have since heard she was inside with the lame one.'

Pip looked at Dalca, but he had his eyes closed.

'Since that day, I have never been back to the churchyard. And I never shall.'

She stopped. The fire in the stove crackled, but no-one stirred. Then, all of sudden, Eva Kirchma sat up.

'Fetch me my scrying bowl!' she said. Anya started. 'Fetch it,' she repeated.

'Not yet, Grandmother. Not until you have told him the rest.'

Not more, prayed Pip, but a little voice inside told him he had to hear all of it.

Anya turned to him. 'Eva did see him again – the Nazi. She believes I have never forgiven her for what happened between him and me, but it is not true. I have told her so many times, but she will not believe me.'

'What about him?' said Pip quietly. 'You mean he came back?'

'I never knew who he was. To me, he was just some German tourist who turned up one day looking for a woman. He was my first man. I was 15 years old.'

Pip stared in horror.

'And he was the Nazi?'

Anya looked across at her grandmother.

'She couldn't help handing me over. She was so afraid when she recognised him. He was the same man who had saved her and my mother's life in 1942. The man who had killed the drunken soldier. But worst of all, the one she had seen as a child in 1916! She didn't tell me that for a very long time, until I asked her why she had let him have me …' Anya's voice shook. Dalca took her hand in his. 'I can never speak of that first time with him. Never. But nine months after, I was delivered of a boy, a white-skinned, golden-haired child, who was physically beautiful but whose nature was evil. I wanted to love my first-born, but I could not. He was cruel from the beginning. And as he grew, I knew I had hold of a little demon. How he could beg! Even as a baby, when I carried him in my arms, with his strange blue eyes looking up into mine, people gathered around to see him.

'A year later, I gave birth to another son, a true gypsy, so unlike his brother, with pitch-black eyes, a loving boy to his mother. It was then I decided to give my youngest away, because it would be better for him. His elder brother was jealous of him and took every opportunity to harm him. I had to send the baby away – and I wanted Nicholai no more!' Pip started as he heard the name. 'Neither of us could handle him. In any case, I could see he would leave us when he was grown. I had no feelings for him after …' She hesitated. Pip could see she was thinking of his conception. 'My grandmother said he was the Devil's spawn. One day, a young woman teacher from Bucharest came to the camp. She had been sent by the government to inquire into the state of child education. She fell in love with Nicholai. He followed her everywhere. Although he was only a toddler, mentally he was old beyond his years. One day she asked me if she could take him back to the city. She said she would pay money. We had nothing. I was glad to see him go, even though he was my first born. I never saw him again.' Anya's lips were set.

'And your second child?' asked Pip.

Anya's face lightened, but her lips were twisted as if she felt the pain still.

'I swear to God it was the worst thing I had to face, but I could not let him grow up knowing his mother was a prostitute. I wanted a better life for him. So I handed him over to a respectable couple in Cluj, who were good to him. I confess they paid me money too. I am not proud of what I did, but I knew that the boy would have had no life with me. Then, after many years …'

'… He found you again?' Pip stared at Dalca. Now he understood who their benefactor was.

'Yes, I was the child,' replied Dalca. 'And Anya has never again had to beg or prostitute herself since I found her.' He put his arm around her shoulders. 'This is my mother, Pip.' He kissed her cheek.

'And your half brother? What happened to him?'

'His adoptive mother was wealthy and educated. He is now a man of wealth and note. You and I,' he looked Pip straight in the eyes, 'have discussed him at length.'

Pip had already guessed who he was.

'*Eisenmann.*'

Eisenmann was Dalca's half-brother and the son of the Nazi, the soldier who never aged, the man who might be Grandsire. Pip could hardly take in the enormity of it all. Then he remembered the photograph in the case of his laptop. The face of Arvarescu, Koppelberg – and Eisenmann. Silence ensued, which was broken by Eva's faltering voice.

'My scrying bowl.'

'Yes, Grandmother.'

Pip lifted his eyebrows and looked at Dalca, who came over to him.

'She wants to tell your fortune,' said Anya. 'She has the second sight.'

'I'd rather not know,' said Pip.

'It can do no harm. And you owe her that much.'

Pip realised that was true. Yet, at that moment, having his fortune told was the last thing he wanted, because he needed some space to think and, afterwards, to discuss with Dalca the implications of what he had just heard. He tried to analyse his feelings. Principally, his annoyance that Dalca had been in possession of that information all along but had not shared it with him. That Dalca was half-brother to the German was something Pip had never envisaged. But from what Dalca had said earlier, he suspected the Professor was of the same opinion as him – that his brother was a murderer. As for Eisenmann being some kind of Jekyll and Hyde, Pip couldn't get his head round that – yet. Although he didn't want to admit it, he knew his opinions about the supernatural were slowly beginning to change

He and Dalca watched as Anya carried in the bowl. It was made of horn with a yellow and black vein running through it. In her other hand, she carried a wooden stand, painted black, which she placed on the dresser. Then she went out again and brought in a jug. Afterwards, she walked over to her grandmother's chair, lifted her up and settled her comfortably. Eva said not a word throughout the preparations.

Anya nodded to Dalca, and he crossed the room, carried over a small table that was placed near the trailer's front window, then sat down. Anya placed the bowl in front of Eva and poured in the water until it reached the brim. 'Pure spring,' she said. 'With a pinch of salt.'

As Anya motioned him to approach Eva's chair, Pip was thinking he hadn't seen any spring that could have been called 'pure' in the environs of the camp. Somehow he felt particularly nervous, more than at any time since he had arrived in Romania. Strangely enough, he had been ready to discount the strange happenings with the computer, to dismiss his visions as the result of stress, and to view with a detached dismay the deaths of people with whom he had come into contact. But having his fortune told by someone who had just recounted a story that made his blood run cold, seemed entirely different.

He tried to analyse his feelings once more as the old lady put out a wrinkled hand and touched his sleeve. Then she bent over the bowl and peered at the water. She sat like that for some moments, then Pip heard her make a thin noise, as if she was drawing in her breath through pursed lips.

'I can see him now.' Pip was about to ask who, when he caught Anya's forbidding glance. 'A boy, but he's a long way away. A lame child.' Her voice stabbed the air and pierced Pip by its sharpness. He wanted to move away, but his feet seemed to be shackled. Eva's voice droned on. 'Now I see a man with a child.' Pip's neck prickled. He wanted to ask her if it was the same lame child, but he was afraid. 'A young girl,' she said, as if she was reading his mind. Pip watched Eva's old face crack into a toothless smile. 'A blessed soul.' Pip's stomach turned over, not from fear but from rising excitement. 'They are smiling at me.' Could it be the man and the child he had seen so long before in Koppelberg's lair? But Pip couldn't ask, because no-one knew about his past. Then Eva drew back from the bowl and closed her eyes.

As Anya hurried forward to take the bowl, Pip felt an acute disappointment. He wanted to know more. He needed to know more. Yet in spite of his frustration, he realised he was at last ready to believe that which, before, had been unbelievable. His instincts were telling him to abandon his scepticism, to open his mind, to become a child again. But he needed one final proof.

Then a wail from Eva Kirchma tore the air apart. 'Danger. Danger! I feel it around me.' She twisted her head from side to side as if looking for something or someone.

'Hush, Grandmother,' cried Anya. 'There is no one here but Simu and his friend.' But Eva could not be consoled. Anya crouched beside her, then looked up at the two men. 'I think you should go. She is overwrought. It is all too much for her. She should never have used the bowl.'

'Yes, Anya, we should go,' said Dalca, picking up his jacket.

'I can't, Professor,' said Pip. 'Before I go, I have to show Eva the photograph.'

Dalca stared at Pip, then at Anya, who shook her head.

Pip didn't move. She had to see it, in spite of what Anya said. He took it out from the case and crossed over to Eva's chair. 'Please, Anya, this is vitally important. To me, to us all.'

'Just what is this photograph?' snapped Dalca.

Pip took no notice.

'May I speak to her? Please?'

To his relief, Anya nodded. He crouched down beside Eva's chair. 'Mrs Kirchma, can you hear me. Eva? Will you help me? You have nothing to be afraid of.' No movement. 'Can you hear me?' he repeated.

Anya stroked her arm.

'Grandmother, wake up.'

'Eva, it's Pip,' he said suddenly – and he didn't know why. 'Pip Durrant, the lame boy.' He didn't notice the looks that passed between Dalca and Anya. 'The lame boy,' he repeated. He shivered as the old lady grasped his sleeve, feeling it as if she were blind. Then the old wrinkled hand came up and waved in the air. He knew she was trying to feel his face, so he bent close and her hand began to explore it. There was a fire in her eyes.

'Pip?' she asked. It was a moment of sheer wonder. 'You've come at last.'

'I'm here,' he replied. She opened her eyes and they were full of tears.

'I have waited for you.'

Pip didn't hear Anya gasp.

'Can you tell me who this man is, Eva?' He brought the photograph close to her face. 'Will you look at this for me?' He seemed to be alone in the world as he waited. 'Is this the man, Eva?'

She screwed up her eyes and stared. Her old face crumpled as she nodded.

'Yes.'

He put his head back in sheer relief.

'Let me see what's she looking at,' cried Anya, breaking the spell.

Pip was still dazed as she grabbed the photograph from him. He felt confused, as if he had woken from a vivid dream. He heard Anya cry out like she was far away. He came to and looked up. She stood clasping the photograph, staring at it and shivering. Dalca had his arms around her.

'It's him!' she sobbed

'Who? Nicholai?' asked Dalca.

'No! My God! No! The German tourist who raped me. How did you get this?' She turned to Pip, tears running down her face. He stood up and his legs were shaky from both relief and emotion.

'Yes, how did you?' asked Dalca, his voice thick with anger. The time had come for truth.

'I first saw this photograph when I opened the Marcu Papers. It is the face of a criminal called Walter Arvarescu. He was a child murderer who escaped from an American prison in 1952.' Anya put her hand to her mouth and shrank against Dalca. 'It is also the face of someone I wish I had never known: Diep Koppelberg, a musician, who tried to murder my family in 1988. It is also the image that appeared on my computer when I was looking up the details of Eisenmann.' He didn't say anything about his visions.

'My half brother,' said Dalca. He looked shaken. 'Anya recognised the photograph you showed her as the Nazi, Eisenmann's father. Not Eisenmann.'

'But Eisenmann is the Nazi's son.'

Dalca studied the photograph. His face was pale. He said:

'You are saying that the image that appeared on your laptop and the photograph that you discovered amongst the Marcu Papers are both of the same man that Eva saw all those years ago? The one who fathered Eisenmann?' He stared at Pip. 'You must believe now, Pip. The thing we have feared is upon us. And you were sent to us; you were chosen to be the witness and our saviour.'

'It's too much to take in,' replied Pip, looking from one to the other. 'It seems beyond belief.' Dalca handed him back the photograph. Pip's mouth was very dry. 'So Eisenmann is Grandsire's child.'

Anya crossed herself several times.

'God forgive me if I gave birth to such a creature!' She turned to Dalca, her eyes wide and full of pain.

'No, Mother,' said Dalca. 'I am sure Nicholai is mortal, although Grandsire's blood runs in his veins.'

Anya shuddered and buried her head in Dalca's shoulder for a moment. The she turned to Pip. 'I too believe that you have come to us to save us.' Dalca glanced at Pip, then looked away.

'How else would my grandmother recognise you, Dr Durrant?' Anya's eyes were red as she looked across at the old lady slumped in the chair. 'It seems she has been waiting for you. She must have seen you before.'

'I don't know how,' replied a dazed Pip. 'In the bowl, I think she saw me when I was a kid. I was disabled in an accident. But I got over it.' He couldn't tell them how he had been buried in the ruins of the chalet. How he had found his voice and his life again.

'But who were the man and the girl she saw?' asked Anya.

Pip shook his head.

'I don't know.'

He was almost sure they were the ones who had appeared in Koppelberg's case. He wanted them to be, because it might mean he would see them again in the future.

'Eva said the girl was a joy. Maybe she is fated to be our Messiah?' said Dalca.

Pip felt a shiver run through him.

'But what does she have to do with me?'

It was Dalca's turn to shake his head.

'I don't know, but now the two of us are working together, we may find out.' He turned to Anya. 'Will you be all right?' Anya nodded, but she was still staring at Pip. 'We'll go now.' Dalca felt in his pocket and handed his mother some bank notes.

'No, Simu, we have plenty.' She tried to give them back.

'They are to look after Eva.'

'I treasure her,' said Anya, 'but I am afraid for her health. It has all been too much.' She turned to Pip. 'Will you come back again? I saw the joy on her face when she recognised you. She hasn't been happy for a long time. Promise me?'

'I promise,' he said, but a voice in his head told him he would never see Eva alive again.

Pip and Dalca drove back to Arva without saying much to each other, except for the necessities. It seemed neither wished to discuss the experience. A strong wind buffeted the car as it battled its way down the road through the open fields. Flurries of sleet assaulted the windscreen, and the wipers struggled to beat them off. Pip stared out of the window, but the savage weather meant nothing to him, because he was absorbed in his own thoughts

The old adage came into his head: *The mind is like a parachute. It does not function until it is opened.* He had no regrets now he had opened up. What he had just experienced, coupled with his own visions, had convinced him that forces were at work in Arva that, as a scientist, he couldn't understand, but he had to believe. He didn't know how Eva Kirchma had seen him in the bowl. Nor identified his lameness. How she had achieved it was a mystery, but that was his past. But her vision of the man and the girl had provided what Pip had been searching for – a release from the old fears, and maybe some hope for his own future. He remembered the confidence the couple had instilled in him as a child. How he had said, *When I'm grown up, I shall see them again.* After that vision he had found the strength to do something about Koppelberg and save his brother and sisters from a shocking fate. Was this happening again? If Eva had seen them – if it *was* them – then perhaps she had been the instrument through which he might discover the power once more, to prevent the shocking things that were happening in Arva? The thought was mind-blowing, but already he was feeling some kind of peace.

He had been lonely without that vision, and he had wanted it back so many times. But it had been a good kind of loneliness, which had been a way of keeping him going when things were at their worst. He realised he had always been confident the couple would return one day, but he could have never guessed that someone else would see them too, or that it would be a hundred year old gypsy woman who lived in possibly the most backward country in Europe. It was incredible.

Armed with such knowledge, he might be able to

complete what Marcu had started and take on Eisenmann. If the German had Grandsire's blood running in his veins, and Koppelberg was in some unbelievable way connected with Grandsire, then – as the Professor had said – Eisenmann must be dealt with.

His mind switched to how Eva had recognised the man in the photograph as the one she had seen in both 1916 and 1942 – and, even more unbelievably, how Anya had recognised him as the one she had seen as a child and had been handed over to when she was 15 years old. So the belief that Grandsire returned every 36 years and had never aged appeared to be borne out. Was Grandsire a demon? Were there such things as demons? They certainly believed in them in Romania. What about devils? Fr Joseph had been convinced that evil was everywhere. Which was true. But had he been referring to a specific evil? A devil within their midst? He had warned Pip to take care, to back off – as had Eva. It all seemed impossible, but he had to press on, to find out more! Marcu must have felt this, as must Robert and Valentin. And look what had happened to them!

Pip glanced at Dalca, whose eyes were intent on the road. He was a part of all this. He had led Pip to it. Was he thinking along the same lines as Pip, now that his own past had been revealed? He had said that they would fight this evil – which both of them now believed existed – together. Pip couldn't yet imagine how they would do that, but he couldn't wait to start planning their next move. He was only sorry that Robert and Valentin were dead, because they needed as many good people as possible on their side.

Pip thought about the Church and Simu's abhorrence of it. To the Professor, it was evil, but Pip couldn't believe that. He was not religious, but he knew the Church had been founded to fight against the dark forces of which Fr Joseph had spoken. Man's nature was a mixture of good and evil. Therefore, there were good priests and bad. He was sure now that Fr Joseph's sudden death was tied in to his disclosures. How much more might Pip have discovered if the priest had survived?

Someone, or *something*, was intent on preventing that

information from being revealed. Pip knew that dismissing the obstacles as bad luck or coincidence was not an option any more. Besides, he didn't believe in either.

15

Ghita was at home when they returned. Her fragility was evident. She looked pale, almost woebegone. He had seen that look on patients' faces as they battled with their demons. In the light of his earlier experience, he wanted to comfort her and shield her from her fears. She was an unwilling victim caught up in a situation that was none of her fault.

'*Tată!* Where have you been?' she asked.

'I've been showing Pip around,' he replied, kissing her on both cheeks. It was the first sign of affection either of them had shown to the other in Pip's presence. 'Where's your mother?'

'In the kitchen. I was helping her with the food.' That too was surprising. Ghita turned to Pip. 'How are *you*?'

'I'm fine,' he replied.

'Good,' she said. 'I was thinking …' She looked at her father. '… I was thinking I might take Pip to the celebrations.'

'Why not?' he replied.

'What are we celebrating?' Pip asked.

'You Americans make a big thing of it. Halloween!'

Pip looked at his watch to check the date. He had completely forgotten. It was 31 Mccober.

'I didn't know you kept it here,' he said, and they both laughed.

'We've been doing it for two thousand years,' added Ghita. Pip was pleased to see her expression light up. 'We students have a great time, especially the foreign ones. They love to hear about Count Dracula, our most famous vampire.' She lifted her eyebrows. 'We're having a party at Uni, where we all dress up. It will go on throughout the holiday, maybe for two days.' Pip had been so wrapped up in the project he had almost forgotten he was even a member of the University. 'I'll take you if you like?' she offered.

He liked!

'I'd love to go along, if your dad doesn't mind,' he replied. He was thinking what would have happened if he had asked Emilia's permission instead.

'You go,' Dalca said. 'You'll have a good time. You'll be staying over, I suppose, Ghita?'

'Miruna will put me up.'

'And I've still my place at the hostel,' said Pip. It was bizarre. He and Dalca had just undergone the harrowing experience of listening to the testimony of Eva and Anya and, now, on the surface, all that seemed to matter was Pip having a good time at Halloween. But Ghita had asked him, and he wanted to go! Not more than anything, but almost.

'What if Mother finds out?' asked Ghita.

'I'll be extra nice to her,' replied Dalca, and Pip marvelled at his duplicity. 'Then when you come back, Pip, we can get on with our work.'

'Thanks, Dad!' Ghita's excitement was evident. Pip was sure she must have looked like that when she was a little girl.

'When are we going?' he asked.

'As soon as we're ready.'

He wanted to ask her what he ought to wear, but she was off up the stairs.

When Ghita was out of sight, Dalca turned to Pip.

'Don't worry,' he said. 'While you're gone, I'll be thinking hard about our next move – and especially about how to tackle Eisenmann. You go and enjoy yourself.'

Pip wasn't anxious at all. At that moment he was experiencing a moment of sheer happiness, brought on by the thought of spending some time with Ghita. Then he caught

Dalca's expression. Did the Professor want to get him out of the way for a while? But he wasn't prepared to stay and find out.

In the privacy of his bedroom he sorted through his clothes. Ghita had said that the students dressed up for the party. *He never dressed up.* He found a clean pair of jeans and a T-shirt with a picture of the Institute in New York printed on it. At least the building looked Gothic from the outside. That was the best he could do. Then he heard a light knock on the door. His stomach turned over like it had on his first date. He opened it – to face a sinister mask!

'Wow!' he gasped.

Ghita pushed the mask up. 'Dracula's daughter,' she quipped. She looked fantastic. Skimpy red top, short black skirt and high boots with heels.

'You look great.'

'No, I look like a tart,' she grinned, grabbing his arm and pulling him onto the landing.

They sat down at a small table in the great refectory, which was decorated in black and red, with fantastic figures from horror movies projected on the walls. Black and red balloons swayed in a net over the ceiling, and disco balls suspended from the ceiling sparkled as they reflected the hellish colour scheme. All around were girls in skimpy outfits, but Pip had no eyes for anyone but Ghita. He certainly didn't notice the man who sat alone a few tables away. He was in full fancy dress and wearing an horrific vampire mask.

'What's all this about Count Dracula?' Pip asked.

Ghita smiled at him, her mask wobbling in her hair. No vestige remained of the worried girl who had met them earlier when they had returned from the gypsy camp. He smiled back.

'They make a big thing over here about Vlad the Impaler,' she replied. 'For instance, look at him over there! Oh, he's gone.'

'Who?'

'*Dracula*,' she said. 'The vampire myth is very good for our economy. Vlad wasn't a very nice man, but he makes us all a good profit. Sometimes, travel agents ask the students to lead tours of vampire country. Anton is doing that right now. Mind you, he didn't want to, but he needs the money. He'll be away until after the holiday.' She smiled. 'Told you I was a tart!'

Pip hoped his face wasn't registering relief. At one point he had thought of asking Ghita why Anton wasn't taking her, but he didn't really care.

Ghita was certainly a girl full of surprises, and he didn't understand her attitude. If he had been Anton, he wouldn't have been pleased at his fiancée asking another man out. And if he had been his usual cautious self, he might have been wary, but he didn't want to consider anything like that at the moment. All he could think of was that he was going to have Ghita all to himself. And that she wanted to be with him, a man getting on for twice her age.

He looked around. Even by American standards, it was a crazy party. Pip felt conspicuous once or twice as he didn't have a mask. Those worn by the other partygoers ranged from the standard ghoul to the bizarre animal, one of which was cavorting about in front of them.

'Bears,' said Ghita. 'People are still afraid of them here. I met a Dutch post-grad recently who was writing a thesis on the wild animals of Romania. He took in wolves as well. He and his team spend their whole time roaming about in the mountains. A bit like you, actually.'

'I don't roam about in the mountains,' Pip protested.

'No, I meant about you being a foreign post-doc doing a thesis. But your research is just as dangerous.'

He was startled.

'What do you mean?'

Instead of answering, she dragged him into the heaving mass of dancers, many of whom appeared to be drunk. A moment later, they were elbow to elbow with a blonde girl, who pushed up her mask.

'Ghita?'

'Miruna!' They grinned at each other, and then the boy Miruna was with pulled her away. Ghita must have guessed what Pip was thinking when she added, 'Don't worry. Whatever happens, she'll cover for me.'

He didn't ask what she thought was going to happen, but it was never out of his mind. He had never been fond of clubbing or dancing, given his past disability, but then he hadn't been with anyone like Ghita. And he was determined not to get drunk, because he didn't want to spoil a moment with her.

'You'll have to indulge tomorrow,' she said, finishing off her glass of wine.

'Why?'

'It's traditional to drink 44 glasses of wine on 1 November.'

'Good grief!'

She nodded and laughed at his expression.

'I think you should try some *palinca*. But I warn you,' she waved a finger at him, 'it is worse than my father's own home-brewed brandy. His is only 40 percent proof. Most bottles of *palinca* are 60 to 80 percent.'

Later in the evening, the band was going crazy, just like the crowd. The music they had been playing all night was a mixture of pop, hip-hop and heavy metal. Then a sudden howl went up. A tall, slim man in medieval fancy dress and vampire mask pushed his way onto the stage. He had long blond hair, which flowed down his back like a woman's.

'God,' said Pip. 'Who's he? The entertainment?'

'I don't know. *Dracula*?' Ghita was laughing. The crowd started to roar and clap.

'What's he got in his hand?'

'It's a *nei*,' she said.

'What's that?' Pip squinted at the curved instrument.

'The pan pipes! He must be a *taraf*.' Ghita noted Pip's raised eyebrows. 'Sorry! A kind of gypsy. They're really famous for playing their folk music.'

The crowd was quietening down as the man began to play. Pip was horrified. He had come from a musical background and had been expecting the sound to be melodious – in any case, certainly better than the god-awful noise the man was wrenching out of the instrument. He almost wanted to put his hands over his ears.

But the crowd loved it. He looked down at Ghita. She, too, had her eyes closed and was swaying in time with the music. He was so glad to be with her, but he couldn't wait for the horrible noise to stop. When it did, the audience went crazy. They were screaming something he didn't understand.

'They want him to take off his mask,' she shouted over the noise. But the man ignored the request. They watched him swagger off the stage. 'That was great,' she said. 'I'll have to take you to a gig with a gypsy band some time.'

'Okay,' he replied, half-hoping she would forget, but, on the other hand, wishing she wouldn't, so he could spend more time with her.

'I'll have to find out who that guy is,' she said. 'He was great. Anyway, how do you like our folk music?'

'Awesome,' he lied.

'I want to go and find him,' she said.

He grabbed her hand.

'You can't. He's gone.' Pip was grateful.

'And he didn't even ask for money.' She grinned. 'Probably knew none of us had any. Except you, of course.'

'I'm not wealthy.'

'Of course you are,' she grinned. 'You're an American!'

She gave him a playful push. And that was what it was like all night. Being with Ghita was like being struck by lightning. They left at around two. Neither was drunk, but they were merry. They stood at the door, the noise still going on behind and the starlit sky and the freezing world outside beckoning them. Suddenly, Ghita snuggled up against Pip, and he held her, his heart beating fast.

'It's going to snow,' she said. 'They'll soon be boarding

up the houses. Although it'll probably be a yellow alert when they do that.'

He didn't want to talk about the weather. Instead, he looked down into her eyes and said,

'What shall we do about – what's-her-name?'

Ghita giggled at the question. 'You mean Miruna?'

He nodded.

'She went off ages ago.'

'Oh,' he said, his hopes rising. 'Where are you staying then?'

'What about your place?'

'Fine by me,' he said. 'What'll your dad say?' He hated himself for being so careful.

'Don't worry. I told you, Miruna will cover for me.' She was giggling and looking down at his shoes. 'You'll need some boots like me when the snow comes.'

'I haven't the legs for it,' he joked.

She laughed and hugged his arm. A moment later, a sudden rush of cold air struck them. But it didn't come from outside. It was the draught from the billowing cloak of the man, who pushed past them and strode off.

'Hey, it's him,' Ghita shouted, 'Dracula! I'm going to ask him about a gig.'

'No, Ghita,' said Pip, grabbing her. 'Don't. You never know who he is.'

She turned, a teasing look on her face.

'I didn't know you cared,' she quipped, looking down at his hand on her arm.

'I do,' Pip replied. 'In fact … I care very much.'

'Come on then,' Ghita said.

It seemed the most natural thing in the world for him to put his arm around her waist. It didn't take them long to stroll, laughing and joking, to Pip's apartment. Once inside, things progressed quite quickly. Both knew what they wanted, and there was no awkwardness about it.

Ghita walked into the bedroom. He hesitated for a moment, imagining her taking off her clothes. 'What's this?'

she asked. She was staring at the cage.

'It's my rat,' he replied, wondering how she would take it.

'Rat!' She screwed up her nose. To Pip, she still looked beautiful.

'Don't you like rats?' Pip didn't want to talk about pets. The only thing on his mind was Ghita.

'They're not my favourite animals,' she replied. He watched as she sat down on the bed and began to take off her boots.

'Here, let me,' he said, crouching down in front of her. When the boots were off, he felt her toes. 'They're cold.'

'Why don't you warm them?' she asked.

He could see by her eyes it was an open invitation. Soon after, as they were lying in bed together, he felt a tiny stab of guilt and said, 'Sure you want to do this?'

She smiled.

'Do you want to?'

'Of course. How couldn't I?' He could hardly keep his hands off her.

'That's all right then.'

The next moment, she kissed him …

He woke in the morning and she was still beside him. It hadn't been a dream after all. He leaned on his elbow, watching her, curled up, looking young and vulnerable. When she opened her eyes, she smiled at him, then stretched luxuriously. He had no regrets, but he was feeling awkward now about what had happened between them. If her mother found out they had spent the night together … He sighed, not wanting to think about the repercussions.

'What's the matter?' she asked. Then she pulled him down and kissed him. 'Why are you looking like that?'

'I don't know,' he lied.

'I'm on the pill, if that's what you're worried about.'

'That's all right then,' he replied, offended rather than

relieved. A few seconds later he asked, 'Do you do it with Anton?'

She frowned.

'Why do you ask?'

'No reason.' He shrugged.

'Well, that's all right then,' she replied, mimicking him. 'Come on.' She swung her slim legs over the side of the bed. 'Have you anything in for breakfast?'

'I never thought about that.'

'Neither did I.' They both laughed. 'Anyway, I know somewhere we can go to celebrate the Day of the Dead.'

'The what?'

'1 November. You people call it All Saints. It's the Day of the Dead for us. You might find it interesting.'

'I doubt it,' replied Pip, grimacing.

She walked over to the window and looked out.

'The snow will be here in a few days. I can feel it.' She shivered.

'Come back to bed?' he asked.

A moment later, she was beside him again.

'You know what I'd like?' she asked.

He shook his head.

'First, breakfast, then to go to Burbor and see Grandma. It's the right day for it.'

He didn't ask why, but her request brought him back to the real world. He wanted to visit Simona too, but for very different reasons from Ghita. Maybe this was his chance.

The hospital seemed more cheerless than ever, because as the two of them walked along the quiet corridors, Pip was remembering Robert. He still felt responsible for his death. It was clear to him now that the nurse must have unearthed some facts about Eisenmann that the German didn't want disclosed; but what those facts could have been was open to conjecture.

'She looks terrible, doesn't she?' whispered Ghita as

they stood by the bed, looking down at the sleeping Simona.

The old woman was very ill, at least in Pip's opinion.

'Maybe she's just having a bad day,' he said. 'Or it could be the drugs.'

He was becoming adept at not telling the truth. Simona Murgu looked only half-alive. It was as if she was in a world where nothing human could touch her. She lay motionless, her wispy grey hair spread out on the pillow, looking much older than her 70 years. Her breath made a rasping sound as she exhaled. He had heard that sound too many times and recognised it was not a good one. It could be the beginning of pneumonia. At her age and in her condition, the illness carried a death sentence.

'Do you think they're looking after her properly?' asked Ghita. 'Robert was so good to her.'

'Perhaps you should go and speak to the charge nurse,' Pip said. 'He's still in his room.'

Another nurse had been about to go into Simona's room with a pillow as they'd arrived, but he had said he would come back later to make the bed, and had then directed them to the charge nurse's office. The new charge nurse, named Wadim, had challenged them as to their credentials and hadn't been particularly pleasant about it. Behaviour like that from a member of hospital staff wouldn't have been acceptable back in the States. It wasn't until Ghita had explained who she was that the man had let them in. He had probably been worried about doing the wrong thing. Or wanted to go off on his coffee break!

'Ask him if she's caught a cold or anything lately,' added Pip.

'I shall,' replied Ghita determinedly. 'Then I can give her this when she wakes up.' She produced the loaf of bread they had bought on the way to the hospital. It was baked in the shape of a bow, and Ghita had explained it was traditional for All Souls' Day. She had promised to take Pip to the traditional rites that evening. He wasn't keen on the idea of spending the time left with her in a graveyard, but he would go along with it, because he might not get another chance to be with her on his own. And, after the night before, he was going to be desperate.

'She'll like that,' he said, thinking that she was too ill to eat it. 'I'll sit with her while you speak to the nurse.'

'Thank you,' she said, kissing him briefly. A moment later, he was left with Simona. He sat down beside the bed and stared at the old lady. He sighed. All remaining opportunities of finding out anything further were slowly slipping away. A few moments passed. The hospital was as eerily silent as he remembered, except for the usual echoing cries and moans. He looked across to the door to see if Ghita was on her way back – and jumped. Simona was clutching his sleeve.

She was like a corpse coming alive. Her eyes were staring and her mouth wobbling as if she was trying to say something. He bent down, trying to think about Ghita's lovely face instead of the grotesque mask in front of him.

'How are you today, Simona?' he said. 'What do you want?' She was scrabbling at his arm and he had to lean right forward to hear.

'Tell ...' she rasped ... 'Tell Claudiu ...' Pip frowned. Claudiu. She must be talking about Basa, the crippled man who had lived by the church. She obviously thought the farmer was still alive. And who did she think Pip was? Marcu again? She was probably hallucinating in her fever, or it might have been the schizophrenia talking. But it was clear she had something urgent on her mind.

'What do you want me to tell him?'

Simona was making an enormous effort to lift herself up, by hanging on to his sleeve.

'You can tell me,' Pip urged.

'Claudiu is Emilia's ...' She gasped.

'Emilia's ...?' He tried to encourage her, but he had a sudden suspicion of what he was about to hear.

'... Emilia's father! Not Murgu!'

Pip had not expected that. But what did it matter now? The man had been dead since 1988. What did it mean?

Simona was still clutching his sleeve. 'Tell him!' she said.

'I promise,' he replied. Pip was not proud of what he did next. He put his face close to hers and asked, 'Do you know who Grandsire is, Simona? Did he kill Anka Petrescu? Simona, do you remember the maiden name of Catina Albu's mother?'

He could see that such answers were beyond her. She was staring at nothing. Of course, she didn't understand. Or didn't want to. But a moment later, she surprised him.

'Tell Ghita to be careful!' The words were quite clear. Then the clutching hand on his sleeve relaxed and she slipped away again. Pip looked round. He could hear voices. Ghita and the nurse were on their way over.

He sat back. Evidently, what Simona had told him had been of prime importance to her. The old lady probably still felt guilty and wanted to get it off her chest. As for telling Ghita to be careful? He didn't intend mentioning Simona's warning. Ghita was afraid enough already of the things she didn't understand.

'Has she said anything?' asked Ghita. Her face was as white as the nurse's coat.

'Not a thing.'

'Wadim says she has a chest infection.'

The nurse nodded his agreement as Pip turned to him. Wadim had thinning hair brushed back neatly and an impatient air about him. He probably thought they were going to report him for his earlier attitude.

'Have you had the doctor in?' asked Pip.

The nurse looked at Ghita.

'No, go ahead,' she said. 'You can say anything to Dr Durrant.'

'I'm only a stand-in over the next couple of days,' the nurse admitted. 'But I've looked at Mrs Murgu's notes. It says the doctor came in yesterday. He won't be around today. It's the holiday.'

Pip was appalled. The guy was useless.

'Holiday or not,' said Pip, 'I think you should call the doctor back as soon as possible.'

'Should I stay with her?' asked Ghita.

'You'd only end up sitting here by the bed all day,' said Pip. He wasn't going to tell her that he thought Simona wouldn't recover. 'But I think you should let them know at home. Maybe your dad will bring your mother over. And they can always phone you, if you're needed.' Inside, he marvelled at how good he was at turning things round to suit himself. It was unlikely Simona would say very much anymore. It was up to Pip now whether or not he told Dalca what his mother-in-law had said – that Emilia was the daughter of Claudia Basa. What would be the point?

'So I should ring Dad?'

'I think so. You can try later.'

Ghita was staring down at her grandmother. She bent and kissed the wrinkled cheek, and Pip was moved by the loving care she showed to someone who had once tried to suffocate her!

'I'll leave the bread,' she said to the nurse. 'Will you give it her when she wakes up?'

'Of course.' He exchanged glances with Pip. 'I'll take care of her. Don't worry.'

'Thank you,' said Ghita.

Pip nodded to him.

'We'll be in touch.'

'My parents will probably be in soon,' added Ghita.

Wadim watched them go, then turning round walked the other way. He paused opposite a door at the end of the corridor, then, looking one way and the other, he withdrew his mobile.

'Hello, it's Wadim, doctor. No, not urgent at all. I'd just like you to look in on one of the patients. Murgu. Yes, the one who is on her way out. The relatives asked me to phone you. Fine, you'll come when you can. Thanks.' He closed the phone and muttered, 'That's that then.'

He crossed over to the door and tried the handle. 'You

can come out now,' he said. 'You better hurry. I've done my bit. Just leave the uniform in there. I'll pick it up.'

Simona came out of her hazy world and looked round for Ghita. She needed to speak to her, to tell her things she had never told anyone. Before it was too late.

'Where are you?' she wailed. 'Ghita?' She tried to sit up in bed, but was too weak. Where had Marcu gone? She needed him so he could warn Ghita. He had always been good at making people tell their secrets. Like Irina. Her friend. Tears started in Simona's eyes as she thought of Irina and little Anka. What had happened to them mustn't happen to Ghita! She struggled to sit up and almost made it. Then she saw a man's shape. He had come back!

'Marcu,' she cried, 'Doctor. Help me, help me.'

'I'll help you,' he said. A moment later, his gloved hands were pressing the pillow down hard on her face. As her face sank into its soft depths, her struggle for air was like drowning. She could feel her head bursting. It was very quick, because, seconds later, Simona knew nothing.

The man withdrew the pillow. He tried the pulse in her neck. *Nothing.* He took her wrist. *Nothing.* He looked at his watch. He had to get out of the place before anyone found her. It had not gone smoothly at first. He was still scared his master would be unhappy because he had been disturbed by the relatives. At least he had kept his cool and waited for them to go, and for the charge nurse to leave his office. He couldn't get it in the neck for waiting.

As he left, he passed the nurses' rest room. He could hear laughter. He grinned. Coffee breaks were very useful to his trade. Especially at holiday time.

Pip took Ghita back to his apartment after the visit to the hospital, but she had reverted to the dejected girl she had been before she had taken him to the party. Still, he wasn't upset.

He would have liked to have gone to bed with her again, but couldn't expect it, given what had just happened with her grandma.

When it was dark, they set out for the graveyard.

'What's the significance of all this?' asked Pip as they approached. The whole area around, as well as the graveyard itself, seemed on fire.

'Over here, we take All Souls' Day very seriously,' said Ghita, hugging his arm. 'It's a time to remember our loved ones who have died. It's a special kind of ritual.' He glanced at her, thinking about another ritual – one he knew too much about. 'Some of our people cook little saints and martyrs.' He grimaced. 'Don't look like that! They're pretzels that form a number eight.'

'Why?' he asked.

She shrugged.

'I can't remember. But you will like the next bit. I mentioned it last night. It's traditional to drink 44 glasses of wine, and supposed to enliven the drinker.'

'I bet it does!'

'Then there is the opening of the graves …' She stopped. 'And – yes – the gates of Heaven. I don't remember what that means either.'

'They don't actually open the graves?'

'Don't worry. It's symbolical. And I can't remember any more.' She indicated the lights. 'Anyway, even the candles are worth a visit!'

He and Ghita joined the crowd streaming towards the gates.

'There must be hundreds of people here,' said Pip, looking round. He had never seen anything like it, except at a football game. But he didn't like it, even though it was spectacular. To him, it was both bizarre and macabre. Each grave was on fire with the flames from candle lanterns, decorated with bright colours. Tall monuments adorned with their owners' images hosted strings of further lanterns. Some of the flat graves were covered in petals, and all around, people were weeping and kneeling beside them. 'What are the candles for?' he asked. He had never been a churchgoer.

'We remember the dead.' She bent down and gestured to him. 'Look how pretty this one is. Each candle is lit to help the departed soul find its way to everlasting light. In the past, families used to have a big feast at the graveside and leave behind some of the meal for their departed loved ones.'

'Shouldn't their souls be in Heaven already?' Pip asked, finding the idea of eating beside a grave repulsive.

'Have you never heard of Purgatory?'

'Yes.'

'So it's just in case the holy souls are stuck between here and Heaven. We pray for them all the time. Mother would kill me if she knew I hadn't gone to Mass today. But I was too busy.' She looked at Pip and smiled. 'I hope they'll be able to come and see Grandma. I wonder how she is.'

'They will,' replied Pip, thinking he would be surprised if Simona wasn't taking up residence here in the graveyard very soon. But maybe she would be buried in Arva. 'Does this happen all over the country?' He was thinking of one place in particular.

'Every churchyard in the country looks like this on the Day of the Dead.'

'What about Arva?'

She twisted her head to look at him, her face pale in the candlelight.

'No-one can enter there except by special dispensation,' she replied. 'The village people still go, but they lay their candles against the railings. Don't let's talk about it!'

'Okay.'

They stood in silence, surrounded by the sound of prayers. A moment later, Ghita's mobile phone bleeped. She grabbed her pocket and moved to a quiet spot to answer it.

Pip waited, watching as a bearded priest in a black robe appeared. He was going round the graves, blessing them, chanting prayers and sprinkling holy water everywhere.

Moments later, Ghita ran over and grabbed his hand.

She was crying.

'It's Grandma! Dad wants to speak to you.'

He took the phone.

'Simona is dead,' said Dalca. 'Can you bring Ghita home? Get a taxi. And, by the way, there won't be only one funeral, but two. Eva Kirchma has gone too. Anya was with her at the end.'

As Pip escorted a tearful Ghita out of the churchyard, he was wondering how she would feel if she had known she had lost a grandmother and a great, great grandmother all on the same day.

When they got back to the house, Ghita went to comfort her mother while Dalca took Pip into the study. 'Eva's funeral will be tomorrow,' the Professor said.

'That quick?'

'Quicker than Simona's. There will be an inquiry about her death.'

'I saw her today. I thought then that she had little time left. I'm sorry you didn't make it to the hospital in time.'

'She was not keen on me,' he replied, 'but Emilia will never forgive me for not taking her over to Burbor straight away.'

Pip would like to have asked what the Professor had been doing, but decided it wasn't his business. Then his unspoken question was answered.

'I was too busy trying to decide on our next step,' said Dalca. 'Then the hospital telephoned. A chest infection, they said.' Pip nodded. 'As for Eva ...'

'I hope that our visit wasn't the cause?'

'No, it was her time,' replied Dalca. 'At least you were able to hear her story. I would like you to accompany me to the funeral.'

'I will if you want me to.'

'It is good to have a friend at such ceremonies,' was the surprising reply. Strangely, Pip had never thought of himself and Dalca as friends. 'I think we should go into the study now and discuss what I have been planning. Before I am needed by Emilia. At least Ghita is with her now. Have you also been considering what to do about Eisenmann?'

If Pip had been entirely truthful, he would have had to admit that for at least a day, the pursuit of Grandsire had become a secondary matter to him.

'Yes, some of the time.' It was a half-truth.

'He must be dealt with before there are any more deaths.'

'You think Eisenmann was responsible for all of them?' Pip wanted to know Dalca's opinion, and if it differed from his own.

'Him or his *alter ego*.'

'Grandsire?'

Back in the States, Pip would have regarded a serious conversation between two academics about the possibility of a man's *alter ego* murdering with impunity, as essentially ridiculous – although it was true to say that plenty of schizophrenics put in a plea for the very same, when they were up in front of a judge.

In Romania, though, he had begun to feel differently. Indeed, he was ready to believe it! And at present, he could see no way that such a murderous spirit could be dealt with! But he wasn't going to venture such an opinion to Dalca.

'The death of Robert from rabies was unusual, but still explicable,' Pip went on. 'Valentin was knocked down by a car, and a hit and run is plausible enough. We have no evidence that Eisenmann was responsible for either death.'

'And the priest? He was an unlikely candidate for suicide. If he had intended to kill himself, why did he take his luggage? And his chalice? I believe he was running to his superiors and somebody got to him first.'

'*Somebody*,' said Pip, thinking this all made sense.

'All these unfortunate people had either spoken to you or were about to impart information to you. Isn't that right?' asked Dalca.

'Yes.' Pip felt guilty. He had not told him about Robert's

accusations concerning Eisenmann. He decided that now was the time to come clean. After he had finished, he said, 'I'm sorry I haven't told you before.'

'What you have told me only corroborates what we have already said. We have to tackle my half-brother.'

'How?'

'We must play him at his own game,' replied Dalca.

'You're surely not advocating murder,' said Pip. 'If so, you can count me out.'

Dalca smiled. 'I am thinking of more subtle means. I know how his mind works.'

'I thought that you and he had never met.'

It was Dalca's turn to level with him.

'We have. I did not know who he was then, but I am sure he knew me. He has the means and the influence to discover anything about anybody. He is a man of great importance. If it was not for him, you would not be sitting in front of me today.'

'What?'

'You look amazed, my young friend, but it is true. You were given his card.'

'So what?'

'You noticed his office was in Strasbourg?'

Pip nodded. His amazement had given way to trepidation.

'His place of work is the Council of Europe, where his business is the promotion of education. He was instrumental in bringing you to Romania.'

'But how would he know about me?'

Dalca looked grave.

'Yes, how. His knowledge was based upon information that we may never discover, unless we take into consideration my *alter ego* theory. This is more evidence that you were chosen. Perhaps you know why?'

Pip didn't answer. He was thinking about all the terrible visions he had suffered when he was 13 years old.

'You were offered the Marcu Papers and they are now in your possession,' Dalca continued. 'Those Papers hold the key to what we have not yet discovered. Let us not deceive ourselves. Eisenmann's criminal actions were prompted by a power or powers that he alone possesses.'

'I applied to go on the exchange,' said Pip, thinking aloud.

'*Why* did you? Remember, I watched you with Eva. I saw what was dragged up from the depths of yourself – a link to Arva and to Eisenmann of which you had no knowledge. Why should it have been you? Why not someone else? I repeat, it is because *he* knew where those Papers lay.'

'Maybe Marcu told him?'

'I think not,' replied Dalca. 'That day in the gypsy camp, you said you believed. Is that belief weaker now? This is time to be true to yourself, Pip. To your instincts. You do not understand what is behind all this yet, but it does not stop you knowing that you have been singled out. This time you were not left behind.'

'I don't understand what you mean,' said Pip.

'1376,' said Dalca. 'A legendary date, but also the date of the founding of Arva by the unknown German. Valentin knew it – he said so in his letter. Riparu probably knew too. I have no doubt that the priest had access to the information. I have not discovered the Church's involvement yet, but I shall not rest until I do. I shall go back again and again throughout the cycle until I find it. So, to recap, it is more than a possibility that Arva's German founder was the Pied Piper, and 1376 is the date the poet Browning gave for his arrival in Hamelin.'

'The date in a fairytale.' Pip couldn't help himself.

'But a fairytale that had its roots in scholarship – not the fancies of the Brothers Grimm. Browning used that date because he had another source. A reliable one. In 1605, Richard Verstegen wrote about ...' Dalca scrabbled through his notes, '... *a most true and marvellous strange accident* that took place in Hamelin on 22 July.

'Verstegen went on to say, *This Jugler or Pide Piper might by necromancy have transported them thither*, and, *The Saxons of Transylvania had so many strange children brought among them ...*

they could not but have memorie of so strange a thing. Note that he used the word "necromancy". This is what we're up against, Pip! By witchcraft, black magic, occultism or whatever you want to call it, the Piper returns every 36 years to claim another prize. An innocent child. But now the lame boy, the child he rejected on account of his disability, has come back to Arva to get even. On account of what you told me of your history and how you obtained the Marcu Papers, I cannot but hold the belief that *you* are that child!'

'But when we spoke of this before, you said a girl would be the Messiah!'

'The girl will be something to do with you,' replied Dalca, 'I don't know why or how, but I am convinced it is the truth. The girl you saw in your vision. The girl Eva conjured.' He sat down. The whole argument appeared to have worn him out. 'You have to fight for that girl – or with her. I don't know which. But the two of you are in it together.'

Neither spoke. Pip was overwhelmed by Dalca's premise, but he knew who he wanted the girl to be, who he was sure it was going to be. *Ghita.*

'So what shall I do about Eisenmann? If he has Grandsire on his side, then …' Pip shook his head.

'You must confront him. You will have God on yours,' replied Dalca.

'You don't believe in him,' Pip retorted.

A wry smile enlivened Dalca's face.

'Once I did,' he said. 'Once I placed all my faith in Him – until He let me down. Until I realised that the Devil was winning in Arva and the Church was responsible. I have not told you what I was before I became a Professor of History.'

'No.' Pip couldn't imagine where this confession was leading.

'I was in a seminary, studying to be a priest! You might well look shocked. You can't imagine it, can you? In fact, I was near to taking my final vows when I discovered the secret of my birth, that I was the gypsy son of a well-known prostitute from Arva, a place cursed by its infamy. From then onwards, I learned more about evil than I had ever been taught in my religious studies. I discovered the Devil is alive and well in Arva and has been promoted by the priesthood. So I turned my back upon Mother Church and its teachings. I could not be a hypocrite.'

'So that's why you hate religion so much.' The remark slipped from Pip's lips before he could stop it.

Dalca nodded.

'I abhor it.'

'Does Emilia know?'

'She never will. And that is the reason I cannot claim to have God on my side. But God and good can be on yours. As they stand on the side of the hero in every fairytale. Your description, Pip. And you must win through.'

'Do you think the Piper has always existed throughout history?'

Dalca nodded.

'Evil is always with us, but I need to discover how to chart its progress. As I told you before, I shall keep searching until I've found out. That is my task at present. Yours is to tackle Eisenmann, who has Grandsire's blood in his veins, which makes him a very dangerous man. I believe he is seeking the roots of his origin as we are. How much he has learned is a mystery. The difference between us is that he is pursuing his goal for aggrandisement. For the power evil confers on its acolytes.' Pip was trying to take in the enormity of what Dalca was saying. 'I can see by your eyes you don't relish the task. But you will be safe. You must be. If he threatens you, then I shall expose him publicly.'

'It might be too late by then,' said Pip, thinking of Marcu.

'If things get nasty, then you will tell him you are well protected; that others know of his exploits. Eisenmann will not risk his reputation. You still hold the Marcu Papers. He has no idea what else Marcu uncovered in his research, which might damage him. And he will not kill you.'

'But we don't know what passed between Eisenmann and Marcu. What Marcu told him. We don't have the notes of their meeting,' said Pip.

'If Eisenmann had known everything, he would not have invited you to meet him,' replied Dalca. 'Hopefully, with the knowledge we have now, you can lead *him* on. Find out what he knows that we don't.'

'I hope so,' replied Pip.

'Best to get it over with as soon as possible, now you have heard what Eva had to say. Then we can get on.'

Pip glanced at Dalca. On the day that Eisenmann's secretary had given him her boss's card, Dalca had been against any hasty action. Now he was eagerly suggesting that Pip should meet the German at the earliest opportunity.

'Maybe I'll phone his office tomorrow,' Pip replied. 'If I have to go to Strasbourg, I might be away for a couple of days.'

'I don't think you'll be going as far as Strasbourg,' replied Dalca. 'I have made some enquiries, and it seems that Eisenmann has a place down here.'

'You kept that quiet,' replied Pip, remembering what Sigi had said: *We come from round here.*

'Well, I've told you now,' said Dalca. Pip raised his eyebrows at the lack of any apology. Dalca added, 'Members of the ACA engaged in cultural cooperation with universities often rent out houses in areas in which they are currently working. I made it my business to find out if Eisenmann did the same. He has a place in Cluj. When you ring his secretary, I suggest you ask for a meeting on home ground. He cannot expect you to travel to Strasbourg, as he was the one who invited you to contact him. Of course, it will be much more convenient for us, should there be any difficulties.'

'That makes sense, I suppose.' Pip had to ask, 'Professor, I want to know if Eisenmann was the stranger I met in the churchyard.'

Dalca looked startled.

'It could have been.'

'Yet when I described him to you, you didn't give an indication that it might be. Why?'

'Because it was not the right time. I wanted you to meet

Eva Kirchma first.'

Pip thought the excuse wasn't good enough. It would have saved a lot of conjecture on his part, and would also have put Ghita's mind at rest, if Dalca had revealed the stranger's identity to start with. However, he didn't remark on the fact. Instead, he asked:

'What do you think he was looking for?'

'The same as you, perhaps?' Dalca was a master of the evasive answer.

'If it *was* Eisenmann, he won't be very happy to see me again,' said Pip.

'Perhaps we should hope it was not then,' replied Dalca. But if he *is* one and the same, then the meeting in the churchyard may have prompted his invitation to you. You must look on it as a happy coincidence.'

Pip frowned.

'Remember he locked me in.'

'That I cannot understand,' added Dalca. 'But everything points to the fact that Eisenmann is eager to question you about what you know; just as we ourselves are impatient for him to pass on his information to us. Now, shall we break?'

Pip was still uneasy and far from convinced as to Dalca's motives when he finally climbed the stairs to his bedroom. The day had been full of surprises, interspersed with the news of two more deaths, albeit apparently natural ones this time. Pip's time at the camp with Dalca had seemed to place them on a different footing with each other – not as professor and student now, but rather as colleagues in arms. But his instincts told him Dalca still had his own agenda.

However, he didn't have time to think about their conversation anymore, because as he passed Ghita's door, it opened to reveal her in her robe, ready for bed. He could see she had been crying. She put a finger to her lips and gestured him to come in. Then she closed the bedroom door.

Pip would have been even more ill-at ease had he known what

was passing through Dalca's mind. The Professor wiped the perspiration from his forehead, knowing he had just played Judas. He was sending the young man on a mission that might lead to his death, as surely it had to Marcu's. But Dalca had to find out what Eisenmann knew. Convincing Pip had not been easy, and although he had become fond of his young colleague, he told himself that protecting his family was his first priority. He had gambled on winning. Whatever outcome the meeting had, he prayed that it would lead to the knowledge, or at least part of it, that would protect Ghita from sharing the fate of those unfortunate women in the past, who had occupied the same position as his daughter. He would have gambled his own soul to do that.

Pip had no idea where Emilia was, but he wasn't going to pass up the chance of talking to Ghita, especially when she looked so upset. A moment later, she had hold of his arm and was drawing him into the room. Neither of them heard her parents' bedroom door open, then click shut again. They sat down together on the bed and did not speak for a while. Pip wanted to give Ghita some time to get her emotions in check. As she wiped her eyes with a tissue, he thought how much she had changed from the perky and mischievous teenager he had first met a few weeks ago, to the woman he had slept with. He put his arm around her, and she let him.

'I wasn't with her when she died,' said Ghita, looking up at him with red eyes.

Pip didn't remind her that her grandmother had once tried to kill her, but waited with the patience he had learned over his own years of loneliness and disability. He put out his hand and pushed back a stray lock of hair that had fallen over her face.

'I needed to be,' she added. 'I wanted her to say something to me. *To tell me.*'

Pip knew that she was referring to the secret. How could he comfort her? In a strange way, he was relieved her tears were derived from more than sadness at Simona's passing.

'Someone has to open up,' she said, 'or I shall go mad!'

'No you won't,' he soothed, feeling uneasy. 'You're far too well balanced for that.'

'You try living in this house!'

'I do.'

He knew exactly what she meant. It sickened him to think that Ghita's unhappiness stemmed from the vagaries of a madly possessive mother and a variety of outward influences, born of an archaic tradition. What was even worse, Ghita felt she had to get married to discover its perverted principles. He suspected that however much her father tried to dissuade her, Ghita was going to ruin her life by allowing her mother to win. A moment of panic overtook him, in case Ghita went the same way as Emilia, but he squashed the thought.

'Anyway, your grandma wouldn't have told you the secret. In your heart you know that,' said Pip.

'I'd have *begged* her. Why did she have to die?'

It was such a childish thing to say that Pip almost smiled. One of the things that endeared Ghita to him was her ability to change from a determined young woman into a confused kid who needed someone to make everything come right. She was like quicksilver.

'We all have to die,' he replied. 'And she was a very sick old lady.'

He wanted to add, *and crazy!* But he didn't. Simona had been typical of all the other Arvan women who had ended up in Burbor. How could he stop this curse happening again and again? He felt very angry. His mind switched to Eisenmann. Did he know the secret? If so, then he would make the bastard tell him.

'Pip, I have made up my mind about something,' Ghita said. 'I shall never have children.'

He stared at her. He knew why she felt like that, but it was a shocking thing for a 19 year old to state in such a determined manner.

'You can't just say that, Ghita. What about Anton?'

'We've talked about it. He agrees.'

Pip shook his head. He wanted to say, *You're both only 19. How can you make up your mind about something as important as that? You might change.*

'I know what you're thinking,' she added, 'but I shan't change my mind! I can't risk my child being put through what I've been through.'

'What would your mother think about that?'

'She'd be glad.'

'How can you be so sure?'

'I just know,' said Ghita.

'And your dad?' persisted Pip. 'He might want a grandchild.'

Ghita shook her head.

'I don't know how he'd feel.'

'And what if it just happens?' asked Pip. He wanted to add, *It's happened to a lot of people*, but he thought better of it. 'Besides, it might be a boy. He wouldn't have to "go-up".'

'It won't!' The tone was vehement.

He decided not to pursue this line of thinking. His sensitivity stretched only so far, and at that moment, he didn't want to be wise.

It was only some time later, when he thought back over their conversation, that an uneasy suspicion began to play on Pip's mind about Ghita's passionate *It won't*. In the first place he had assumed it was simply an emphatic reiteration of her determination not to get pregnant, which was credible. But might Ghita have meant that she believed the child whom she was determined *not* to bear, was destined to be a girl? How crazy was that? The idea that she might have been talking with such feeling about something she was sure *wasn't* going to happen, provoked a shiver in Pip. Once more, his fleeting thoughts about Ghita's possible state of mind in the future made him go cold all over.

16

'Two funerals,' said Dalca. 'I think Eva's will be the most interesting for you to attend. I would like you to come.' Pip winced. Dalca's dark eyes probed his face. 'I can see that you think I am being tasteless – maybe even callous to talk of my great grandmother in that way. But we gypsies do not weep at the funerals of our dear ones. We celebrate. If I was a believer, I would say she has gone to a happier world. For her sake I hope that is true. It certainly could be no worse than the miserable life she has had on this Earth.' Dalca's expression was dark and bitter. 'Will you come?'

'I'm not keen on funerals, but yes, if you want me to.'

'I do. You are fortunate to have the chance to see another ritual take place in Arva. One that I believe has not taken place in Romania since 1993. Of course, there may have been some that were undocumented.'

'How come?' Pip was surprised.

'Anya tells me that her grandmother wished that the old rites be performed at her funeral. She had no more love for the Christian Church than I. And she had good reason, don't you think?' His lips twisted.

'Yes.'

'Many of our race belong to the Gypsy Church, but Eva did not. It will be a huge gathering, as a hundred years of history has passed away with Eva and many of our people will be there to honour her. Also some will attend simply because of what she was.'

'You mean – a prostitute?'

'No, I mean a seer, a teller of fortunes. There are those who fear her spirit might return to haunt them or be brought down in the wind to plague them.' Pip thought that an interesting idea, though macabre. He was convinced of the latter when Dalca added, 'The superstitious believe a misty light will stream out of her corpse and she will sit up in her coffin and prophesy the future. Such rites must be observed to prevent that happening.

'I am happy to say that Eva's poor old tongue will not be cut out and her mouth filled with garlic.' Pip lifted his eyebrows. 'Oh, yes, Pip, I can see you don't believe me. But that is what used to happen. Shall I explain a little further?'

'I think I'd rather see it for myself,' replied Pip.

'The piercing I think will interest you,' added Dalca, taking no notice of what Pip had said.

'*The piercing*?' Pip frowned.

'The enactment of resurrection; a theme pertinent to our present studies.'

'You mean Eva's funeral has something to do with Grandsire?'

'All rituals have much in common. However, Anya, who in spite of her past profession, became a Church member, has now insisted that after the old rites, her grandmother is to buried in the Christian fashion. So there will be no burning. Have I disappointed you?' Dalca didn't elucidate as to whether he was talking about cremation or something else.

'I'm certainly not disappointed, but very interested.'

At that moment, Pip wondered if he had ever liked Dalca, who seemed to be impervious to any distress regarding the death of his great grandmother. Pip, on the other hand, felt apprehensive, as he was not quite as ready to observe the rites in company with Dalca, as he had been with Ghita on the Day of the Dead.

As Dalca had said, the gathering was a huge affair. Under the pewter-coloured sky, between the fields dusted with snow, they crawled in the car towards the camp, caught in a queue of vehicles, a mixture of old and smart cars, trying to pass carts drawn by horses. Some of the wagons were covered and decorated with flowers. Pip was amazed to see a festooned float carrying a band of musicians. As their turn came to manoeuvre past the float, Pip remembered the masked gypsy musician who had played the pipes at the University party. *Let's hope their music isn't as dire as his*, he thought.

'How did they all know when to come? And where are they all from?' He was amazed.

'The gypsies can always find each other in their hour of need,' replied Dalca. 'We all do our bit. I was the one who called the undertaker. Anya spread the news in the camp, and then it was up to everyone else to contact their relatives, some of whom have travelled considerable distances in their eagerness to be here. Eva was well known throughout Romania for her age and her talents.'

'What about the band?' asked Pip.

'I hired it. They will march in front of the coffin before Eva is buried. But I have no doubt other musicians will turn up too. It is traditional that the *bosavenos* – the fiddlers – attend a funeral. They're probably up front somewhere. It's a good living for them, drawing out spirits.'

Pip glanced at him, but Dalca appeared completely serious as he drove carefully on. Once they reached the camp, it seemed more like a football game than a funeral.

'Where are we going to park?' he asked.

'We have a reserved place,' said Dalca. They drove through the crowd, which consisted of people of all ages. Although it was very cold, some of the men had their shirts open. Great crosses hung on their bare chests, suspended from golden chains. Many of the women were dressed in red, and the men wore black, wide-brimmed hats. As Pip and Dalca passed them, a man peered in through the car window and grinned. Pip was both impressed and repulsed by the amount of gold fillings in his mouth.

Dalca caught Pip's look.

'A lot of gypsies are wealthy,' he said. 'Their money comes from begging, or more often through dealing in scrap metal. Here in the countryside, they tend to be poor.'

'Why are a lot of the women dressed in red?' Pip asked.

'It's the colour of celebration. Sometimes, they all wear white to a funeral. I expect they think it more appropriate to use red for my greatgrandmother.'

Again Pip was surprised at the tastelessness of his sarcasm.

They pulled up a short distance from Eva's trailer. Not far off stood three wild-looking men on horseback. As he and Dalca got out of the car, Pip felt uneasy. A lot of people were staring at him in particular.

'So they have come too,' said Dalca, indicating the horsemen.

'Who are they?'

'The Berber *tzigane*. I was not expecting them. It's their tradition to gallop around the coffin.' He gestured, and Pip saw the open casket. He was relieved to see it was empty. His respectful nod towards it was far less than impressive as Dalca's, who bowed. Then the gathered crowd stood back as Anya came out and greeted her son with warmth. She also placed her arm on Pip's sleeve, for which he was grateful, given the curious way the crowd was watching him.

By then the band had come up and was playing music that to Pip was a mixture of recognisable and unrecognisable sounds, which provoked some people to start dancing.

'The grave has already been dug at the church,' explained Anya to Pip. 'But we cannot hold the rites anywhere but here. Then we shall take her on the wagon into town.' It was the first time he had noticed the large decorated cart covered with a canopy, with a horse standing at the shafts.

'Eva is not being buried in the village?' asked Pip.

'No, there is no other church there but Arva,' replied Dalca, 'and she would never lie in the churchyard there!' He gave Pip a look that turned his stomach over. The thought of Eva being laid to rest at the scene of her terrible misfortune made Pip shiver. 'The funeral will go on for a long time, and when we reach Arva, I suggest you go home and forgo the rest of the burial. This is the part you should see. Unless of course you *wish* to attend the *pomana*.' He smiled at Pip's lack of understanding. 'The dinner.'

'Oh, the wake?'

'Just so,' replied Dalca.

Anya interposed:

'We have Simu to thank for that. He has organised it all – and paid for it.' Dalca put a finger to his lips. 'Will you come with us to the feast and celebrate?' she asked Pip.

'I'm sorry, Anya,' replied Pip. 'I have a lot of work to do.'

'In the past you would have had the opportunity to attend more than one feast,' said Dalca. 'Isn't that right, Anya?'

'Yes,' she smiled. 'But, today, one will do.' Pip looked puzzled. 'Sometimes feasts are held for every year of the deceased's life. Which would be very many in my mother's case.'

'One hundred would be expensive,' Dalca agreed. They smiled at each other. In spite of what Dalca had said earlier about not mourning but celebrating, Pip was still surprised at their easy behaviour.

'My grandmother had a hard life,' said Anya, reading Pip's thoughts, 'but her death was peaceful. I am grateful for that. Come.'

Pip went to step forward, but Dalca stopped him.

'No, she means me. Sorry, *you* must not touch the trailer, as you are not one of us.'

Pip drew back awkwardly as three more men followed Dalca into the trailer. A few minutes later, the four brought out the body. A sigh arose from the huge crowd. Pip watched as the bearers lifted the slight corpse of Eva and laid it in the coffin. The crowd was silent. Dalca withdrew and stood beside Pip with Anya. Once the lid was in place, a man stepped forward and began to drill holes in it.

'The piercing?' whispered Pip.

'Seven times,' whispered Dalca. 'One hole above the forehead for the soul to slip through. Two for the eyes so that they can see. Two for the ears so they can hear the *basaveno* playing the death music. And the last two below the heart, so that when the earthly body beneath disseminates, it can pass through.'

Pip had never seen such an eerie sight. He could feel the crowd shuffling and moving back behind him, making a wide circle around the coffin. Then the melancholy sound of a solitary fiddle was heard; a dismal scraping that made his flesh creep. The hand on his arm made him jump.

'This is the Dance of Death,' said Anya. 'The Death of the Spirit. Eva will hear the music and be drawn out of the coffin.'

Pip breathed in deeply. He had never expected to be reeled into the ceremony the way he was now. He was enchanted. Other fiddles had joined in now and the music was becoming quicker and wilder as it increased.

'She can see everything now, more than she could in life,' added Anya.

Pip wanted to ask if Anya really believed that, but he could not break the spell. Then, all at once, he couldn't see anything, as a mist obscured the onlookers opposite him. It seemed to be hovering over him. He blinked, thinking his glasses had misted up, and took the small cloth from his pocket to rub the lenses clean. He didn't want to miss a thing!

'She can hear the music,' whispered Anya, 'and soon she will be gone. She will wrench her body through the holes.'

Then Pip felt the cold rising in his body, making him shiver. He pulled up the hood of his parka, but it didn't make any difference.

'Can you see the mist?' he asked Dalca, although he was almost ready to believe what was happening.

Another vision was coming on! He felt sick, as he always did; ready to panic at losing touch with reality. He heard Dalca's reply only in the far distance as the mist wrapped itself around him like a wet shroud ... Then the old woman's eyes were peering into his through a watery film. They were reflecting the fire he had seen within them when she was scrying ... When she had prophesied his future ... He was afraid ...

He came to suddenly, the sound of hooves thundering in his ears. The mist dissipated and he saw the three horsemen part the crowds and begin to gallop towards the coffin. He could hear people cheering as the riders entered the circular space and wheeled about.

'*Did you see the mist*?' he repeated, unable to disguise the fear in his voice as the horsemen rode around the circle. Then the music stopped and the horses thundered away. Anya looked at him.

'You have seen the *mullah*,' she said. 'Her spirit. You are blessed with the second sight, as she was.'

Pip shivered and looked at Dalca, who with the rest of the crowd was staring at the trailer. Evidently Anya was the only one who had heard Pip's question.

Dalca turned to him. 'In the past, scraps of fat and oil were thrown in, and then the trailer was set alight with the dead person in it and all his or her belongings.' Dalca's dark eyes looked lighter than usual and glittered with what Pip recognised as tears. *So he is upset after all*, thought Pip.

'I shall destroy everything she owned, but I shall still need the trailer,' explained Anya. Pip saw the warning in her eyes. He knew that what had just happened to him was to remain their secret. 'In spite of her wishes, I shall see my grandmother buried near to the gypsy church. It will give me comfort. Eva will have the best of two worlds. She has had the rites she wanted and I will have my wish granted for a

Christian burial.'

Anya left the two of them standing there, and made her way slowly towards the trailer. The crowd broke the circle and drew back respectfully as Dalca and the other three men stepped forward and carried the coffin towards the canopied cart and the waiting horse.

A moment later, Anya emerged, carrying something hidden under a cloth. 'I, or any other gypsy, may not own anything of hers anymore. You are not one of us, so I bequeath it to you.' She took off the cloth and handed Pip the scrying bowl. He stared at it. 'You will make good use of it. Now cover it.' Then, as Dalca approached, she said. 'I have given him her bowl.'

The Professor nodded.

'Look after it. It might be the most important present you ever get,' he said. Pip was too overwhelmed to speak as he looked down at his gift. 'Now, as Eva's nearest relatives, we shall walk as much of the way to the church as we can, then others will take us on to the burial. You can take the car back to Arva. Here are the keys. And don't say anything to Emilia!'

Pip stared at them. The last thing he wanted to do was drive, and the idea of lying to Emilia did not attract him at all. But there was no option as the funeral wagon was already being driven slowly away, accompanied by the band. He waited until the crowd had dispersed, then made his way to the car, which was now surrounded by parked vehicles. He set the bowl down on the passenger seat and covered it with the tea towel. He couldn't get out of his mind the memory of Eva's wizened face as she had stared into its depths. Nor the misty vision.

All he could do was sit and wait until those that were hemming him in were ready to move. Finally, he managed to join the cavalcade following the coffin. He didn't notice the Mercedes slide into the procession behind him. If he had, he would have been more uneasy than he was already. A woman was driving, but the passenger, if there was one, could not be seen behind the smoked glass windows.

But Pip would have been more than agitated if he had glanced back at the silent, empty camp and seen the figure of a tall man standing beside Eva Kirchma's trailer. He was wrapped in a dusty black cloak streaked with red, over which straggled long blond hair. And he was smiling.

Pip left the car outside the house and unlocked the door. He had rehearsed what he would say to Emilia if she caught him on the way up to his bedroom. He would just lie! He put one foot on the stairs and she came out of the kitchen.

'Is Simu with you?'

'He's gone into town.'

'Why hasn't he taken the car?'

Once again, Pip was reminded of the Inquisition. In fact, Emilia looked even more forbidding than usual. She seemed to wear nothing but black, which did nothing for her, only accentuating her tall, thin form and black-ink eyes, which at that moment were fixed on the tea towel containing the scrying bowl. What would she have said if she had known what it was? It certainly wouldn't fit in with her strong religious principles.

'I believe someone has given him a lift,' Pip answered. Which was true.

'I know he's been at the gypsy funeral,' she said, 'attending pagan rites.' Pip didn't reply. 'I don't approve. But my husband continues to do many things that give me pain.' Her eyes glinted as she stared at Pip, who stood there awkwardly. 'While I'm being disapproving, Dr Durrant,' she said, 'will you keep out of my daughter's bedroom.'

So she *had* seen them together! He didn't feel a need to reply to the accusation, only inclined his head slightly and began to go upstairs. He could feel her watching his every step. Her over-protectiveness was getting him down. If it went on, he would have to leave. Then he thought of Ghita. He could put up with a lot if he was still near her. It was only when he had closed his bedroom door behind him that he began to analyse his feelings for her.

He was very fond of Ghita. He would go even further and say that the night they had spent together on Halloween had been the best experience he'd had. He couldn't remember enjoying anything so much for a very long time, although he wasn't sure how she had felt about it. He had asked her if she did it with Anton, which he knew had upset her. Of course she did! And what would Emilia say about that? Was it all right because they were engaged? He smiled. But what would she have said if she had known *Pip* had slept with her? Probably gone crazy. But maybe Emilia was crazy already? Maybe that mad glint in her eyes was a hint of things to come? But he wasn't going to think about that. Perhaps he was misjudging her? After all, she had just lost her mother.

He was determined not to go to that funeral. One was enough. But Eva's had been an eye-opener. A bizarre experience that he wouldn't forget. He had been hoping he wouldn't have any more visions, but after what had just happened, clearly he was not free of them. They would not come frequently, but still soon enough for him. He didn't want to see them anymore. He only wished to get on with the project. Eisenmann was the next on his list. He felt both apprehensive and excited at the thought.

Pip lay down on his bed and made a plan. He would phone Eisenmann's secretary. He withdrew the card and took out his mobile. Then he wondered if he should tell Dalca first. Perhaps. He replaced his phone in his jeans pocket. He decided he would ring the next day instead. He kept looking at the door, hoping that he would hear a knock. But not Emilia's! He wanted Ghita to confide in him again. But nothing happened.

Sighing, he got up and sat down at his desk to make some notes. But he couldn't settle, and it was cold in the bedroom. If he had been in a different house, he might have gone down to the kitchen for warmth, but he couldn't do that

there. He had to put up with the inconvenience until Dalca –
or Ghita – returned. He thought of Emilia sitting down there
all alone, facing her mother's funeral the following day, and
felt some regret. Not only because of her bereavement, but
also because the opportunity of questioning Simona about
the secret had been lost. *I suppose that's what Marcu felt, when
Irina Petrescu died*, thought Pip. *That's why I have to make the
meeting with Eisenmann count, or I'll never get anywhere with the
Marcu Papers.* So many questions filled his brain that he gave
up what he was trying to do, went over and lay back down
on the bed, hands clasped behind his head, listening to the
wind and wondering what demons it was bringing down to
Arva. Hopefully, Eva hadn't been turned into one.

Pip went into Cluj the day of Simona Murgu's funeral. He felt
he needed to get away from Arva for a short time. He had
always been careful about security, so he took the Marcu Papers
with him as well as his personal possessions, all stuffed into his
backpack, leaving only a few clothes in the wardrobe. He
questioned himself as to why he had done that, but it had
seemed the right thing to do at the time. He was amazed to see
several people on the outskirts of the village boarding up their
houses as he left. He remembered what Ghita had told him
about them doing it in preparation for a heavy snowfall. 'It'll
probably be a yellow alert when they do that,' she had said. He
had wanted to ask her what that meant, but they'd been too
engrossed in each other. Later on, he had Googled it and found
out it was a national alert of bad weather on the way. Red for
the highest risk, down through yellow and on to green. So
heavy snow was expected.

Simona's death was on his mind as he huddled himself
up in his seat, while the draughts in the rattling bus cut around
his ankles, but he would have been even colder if he had been
aware of the bizarre stipulation Simona Murgu had made
regarding her death …

Simona's body had been released from the hospital and her sudden demise put down to pneumonia following a serious chest infection. Arva churchyard had been opened by special dispensation from the bishop for an aged parishioner, who had led a blameless life and was the mother-in-law of a well-known academic, whatever his beliefs. Arva church itself was not fit for holding the Requiem Mass, which was sung instead in Cluj. But, on the day of the funeral, Emilia stood by Dalca in the churchyard, raging inside.

'I don't want this,' she said. 'I don't want Mother to be buried here.' She looked down at the plot next to her mother's, then up at the church tower. Simona's request had rankled so much that she had cursed her mother for embarrassing the family. A second later, she was sorry, but with Fr Joseph gone, she couldn't go to Confession. 'I really do not!' she appealed, her eyes red from crying.

'Hush, Mother,' said Ghita, laying her hand on her arm. 'Don't upset yourself.'

'I don't want her next to *him!*' repeated Emilia hysterically. 'I don't want her here.'

Dalca and Ghita exchanged glances.

'You know she was always up in the churchyard!' replied Dalca. 'She spent a lot of time looking after the graves.' It was a well-known fact that Simona Murgu had an obsession with talking to the dead. He glanced over to the place where 'Grandsire's Girls' were buried. When he had been desperate to find out how many little unfortunates had been laid to rest there, he had tried to get permission for them to be exhumed. But that had never happened. The girls had rose bushes all to themselves – only red and gold, of course. Dalca's smile was bitter. *It was the custom.* No-one had attended the funeral of Grandsire's last victim, Anka Petrescu, except her parents, the priest, and Inspector Valentin. *The custom again.* Now that particular policeman had himself come to a nasty end.

At least Ghita had come through the ordeal of 'going up'. But he had to admit he was worried, very worried, after what Pip had told him about the records. He looked down at Ghita, and she, sensing his unease, took his hand. He thought black suited her much better than her mother.

Quite a few people had gathered in the churchyard, including many of the villagers. Simona had been well-liked. But her stipulation that she be laid to rest next to the farmer, Claudiu Basa, had really upset Emilia, who would have preferred – naturally – that her mother be laid to rest by her father! Like many others there that day, Dalca thought the situation was more than peculiar, and he cast several glances at his wife during the burial. There was village gossip about Simona and Basa having been lovers. Dalca believed it was more than idle talk. In fact he had learned from his mother that Simona had been the 'plump and pretty' girl who had been waiting at Basa's front door that day in 1952 when Catina Albu had been Grandsire's victim. As they lowered his mother-in-law into her grave, he wondered how much she had really known.

Then he felt Emilia slip her palm into his, which surprised him. It had been a long time since she had needed his comfort. When, much to Dalca's relief, the service had finished, both his wife and daughter were clinging on to his arms as they walked down the stony path. But Emilia was talking to herself under her breath.

'It goes on, old man, it goes on,' she muttered.

How often had she heard her mother say that, when she had tended Basa's grave? Too many. As for Ghita, Emilia knew she had do something to save her from the fate that would undoubtedly ruin her life. She had done all that she could so far, but how long could she go on protecting her? Ghita was wilful, and her liaison with Dalca's student boded no good. If her grandmother had known what Ghita was getting up to, she would have had plenty to say about it.

Sometimes at night, the voice in Emilia's head insisted that she herself should act. It troubled her. It was coming too often, reminding her that *she* was the one to blame for the family's terrible predicament. The voice was insistent, plaguing her, reminding her it was all her fault, urging her to put a stop to what was going to happen in the future and telling her how to do it. When she had begun to hear it in the daytime too, she had become even more afraid. She couldn't confide in her husband, though, because he was too wrapped up in his books, trying to discover the secret with which *she* was burdened.

Emilia's eyes darted from side to side as she stumbled down the path from the church. Over there was Basa's old house, which had been fired by the village men after his death on the day Petrescu's daughter had died. It had been a fitting end to a place that had been cursed by his presence. Her mother had thought she had hidden her secret from Emilia, but Emilia had suspected for a long time that the old cripple was her father! She had been conceived on the day that Catina Albu died! And, now, her mother had betrayed her, by revealing Emilia's shame to everyone else by her choice of grave.

'Ghita will pay for my mother's sin,' she murmured under her breath. 'I would rather she and I were dead.'

At that moment, Emilia hoped she would not live long enough, or be sane enough, to witness the horror that was bound to come again to Arva, unless she did something about it.

Pip wondered how the funeral was going back in Arva and how Ghita was taking it. With the old woman's death, another avenue for discovering the secret had been closed. Ghita thought that by marrying Anton she was going to find out, but Pip had his doubts as to whether or not Emilia would tell her. He couldn't imagine that woman getting close to anyone. And she was certainly behaving strangely. It slipped into his mind that Emilia might be heading the same way as her mother. How he wished that Marcu had found out more about Arva women's schizophrenic tendencies and documented the voices they were hearing. But the similarities seemed to have baffled him.

Instead, Marcu had taken a wider view, concentrating on Irina and what had happened in Arva, rather than the mainspring of her illness. Pip supposed that he had intended to turn to the latter in his coming research – that is, if his life hadn't been cut short. He thought of Robert then, and whether or not there could be any truth in his suspicion that Eisenmann had killed Marcu. It seemed preposterous, but he would never know that either. Pip wasn't afraid of dying like his predecessor, but he realised that the German was dangerous. He had to take precautions and cover his back. He remembered the joke his American supervisor had cracked: *Watch out for vampires!*

As he smiled to himself, his mobile phone rang. He couldn't believe it. Professor Wright! Talk about telepathy! If there was such a thing.

'Glad I got you,' the Professor said. It was good to hear an American accent again. Pip had almost forgotten all about the Institute.

'Great to hear from you, Prof.'

There was a pause.

'You may not think so, when you hear what I have to say. I want you home.'

'What?'

'I'm not going to explain everything now. In brief, the Institute has received a letter. A very surprising one. Knowing you, I was more than surprised when it was handed to me and, although I don't want to sound judgemental, I was somewhat …' He paused '… Disappointed.'

'What am I supposed to have done?' Pip was genuinely puzzled.

'The letter accused you of antisocial activities. I can hardly believe it, but it mentions you have been investigated by the police …'

Oh, shit, thought Pip. *The letter from Valentin.*

'I can explain,' replied Pip.

'That's what I told the Board. But they're in a sensitive position, seeing as you are the first student they have sent on this exchange. You're the flag bearer – and we can't have students getting into trouble. It gives us a bad name.'

'I have nothing to hide,' retorted Pip.

'You can explain all that when you get back. I have every confidence in you. I guess I know how you feel, but as I'm your supervisor, this thing has to be settled. My advice to you is to book yourself on the next plane. Or ...' The pause was significant. '... They might withdraw your grant. And that wouldn't be pleasant for either of us. I assume you've been getting on with your research?'

'You don't have to ask me that.'

'I do and, in spite of this conversation, I do have a lot of faith in you, or I wouldn't have put you forward for the project. You just have to come home and defend yourself.'

'I shouldn't have to,' said Pip, 'but you're the boss. All I can say is it's very inconvenient at this stage.' He thought of the meeting with Eisenmann.

'I know, but I'm confident you'll do the right thing.'

'I can see I have no option. I'll get myself on the next plane.'

'Good man.'

Pip stared at the phone as the Professor hung up.

'Shit,' he said. 'I could have done without that right now. But I'm going to see Eisenmann first.' He sat thinking about the whole thing for a few minutes, but he couldn't see any way out, so he got on the internet and booked a ticket for a flight the following evening. His head was full of what Wright had told him. He could understand the concern of the Institute trustees, but as he had told the Professor, he had nothing to hide.

Then it crossed his mind that Wright might have been economical with the truth. Maybe Pip had been implicated in the other strange deaths of Robert and the priest? His imagination started to run away with him. He had been worried about getting mixed up in Riparu's activities with Eisenmann in the first place, although it had to come to nothing. Maybe the State Police had something on Robert? Over here, they couldn't be described as friendly. And they knew that he had wanted to meet Valentin!

'Stop it,' he said. 'When you come back, Dalca will put it right. After all, you've been working with the guy all this semester. You've nothing to worry about.' Except, perhaps, the possibility that the Institute might not let him back, and throw him off the project. That was why the most important thing right then was for him to contact Eisenmann. He consulted his watch. It wasn't too late. He would ring the German's secretary. At least he now had an honest reason to say he must meet him in Cluj, because he was leaving for America the following evening.

The conversation was friendly. Sigi said she understood the dilemma perfectly and she would put him in the diary for the following afternoon. Then she gave him precise directions for how to get there. He felt relieved at her attitude. How could he have imagined that Eisenmann was going to kill him?

As Dalca got ready for bed, he thought to himself that Emilia had been behaving strangely. He had tried to persuade her to retire early, given the state she was in after the funeral, but she had refused. He could hear her roaming about the house, then clattering about in the kitchen, but he knew better than to go down to try to persuade her while she was in a mood.

Ghita had not gone out. Although she had assured Dalca that she was fine, she didn't look it. She was taking her grandma's death badly, and no wonder. She had spent a lot of time with the mad old woman, and whatever had happened between them in the past, she had managed to put it behind her and save Emilia the regular trip up and down to Burbor, which always unnerved her.

Half-undressed, Dalca shivered. The heating was playing up, so he switched on the fan heater in the bedroom. Then he went over to the window, put his hands on the sill and stared out into the night's whirling blackness. He was sure there was going to be a heavy snowfall. The skies had been a sombre grey all day, fitting for a funeral. He felt as if a burden had been lifted by Simona's death. She had been a liability ever since she had cracked up. He had seen it coming on for a long time in her fight against her own particular devils. None of it had done any good to Emilia nor Ghita.

Sighing, he thought of his great grandmother. At least

they had given Eva a good send off. The *pomana* had been received well, and the dancing afterwards had been wild. He had left fairly early, as he had thought Emilia would be surly with him. Strangely enough, she had seemed withdrawn, which he supposed was only to be expected after receiving the news of her mother's death. He had known then that he was destined for a bad few days. All in all, it had been a week he wouldn't forget.

However, he had to get back to work. He still had several lectures to prepare. Luckily, his timetable was light enough for him to be able to pursue his work with Pip, which now was a matter of the greatest urgency. Sooner or later, he was going to have to tell his young friend the truth about Eisenmann – and Ghita! He should have told Pip before that the stranger he had met in the churchyard was the German, who would stop at nothing to wring out any information he could glean about the project. He too was on a quest. No way would he allow his true origins to be made public. It wouldn't do much for his career if it was made known that his father was a Nazi and his mother a Romanian gypsy. Eisenmann had built up an international reputation, which he had no intention of tarnishing. Added to that, there was the Grandsire element of the equation. Dalca did not know how far his half-brother had advanced with the theory that the Nazi was his father. When he was a child, he must have heard something of the man's reappearance from the lips of Eva Kirchma. As Anya had said, Nicholai had not been an ordinary boy. Far from it. Dalca did not know how much he resembled the Nazi officer, aka Grandsire. He could only guess. But what he did know was that all those who could have possibly aided his and Pip's work had been eliminated.

Would it be safe for Pip to meet his half-brother? Dalca couldn't be sure that nothing bad would happen. Eisenmann was undoubtedly their enemy but, in the end, he had to be faced. Dalca still hadn't made his mind up as to Marcu's fate. Maybe it *had* been just a heart attack. All at once, he decided that he couldn't leave his young friend to face Eisenmann alone. He would tell him the next day that he would go to the meeting as well – and also tell him what he ought to know about Ghita. He had put that off because he could hardly bear to think about it, never mind frame it in words.

Dalca left the window and went off to brush his teeth. As he looked at his shaggy reflection in the bathroom mirror, he grimaced. He'd had no time to attend to personal matters recently.

'It's best you tell him all of it soon,' he said to himself.

The fan heater wasn't doing a lot of good, so Dalca left on his vest and underpants under his pyjamas and kept on his socks. He also left the heater on for Emilia to switch off when she came up. Trying to put everything out of his mind, he hugged the blankets around him and, having made the decision to confess, fell asleep very soon.

Downstairs, Emilia continued to roam, trying to get rid of the insistent voice in her head. She didn't want to go into the kitchen, but she couldn't bear the living room either, because Dalca had left on the television. She had tried to avoid looking at it. Even the people on the screen had joined with the voice, telling her what she should do, urging her to finish it, telling her that if she did, she would be free. The old red rooster on the rug had cackled in agony when she had stepped on it, and she had run out into the broad hall corridor. But even there, the black shapes stencilled on the walls made faces at her, jeering at her, taunting her, telling her to do it.

She could hear them laughing behind her as desperation drew her back towards the kitchen. She looked up at the ceiling, and drops of perspiration ran off her brow and dripped down her face. She had to go upstairs, but she was afraid.

'Go on,' said the voices. More than one was urging her now. 'You'll be free. Nothing will ever worry you again. It's the best thing. The best you've ever done.'

She walked slowly over to the cooking range, pulled the big meat knife from its block, then turned and looked towards the door.

The knife felt cold in her hand. Its coolness comforted her. Emilia withdrew her feet from her slippers and crept quietly out of the kitchen with her voices singing in her ears. They were happy. *She* would be happy. She put her hand on the banister and began to climb the stairs.

Ghita turned over in bed and opened her eyes. She had always been a light sleeper. She stared up at the ceiling, her eyes slowly adjusting to the dark. She had been dreaming about Simona, and it hadn't been pleasant. She sighed, but a sudden streak of light illuminated the ceiling. It was coming from the door!

'Is that you, Mother?' But there was no response. She rolled over. The door was open a crack and was opening further. 'Mother?'

Ghita felt a pang of guilt. She should have been more supportive at her grandma's funeral. Her mother was bound to be upset. Maybe she had gone across the landing to the bathroom? But why open Ghita's door? Perhaps she was looking for comfort.

Ghita sat up in bed. She felt so tired that all she wanted to do was go back to sleep. Sighing again, she was about to get out of bed and close the door when a dark figure slipped through. 'Mother?' she repeated.

A moment later, the shape darted forward and flung herself at Ghita, who screamed as she threw herself over to the other side of the bed. She scrabbled to get the bedclothes off her as her mother wrested herself from off the bed. Ghita was terrified, seeing the big knife in her mother's hand. A second later, Emilia lunged. But Ghita was quicker, and ducked out of the way.

'*Tată!*' she screamed, her voice piercing the air.

Emilia stood as the scream resonated in the room. In that silent moment, Ghita took her chance. She hurled herself towards the door. Her mother was blocking the way, with madness in her eyes, but the violence of Ghita's push sent her staggering back. The girl flew to the door and through it, to see her father stumbling along the landing.

'*Tată!*' Ghita launched herself at him and burst into tears. 'Mother tried to kill me. She's in there. She's got a knife.'

'No, darling, no!' he soothed. But it wasn't a nightmare. As Emilia came through the door, he saw that she had a kitchen knife in her hand. She raised it. Dalca pushed Ghita aside and stepped towards her. 'Emilia, what are you doing? Put the knife down!'

He approached her. All the sleepy confusion had gone from him now. So it has come to this, he thought. 'Put the knife down! Are you going to stab *me*?'

Emilia stood still, while Ghita cowered behind him.

'She has to die,' said Emilia, her voice coming out of her as if she was in a trance. 'My voices told me.'

'Then your voices were wrong,' said Dalca in a measured tone. 'Be calm, my love.' He was still approaching and she was retreating, waving the knife. 'Just give it to me,' he said, 'and everything will be all right.' She had her back to the stairs now. He put out his hand and she slashed at him. The blow was of such force that she toppled backwards, and with a scream – *fell*, her body bumping down the stairs. Then Ghita launched herself into his arms.

'Why did she do it, Tată? Why?' She was hysterical. He held her in his arms, but, all the time, his eyes were on the bottom of the stairs.

'Shush, darling,' he said, putting her aside gently. 'I have to go and see how your mother is.' An overwhelming trepidation seized him. He breathed in as he prepared himself to go down and look at the motionless body of his wife. But Dalca would never forget what he felt in his heart that night as he walked down. He was hoping that Emilia was dead.

17

The wind woke Pip up in the night. He went over and stared out of the window to discover it was blowing a blizzard, with great flakes of snow being hurled out of the sky. It was four in the morning when he sat down with a cup of coffee, thinking about the meeting with Eisenmann that had been arranged for the following afternoon, before he caught the plane. Afterwards, he went back to bed, and it was after eight when the phone woke him.

'Professor,' he said. 'I was going to ring you soon.'

'I have some bad news, Pip. Emilia has had an accident.'

Pip felt a shiver down his back.

'What happened?'

'She fell down the stairs in the night. She has been taken to the hospital. I am still here sorting out things.'

'Is Ghita with you?'

'No, Anton has driven her over to stay with Miruna. She's very upset.'

That's strange, thought Pip. *I would have thought she would have wanted to be with her mother. And why isn't Dalca at the hospital?* His instincts were telling him things were not quite as simple as the Professor was making out.

'Enough of me,' added Dalca. 'What is happening with you? Have you contacted Eisenmann?'

'I am seeing him this afternoon,' said Pip. Silence.

'So soon?'

'Yes. I have something to tell you, Prof. I have to go back to the States.' Pip told him about the phone call.

'But no-one has mentioned this to me,' replied Dalca.'I am sure I can do something about it.'

'It's best I do as they say, or the project will be scrapped,' warned Pip. 'Anyway, I'll be back soon. I would like to say goodbye to Ghita though before I go.'

'That won't be possible,' replied Dalca.

So I was right then, thought Pip. *There is more to this.*

'Best leave it until you return,' Dalca continued. 'She's very upset about her mother. How are you getting to the airport? I could get Anton to take you. He's back in Cluj.'

And no doubt he's comforting Ghita, thought Pip. *Well, I can ring her.*

'Are you still there?' asked Dalca.

'I suppose this means I'll have to go and see Eisenmann on my own then?'

'You should put it off.' The statement sounded more like a command.

'I don't think so. In any case, if I get anything from him, I can work on it while I'm back in the States.'

'I could meet you at the airport. As I told you, I have something important to tell you, but I can't this afternoon. What time does your plane leave?'

Pip told him.

'I suggest this,' said Dalca. 'I'll arrange for Anton to take you to Eisenmann's, wait for you, and then take you on to the airport. I'll meet you there. I should be finished by then. By the way, have you looked out of your window?'

'I'm still in bed.'

'The first real snow of the winter,' said Dalca.

'What about driving in it?'

'The E road will be clear. The airport is only eight kilometres anyway.'

'No, I mean you!'

'I shall make it, don't worry. We are used to snow here.'

'By the way, I have left a few things at your place.'

'I'll look in your room and bring them.'

'No, it's fine. I don't need them. See you at the airport then.'

'Anton will ring you before he comes round. Keep safe,' replied Dalca, cutting off the conversation.

Pip stared at the phone. *So that's it. I meet Eisenmann alone, and with only Anton for back-up.* He shook his head. So much for Dalca's histrionics about evil. Now he would have to arrange with Anton what he would do if he found himself in trouble with Eisenmann. Ghita's fiancé had made it quite clear what he felt about the man he saw as his rival. They'd never said two words to each other. And now Dalca was suggesting Anton would back him up. 'He would probably be happy if I got my throat cut,' said Pip.

Later on, he rang Ghita, but she didn't answer. So he left her a message:

'Ghita, I hope you're okay. Sorry to hear about your mother. If you don't want to stay with Miruna, you can use my flat. I'll tell your father when I see him. I won't be there, as I have to go away. I'm sorry, but I'm leaving you a note with the concierge explaining it all.'

It took him some time to write the note, although it was only a few lines long. He was used to getting things down on paper, but anything personal was different. He didn't want to screw it up.

Dearest Ghita,

I want you to know I'm thinking of you. I have had to go back to the States to sort out something urgent with my supervisor. Dare I say that as your mother is so ill, maybe you won't be tying the knot for a while. You don't have to, you know. If, for any reason, I can't get back (although I don't expect to be gone for long), and you change your mind about Anton, you could always come over and see me in New York. You have my number if you want to call me. I shall miss you.

Yours, Pip.

He stared at it and shook his head. This was as near as he had come to declaring his feelings to anyone. But he needed to tell her, just in case. The idea of leaving Romania was unpalatable in one way, but welcome in another. He wanted to get back to all things familiar; but, on the other hand, not like this. How the Board of the Institute could believe he had been mixed-up with shady dealings was beyond him. Wright should have been able to sort it out. Dalca would have done! He felt angry with his university being influenced by the politics of the thing. 'Flag bearer, my ass!' he said. Then he saw the other side. They had no option but to check him out. Pip had always been known for his tolerance.

Whatever happened, he was going to hang on to the Marcu Papers. A sudden thought pierced him. What if they wanted to give them to someone else to finish the project? That would be death to him. He had come to consider them as his own. The thought spurred him on. He packed all his personal items into his backpack, then took the Papers down to the students' office to use the photocopier. He was going to take a copy. It wasn't ethical, but he intended to do it. Luckily, the secretary was out. It would just cost him.

When he had finished and gone back to his room, he tried to decide what to do with the material. Should he entrust it to someone, like Marcu had to Robert? But Pip had no-one. *He was not going to hand over the copy to Dalca.* Part of Pip argued that would be the right thing to do; the other, which he recognised as a mixture of pride and the mark of the solitary researcher, precluded such a step. He decided he would take everything back to America with him and, if the worst did happen and the original Papers were handed over to someone else, he would still have his own copy – although he wasn't sure what he would do with it. Hopefully, that would not happen. Briefly he had thought of asking Ghita to keep the Papers for him, but he had decided against it. He didn't want her looking at them and becoming even more scared. She had enough to cope with at present.

He placed both the copy and the original in his briefcase, which he would take onto the plane as hand luggage. That way, they couldn't be lost. He felt relieved he had completed the task. The memory brought back the vision of Koppelberg, and made him feel a bit sick. Then he thought of the horror he had felt when he had been looking up Eisenmann on his laptop and had seen Arvarescu's face merging with Koppelberg's in the blank photo frame. And when he had seen the note on the lawn – and the message on the laptop. What had that been about? He could think of no explanation for it, except imagination; but whatever it had been, it had really spooked him at the time. Like too many other inexplicable things he had experienced in Romania. He wondered what he would do if Eisenmann looked like Koppelberg. Shiver-making.

He did something then that he had never thought he would. He looked in his wallet and found the little silver cross his mother had sent him after he had gone to live in New York. After he had fastened the chain around his neck, he pushed the cross under his T-shirt, feeling rather foolish. He couldn't imagine what he was going to do with it. Hold it up to protect himself? Like they did in a vampire movie? Ghita still hadn't returned his call, and by the time he had been downstairs to the kitchen and made himself a sandwich, it was getting late. What if Anton didn't turn up? Then his cell phone went. It was the man himself.

They made an arrangement for Anton to pick up Pip outside the hostel in time to get to the meeting. A few minutes beforehand, Pip went down to the entrance hall to wait. After he had given the concierge his note addressed to Ghita, he thought to himself how pleased Anton would be to see the back of him, and how angry he would be if he knew what Pip had written in the note. Before leaving the flat, he had decided to take a chance on asking Ghita to look after Cass. She had said that rats weren't her favourite animals, but he couldn't help it, because he couldn't take a rodent back with him to the States.

When Pip, burdened with his backpack, his briefcase, his laptop and Cass's cage, struggled out to Anton's car, he was surprised to see just how much snow there was on the ground. He did not ask Anton to help him with his luggage, and he realised the other wasn't inclined to offer.

'What am I supposed to do with a rat?' Anton was staring at the cage.

'Sorry, but I can't take her with me. Would you ask Ghita to look after her for me?'

'Did she say she would?'

'I think I mentioned it,' said Pip. Anton was still staring. 'Shall I put it in the back?'

'If you have to. I've never liked rats.'

'You've missed something then,' said Pip. 'They're friendly.'

He stowed the cage in the back seat, propping it up against some stuff of Anton's. Cass wouldn't like it if Anton stepped on the brakes too hard. The pavements had been partly cleared, and the snow was piled high on each side, leaving only a narrow path to walk through. *Not many people in the park today*, Pip thought. Then he remembered Ghita's remark about the boots, as his trainers splashed through the slush at the side of the road. He noticed that Anton was well-equipped for the weather, with high boots and a heavy jacket. When Pip climbed into the passenger seat, his feet were soaking, as were his trousers. He decided he would change at the airport, or on the plane; but he reminded himself that such trivia were unimportant compared with his present worries. All he could do now was prepare for the meeting with Eisenmann. Why did the man want to see him? But Pip had his answers ready and was determined that Anton, however sullen he was, had to provide the back-up he needed.

The teenager seemed to have quietened down a bit, as he seemed to be taking care on the road. It was certainly not the hair-raising journey that Pip had suffered before, when he had travelled back to Cluj with Ghita, which seemed an age ago.

They drove on through an exclusive neighbourhood as expected. Many of the houses were grand and imposing and, ornamented by snow, their red-tiled roofs were fairytale-like. The road into which they turned was a broad sweep flanked by a wooded hillside on one side and flat woodland and smaller houses on the opposite. Anton and Pip had reached their destination without even exchanging a word. As they came to a tall column flanked by two black statues, which Pip assumed was a war memorial, Anton drew into the verge and stopped. Two very large houses bordered the road on the hill side. Between them was a small wood. At the very top of the hill was a building that looked like flats or a hotel. Lower down, he could see high gates at the entrance of a drive, which vanished between the trees, but no house was visible beyond.

'That's it,' said Anton, bending his head to look across to the other side of the road and pointing at the gates. 'I could park over there.' Pip was relieved to hear him speak, but not at all happy when he added, 'I'm not driving up there. The car won't make it in this weather.'

'I need you to take me right up to the door, and then wait for me. You have chains on the wheels.' Pip didn't want to sound accusatory, but he knew Anton was being obstructive.

'So?' retorted Anton.

'Professor Dalca said you'd take me – and you will.'

'Will I?' Anton made a face. 'It'll cost you.'

'Fine by me.'

'How much are you offering?' said Anton, looking interested.

Pip put his hand into one of the inside pockets of his parka and brought out his wallet. 'One hundred bucks. Including the fare to the airport. That's as far as I'm prepared to go. If you're not satisfied, I can ring Dalca.' He took out his mobile phone.

'No, that's fine,' said Anton, pocketing the cash. 'But don't blame me if the car doesn't make it! She's not keen on slopes.'

Pip was soon to realise that Anton knew his own vehicle better than he did …

A few minutes before Pip and Anton arrived, Heine Muller loaded up Sigi's car with luggage as instructed. He felt like he was boiling up inside as she ordered him about.

'Put those in the car!'

'Very good, madam,' he said, seething.

His job wasn't good anymore. Her car was another Mercedes, a black open-top sports. He was not allowed to drive it, only the master's. But she drove his master's as well, whenever she fancied it, and whenever he needed her to accompany him on his secret business. Then, Heine was superfluous.

Sigi had a petulant look on her face as she drove slowly out of the courtyard. *She'll soon need a bigger car*, Heine thought, with a scornful look on his face. He had used to think she was pretty, but pregnancy didn't suit her like it suited some women. As well as being fat, she looked ugly. She was probably going to meet up with Eisenmann when he followed her on to the airport – because they were both about to go off again in the private jet, leaving him to mind the house. They rarely travelled together. Heine shook his head. Who did they think they were? Royalty? But he knew. If one had an accident, the other had to carry on with the dirty games.

This time it was New York! Maybe this was the end of the line with Eisenmann's PACE business, which was winding down. Heine suspected that the work in Strasbourg would soon be finished. The States are probably more lucrative, he thought jealously. Maybe they were legging it – which they could afford to do – and leaving him to clean up their shit. Heine knew they kept most of their money in a Swiss bank, and up to a quarter of a million in the house safe. It cost to do what his master did. He could buy anyone.

How Heine had dreamed of getting his hands on the contents of that safe! He and one other member of the staff, a brainless thug named Hermann, held keys to the safe and to the house, but neither had the combination to the former. Or at least Heine thought Hermann didn't. He suspected his master's decision to withhold the combination from one or both of them stemmed from some warped desire to turn him against Hermann. That wouldn't take very much. He and Hermann didn't get along!

Nobody ever knew what Eisenmann was really up to, except Sigi. Maybe he had arranged to take Hermann with him to the States instead of Heine? And what was he supposed to do when they'd gone? Sit there twiddling his thumbs until Eisenmann phoned him up and ordered him to knock off a few more people? Heine was done with killing for a pittance.

Besides, he didn't trust either of them anymore. There was no place in their lives for him. Once, he had been loyal, but where had it got him? He was the butt of their jokes, and he had a terrible feeling that they were going to drop him in the shit. Or worse. He hadn't done anything about it up until now, because he was afraid of what they might do to him. He was also scared they'd discover how he felt. Eisenmann had a way with him, almost as if he was reading his every thought. Then he would be done for. But his dissatisfaction had been escalating at a steady pace, ready to burst out into something far worse – which had become an alarming possibility since he had realised they were taking off for New York in the private jet.

He could see the roof of Sigi's car as it nosed its way along the broad path at the side of the house. 'Thank Christ she's gone,' he muttered, and went back in, hoping she wouldn't scratch the side of Eisenmann's Mercedes as she squeezed past it, because he would get the blame if she did.

A few minutes later, he heard the noise of a painfully labouring engine as it crawled its laborious way up the drive. He could tell it was an old car. Certainly not a Mercedes. It must be his master's visitor!

Heine made his way into the hall, where he examined his reflection in the great French mirror – one of the many trappings of Eisenmann's enormous wealth. All at once, Heine wanted to smash in its self-satisfied face. He was a dangerous man when roused.

He unbuttoned his suit jacket and felt a throb of pleasure as he checked the gun strapped into its holster, stark black against his white shirt. Heine dressed well. It was the only part of his job now that he liked, wearing his uniform. Once, when he was young, he had a dream of joining the army. But he had ended up working as a waiter in a Cologne hotel, until his potential for violence had been spotted by his master. He had been green then! Malleable. Now he wished he had refused the job, because he was little more than a slave to them. But he was still a force to be reckoned with, and not a minion to be abandoned at will.

The old car's engine groaned as its wheels slipped and skidded on the slope. With an I-told-you-so look on his face, finally Anton made it up the drive. The house looked straight out of a Gothic novel, its turrets glowering at them through the snow, which was beginning to fall again. *Where else would the man live?*, thought Pip. He turned to Anton, 'You wait for me,' he ordered, 'and if I don't come back in an hour ...'

'An hour!' burst out Anton. 'I'll effing freeze to death!'

'Well, keep the engine running!' snapped Pip. 'You look as if you've enough clothes on! I'm leaving the backpack here, my laptop and my briefcase. Whatever happens, don't let anyone have them!'

Anton looked interested.

'Why? What are they worth?'

'Look here, Anton. You're doing a job, so shut it. I intend to get to that airport on time. I'm leaving for the States and you're marrying Ghita, so what's your problem?'

They faced each other.

'I suppose,' Anton backed down.

'Lock the doors when I'm gone. And swing round in the drive – in case we need to make a quick getaway.'

'Who are you expecting? *Dracula*?' Anton peered at the house.

'Very funny. Just do what I say, please.'

'Okay, you're the boss,' Anton replied, getting out a pack of cigarettes. Neither of them noticed the bronze Mercedes parked up at a distance next to a side door, and in front of it, a smaller Mercedes, this one a soft-top sports, its fur-clad woman driver flipping through a magazine.

A few moments later, Heine was letting in the visitor, noting that he wore fashionable spectacles and looked sharp, but was dressed poorly in a T-shirt and jeans under a parka! Their usual callers were politicians, bankers and other businessmen who had come to impart and receive the kind of information only Eisenmann had. But it cost. The chauffeur had met plenty of *them* in his time. The crooked kind, who would do anything for money and had plenty of it. But this young man looked like a student.

What does my boss want with him? Heine thought. *He doesn't look as if he has one mark to his name. No wonder he's expendable.* His feet were in dirty trainers and his jeans wet to the knee, even though he had come in a car. Before he closed the door, Heine's scathing eyes rested for a second on the small, scruffy vehicle and its occupant, a cigarette dangling from his mouth, who was attempting to turn the car in the snow. He was a poor-looking specimen too. It would be no problem dealing with both these men, if needed. For a moment, Heine felt sorry for the two of them. Which surprised him, as he wasn't given to sentimentality.

When the man opened the door to him, Pip was almost expecting the creepy old retainer from a horror film, which would have fitted the aspect of the building very well. Instead he was confronted by a black-suited man wearing black leather gloves. He had the kind of average face and build to which no-one would give a second glance. But as he looked again, Pip had a sudden instinct he had seen him somewhere before. The servant was so unprepossessing that Pip couldn't place him, yet the suit's funereal aspect and his grim demeanour smacked of the hit man. He certainly wasn't a butler, although he sounded like one when he said,

'The master is expecting you.'

'Thank you.' Pip could feel himself sweating. He was longing to take off his parka as he followed the man across the tiled hall with its great French mirror, which was definitely Louis Quatorze. *Eisenmann lives in some style*, thought Pip, glancing around. *Probably at the taxpayers' expense.* He wondered if Marcu had been intimidated when he had gone to meet the German. The idea made him sweat a little more. He didn't intend to end up like his predecessor. He had to get this one right. To take control.

'Who shall I say?' asked the man.

'Dr Durrant.'

The heavy door creaked as the man opened it and stood with his back against the wood. 'Dr Durrant,' he announced, like they do in the movies. Then he gestured Pip to enter.

Pip walked through, looking as cool as he could. He had not been prepared for the beauty of the room, nor its spaciousness. It even had a gallery. In spite of its ancient aspect and its dark and heavy panelling, lined with thousands of books imprisoned behind meshed golden grilles, the place was a power house of modernity. This was an office of some proportion, more suited to a city block than to a private house. At the far end was a large glass display case, but he couldn't see what it contained. He swallowed. He had always been wary of cases like that, ever since his past encounter with Diep Koppelberg.

Pip glanced away and concentrated on the centre of the room. Several desks were arranged in a huge semi-circle, which could have housed as many delegates as secretaries, but the luxurious, red velvet swivel chairs were empty. The huge seat at the focal point of the conference room – for it was that rather than an office – was empty of its occupant. In front of the chair, which faced the gap in the circle, was a table on which was set a fine cut-glass carafe containing water and two glasses. Pip could imagine how the boss strode in and out, leaving his minions overawed. The computer screens exuded a panoply of special effects that sprinkled coloured light on the ornate ceiling and the solemn bookcases.

'Mr Eisenmann?' called Pip. He couldn't see his adversary.

'At last.' The voice came from above! Pip looked up to the gallery. A man appeared. He was wearing black as well. 'I'll be with you directly. Please sit.'

'Thank you.' Pip made his way to a chair as near to the table as possible. He didn't intend to be intimidated. He watched the tall man leaping down the spiral staircase, his movements so graceful that he seemed to be suspended in mid-air. He was carrying a black book and his lithe action seemed remarkably boyish from a distance. But when he approached, Pip recognised that floppy golden hair and blinked. Then those eyes, snake-like and unblinking, fixed him as they had done *in the churchyard*.

'We have met before, I believe,' said Eisenmann. 'But in a less pleasant environment.' He extended his hand, which Pip was forced to take. The man's talons scratched him as his palm slipped through Pip's, reminding him of the sensation of trying to hold an ice-cube when he was a kid. Pip decided not to comment on their earlier meeting. If he had the chance, that would come later. But what the hell had Eisenmann been trying to find in the tomb at Arva?

Facets of light glanced off the German's diamond ear studs as he settled himself into the central chair, which Pip knew was meant to give a psychological advantage to anyone who sat there. Eisenmann put the book down and left one hand upon it. It was evidently of great value to him.

'Please take off your coat. You look hot. Would you like a drink?' said Eisenmann, indicating the carafe. 'We have ice cubes.'

Pip, who was perspiring freely now and beginning to feel stressed already, started to employ some of the preventative measures he had learned in his training.

'I am, but no thank you,' he said. 'I'll keep my coat on for now.' He wasn't going to leave his parka behind if he had to make a quick getaway. He stared Eisenmann straight in the eyes. 'Can we get to the point, please? I have a plane to catch. Why did you want us to meet?'

'I am interested in your research.'

'Why? Are you in the business of furthering it?' replied Pip, turning the question with skill. He stared at the book. Did it hold any of the clues he was looking for? Then he noticed two large holdalls behind Eisenmann's chair. Maybe Pip wasn't the only one planning a trip.

'I am in the business of facilitating,' said Eisenmann. 'In that area, I am much in demand.'

'In that case, I'd welcome hearing anything to my advantage. That is, if you already know the nature of my business.' Pip wondered how Marcu had approached the man. Was verbal fencing the style to adopt? Or was he being too eager?

'Your fame has spread, Dr Durrant. And not only in the University.' Eisenmann's eyelids seemed to droop, ageing him. Until then, his physical aspect had transmitted an impression of utter youthfulness, but Pip knew he must be nearing 50, according to Anya's account. Ever since the Arvarescu apparition had appeared on his laptop, the memory of Koppelberg had haunted Pip, and now it had been reinforced by the sight of the glass case at the end of the room.

How old was the inhuman part of Eisenmann? Pip's extreme imagination flicked back the answer. Five hundred years?

'I'm flattered you've heard of me,' replied Pip. 'But I'm sure University gossip wasn't responsible. I'd like to know who's been talking about me.'

'The police,' snarled Eisenmann, catching Pip off balance. He was an adversary who went for the jugular! Eisenmann must have foreseen the effect of his words, as he added suavely, 'But I am sure that is all hearsay.' Yet even this comment veiled a subtle threat.

Pip recovered himself.

'I have nothing to fear from the police. But I'd like to know how you obtained the information?'

'I have my sources. *And* you are leaving the country.' Eisenmann leaned back in the chair, swinging it with a black, perfectly-shod foot.

'Not for long,' retorted Pip. 'Also, I assumed police matters were private – unless of course you're trying to blackmail me.'

'Why would I do that?' A sinister smile hovered, then vanished. 'I would much rather we were friends, seeing that we are prosecuting similar avenues of knowledge in pursuit of the same goal.' He was tapping the book as he spoke. *I'm right,* thought Pip. *The evidence must be in there. And he is probably taking it with him, wherever he is going.*

'If you are sure of that, then why would you want to meet me?'

'We have the same goal,' said Eisenmann. 'I'd like to discuss the implications.'

Pip was ready to play the German's game to glean as much information from him as possible. 'The same goal,' he echoed. 'I'm interested in your opinion as to its nature.'

'Historical authentication of an ongoing problem that affects us both.'

He's a clever bastard, thought Pip. He isn't going to define it. But neither am I. It was like dog sniffing dog.

'I am not affected by any of the material personally,'

said Pip. 'I'm a researcher, Now in your case ... it *is* more personal.' He could see that he had hit a nerve, as Eisenmann's expression changed. If the man *had* been a dog, he would have snarled!

'This personal knowledge of me – what are your sources?'

'Reliable, but I'm not willing to reveal them.' Pip relaxed in his chair. He could feel suppressed anger emanating from his adversary.

'Then I shall guess. The gypsies, and one in particular?'

'I can't answer that.' Whether he knew about the visit to the camp or he was just bluffing, Pip couldn't tell. He added, 'But I have complete faith in my information, which has allowed me to fill in certain gaps.'

'So intelligence has not yet quite decayed,' Eisenmann rasped.

'An apt quotation,' returned Pip, smiling a little himself. He had a memory for the smallest details. The German was quoting from what had been Browning's primary source for the Piper.

'From an old acquaintance!' Eisenmann snapped.

'You've read the Verstegen tract? Written I believe in 1605?' Pip could be sarcastic too.

The German let the tip of his tongue flick over his lips. The atmosphere was heavy with hostility. 'Yes. The manuscript is in my priceless collection.' He touched the book. 'You may have heard I was a bookseller, *once!*' Pip could see the acquisitive gleam in his eyes. 'You're a clever young man, Dr Durrant, but watch out, you may be tripped up by your quick wit.'

'You think so?' asked Pip. 'I didn't come here to play games, Mr Eisenmann. I think we both know we are referring to the Arvan ritual. I may be a scientist, but my interests extend far beyond, and I have progressed with the help of a medievalist in that area.' Eisenmann glowered. 'I have also discovered I have a particular interest in theology. I met with a priest recently, and our discussion was enlightening, though I am not a religious man. I'm sure you know that anyway, or I wouldn't be here.' Eisenmann made a small noise, resembling a growl. 'In these fields, I can say that my studies are going very well at present, unless of course you were hoping to add something to them. If so, I would be delighted.' He looked at the book again. What he would give to get hold of it! He felt an almost irresistible urge to lean over and grab it.

Eisenmann took his hand off the book and, interlinking it with the other, flexed them while staring at his talons.

Pip continued, 'But I assure you, I have obtained my knowledge through proper academic channels. I am not a criminal. As to the latter, I don't know where you stand!' Pip knew he was being reckless, which had always been his weakness.

Eisenmann jumped up from his chair. 'You think you have come up with the answers, Dr Durrant.' It was not a question. 'But I fear you're wrong, and you have still much to learn.'

Pip inclined his head, giving himself time to regain his cool.

'I'd be willing to, if it were possible,' he said. Pip knew Eisenmann was needled now. The trap was open and he was playing a dangerous game.

The German came round the table. Near to, a scent of freshly-turned earth came off him – and he hadn't been digging the garden! For a second, Pip panicked. He recognised that smell. It always figured in his visions. But he put his fears aside and looked Eisenmann straight in the eyes, challenging him. Something deep within Pip was priming him on how to proceed. It was as if someone else was taking him over.

'You think we could work together, boy.' The sarcasm was brutal.

'I think it might be a good idea to pool resources. Given your background.'

Eisenmann threw back his head and laughed. But it was not melodious. *My God,* thought Pip, *how much of Grandsire is in him?*

Then the German loped back to his seat, his very gait exuding anger. 'You know my background,' he repeated, sitting down. He stared at the book.

'I know you wouldn't like it made public. So I suggest we join forces!' Pip gasped inwardly as Eisenmann smiled, showing pointed incisors.

'You'd like to join forces with the devil, would you?'

'I don't believe in that shit,' said Pip in a brave voice. 'But a man who would hide his lineage at any cost, who would remove anyone who was a danger to him, might find that joining with another academic in cultural co-operation would be of advantage to both.' He paused. Eisenmann stood up.

'You think I would co-operate with a boy who has something I need in his possession. An arrogant brat who is dedicated to the destruction of Arva and all I hold dear. No, Dr Durrant, *I* do not co-operate. Nor am I in the mood for spreading your particular brand of altruism. You won't win *me* over. I am what I am. But I admire you for your insolence.' He stared hard at Pip.

'What *do* you need?' Pip could hear his voice shaking and his resolve fading. He could feel his earlier courage being sucked out by those hypnotic eyes. But he couldn't back down now.

'The Papers.' Eisenmann's voice was hollow. It echoed from the dim corners of the room. 'I want the evidence that Marcu gathered from the lips of a madwoman. Whatever Irina Petrescu told him, I need to know. Marcu cheated me. You have more fight in you than him, but like him, you're human. Believe me, Dr Durrant, you could go down the same road as your predecessor if you deny me what is mine.'

So Robert had been right! Eisenmann had killed Marcu. But how had he instigated a heart attack? Maybe a colourless poison? Pip flicked a glance at the tray with the carafe and two glasses. He was glad he had refused the water.

'And, if I refuse to hand over the Papers, you'll silence me?' Pip said. 'How?'

'It won't come to that if you play ball. Where are they?'

'I don't have them anymore. They're in a safe place,' lied Pip.

'I don't believe you. In your luggage?' The black eyes narrowed.

'That's my business.'

'Well, I shall make it mine,' threatened Eisenmann. 'You think you're smart. If you had been, you wouldn't have accepted my invitation.'

'I'm not afraid of you,' said Pip, getting up. 'Several people know where I am. They'll call the police if I don't come back.'

'Do you think that would be of any use in your present situation? The police are already looking for you.'

'That's not true,' replied Pip, braving it out, his quick brain searching for an escape route. Evidently nothing was going to be learned from this meeting. His interests would be best served by getting away from there as soon as possible. Dalca had been right. The man was both evil and dangerous.

'Now – the Papers,' repeated Eisenmann. ' Where are they?' His voice was more threatening now than at any time in the meeting.

'I told you, I don't have them,' stalled Pip, hoping that Anton was still outside. It was time to make a run for it.

'Then, if you will not give me the information, someone else will make you,' growled Eisenmann.

At that moment, Pip launched himself at the table and grabbed the book. He couldn't believe he had done it as he headed for the door.

He heard Eisenmann scream,

'Muller!'

As Pip reached it, the door was flung open, and he found himself staring at the barrel of a gun. He backed. Eisenmann sat down. 'Now what are you going to do, Durrant? Give me the book!'

'No,' said Pip, hugging it to him, looking from one to the other. But he could see no way out.

The German laughed out loud.

'You will let it go.' He turned to Heine. 'Take him out. Kill him! Afterwards, bring in his luggage.' He leaned back. 'And don't damage the book. Or you'll pay for it.' The man glowered. Pip was trembling all over.

'What about the driver?' replied Heine.

'Deal with him too.'

Heine nodded and waved the gun at Pip, motioning him to walk out of the door.

'You won't get away with this, Eisenmann!' Pip shouted as he was forced out into the hall, still clutching the book.

'I can assure you I will,' he called. 'And *you* won't! Shut the door behind you, Muller – and clean up your mess afterwards.'

Pip shuddered, but he pulled himself together in the hall. Whatever was going to happen, he wasn't going to give up without a fight. At least he would try to talk himself out of this.

'You don't want to do this,' he told Heine. 'I wasn't invited here to be shot. I came here for *this*,' he lied.

'What's with the book?' asked Heine.

'It belongs to the University,' said Pip. 'They sent me to get it back.' He knew he had caught the man's attention. Maybe he could be bought? But by the look on the man's face, there wasn't much chance. 'Your boss stole it. He wants it more than anything. The University will reward you, if you let me keep it. They know I'm here. If I'm harmed, the police will be on to *you*. Not him. You'll be in deep shit, and he'll get away with it.' Pip went cold all over as the man stared at him. There was no mercy in his eyes. 'Just let me go,' he pleaded. 'The book isn't his!'

'I'm not interested in the book,' said Heine. 'Outside.' He gestured to the front door.

'Are you going to kill me?' Pip was trying to think of everything he could. 'He wants my papers as well. They belong to the University too. If you shoot me, he won't ever know where they are. They're not in the car.' He knew he was gabbling. The man's face was expressionless, but recognition came to Pip like a flash. He knew he had seen him before! He had been the junior nurse on Simona Murgu's ward. He must have killed her too. Perspiration burst on Pip's forehead and rolled down his face. 'Your master won't be very happy if you don't bring him my papers. You might even end up dead.'

'Shut up,' growled the man.

I'm going to die, Pip thought as he felt the gun pressed into his back. *This is the end.* He felt sick, and his bowels loosened. He cursed Dalca for abandoning him. They crossed the great hall and reached the door. The man jerked the gun at Pip, gesturing him to open it.

As he did, his head was trying to compute his chances. What would his dad have done? How many hit men had he faced in his time? The cold air froze his face. *Soon I'll be colder*, he thought. *I'm not going to get out of this.*

'Move!'

Pip could see that Anton had turned the car round. It was on the slope facing down. At least he had *some* sense. Should he make a run for it? But then the bastard would shoot him in the back. Best to do what he said. *While there's life there's hope*, squeaked a lying little voice in his head.

He felt the gun prodding him towards the car. He couldn't see Anton. Where the fuck was he? He stumbled on, still clutching the book. Then he felt the gun withdraw from his back, and he screwed up his eyes, waiting for the bullet.

'Now get the hell out of here! And don't switch on the engine.' He opened his eyes, dazed at the command. A moment later, he heard two shots in succession and saw the trees frantically shake down their burden of snow as the bullets crashed into them. Pip made a dash for the car and hammered on the window. Anton looked terrified.

'Open the goddamn door. Move!' Pip screamed, jumping in. 'No, don't switch on the engine. Roll her down!' With the door hanging open, the little car responded as Anton let out the handbrake. Then it was crawling down the slope, gathering speed all the time.

Pip, still dazed and sweating heavily, heard Anton scream, 'We're fucked up now.' All he could think of was that he had got away – and he had the book! He stared at it with disbelief.

'I've still got it,' he said in a daze, as they crashed out of the drive and into the silent road.

Heine stood and watched the little car's crazy progress, his black shape stark against the snow. Now he had let them go, there was only one way out for him. Buttoning his coat and still holding the gun, he walked back to the house. He knew what he had to do. How many years had he wanted to get his own back? His head was so full of his plan that he didn't notice that the smaller Mercedes was still there, parked in front of Eisenmann's. As Heine made for the front of the house, the car door opened and the woman, swathed in the heavy fur coat, lumbered out like some predatory animal and disappeared through a back door.

Heine waited outside the main door for a while. He knew Eisenmann would have heard the shots. He had to make everything seem authentic. It had to look as though he was cleaning up. Finally, he entered the house and crossed the hall to the study. He waited outside the door, still playing for time, then knocked. But the command to enter didn't come quickly.

When he went in, his boss was standing before the open safe. Heine couldn't believe his luck. He was cleaning it out! Eisenmann swung round and stared at him and the gun. 'Is it done? It took you long enough! Put that away!'

'Yes, sir.' He lowered the gun to his side. He looked down and saw the stacks of banknotes piled on the floor next to the holdalls.

'You can clear up the mess in here when we've gone,' said Eisenmann. 'Where are the Papers? And the book?'

'The Papers were in his luggage. It's all outside the door,

including the book,' lied Heine.

'*Verdammte Arschloch!*' swore Eisenmann. 'Go and fetch them!'

'Who are you calling an asshole?' said Heine. It was now or never. He saw Eisenmann stiffen.

'What?' He took a step forward, and Heine raised the gun. 'Don't be a bloody fool,' Eisenmann snarled.

'That's the last thing I am,' retorted Heine, his voice cold and grim. 'But you've been playing me for one. Don't you think I know you're taking off for good?'

Eisenmann moved a step closer. His expression was ugly, uglier than Heine had ever seen. Inside, Heine could feel himself shaking.

'Do you want money?' Eisenmann bent and threw a wad of banknotes across the floor. 'Take it – and then I won't make you pay for what you just said.'

'You're the one who's going to pay,' retorted Heine, controlling his fear. 'I've done disgusting things for you – and you've treated me like shit.'

'Then I was wrong, very wrong,' replied Eisenmann, his voice changing from threatening to silky. 'Now put the gun down, Heine. I made you what you were. Didn't I raise you up from an obscure waiter and turn you into …'

'A killer,' cut in Heine. 'Well, I'm finished with doing your dirty work. I'm the one who's going to take off. With that!' He waved his pistol at the money.

'Shoot me then,' hissed Eisenmann, his sharp teeth showing. 'Right here!' He approached, indicating his chest. 'You wouldn't dare, because you're yellow!'

Heine had done with being mocked.

'You asked for it.' The bullet hit Eisenmann in the sternum, taking the German off his legs.

Heine was shaking and breathing hard. 'I did it,' he said, looking down at the pistol. His hands were wet with perspiration inside his gloves. He turned, as if seeking some witness to corroborate the act, and then looked across at Eisenmann, who was lying on his back. He couldn't bear to check to see if he was dead. He collapsed into his master's chair and took a swig of the iced water. When he felt calmer, he began to stuff the bundles of cash into the two holdalls.

He cleaned out the rest from the safe and, after leaving it open, kicked over a few chairs, wrenched out drawers, overturned the desk and smashed a lot of the bookcase windows, making it look like a robbery. He was used to destroying evidence, so it didn't take long. His heart was thudding in his ears, but his head was clear now. By the time Sigi discovered Eisenmann wasn't going to make the rendezvous at the airport, he would be over the border with the cash. Then he would dump the Mercedes and disappear. He'd had plenty of practice. He felt drained but triumphant. He had killed Eisenmann. He'd done it. He grabbed the two holdalls. They were heavy.

As he straightened up and turned, he found himself staring into a gun barrel.

'You! How …?'

It was the last thing Heine Muller ever said, as Sigi shot him, punching a hole as neat as a rat bite right in the middle of his forehead. Then she waddled over to Eisenmann and caught his shoulder. He stirred, sat up and tore open his shirt. He was grinning.

'Kevlar! A masterly invention by a "modern day alchemist." Unfortunately she was an American! And the stupid fool aimed right for the chest. You didn't, did you, *Mausl.* You went for the head! What? No tears?' He lifted her chin. 'No, I didn't expect them.' He stared into her bright little eyes. 'I'm sorry you were forced to kill him, but we had to make sure. In any case, the water would have done it.'

'I was worried for you,' she said. 'Not that idiot.'

Eisenmann stood up and began to unstrap himself from the bulletproof vest. Then, going over to Heine's lifeless corpse, he kicked it hard. 'Ignorant pig!'

'What shall we do with him?'

'The usual thing.' He saw Sigi's eyes flick to the phone. 'Not that one. Use the mobile they can't track. Tell Hermann to hurry and bring a couple of the others with him. The place needs clearing up. I'll sort out the cash. Then get on to the pilot and tell him we'll be late.'

Sigi nodded and soon began carrying out instructions. Then she flipped the phone shut.

'They'll take about 20 minutes. What shall we do about the American? He has the book.'

'Come here,' he ordered. She obeyed. He put out his hand and caressed her stomach. 'Don't worry about Durrant. Let him do some of the work now. In spite of his insolence, he has a good brain, although it's muddled at present.' He laughed. 'He doesn't understand his visions – yet. Nor what danger he faces. I believe that the end will come in our time, and my share in the revelation will be rewarded. Only then will Durrant's trivial role be dispensed with. So let him go blundering on through history and may the best man win, as the English say.

'We will never let him out of our sight. He will be watched every hour of every day. Believe me, I shall be with Durrant in spirit.' He brushed her hair with his hand. 'We have a greater weapon, dearest.' Eisenmann bent down and kissed her stomach. A moment later, he straightened. 'Soon *he* will be here, and we shall teach him well, *Mausl*. We shall be attentive parents, although he will not know who his father really is. And he will be beautiful.'

'Like you,' she said, her eyes shining.

'Not quite,' he replied.

Anton waited in the car while Pip fetched an airport trolley. 'What went on up at the house?' he asked when Pip brought the trolley back. 'You nearly got us killed!' Strangely enough the teenager hadn't wanted to talk about their frenzied getaway before, but he seemed to have loosened up on the way to the airport. He had also proved to be a very good driver. Anyone else would have turned the car over on that slope!

'Best you don't know,' said Pip. 'All I can say is, thank

you.' He held out his hand. 'If you'd gone off, I'd have been in the shit.'

'Okay, man.' Anton grinned, shaking his hand.

I guess he's just happy I won't be seeing Ghita again, thought Pip.

'Tell Ghita I was asking after her,' he added out loud.

'Wait,' said Pip, 'can you check on the rat?' He'd forgotten about Cass.

'Will do,' replied Anton. 'See you then.'

'Now!' yelled Pip, but a moment later, Anton accelerated away, leaving Pip standing outside the airport entrance. Feeling a mixture of happiness that he had got away, and regret for his pet, he paused. Then a police car screeched up. Pip swallowed. This time he really had something to worry about from the authorities. He was in possession of stolen goods. He attempted to look nonchalant as he put his backpack, briefcase and laptop onto the trolley. As the policemen got out, they were joking with each other, and they passed him by and went inside the building. Loaded up, Pip followed them through the revolving doors into the complex.

Once inside, he stared at the departure boards. His flight was on time. But he still had to wait for Dalca. He couldn't check in until they met. But he had plenty of time. And he needed it. He felt drained after his experience. He couldn't believe Eisenmann's hit man had let him go. He must have had his own agenda.

He found somewhere to sit down on the concourse and stared at the check-in desk. He'd put the book into his briefcase alongside the Marcu Papers, and was sure he would be allowed to take that and his laptop onto the plane as hand luggage, along with his backpack. He was a bit worried about being searched, but, after all, he was an academic, and they all travelled with books. *But not like this one*, he thought. He wanted desperately to pore over the book, but this wasn't the time. Nevertheless, he couldn't resist a quick look.

To his utter surprise, when he opened it with careful fingers, he discovered it wasn't a book at all. It looked like one, but it was actually a box. He lifted the lid – and gasped. Inside, he could see the brightly-coloured page of an illuminated manuscript, covered by special paper to protect it from the light. Beneath were several more. Eisenmann must have brought them down to pack.

How was Pip going to get them through the security check, and at the other end of the flight as well? He closed the box and straightened. He decided that if he was asked, he would lie and say they were facsimiles, hoping the security people wouldn't know the difference.

At that moment he couldn't believe he had stolen the manuscripts. He was a thief! What would his dad say if he knew? But he would never know. Nor would anyone else. He would have to keep the manuscript pages secret from everyone. His shook his head, thinking of all the possibilities. But it was no use now. He would formulate a plan afterwards. At that moment, he only wanted to get on the plane.

He replaced the box in his briefcase, placed it back in the luggage trolley and wheeled it along the concourse. He was thinking about Simu. He looked at his watch. The Professor should be there soon. Still feeling a little sick, he went to sit in the agreed place. He only hoped Dalca would show.

But Simu hadn't arrived by the time to check-in and Pip couldn't risk missing his flight. He imagined it was probably because of the snow. He had tried calling Simu several times, but had got only his messaging service. Possibly the snow was causing bad reception too. Pip wasn't that worried. Whatever Simu had to tell him could be discussed later. In any case, he felt a tiny bit relieved, having feared that his sensible side might prevail and cause him to hand over the book. In the end, he gave up thinking about anything but the task in hand and walked over to the desk.

Once he had checked in without any problems, he felt even more relieved. Evidently Eisenmann had thought better of calling the police. He probably had too many skeletons in his cupboard. The idea made Pip smile, although it wasn't at all funny. The first hurdle was over. Only the security check now.

Getting the box through was in the lap of the gods now – and Austrian Airlines, as he had to change in Vienna. But he wasn't questioned! As the briefcase went through the scanner, he thought, *Only one more at the Austrian capital and I've made it.* Only then could he relax.

He made his way to the bar and bought a plum brandy to remind him of Romania. But it reminded him too much. So he moved over to a chair near the gate and closed his eyes, trying to shut out the memories. He had never had a day like it, and he didn't want another. But he was going home, and, once there, he was sure everything was going to be all right. He had cheated Eisenmann and now it was in *his* hands to nail Grandsire. And he was getting nearer all the time. He was probably going to find some more answers in the stolen manuscripts. He breathed in at the amazing thought, and called Simu again. No answer.

God, I've been lucky, thought Pip. He was sweating. As soon as he was inside the plane, he would make one last attempt to reach Simu.

Dalca swore out loud as he drove from Arva in the direction of Someşeni. He had given himself plenty of time, as he had known the journey would be treacherous, but he hadn't expected to hear on the radio that the E576, the main road to the airport, had been closed on account of an accident.

He was afraid he wouldn't make it before Pip checked in. He hadn't time to stop and phone him, and he was faced with a difficult decision. Should he take the rat run? It was a second class road that would circumvent the accident, before it snaked off the mountain to join the major one again. He knew it quite well and there didn't seem to be any other option.

Still cursing, he turned, gambling that the snow ploughs would have done their work. Quite a few people used that country road when traffic problems prevented them getting out of the environs of Cluj, which had now sprawled its way almost to the limits of the airport. Dalca was pleased when he found he had made the right decision. The road was fairly clear as he drove through a white world. Heaped piles of slush along its sides were backed by dense forest trees, themselves crowned in snow, their lowering beauty still visible in the misty dusk of the November evening.

He had a lot on his mind as he drove. Emilia. He shook his head. She was fighting for her life, with serious head and back injuries. But he was more worried about her state of mind. It would be better for her if she didn't recover. He thought of Ghita, who didn't understand where she fitted into the black equation of Arva. He was going to have to tell Pip the truth. How would *he* feel? Dalca couldn't help but know that the American was sweet on his daughter, which complicated matters, as Ghita certainly thought a lot of him too. But now that Emilia was no longer in the picture, was it possible the two of them would get together? If Ghita married Pip, he could take her to America with him. That was if he came back, of course.

Dalca had his suspicions as to who had written that letter to the Institute in New York. He swore again, longing for the miles to fly by so that he could hear from Pip how the meeting with Eisenmann had gone. After that he felt cold, in spite of the car's heater. What if the boy never turned up for his plane? Which would mean that something had happened to him, like it had happened to Marcu. If it had, then Dalca would be responsible. It didn't bear thinking about. He upped his speed.

The road was strangely empty as it climbed, before it swooped down the mountain again onto the plain where the airport was situated. He had expected some other cars to have risked it. But it was dark now and the night shadows thrown across the windscreen from the windswept trees were disconcerting. He kept the headlights on, ready to switch to dim if need be. But there was no need. No traffic! At the highest point of the drive, he rounded the coil of a snake-like corner – and braked.

In front of him crawled a station wagon, taking up the middle of the road. Its roof was covered in deep snow and it looked like a Logan MCV – a big one, a seven-seater. Dalca didn't want to blow his horn. He hoped the driver would notice him in the mirror and move over. But now it was almost at a stop, yet still it kept creeping along in front of him. Dalca felt his colour rise. Whoever the driver was, he hadn't any consideration for other road-users! But he couldn't overtake, because of the snow and the bend. So he was forced to crawl behind the station wagon, like in a funeral cortège.

He found himself getting angrier and angrier. Was the driver being obstructive on purpose, or was he just plain scared of skidding? It didn't make sense. He blew his horn once, then twice. The second time worked, because at the very apex of the bend, the station wagon moved slightly to the right, giving Dalca the chance to squeeze past.

There were no lights indicating any vehicle coming in the opposite direction, so Dalca stepped on it. But not too fast. *Just in case.* As he passed the station wagon and his lights hit its side, its window shot down and he found himself looking into a face he knew only too well.

'You!' he cried, and in that moment of shock, he lost control of his vehicle and swerved sideways. A second later, Dalca's arm went up involuntarily to shield his head from the glass as his car hit the barrier and toppled over the edge. All he could feel was the airbag exploding with a thud against his chest, a massive pain and a crashing sound as the roof of the car was ripped back by the bushes on its way down the side of the mountain. Then all went black …

The man got out of the car and walked over to the barrier. He was very tall and his cloak billowed in the fresh night air. His face was slapped by the strong wind, but it caused him no more trouble than a summer's breeze. His blue eyes resembled a young wolf's as the mirror-like layer at the back of his eyes penetrated the darkness and fixed on the crippled car. His acute sense of smell could scent burning rubber and metal, and he was satisfied with his work. His ears, which were so sensitive he could pick up sounds from half a mile away, caught the trill of a mobile ringing insistently at the bottom of the ravine. He grinned as he loped back to the station wagon and switched on the engine. Then, with a lithe movement, he closed the window and drove down the hillside on his way to the airport.

Pip settled himself in his seat in the plane. He had taken out the book from his briefcase as soon as he had boarded, then he had called Simu again, to no avail. He was worried, but he could hardly wait to look at the material on his lap. As he opened it, though, he was sweating even more, this time with guilt.

But, like any good thief, he was well rewarded. What would Simu have said if he'd had the opportunity to see this? The only problem was that, from what Pip could see as he flicked through, the documents in the box all seemed to be written in Latin. He had learned the language, but he was no scholar. *That's a bit of a problem*, he muttered under his breath. He would have to think very carefully before he showed the documents to anyone else. They were priceless manuscripts. Each was packed in the same special material to prevent the light affecting it, and labelled with a flowing italic hand in red ink.

His Old French wasn't good either. He found one manuscript labelled *Les Chroniques de St Denis. The Coronation of Charlemagne. Charlemagne Enthroned.* The beauty of the frontispiece made him catch his breath. It depicted a square, the top half and sides painted red and gold, the bottom a deep night-blue. The picture showed a priest seated on a white throne. He was wearing a mitre on his head. Pip knew he had seen something like the depiction before – but where and when? In front of the figure knelt a king who had just been crowned. Behind him, two monks – one small and the other mighty in stature – dominated the half square. Pip stared at the plate again, but he couldn't take his eyes off the man and his mitre. Why did the illumination seem so significant?

He shivered as a sharp memory returned, stabbing at him. It was the same priest he had seen in his vision, when he had looked into Koppelberg's case in the chalet all those years before in Sunny Mead. The man who had blessed the children and sent them off to their deaths. He swallowed the lump in his throat and covered the page, feeling the same as he had when he had opened the Marcu Papers and recognised Arvarescu. Perhaps he had been meant to steal the manuscripts? The responsibility of discovering the reason why seemed more of a burden now than it ever had since he had been given the task of finishing what Marcu started.

He was about to put away the manuscripts and close the box when he caught a flash of white. What had he missed? He caught hold of it, but it was stuck. Why hadn't he noticed before? The scrap of paper was the corner of something. All at once, he realised that the box must have a false bottom. After much searching he discovered how to remove it. An envelope. He could hear his heart thudding. But they were about to take off. He stuffed the manuscript pages back into the box, returned it to his briefcase and stood up to put it in the luggage locker. At that moment, he was happy he had obtained an aisle seat.

After he had sat down, the hostesses came round to check all was good for take off. He had his eyes closed through the safety drill, trying to calm himself.

After the breathless rush of take off, they were in the air and climbing steeply.

All Pip wanted to do at that moment was sleep and forget everything – for a while. But he couldn't rest. He had been overwrought before the plane took off, and he kept thinking of Ghita, of what was going to happen to her. All the events of the last few weeks plagued his mind. What would happen if he was forced to give up the Papers? He had a copy, but how could he proceed with his research? How could he help Ghita? But maybe she wouldn't need his help? He had wondered so many times if she had been the young girl Eva had seen in her vision. If so, she was happy; she was going to be all right. But who had been the man carrying the girl?

Maybe he would find the answers in the manuscripts he had stolen? He had to make sense of the puzzle somehow. But in his heart he knew that he didn't want to be alone on the journey. He wanted Ghita beside him. But how could that happen? She was marrying Anton, and he was on his way to New York.

When the light came on, he stood up again and retrieved the box. With a surreptitious glance at the man beside him, who had his eyes closed, Pip opened it and took out the letter and looked at the address.

In Business Class, the man was asleep. Larry, the steward, had been very relieved to see the blond passenger. He had been called on the airport tannoy several times, but hadn't turned up until the last minute. At least he hadn't had any luggage to check in. All he seemed to have with him was a long case containing a musical instrument.

The man was a natty dresser. Gloves and a stick. The profession on his passport indicated he was an *entertainer*. And he looked it. As well as something else. Larry grinned. He was very handsome in the way Larry liked. But he had seemed arrogant, as he had only nodded dismissively in response when Larry had greeted him. It was like he had hardly noticed. Having taken his seat, he had wrapped himself up in his black coat, then closed his eyes, which were the strangest and most attractive the steward had seen for a long time!

When they were well on their way, Larry decided he would go and ask the passenger if he wanted a drink. He was hoping to have a few words. He felt instinctively that this guy was going to make the tedious journey bearable.

'Drink, sir?' Larry asked, smiling.

The man yawned, stretched out his legs and smiled back, revealing peculiarly sharp incisors. But he had a very nice smile. It kind of curled round his mouth.

'Nothing now, thank you,' he said. He was looking at Larry's name badge. 'Maybe later – Larry.'

Larry felt happy. The passenger wasn't arrogant at all. *And he had noticed him.*

'Thank *you*, sir,' Larry replied.

As the young steward turned, the man stretched. He was feeling happy. It had been a good day's work and he was even stronger now. Once more, he was free to go wherever in the world he wished. But he would never rest until all those who sought to destroy him were annihilated.

ABOUT THE AUTHOR

Helen McCabe is a highly regarded author whose love of writing and powerful imagination, coupled with a determination to succeed, have ensured a long and successful career. Her lifelong fascination with literature, history and research and an interest in the paranormal have enhanced Helen's immense gift for creative storytelling.

She graduated with Honours from London University, where she read English, and holds an MA degree in 18th Century English Literature from the University of Keele.

Her long career began with her first novel at the age of seven, with poetry published at 13 and read on the BBC. She started her true career as a novelist after becoming well-known for her short stories and serials in popular magazines. In 1995 her first full-length novel – *Two for a Lie*, about the 19th Century Princess Caraboo – was published, gaining much interest and critical acclaim. Since then, in tandem with work and family, she has written more than 30 novels in various genres, including historical, romance and more recently horror/thriller and crime. She also writes scripts for film, television and the stage.

Alongside her writing, Helen has worked in a variety of jobs, beginning as an assistant librarian and finally as a lecturer and teacher. She is a member of the Romantic Novelists Association, the Crime Writers' Association, the Horror Writers of America and the West Country Writers' Association.

Helen was invited to join Mensa, the high IQ Society, in 1989.

Helen lives in Worcester and has three grown-up children and a grandson.

Her website can be found at www.helenmccabe.com.

ALSO AVAILABLE FROM TELOS PUBLISHING

HORROR/FANTASY

HELEN MCCABE
PIPER
THE CODEX (Coming 2015)

GRAHAM MASTERTON
THE DJINN
RULES OF DUEL (With William S Burroughs)

SIMON CLARK
HUMPTY'S BONES
THE FALL

DAVID J HOWE
TALESPINNING
Horror collection of stories, extracts and screenplays

URBAN GOTHIC: LACUNA AND OTHER TRIPS edited by
DAVID J HOWE
Tales of horror from and inspired by the *Urban Gothic* television
series. Contributors: Graham Masterton, Christopher Fowler,
Simon Clark, Steve Lockley & Paul Lewis, Paul Finch and
Debbie Bennett.

RAVEN DANE
ABSINTHE & ARSENIC
16 tales of Victorian horror, Steampunk adventures and dark,
deadly, obsession
DEATH'S DARK WINGS (Coming in 2015)
Exciting alternative history with a supernatural twist

CAPTAINS STUPENDOUS by RHYS HUGHES
Steampunk humorous adventure about the Fantastical Faraway
Brothers

<u>SAM STONE</u>
KAT LIGHTFOOT MYSTERIES
Steampunk, horror, adventure series
1: ZOMBIES AT TIFFANY'S
2: KAT ON A HOT TIN AIRSHIP
3: WHAT'S DEAD PUSSYKAT
4: KAT OF GREEN TENTACLES (Coming in 2015)

JINX CHRONICLES
Hi-tech science fiction fantasy series
1: JINX TOWN
2: JINX MAGIC (Coming Sept 2015)
3: JINX BOUND (Coming Sept 2016)

THE DARKNESS WITHIN
Science Fiction Horror Short Novel

ZOMBIES IN NEW YORK AND OTHER BLOODY JOTTINGS
Thirteen stories of horror and passion, and six mythological and
erotic poems from the pen of the new Queen of Vampire fiction.

<u>KIT COX</u>
DOCTOR TRIPPS SERIES
A Neo-Victorian world where steam is pitted against diesel, but
which side will win?
KAIJU COCKTAIL
MOON MONSTER (coming in 2015)

BREATHE by CHRISTOPHER FOWLER
The Office meets *Night of the Living Dead.*

SPECTRE by STEPHEN LAWS
Something is stalking the Chapter, picking them off one by one,
something connected with their past, and with the girl they
used to know.

TELOS PUBLISHING
Email: orders@telos.co.uk
Web: www.telos.co.uk

**To order copies of any Telos books, please visit our website
where there are full details of all titles and facilities for
worldwide credit card online ordering, as well as occasional
special offers.**

www.ingramcontent.com/pod-product-compliance
Lightning Source LLC
Chambersburg PA
CBHW070434170726
48291CB00002B/497